Dame Fiona Kidman OBE is one of New Zealand's most acclaimed novelists. *New Zealand Books* said of Kidman, 'We cannot talk about writing in New Zealand without acknowledging her.' Born in Hawera, she has worked as a librarian, radio producer, critic and scriptwriter. Her first novel, *A Breed of Women*, was published in 1979 and became a bestseller. She has since written more than 25 books including novels, poetry, non-fiction and a play. Fiona Kidman lives in Wellington, New Zealand.

For Ian Kidman
aviator, adviser and dear companion

And so the sky keeps,
For the infinite air is unkind.

From 'The Wreck of the Deutschland'
Gerard Manley Hopkins

The Infinite Air

A novel about the enigmatic Jean Batten

Fiona Kidman

Aardvark Bureau
London

An Aardvark Bureau Book
An imprint of Gallic Books

First published by Random House
New Zealand Ltd in 2013

First published in Great Britain in 2016 by
Aardvark Bureau, 59 Ebury Street,
London, SW1W 0NZ

A CIP record for this book is available from the British Library
ISBN 978-1-910709-08-5

Typeset in Garamond by Aardvark Bureau
Printed in the UK by CPI (CR0 4YY)

2 4 6 8 10 9 7 5 3 1

Part One
Prelude to a Flight

1909–1934

Chapter 1

1934. The young woman, in a sleeveless white silk dress, stood at the window of a small apartment gazing out over the warm organic colours of Rome, its ancient earth and stone. It was evening, and across the roofs of buildings she saw another woman sitting at a window, level with her, looking out as she did. This other woman sat quite still most of the time, reading a book perhaps, for she glanced down at her hands now and then as if turning a page. She wore her hair in a chignon, and from the poise of her shoulders, Jean guessed that she was one of those elegant older women whom she saw making their way to the shops in Trastevere. Jean wished that she would look up, give her a wave, although perhaps that would be considered improper here in Rome. Just some acknowledgement would have satisfied her. She longed for her mother at this moment; the stranger had the same familiar imperious tilt of the head.

The apartment where Jean Batten stood was the home of Jack Reason, secretary to the air attaché in Rome. The walls were pale and sun lit up the room during the day. Otherwise, it was a plain place with little ornamentation beyond a vase or two, a pretty enough rug and some light raffia furniture, as if the owners were used to shifting house often and everything they owned could be easily transported to some other posting. It had surprised her at first that in spite of the ancient buildings beyond, and the difference of the city, she was surrounded by the odours of tobacco and talcum powder, bacon fat and disinfectant — the smells she and her mother had been accustomed to in London, in cheap, temporary lodgings.

The trouble had begun in Marseilles, on the first day of the flight. Just a year before, she had destroyed a plane in Baluchistan, a plane that had not belonged to her. That had been misfortune, she believed, pure and simple, but this time there was no avoiding it had been her fault. The Gipsy Moth had ended up squatting in a field of grass on the edge of the Tiber, its undercarriage shattered, the wings crumpled. As she had glided through the night, with only a torch to show her the way, twisting and weaving, like a firefly in the night, she had somehow avoided tall wireless masts on each side.

It had been after midnight when she was taken to the *pronto soccorso*, a Red Cross station of sorts. The petrol tank had been empty, but then it had been for some time, and that should not have happened. How could she have been so utterly stupid? How could she have failed her mother, whom she loved more than her life, and who had given her so much? But that didn't bear thinking about. That was the dark bird perched on her shoulder, the haunted dream that made her cry out in her sleep some nights, the creature she had to kill. Her mother knew the bird was there, and

8

only her mother could drive it away. But she was not here, she was in London, waiting to hear that Jean had made the next stage of her journey. What she would receive in the morning was news of a disaster, one that could have been so easily averted, had Jean but listened to the men in Marseilles. Perhaps it was the city of Marseilles itself, unpredictable and dangerous, full of seafarers and gypsies, because she had not wanted to stay in the old port town for a night. But that was not true. She was scared by very little on the ground, it was only in the immensity of the air that she sometimes understood danger. And that was what had driven her on, the need to conquer fear. She had done this to herself, succumbed to her own craziness, a strange light-headed madness that leapt out of control. She should have known.

Behind her, Molly Reason entered the room. She was a plump woman in her late forties or thereabouts, with frizzy hair parted in the centre and anxious eyes, as if her guest made her nervous. She wore a floral frock, pleated over her bosom in a way that made it look heavy. Her husband had been called directly after the crash, and now he had taken charge and installed Jean in their apartment.

'Excuse me, Miss Batten,' Molly said. 'The doctor is here to see you.'

Jean turned from the window, trying to conceal her regret at having her thoughts interrupted. 'The doctor? What doctor?'

'The one who attended you last night. He's come to check that you're in better health.'

As if Jean had already agreed to see him, the doctor followed Molly in.

'Doctor.' Jean extended her hand. 'It's very kind of you, but as you'll see, I'm perfectly well. Certainly much better than I was last night. Or was it early morning? I'm very sorry you were woken up so late to attend to a foolish girl like myself.' She forced a small laugh.

When they had met, her left eye was as swollen as a Black Doris plum, while her lip hung loose over her chin. The doctor had been summoned to the aid station, where she had been taken by a group of men who had found her, sodden from stumbling in the rain through marshland. As he stitched her lip together the pain was intense, but she would not cry, would not scream. This was her night of folly and whatever she might feel, she did not wish to reveal it. She knew her mother would say, 'Chin up, dear. Grin and bear.' Nellie had no time for complaints. She had, she said, suffered in her time and now that was behind her, and she and Jean could conquer the world together.

'She'll be as good as new in no time, won't she?' Molly Reason said to the doctor, in better Italian than Jean expected.

He looked at his patient with an appraising eye and spoke rapidly. The older woman lifted one shoulder in acknowledgement and seemed at a loss.

'What did he say, Mrs Reason?' Jean asked. She knew she owed it to the doctor to at least listen to his advice, for he had stayed up all night holding cold compresses to her eye, helping the swelling to go down.

Molly Reason hesitated. 'He says the signorina is immensely beautiful, and if she looks after herself, her appearance will soon be restored. He says her hair is the colour of falling night, her skin like almond petals. He recommends, Miss Batten, that you spend a few weeks resting, and hopes that you'll remain in Rome while you recover.'

'A few *weeks*. That's ridiculous. I have to fix my plane and fly to Australia.'

'Well, the world is full of good intentions.' Mrs Reason seemed to assert herself. 'But it's hardly the first time you've set out for Australia, is it? I suggest that you climb into bed and get some rest. The doctor says you're still in shock.'

With that she turned to leave the room.

'Mrs Reason,' Jean said, 'have you not spoken with your husband today?' She chose her words with care, knowing that the other woman was not happy about her unexpected guest. Quite early in the morning she had left the apartment for Matins, and had not returned until much later.

Molly paused. 'He didn't go to church this morning,' she said, with starch in her voice.

'That's because we've been hard at work. The Italian Air Force transported my plane to the aerodrome this afternoon. They're already making a list of the parts needed to repair my machine. Mr Reason has been very kind.'

'My husband telephoned me after lunch. I understand there are no wings available for your plane anywhere in Rome. You won't get far without wings.'

Jean glanced down at her pretty dress, swirling around her knees, and laughed again, this time with real humour. 'Don't you believe it. I know where there are wings. I've seen some in the hangar.'

'You haven't got them yet,' Molly said.

On reflection, The trouble had really begun the week earlier. It had been an inauspicious beginning. She and her mother had risen and breakfasted at the small inn in Kent where they were staying in readiness for Jean's flight from Lympne aerodrome. Nellie sat opposite her, encouraging her to eat well because, as she said, she didn't know where she would get her next decent meal and she must keep up her strength. Her mother, the most handsome of women, was tall and strong boned. She ate what she liked and always looked as if she exactly fitted her skin. When they walked along the street together, Jean, small and neatly put together, barely came up to her mother's shoulder. Heads turned to look at the pair, alike yet so different. Nellie Batten had regular features that her daughter had inherited, a big sensual mouth, heavy-lidded eyes, a strong chin that she held at an angle as she strode along, her back very straight. To look at her, one would think she had the capacity to laugh but she seldom did. There was a time when she had walked the boards of theatres — very small theatres, she said with a hint of wistfulness that was outside her usual demeanour. New Zealand theatres. As if that said everything. Little theatres in little towns.

'Darling,' Jean had said, 'you know my next meal will be in Rome. I'm sure I'll eat fabulously well.'

At that point they had been joined, rather later than he was expected, by Jean's fiancé Edward Walter, who had come from London to say goodbye, and to try once again to persuade her not to go. He was still rubbing his eyes, apologising for sleeping through his alarm. Jean watched him across the table while he ate his way through fried kidneys and three eggs, stopping long enough to remind her that he had bought her the axe, so that if she came down in the sea she could hack the wings off her plane to make a raft.

'I've packed it, Ted,' she said.

'Well, thank goodness for that. You know I wanted you to take a life raft.'

'Much good that will do me if I'm truly lost at sea. You know how little room there is in the cockpit — goodness knows, you've flown often enough yourself. I've got all the essentials.' She hesitated, on the point of reminding him that he was a weekend flyer, an enthusiast rather than a real pilot, and that although he, too, owned a Gipsy Moth he had never flown further than the next town, or even over the English Channel. Nor did she itemise what she did consider the essentials, although her mother had given a small conspiratorial smile as Jean mentioned them. She had helped her daughter buy face cream and talcum powder, several changes of underwear, a white silk dress for the evenings when she landed. In her breast pocket she carried powder and lipstick and a small bottle of perfume, along with her comb. 'Make sure your hair is always neatly parted when you land,' Nellie had advised her. 'Make sure you look as if it's effortless.'

'I'd like you to take the revolver I offered you,' Edward said. 'It's in the car.'

'Ted, no. I managed without a gun in Baluchistan. If I start shooting people they'll shoot back, rather than help me. You're being dramatic.'

'That's not what I had in mind. If you go down in the water, and there are sharks, what then?'

Jean studied him, noting from the angle of his head the bald patch that had begun to spread, the pink gleam of his scalp. He was good-looking enough, with that air of a refined Englishman about him that had attracted her at first, but although his face was lean his chin was collecting soft folds that made him look older than his thirty-three years. 'You mean I should commit suicide?' she said.

He pushed his plate aside with an angry gesture. 'Now you're the theatrical one.'

Jean got to her feet. Not for the first time, it crossed her mind that this man she had promised to marry might become someone with whom she could share too many breakfasts. His first wife seemed to have tired of him very quickly. An ageing stockbroker who might expect what? A wife who gave dinner parties and talked about shares and bonds? She twisted the ring on her finger, a half-circle of very good diamonds.

'We should get going, it's nearly dawn already,' she said.

Nellie nodded. 'Yes, come on, darling. You're off to Australia today. If you're going to get there faster than Mrs Mollison.'

Jean sensed that, at any moment, her mother might launch into another recital of Amy Johnson's achievement in flying from England to Australia in nineteen and a half days. Nellie always referred to the other aviator by her married name, as if to indicate that a domestication had taken place since her marriage, even though Jean's rival continued to set records. The record for a woman's solo flight from one side of the world, and the only such flight at that, had stood since 1930, four years earlier. Nellie's eyes blazed as if in anticipation of the triumph to come. How long is it going to take you, she was in the habit of asking Jean, although the question was always rhetorical. To which her daughter would reply that she hoped, all going well, it would be ten or twelve days.

And now, instead of breaking records, here she was in Rome, alone to all intents and purposes, with Molly Reason needling her about her plight.

'My husband says that Signor Savelli, who owns the Gipsy Moth, is not keen on parting with the wings of his plane.'

Jean looked across the rooftops, rose coloured in the

deepening day. For an instant she thought the woman sitting at the window inclined her head ever so slightly towards her. 'I assure you,' she said, tilting her chin, 'that before today is done, I'll have wings.'

Chapter 2

1909. When Jean was born her mother, Ellen Batten, who was known as Nellie, pinned a newspaper picture of Louis Blériot and his monoplane above her cot. Just eight months before, the Frenchman had flown across the English Channel, the first person to achieve this feat, in the time of thirty-six minutes and thirty seconds in a two-seater monoplane. A year to remember, the family said — Blériot's triumph, and the birth of Jean.

The story of the aviator was often told in the Batten household, when they all lived together in Rotorua. It would come up in conversation each time there was some new and amazing exploit by an aviator. 'It struck me very forcibly,' Nellie would say. 'Perhaps because of my condition, I was very impressionable at the time. But you know, when I read about that man, launching himself across the sea, right on the moment of sunrise, and what he had to say about the loneliness of it all, it struck my heart. As he told it, he was alone, isolated, lost in the midst of the immense ocean, not able to see anything on the horizon or a single ship. Such courage. Just imagine, his wife was on a following ship, and she couldn't see him either. What must she have thought?' She would pause then, and marvel. 'Yet he did it,' she always said, completing the story. 'He made it across the water and survived.' When her daughter was older, she would add: 'How I wish I could do that.'

During that time in Rotorua, they believed they were happy: Fred the dentist, with a flourishing practice, and his exuberant wife, Nellie, two little boys, and Jean, the baby. True, there had been a loss along the way, a boy who had died, and, sometimes, later on, Jean wondered if that might have been when the family's problems began, the first hint that sorrow might besiege them. But when she was born, tiny and frail, her parents rejoiced in a girl, swaddling her with care and constant attention, lest this one be lost. Jean imagined, later, that she must have been born prematurely, for just two nights before the birth her mother had danced at a ball. Nobody knew my secret, she boasted. They couldn't tell that I was having a baby. On the night of her birth her father played the flute in the room next door to where her mother laboured. They called their daughter Jane Gardner Batten, in honour of Fred's mother, but somewhere along the way her name eased itself into Jean, and it stuck. It was the name she called herself when she began to talk.

Rotorua resembled a frontier town, with long unpaved streets, hitching posts for horses, small houses made of wood and roofed with iron. What made it different from other central North Island settlements were the thermal pools, volcanic steam rising in unexpected places from the turbulent earth. Geysers erupted, spewing hot water into the air, and mud bubbled on the corners of the streets. The air was suffused with the pungent smell of hydrogen sulphide. Although visitors to the town spoke of the stench of rotten eggs, those who came to live there soon stopped noticing it. Because of the curative properties of the water, a spa resort had been built at the eastern end of the town, a sprawling mock-Tudor bath house with its back to a lake, and also a number of large hotels to accommodate those seeking cures. Beneath the charming entrance to the bath house, with its grand sweeping staircase, and an orchestra playing soothingly on a balcony, lay a complex subterranean basement where patients underwent therapies intended to remedy all manner of ailments. The lights were dim, and the powerful reek of sulphuric gases caught one in the back of the throat.

Amohia Street, where the Battens lived, ran close to the large public gardens where the bath house stood and was just around the corner from the Prince's Gate Hotel where prime ministers and royalty had stayed. Fred and fellow musicians sometimes entertained guests in the reception hall, just for the hell of it, not for money. The Prince of Wales and his wife, Mary, who were soon to be king and queen, had stayed there and, in their honour, large steel archways were placed at the entrance to the gardens. In spring these arches foamed with purple wisteria, the vines turning into green canopies in the summer. Just think, Nellie murmured to Jean, we are walking in the same footsteps as their majesties.

The house in Amohia Street was rented, but Nellie had furnished the front room in what was already dubbed the Edwardian style: bamboo and wicker furniture with delicate legs and curved backs, except for one solid, dark green easy chair with a comfortable back so that Fred could rest at the end of a day's work. The chintz-covered cushions were colourfully patterned, the walls papered a dark gold colour, with deep red floral friezes, not flowers all over like most people had — so very modern, Nellie enthused, and look how large this made the house look. The tall vases that had come from Fred's mother were always spilling with flowers. In the corner of the front room stood a piano which both she and Fred played. Fred, a swarthy man, with eyes the colour of licorice, had discovered Debussy, whose music he described as sensuous, although Nellie found it discordant. 'Besides,' she said, 'that man leads a wicked life in Paris, if the newspapers are anything to go by.' 'You're one to talk,' Fred had said with a laugh, for Nellie was known as high-spirited. Her musical repertoire was varied, some of it classical, but she liked playing old tunes that people sang around pianos and, for the children, she had picked up tunes like 'The Teddy Bears' Picnic', which was all the rage. She held Jean in her lap and helped her finger chords on the piano.

The nearby lake, known to Maori as Rotorua-nui-a-Kahumatamomoe, though Europeans called it Rotorua, was an expanse of water so large that it was difficult to see the far shore from the town, dark blue in summer, purple and chill in the winter, with an island lying at its centre. On Sundays the Battens walked along its shore, dodging eddying bursts of sulphur gases. They never entered the pa, home to local Te Arawa, who wove feather cloaks and cooked their meals in the hot pools. An Anglican church crouched on the side of the lake, and from it billowed exquisite renditions of familiar hymns, sung in a different language. Jean listened longingly to this distant music, but her mother said that although they meant well in their Christian endeavours, the Maoris still had a long way to go to escape their heathen ways. 'My father fought them during the wars,' she said, her voice cool.

Some Saturday nights in wintertime, the family went on expeditions to the bath house and hired a family hot tub. Nellie was a strong believer in natural remedies. 'Off we go,' she commanded them, in a loud, cheerful voice. 'Let's all get healthy.'

The tub was so deep it was up to Jean's chin. There were seats around the edge so they could all sit with their feet floating in the middle. Only Jean did not wear a suit that covered her completely, being considered too small for it to matter whether the little flat buttons of her nipples showed or not. When they had soaked, they went off to the changing rooms, and exchanged swimming trunks for their pyjamas and dressing gowns. Afterwards, with much laughter and whispering, they all scampered up the street back to the house, and leapt into their beds.

Fred was in constant demand in his dental practice, a man with presence. He was a captain in the Taranaki

Territorial Army, which he had joined some years earlier, and could lift a cannon ball aloft in each hand. Nellie massaged his broad shoulders when he sat in the green chair in the evenings, pipe in his mouth. His chest muscles rippled beneath his shirt; his dark hair, swept back in regular waves, met in a widow's peak above the high plane of his forehead. 'You have your father's cheekbones,' Nellie would say to Jean, admiring father and daughter as her caresses lingered on her husband. Jean would sit at Fred's feet on a low stool engraved with poker-work. His hand would fall on her head while he dozed, fingers entwined in her hair, twitching awake with sudden little spasms of his grip on her skull, like an eggshell about to break open. 'She is so delicate, our little Mit,' he commented more than once to Nellie. Mit. It was his name for her then. She used the word when she wanted her mittens on cold winter mornings. There were many of those: it was hard frost country.

'You've had Mrs Hardcastle in again,' Nellie said one evening.

'Now why would you say that?' Fred asked.

'I'd recognise that freesia perfume anywhere.'

'Oh that,' Fred said. 'I don't notice things like that. It's all disinfectant and soap when I have someone in the chair.'

'She bought it in Grasse, on her grand tour of Europe last year. It's very distinctive. She wears it to meetings. Her teeth must be in a terrible way, the number of times she visits you. Not that you'd think it to look at her. She's not a bad-looking woman.'

'I'll take a note of it next time, pay her a compliment if I think of it,' Fred said easily.

While her husband was at work, Nellie was busy about the town. She rode a tall white mare from one committee meeting to another, seated side-saddle and dressed in a green jacket, a plaid riding habit and a hat with a brave red feather tucked in its band. The committees were mostly for theatrical societies, but also for the rowing club. She and Fred both rowed on the lake. Then there was the organising committee for the annual military ball, and for the flower show. Her blooms won the sweet pea division every year. She grew vegetables, too, lettuce and spinach in abundance, believing as she did in healthy nutritional diets. But, really, the theatre was Nellie's first passion, begun when she was a girl in Invercargill. She was a regular feature at the Theatre Royal, the Fairy Queen in *The Sleeping Princess* when she was just fourteen, and then there were musicals at the Opera House in Wanganui where she kicked up her heels, and showed a little ankle, and met her husband in the process. And now here she was in Rotorua, at the Lyric, playing the lead role in *Lady Frederick*, a widow with a past, and she loved the way the part made the audience laugh. People could think what they liked of her, say she was wanton and abandoned, because of the way she threw herself into every activity, but she knew the truth, that nothing would happen if someone didn't lead with a bit of spirit.

Louis Blériot's exploits stood for everything she had ever imagined, the power to propel oneself through the air. In her dreams, she would confide to Jean, she sometimes found herself walking around a room, a library perhaps, with very high walls lined with books, and she would be reading the volumes on the top shelves, her feet just walking along the air beneath her. After Blériot's flight, she told astonished members of the gardening circle committee that she saw herself as he did, alone in space. Only the other side remained unattainable, the far shore.

The horse she rode was lent to her by an American called John Hoffman, a big man with a crest of hair already turning white, although he was of an age with Nellie. He had emigrated at the turn of the century and 'gone native', as it was said, marrying a Maori woman, and already there was a child every year. Nellie found it most peculiar, but she needed a horse and liked Hoffman. He kept two or three and raced them from time to time. He needed his horses to be ridden, he said. The white mare had nice shoulders and a good steady eye, nice for a lady to ride, especially as she took her little girl with her more often than not. Sometimes he would wink, and whisper in Nellie's ear as she dismounted at his stable. 'A bit of a flutter?' he would ask, and laughing she would hand over some coins. The next time he saw her, he would press the palm of her hand. 'You've got a good eye for a horse,' he often said in his soft drawl.

'And you're leading me astray,' she invariably responded.

Once she said, 'Now don't you dare tell my husband. He thinks I'm cleverer with money than I really am.'

'Oh, but I think you are. I think you study form more than you're letting on.'

By the time Jean was four she had grown strong, with wild unruly curls that reached to her shoulders. She and her second brother, John, bore a close resemblance to each other, small-boned and dark-featured, with the same alabaster complexion that came more from their mother than Fred. Harold, the older of the two brothers, was taller and, in a way that was hard to define, more awkward in his skin, as if something were slightly broken in him already. Sometimes Jean noticed displeasure in her mother's voice when she spoke to Harold that was never apparent when she talked to her and John. It was years and years later, after flights that circled the globe, after fame, and loss, and despair, when Jean came to bury her mother in a foreign country, that the marriage and birth certificates she carried revealed that Harold's birth had occurred a few short months after her marriage. This had happened in a town down south, before Fred and Nellie's move to Rotorua. Not that this could have accounted for the way Harold was, except perhaps for an inner core of desolation Jean sensed, which might have stemmed from this beginning, the embarrassment he would have caused his mother.

Still, it was Harold who wanted an atlas, to study maps of the world. He wanted to become an explorer, like Dr Livingstone. His father sent away for a *Times Atlas* and, when it arrived, Harold invited John and Jean to join him in poring over more than a hundred coloured maps of the world. He traced his finger over country after country, noting where there was still not enough information for the cartographers to fill the gaps. Africa, thanks to Livingstone, looked well coloured in. 'There's Russia. And Asia. Look, I could go to China, there's lots to discover there,' he said, full of longing. His voice had just broken, and his limbs gangled across the floor.

'There's a hole in the middle of Australia,' John said.

'Oh, that's not far away, someone will find it soon I expect.' It was Harold's habit to contradict nearly everything his brother said. He never 'played' with John, the way his mother hoped. The distance in their years had opened up, so that John and Jean seemed more of an age than the two brothers. Harold let Jean trace her finger across the Nile. 'You couldn't go there,' he said, 'too many crocodiles, and besides, girls can't be explorers.' After a while he got bored with the younger children's company and went to his room, taking the atlas with him. He was a boy who often got tired, or that was what Nellie said, although there was something worried in her tone.

One day, Jean managed to open the front gate, and escape down the road on her own. It was Harold who found her, amid the panic that ensued in the household when her disappearance was discovered.

'I was going off to explore,' she said. 'It sounded really interesting.' Harold grabbed her fiercely by the arm and dragged her back along the street, Jean yowling like a stray cat.

'Trust you to get me in trouble,' he said, as he handed Jean back to their mother.

Nellie looked the situation over, dismissing Harold with a wave of her hand, barely a thank you. 'Now stop that noise, Jean,' she said. 'We're British. British people don't cry.'

Jean and John created their own diversions. Nellie had a tin cabin trunk that she had used to transport her belongings from the South Island before she met Fred. It had come all the way from Scotland when her mother was a new bride, just seventeen years of age. Her name was Mary Anne Shaw and she married a military man called John Blackmore. Nellie spoke of her parents and her eight brothers and sisters with pride, although the family had dispersed since she was a girl, and she had lost track of most of them by then. But Mary Anne's cabin trunk had been given to her, and now she filled it with an assortment of her and Fred's old clothes, his raincoats and worn-out dentist smocks, a baggy pair of trousers, a tie on which he had spilled tomato soup that his wife had failed to remove, a shapeless trilby that had sailed off his head and landed in the lake when he was trout fishing; old petticoats and some dresses Nellie had discarded after a season or two of wear because the fashion had changed, a pair of green velvet dancing shoes with one broken heel, a rope of beads.

These were the children's dress-up clothes. 'Don't be

shy,' Nellie cried. 'I was never shy about what I wore when I was a girl. Do you know, for a dare, I once rode a man's bicycle down the main street of Invercargill, wearing a pair of serge bloomers? My brothers were horrified but people laughed and cheered. They thought it was hilarious.'

John was nine when Jean turned four, but he still loved the game. He dressed his sister up in his mother's cast-off finery, even though the skirts trailed along behind her, and she tripped on their hems. John put on his father's clothes, playing the part of a young man taking a girl to a dance, bowing low to her, and offering his arm, and they would skip along together. One day John said that, just for a change, she could put on their father's clothes and he would wear a dress. He put on the old ball gown, gathering up the skirts as far as he could, telling Jean to play the father's role, while he was the mother. It was while John was swinging the rope of Nellie's beads in one hand that Harold entered the room. He stood there with an odd smirk on his face. That evening at dinner, he told his parents what he had seen.

There was an uneasy silence in the room. Fred said, 'Nellie, don't you think John is a little old for dressing up?' Nellie hesitated for a moment. 'I think the children should be allowed to express their personalities however they wish really. Men play all sorts of roles on the stage. Imagine Gilbert and Sullivan if the men could not wear frills at their wrists.'

'Trust you not to listen to Father,' Harold said, full of vehemence.

'I played the fool a little myself when I was a girl,' Nellie said.

'No wonder they shipped you out,' said Fred, not amused.

'Oh Fred, where's your sense of humour?'

Fred had merely shrugged and changed the subject. Later that evening he stood up and put his hat on. He was, he said, going for a walk by the lake.

Did Jean imagine it, or did her mother mutter the name Mrs Hardcastle under her breath? Harold, who was angry, said so, but his mother turned away as if she hadn't heard him.

All the same, when summer came, the children were sent outside more often. Nellie insisted that Harold accompany John and Jean on picnics, even though he had turned thirteen and he resisted the company of the children as much as he could. His parents didn't always know where he was, and in the evenings, if he were late home, they would exchange anxious looks. It was after one of these late nights that he had agreed with reluctance to a picnic at the lake. Nellie was tired, she had said. Or was she? Jean was too small to know what was really wrong with her mother that day, just that she needed to lie down in a darkened room.

There was a suffocating quality about the air as Harold and John set off with Jean, accompanied by strict instructions from Nellie for the boys to look after their sister. They went to the lake carrying a picnic basket containing sandwiches and crusts of bread in a separate paper bag to feed to the ducks and swans gathered at the water's edge. When they had eaten, Harold suggested that they walk on along the shore to the place they called Sulphur Point, which lay behind the bath house. People came down here to do secret things, he said. When John asked what things these might be, Harold was mysterious and elusive. 'Things,' he said. They might see things going on. They walked along to where a scrubby plantation jutted out into the lake, and bands of rough yellow mineral encroached on pools of water in the rocks. This was further than they had ever been, but Harold was intent on leading them on.

John said, 'I think we should go back.' He was ten, and beginning to act in a more grown-up fashion.

Earlier, they had fed all their crusts to the birds. Now a group of swans emerged from the water and began to circle the trio.

'They've followed us,' John said in a small frightened voice. 'They want more bread.'

One of the swans arched its neck and raised its wings, beating them fiercely as it approached Jean. The bird's hard beak was extended, as if aiming straight for her eyes.

She screamed, putting her hands up to defend herself, while John ran towards her, waving his arms up and down. Harold stood still, shaking in an odd way as if he were helpless, unable to move. Then Jean pulled herself together, shouted for the swan to go away and put her fingers straight out in front of her. The creature stopped in its tracks, wings hovering in the air for some seconds, before folding them away and drawing its long neck back into the cushion of its breast.

A moment or two later it was gone. Now that the danger had passed, Jean gave one or two shocked sobs, John's arm around her shoulder. Harold seemed to recover himself and stuck his hands in his pockets.

'So what do you want to do now, cry baby?' Harold demanded.

'Home,' Jean said. She didn't know where her bravado had come from, but she was still afraid, whether of the bird, or her brother, she couldn't be sure.

'Play mothers and fathers?' Harold said, a strange smile playing at the edge of his mouth.

John said no, that wasn't what they wanted to do, his voice low and urgent.

'I could be father today,' Harold said, laughing now.

John and Jean had fallen silent. She saw the shadow of the swan's wing again, lifted against the heavy clouded light, like a dark cape. When they got to the house, John ran in, calling out to their mother that Jean had been brave. But the house was quiet, and Nellie wasn't there. The two younger children sat in silence in the front room until she returned, though neither could have explained the sense of dread they felt. Nothing more had happened, except that they had walked home and then Harold had left, and somehow this felt as if it were their fault. He stayed away until nearly midnight. Nellie came home but she and Fred were not speaking to each other. In the morning, their father took his strap to his eldest son, his strong arms coming down with thwacks that could be heard all over the house. Whether Harold's misdemeanours were related to Nellie's malaise was impossible to tell. The explosive word 'frigging' hovered in the air, but Jean didn't know what it meant.

Frigging. That was Harold's problem. He'd been trying to frig around with housemaids at the Prince's Gate Hotel. And him only thirteen, the manager said when he returned the Battens' son to them. He didn't know what the girls saw in the kid, the way they egged him on. Too cocky for his own good.

Fred frigged around, too. Like father, like son, Nellie shouted. She had caught Fred frigging with a patient on the floor of his surgery on a Friday afternoon.

'More services rendered?' she said when they got home, her voice as bitter as aloe.

Frigging was what got people into trouble, what broke families up. In time this is what would happen to them, in yet another town, Fred and Nellie living in different houses, Harold gone, disappeared abroad, taking his atlas with him. But by then, John would have gone, too. At least Jean and Nellie would be together.

That is how it would be. Jean and Nellie.

Chapter 3

At first, the family lived in Auckland, Rotorua firmly behind them. If Nellie missed the old life of horse riding and theatre, she didn't say so. The Battens had stepped up in the world as Fred moved into the London Dental Institute to become a dental surgeon rather than just a plain dentist. They rented a house in Parnell, with a garden that had a large pepper tree at its centre. After they left Rotorua, for that brief time when Fred and Nellie still believed they could forgive and forget, Jean thought of herself as content. Nellie and Fred joined a rowing club again; the boys went to school. Her father made a swing for Jean, attaching it to the pepper tree. They were happy, they said. Happy. This is what families are. The past is just that, a place where we lived when we were young and foolish.

Harold was enrolled at Auckland Grammar School, a great opportunity for him, his parents said. It was next best thing to a private school. Parents fought to have their sons enrolled there. It had a grand brand-new Spanish-mission-style reception area, and the school motto 'Per Angusta ad Augusta', which meant 'Through Difficulties to Greatness', appealed to Nellie in particular. Harold didn't find school easy. Here, he would be understood, she was sure.

Jean started school at Melmerley College, a private school for up-and-coming young ladies, housed in an enormous building in Parnell. She wore a navy blue gym-slip, black stockings and a wide straw boater hat kept on by an elastic band under her chin. She learns very quickly, her teachers told Nellie, noting in her first report how well organised Jean was, always having her pencils sharpened, and her desk neat as a pin. John, who was going to a state school, but would be enrolled at King's College as soon as a place came up, was a Boy Scout now, and in the evenings when it got dark he would take Jean outside and show her how to signal Morse code with his torch. Short long, that's A, three shorts, that's an S and so through the alphabet; then he would flick a message out that might say, 'Batten calling from Parnell', his fingers flying so fast on the button that she couldn't keep up with what he was doing. Over the weeks that followed, whenever John was out, she crept into his room and found his semaphore book, then studied it in her room. One night she asked John to lend her the torch. 'Jean Batten here, Jean Batten calling from Auckland.'

'How did you do that?' he asked in wonder. When she didn't reply, he grabbed the torch from her. 'You monster, you've been in my room, haven't you?' And Jean, laughing and exultant, rolled away in the grass, crying, 'Beat you.'

John jumped up and ran into the house to tell his mother that Jean had been sneaking around, looking at his things. But when the crime was described to her, Nellie seemed pleased with Jean, not angry at all.

Fred worried about the swing he had improvised in

the back yard, suspended from the branch of the pepper tree. Jean swung higher and higher, becoming increasingly reckless. He implored her to let him replace the swing with something stronger, but she told him, 'I'd rather use this one. It's lighter, don't you see, and the angle is just right.'

When he appealed to Nellie, she said that Jean was a tomboy right now, and she thought she would continue whatever they said. Fred threatened to remove the swing, but Jean took little notice. The sensation of soaring towards the sky was so exhilarating that she couldn't stop, even when she glanced down and the earth seemed a long way away. She simply waited until Fred was out of sight and resumed her aerial games.

Still, in spite of her dismissive tone to Fred, Nellie kept an anxious eye out the kitchen window.

There was talk of war in the air, but nobody believed it would happen.

Fred still took part in army manoeuvres, on stints of duty for his Taranaki regiment, but what was happening in Europe was so far away from New Zealand, it was impossible to think that anything could make a difference in Auckland. Then the Austrian ruler, Archduke Ferdinand, and his wife were assassinated, and all of a sudden the torch was lit, the proclamation made. Britain was at war, and so was New Zealand. 'There's nothing for it,' Nellie cried, her eyes blazing. 'Of course we should follow the mother country.' Fred was standing very tall by the breakfast table, his fists clenching and unclenching.

Harold looked gleeful, as if he could already see himself

on his way to fight, no matter that he was still a school boy. He and Auckland Grammar didn't agree on much; in fact the school would be more than ready to see the back of him. Nothing they could put their finger on, just that he was a disruptive influence in every class, and he had a menacing tongue. Some of the boys were afraid of him, and the ones who weren't came off worse when they did resort to fists.

'Thank God,' Nellie said suddenly, 'none of you will have to go.'

'What sort of talk is that?' Fred said, shaking his head vigorously.

'I mean ...' Nellie's voice trailed away. 'It's all very well, war, isn't it? But I couldn't bear to think of you going away.'

'I'll have to,' Fred said. 'It's duty, Nellie. One does one's duty.'

'You're too old, Fred. Don't you see?'

Fred didn't say a word, just turned and walked out the door.

The city began to empty of young men. Troops dressed in khaki marched through the streets, hemmed in on either side by cheering crowds. Fred was thirty-five, and nobody expected him to join up. Don't be ridiculous, Fred, Nellie repeated whenever the subject was mentioned. Fighting was for the young and fit. Still, Nellie watched him anxiously for any sign of a sudden move.

For a while there was a run of young men getting their teeth fixed before they went overseas, paid for by their parents, or, more often than not, having all their teeth pulled and replaced with artificial ones so that they wouldn't have trouble while they were away. Sometimes Jean was allowed into her father's surgery when he was working in the evenings making dentures. The porcelain teeth sat in rows in small flat containers, gleaming like polished fingernails. Fred would pick them out delicately between tweezers, fixing them one after another into the gum that would fit inside someone's mouth. Jean liked to touch them, imagining the smile that they would make. Or the bite. 'Can you make them sharp?' she asked once, making both her parents laugh. After a while this work began to run out, as people gave their money to the war effort instead. There was a restlessness about her father, as if he would rather be anywhere but at the London Dental Institute in Queen Street. The first waves of men who had gone away were coming back now, arriving on hospital ships bearing the wounded and maimed, unrecognisable as the laughing boys who had left. Fred turned his face away, unable to look at them.

'The Medical Corps are crying out for more hands,' Fred said to Nellie, on one of these evenings when she had brought his dinner to the surgery, because he had had a sudden urgent order to fill, a rich woman who wanted new teeth before her daughter got married. It was 1916 and the war had already been in full swing for more than two years. 'Fred, you can't,' Nellie said with exasperated patience. 'Perhaps at the beginning of the war it might have been different.'

'You told me then I was too old,' Fred reminded her. 'Everyone is getting older. I'm in good health.'

'What would we do without you here?'

'You'd manage,' Fred said. 'That's what you'd do. You always have.'

'Are you sure it isn't that you just want to get away from us?'

Jean stayed very still, waiting to hear the words she dreaded. Finally, Fred said, 'Nellie, you know you want the children to have good educations. We can't afford that. They'll have to go to ordinary schools like everyone else. At least the army means regular pay.'

'You've enlisted, haven't you?' Nellie said, her voice dull.

When he agreed that, yes, this was so, she told him how much she loved him, that she didn't know how her life would carry on if he didn't come home. They seemed to have forgotten Jean standing there, as they folded their arms around each other, and Nellie wept. 'Buck up, old girl,' he muttered, bent over her shoulder. 'You'll be all right, you'll be splendid.' Then he put down the teeth he had been creating, little neat teeth. 'Someone else can finish those,' he said. He gathered Jean and Nellie together, locking the door of the surgery behind them. They walked down Queen Street, along the wharves, rank with the smell of fishing boats and noisy with sailors on leave, and home. In the morning, he packed his kit and left for camp. He was being seconded for duty with the 3rd Auckland Regiment, retaining his Territorial captain's rank.

Before he left New Zealand, Fred made arrangements for Harold to go to a boarding school in Wellington. It was for the best, they agreed, as they all saw Harold off on the night train that would bear him hundreds of miles away. A fresh start. John gripped Jean's hand tightly, holding her back from the edge of the platform.

When Harold was on board, Jean heard Nellie murmur, 'A relief,' but there was something shaky about her voice. Steam billowed in their faces as the train snorted, heaving into life. The whistle blew and the guard said, 'Stand back, please.' If Harold minded, he wasn't showing it. 'It'll be a lark,' he'd said. He didn't wave back to them standing there on the platform, just stared straight ahead. In his shiny new Wellington College blazer, he looked young and vulnerable, his hair cut very short back and sides, like a plucked chicken. For a moment, Jean had an odd feeling of remorse, as if it were she who had sent her brother away. The family had begun on their separate ways.

Next it was Fred leaving, only this time there were streamers to hold onto as the ship pulled out from the shore, and a brass band played, while the men on the decks of the ship tossed their lemon squeezers in the air. Nellie, who wore a particularly large navy hat, adorned with ostrich feathers, pulled the veil over her eyes.

Mail arrived from the other side of the world, two letters from London, the other from 'Somewhere in France'. Nellie had bought them some maps of their own, and John and Jean traced lines across the world, working out the location of the cities from where the letters were written. 'All the way across the sea to Australia, and across the equator, right away up there,' John said.

Harold came home for the May school holidays, and joined in these searches, just as he had when they were small, his yearning to be far away as strong as ever. In his first months at his new school Harold had been writing home saying he hoped the war would last forever because soon he would be old enough to join up and he could put this *b_____ school* behind him.

'I'm going to London some day,' Jean said. Her brothers thought this funny.

'I'm not going back to Wellington,' Harold said to his mother one morning, when the time for him to leave drew close. 'I told you I was going to join up.'

'Stop that nonsense,' Nellie said. 'You're too young.'

'Too old, too young, that's all you ever think about,' Harold said, venom in his voice. 'There're kids in the trenches who are fifteen I know, I've heard about it. One of the boys in my house has a cousin in England and he ran away to the war.'

'Yes, and they would have caught him and sent him home,' Nellie said.

'Oh no they didn't.'

'I knew I'd have this trouble with you when your father went away,' Nellie said, her face red with exasperation. 'He's hardly gone and you're trouble. I don't know how he ever expected me to keep control of you.' She was standing at the kitchen bench, peeling potatoes. Her hand lifted, holding the knife, as if she were about to strike her son.

'You wouldn't dare,' he said. There was something about his face that reminded Jean of the day by the lake, when she had been challenged by the swan. She was eight now, and had forgotten about it until then, but the memory bubbled up unbidden.

'Listen,' Nellie said, as if exhausted with anger, even though they had been quarrelling for only a minute or so, 'let's all go down to the harbour this afternoon. We can look at the flying boats at the training school. They're training pilots to serve with the Royal Flying Corps, you know. They'll go to France, just like your father.'

This seemed, temporarily, to appease Harold. The seaplanes and their pilots were a fast-growing Auckland legend. A youth called Malcolm MacGregor had made a name for himself doing crazy stunts and aerobatics, swooping low over the city's buses and trains, as well as trying to knock the tops of church spires. He was known as 'Mad Mac'. When interviewed, he said he was just letting off a bit of steam because he hadn't been allowed to go to war on account of his age. Harold's eyes lit up when he heard of these exploits.

A dozen young men lived in rough huts and tents, between the bush and the water, flying from morning until night. Mac had gone off to war, of age now. The trainees, handpicked by the Walsh brothers who ran the school, dazzled and burned with risk and daring. When the Battens reached the water's edge, they saw small seaplanes skimming across the water, showering spray behind them before rising into the sky. Like seagulls, Jean thought. The spindly flying boats flew back, circling the bay, sun gleaming on their wings.

Jean stood on the tips of her toes. 'I want to do that. Mother, I want to fly aeroplanes.'

'Oh yes, darling, yes,' Nellie cried. 'You know how I'd like to do that, too.' Her face was shining with excitement, the upset of the morning forgotten.

'We can go flying together, you and me. I can drive the plane,' Jean said.

On the shoreline, a pilot was beckoning the two boys over to look inside his machine. They ran across the grass to where it was anchored.

As Harold and John climbed into the cockpit Jean stamped her foot. The pilot saw her and called out, asking if the little girl wanted to look as well. When she ran forward he swung her up easily above his shoulder to join her brothers. She saw the shadowy recesses of the plane's interior, noting the deep metal seat and the rudder bar, the control column and the instrument panel.

'Is it hard to fly a plane?' Jean asked.

'Easy as riding a bike,' he said, laughing.

That night she dreamed of flying, and though often given to nightmares, rested easily, lifted in sleep into the blue blaze of a summer sky.

Another letter came from Fred, this time just for Jean, bulkier than the ones that had come before. On opening it she found a bunch of wild blue violets pressed between its pages. 'Do they really grow wild in the woods?' she asked Nellie. She remembered the violets her mother had tended with care when they still had a garden. There was a garden of sorts where they lived now, a two-bedroom house at the rough end of St Georges Bay Road. It wasn't big enough to contain all their furniture and some of it had to be sold. Nellie wept the day the piano went, not consoled by the good price it fetched at auction. At night, soldiers lurched down the road singing beery songs in ragged off-key bursts. There were houses where dim lights shone at night, even though they were supposed to be blacked out. When a drunken man banged on the Battens' door one evening, lurching against the verandah post, Nellie said in a blistering tone that though women did have the right to choose what they did with their bodies she wasn't one of them, thank you, and if the man wanted a disgusting illness, that was his business and may all his bits rot off. She slammed the door hard, and leaned against it. Then she saw Jean's frightened face, heavy with startled sleep, in the passageway.

'Get back to bed this instant,' she cried, as if she were scolding. 'Jean, go back to bed.'

'I want Dad to come home,' Jean said.

In the morning this seemed like one of the bad dreams, the sight of her mother shaking from head to toe, collapsed against the wall. She caressed the violets her father had sent her, their slender stems dried out already and brittle, but when she held them to her face she was sure she detected some wild woody scent.

Harold ran away from school. In Wellington, he caught the north-bound night train, but somewhere along the way he had got off it. Nellie had gone straight to the police station with the constable who delivered the news. The police there had their hands full, they said. All these soldiers coming home and there was trouble of one sort or another everywhere. Did she think her son might have tried to join up? Of course, that was the first thing that had crossed her mind. She had to confess that. But, could they not, at least, ask the people at the railways if anyone had seen him? What if he had fallen from the train between the carriages, somewhere on the high central plateau, his body lying on the side of the tracks? By this time, at least a week had passed since his disappearance.

The sergeant on duty said that yes, they could, at least, do that. In the meantime she should check the recruiting office. This wasn't as easy as it sounded. Harold could have enlisted in any little town between Wellington and Auckland. Jean came home in the afternoon to find her mother standing in the parlour of the front room, white-faced. The sergeant stood with his notebook in his hand. Yes, he told her, the boy had been seen getting off the train soon after he left Wellington. The guard remembered him, because Harold had chatted to him, not long after the train left, although, as he recalled, the boy was fidgety. Harold told him he was eighteen, and reckoned he could do any man's job — shovel coal, drive a jigger. Perhaps, he said, he could get a job on the railways. The guard had gone away to clip tickets and when he came back, after the next stop, Harold was gone.

'Did you know what he was planning to do?' Nellie demanded of John.

John looked evasive. 'Did you, or didn't you?' Nellie shouted, and to her daughter's astonishment, began raining blows on her brother's head. She was bigger and still much taller than John. John, the delicate dark boy who, it seemed, never caused anyone trouble. 'Truth,' she cried, 'I want truth out of you.'

John put his hands up to stop her. 'He took some money from milk buckets when he was home in May. He told me they didn't feed him properly down south.'

'Did he just? Well, bigger fool anyone who leaves money lying around these days. What else?'

John stood up, regarding his mother with his cool, beautiful eyes, seeming all of a sudden to be much older. 'You didn't notice he went down to the shipping office every day that he was here?' he said. 'I reckon he's gone off to sea.'

Nellie sank into the now-battered green armchair. 'What will I tell your father?'

'So what did you expect?' John was talking like an adult, the man of the house, as if he were acting a role. He was fourteen but he had developed a certain elegance in his manner. Since the beginning of the year he had gone to King's College. 'You think Harold could become a lawyer or an accountant, Mother? You really think he's that special?'

Nellie rested her chin on her hand. 'I thought that he

45

might be able to make something of himself, that's what I thought. If he tried.' She corrected herself. 'If we all tried hard enough. It's this war, I suppose. Why didn't you tell me, John?'

'I wanted him to stay away.'

'Oh you did, did you? Why was that?'

John looked away, a child again. 'He said nasty things.'

'Nasty things. Sticks and stones can break my bones, but words never hurt anyone. John, I thought better of you.'

This, too, was a moment that marked change. Nellie and John's relationship slid downhill after that. John, the traitor. Not that it was remarked on again, it was just that the closeness melted away between them, as if John might be as capable of misdeeds as Harold. Besides, Nellie couldn't afford to keep him at his new school, and so he had the humiliation of returning to his old one. But then, neither could their mother go on paying for Jean at Melmerley. All round, it was a disaster. No news of Harold emerged. Nellie wrote to Fred, but as she said, he could hardly catch a boat home. When some weeks had passed, she decided that perhaps no news was good news. Harold was a big boy and strong. Somewhere, he was sure to be all right.

Something else happened.

An extraordinary lead story in the *Truth* newspaper

reported that a twenty-year-old Sydney student, described as looking very young for his age, had appeared in court on forgery charges. He called himself William Sanders but in the box he gave his name as Harold Batten. When arrested, he was found to be carrying several letters he had written to insurance companies, threatening and wheedling them for discharge documents from a merchant shipping company, in exchange for information about threats to blow up their ships.

'I was just being silly the day I wrote those,' the boy told the detective who interviewed him. 'Someone did want me to blow up ships, but I wouldn't do that; I'm British, you know. There're lots of Germans here that you don't know about. They're always plotting to get people to blow up ships. You know, I just wrote those to let the insurance companies know.'

At his lodgings the police found more letters, and plugs of gelignite, fuse and powder, as well as detonators, enough to blow a hole in the side of a ship.

'It can't be him,' Nellie said. The police in Auckland didn't seem to think so either, although nobody could be sure. 'His name is Frederick, it's only the family who call him Harold.'

But the harm was done. The daily newspaper picked up the story and roaring headlines followed them. At Jean's new school, the first thing the children asked the next day was whether she had a brother called Harold. She said she had a brother called John. Her face was set in a stony stare. Miss Stand-off, they called her. A boy asked in front

47

of his mates if she were planning to run away to sea any time soon. Voices followed her around the school ground as she walked on her own. 'Harold, Harold,' they chanted. 'Where are you, Harold?'

She considered going to the swimming baths for the day, but if she did that she would miss the geography lessons that made sense of the maps she and John studied, the arithmetic she excelled in, and English, which always earned her the best marks in the class. If she learned what she needed to know, she decided, she would rescue herself, in time.

Her teacher, a skinny older man with a hairless head, told Nellie, grudgingly, that her daughter had a gift, but there was no need for her to be forward. She shouldn't get ideas above her station. Girls needed to be practical in their disciplines, and when it came to being top of the class it would do her no good at all if she let the boys see how clever she was. Besides, with trouble like theirs, it didn't do to stand out.

'We do not have troubles at home,' Nellie said.

'Oh, then please accept my apologies, Mrs Batten,' the little man said, his eyes glittering with amusement.

The truth was, they still didn't know where Harold was. The scandal, real or imagined, wasn't going away easily. The 'case of Harold Batten' rumbled on through the news for several weeks. The boy in Australia was now reported as having been born in Melbourne under a different name again. It didn't seem possible that he was their Harold Batten. Nellie said that Jean must remember to refer to Harold as Frederick if she were ever asked about him.

It was around then that Nellie began betting on the horses, going to the tote on her own, carrying a big bag with a brass buckle.

Chapter 4

Jean learned to use a compass after her father returned from the war.

The letters from Fred had continued to arrive in bursts from overseas. There would be long silences and then a flurry of his correspondence. Some contained descriptions of places he had visited, though little of the horrors he witnessed, just a passing reference now and then to 'some poor devil with both his legs blown off'. He told them about Paris and the Eiffel Tower and the Arc de Triomphe, about the way the French drank wine and ate well even though food was scarce, but it was amazing what they could do with a snail or two, and food gathered from the countryside, about the lilac trees blooming, the little chimney pots on the roofs of the houses, the horse-chestnuts greening all along the vast length of the Champs-Elysées, the most beautiful avenue in the world, though by Jove he wouldn't mind the sight of the oak trees along Symonds Street.

Elysées was the French name for the Elysian Fields, he wrote, the place of the blessed dead in Greek mythology. This elicited a sharp snort of laughter from Nellie. 'He needn't give us the Greeks and French wine,' she said. 'We actually need more food of our own.' All the same Nellie wrote steadfastly every week whether there had been a letter from Fred or not. 'Although what have I got to tell him?' she asked Jean one Sunday. Sunday was her day for writing letters: to Fred, and also to one of her two brothers still fighting overseas, and to her mother in Invercargill, failing in health and still longing for 'the old country'. Her mother had never got over homesickness, and now, Nellie said with a catch in her voice, she would never go home.

'Nothing but gloom,' Nellie continued, answering her own question. 'Harold in trouble and nowhere to be found. John gone all peculiar on me, up and staying out late. And never enough money. No wonder Fred doesn't write much. What can he say about our problems?'

Jean stroked the side of her mother's face. Nellie took her hand in hers. 'I've got you, my darling,' she said. 'I write and tell Father every week what a good girl you are.'

Then a letter came from London, not long after Armistice Day, full of endearments and news of Fred's anticipated departure for New Zealand. He wished he was coming home for Christmas, but he thought it would take a bit longer than that. He couldn't tell his dear wife how much he longed to see her. As Nellie read this letter to Jean and John, over breakfast, her eyes filled with tears and longing.

'He'll have to say goodbye to all his French girlfriends, won't he?' John said.

'Don't you say that about our dad,' Jean said.

'I think you'd better leave the table, John,' his mother said, her face rigid, throat crimson.

John, now sixteen, uncurled himself from his chair like a graceful cat. Jean would remember the way he carried himself then, the poise of his shoulders, the eloquent gestures of his hands. There were days she wanted to go after him when he left the house but somehow he had outgrown her, making her feel childish and small.

Fred's discharge didn't arrive until early in January and it was April before he made it home on the *Ionic*. When he showed them his British War Medal and Victory Medal, Nellie's face shone with pride. She softened and mellowed, made plans to help Fred restart his dental practice. He would go back to his old rooms and she would be his nurse. Fred had rented a house in Epsom for them all, a step up from their lodgings during the war.

Fred's trunk contained treasures that Jean seized on as they were unpacked. There were manuals about warfare and maps and a compass. She watched its needle slide this way and that. When her father explained that it showed the direction between one place and another, she demanded to be shown how it worked. 'Why, little Mit, I think you're serious,' he said. 'We'll have to see about that.'

He had bought a motorbike, and now he took her on his pillion for a ride into the bush on the edge of Auckland, equipping them with maps and a compass so they could determine their route. He showed her how to orientate a map, using the compass to work out a heading for their destination. And straightaway, it seemed, Jean had worked out that they must travel south-east from the Waitakeres if they were to get back to Epsom. 'Amazing kid,' Fred told Nellie on their return. 'I can't believe how well she got it. She understands navigation.'

He took her on more expeditions in order to test his first impression of her skill. She never failed him. On the motorbike, her arms wrapped around her father's waist, Jean had her first real sense that she was flying. The feel of the wind rushing past her face, the road uncurling beneath the tyres of the motorbike, made her so happy that she never wanted to let go. Her heart, pressed against Fred's back, waltzed with the pleasure of his nearness.

That same year, 1919, news came through that two men had crossed the Atlantic in a plane. John Alcock and Arthur Whitten Brown had taken fewer than sixteen hours to fly from Newfoundland to Ireland, in a former wartime bomber modified to carry enough fuel for a long-distance flight. It was June, summertime in the Northern Hemisphere.

'Hurrah, for Jack and Teddy,' Nellie cried, brandishing a newspaper at dinner as rain pelted against the windows and damp seeped under the eaves. A flickering gas fire added little warmth.

'You don't know them, Nell.' Fred's tone was caustic.

'That's what everyone calls them,' she said. 'Oh my goodness, they've won ten thousand pounds. Can you imagine it? And the King has given them knighthoods. They're heroes.'

'They crashed their plane in Ireland. Hit a bog in Galway. They just got lucky,' Fred said.

'What's eating you, Fred? They're brave, they served in the air force in the war. Alcock was taken prisoner.'

'People did what they had to in the war,' he said, sounding weary and a trifle defensive.

When he and Jean were next in the Waitakere Ranges, plotting their way back to Auckland, Jean said, 'Did you see the planes fly in the war, Dad?' They were deep in bush, along a gravel track near one of the waterfalls, a cavalcade of water prancing on dark rock.

'Of course I saw them,' Fred said. 'They were all around and above us.'

'I love planes,' Jean said.

'I know you do. But aeroplanes fall out of the sky. I saw that, too. I saw flames overtake them, and men spin out of them like flies on fire, and when we picked them up, there was nothing left of them, just teeth and bones and the rags of their clothes. And the smell of what was left of them.'

Jean was silent.

'I'm sorry. You're too young to know about such things. Just don't think about aeroplanes.'

'I can't help it.'

'You mean your mother can't help it. We all have our weaknesses. Now come on, concentrate on what you're doing, or we'll have to spend the night in the bush.' A shock of wind was jostling the trees around them. Dusk was closing in. Between the branches of tall trees and the tangle of ferns, Jean could see the light leaking out of the sky. 'There are bats out here,' said Fred, 'and you'll get flying lessons if you run into them.'

Nellie was no less excited when, that same year, Australian brothers Ross and Keith Smith, with two other men, flew from England to Australia for the first time, over twenty-eight days. One hundred and thirty-five hours in the air all told. Nellie was ecstatic when she read these items aloud to Jean. 'Oh, it's really possible,' she cried. 'Imagine, flying all that way from one side of the world to another. Wouldn't you like to do that, Jean?' She held her arms out as if they were wings and bobbed from side to side.

This was in December. Nine days later, John Alcock, the Atlantic flier, was dead. His latest plane had crashed in France, near Rouen.

Fred didn't say anything when Nellie announced the news in a subdued voice. Still, it was nearly Christmas, and it was agreed there would be turkey and plum pudding with threepences. The war was over. They were all safe. The world would go on.

None of this rediscovered domesticity would last for long.

First, a letter arrived for Fred, addressed in unusual handwriting, postmarked Paris. The letter had been sent care of army headquarters and forwarded to Fred at their new address. Nellie was at home on a Saturday morning with Jean when it arrived. She put down a sock she was darning, held the letter up to her nose and sniffed, then put it down quickly, as if it might burn her hand.

'Dad's friends are writing to him from France,' Jean said excitedly. 'That's nice, Mother. Isn't it nice?'

'You seem to have mail from a friend in France,' Nellie said when Fred came home, and Jean knew that somehow this wasn't nice after all.

Fred stood looking sheepish in the hallway.

'Well, Fred, aren't you going to open it?'

'After dinner,' he said, pocketing the letter.

'After dinner,' she mocked. 'After the roast beef and Yorkshire pudding. After the apple sponge. Then what? Something a little decadent, perhaps.'

'You're being silly, Nellie. We New Zealanders made a lot of friends in France.'

'Oh, friends. Well, we all want to share your French friendships. Could we have a reading over dessert then? We could all write letters from New Zealand to your new French friends. Who knows, they might want to come and visit us.'

Fred picked up the hat he had laid on the chair and walked back out without saying a word.

'Fred Batten, you come right back here,' Nellie shouted, racing to the door and calling into the night.

Fred didn't return until after midnight. Jean knew, because she lay awake listening for him. In the morning, the house was quiet and Nellie was red-eyed and shiny-nosed, but on Monday morning, Fred dressed with his usual care. Over breakfast, he asked his wife if she would be joining him at the surgery. If she didn't intend coming in, he'd like to know because he would have to make other arrangements. When she said that yes, of course she would be in, Jean could feel the relief in the room. John had been kicking the leg of the table, and pretending to read a book. A Shakespearean play, Jean thought. She had an idea his class was studying *Macbeth*.

Life continued quietly for some months. No more letters arrived for Fred. Nellie had stopped going to the races, a pastime Fred disapproved of. Sometimes she seemed heavy in her movements, but Fred acted more or less as if nothing had happened. He took Jean out on his motorbike and spared nothing to make her smile. When there were silences between him and Nellie, Jean found something to fill them, rushing to tell them about her school day, what she had learned in geography, her favourite subject.

John had become more withdrawn and took little part in these conversations. His age, Nellie would sigh, if Fred mentioned the boy's silences. The company of his drama group preoccupied John, and when Jean talked volubly at the table, he was inclined to cast his eyes towards the ceiling and start mouthing in silence, as if he were reciting. When Fred asked him about his day, John was as likely to tell his father that he wouldn't understand. As if Fred was at best ill-educated or, at worst, an idiot. Talking down, Fred said one night, fury in his voice.

'What do you know about Shakespeare?' John said, in the same cool way he had been addressing Nellie since challenged, years before.

'It is a wise father that knows his own child,' Fred said. '*Merchant of Venice* Act 2, Scene 2.'

'War, is it, Father? You only think you know me.' John looked worried all the same. 'I thought it was Mother who was the actress in this house.'

'And you think I'm a nincompoop.'

'Oh, leave it be, Fred,' Nellie said, throwing up her hands. 'What difference does it make if the boy wants to be a know-it-all?'

'Truth will come to light; murder cannot be hid long,' John said. 'Same scene.'

Nobody said anything. After a while, John got up and left the room. A house full of exits and entrances, or so it seemed. It wasn't murder that was about to be uncovered, but, on another evening not long after this, a woman knocked at the door. She held a child of perhaps six or seven years of age by the hand.

She was a Maori woman, dressed in a white high-necked blouse, and a long dark skirt beneath a heavy coat missing buttons. Her hair showered her shoulders in a thick black mass, a small headscarf holding it back from her face. The little boy was fairer than his mother. The woman spoke in a quiet voice when Nellie opened the door. 'Mrs Batten, perhaps you won't remember me. I've come to see Mr Batten, if you don't mind.'

This time the actress in Nellie was to the fore.

'But of course I remember you,' she said, smiling and addressing the woman by name. 'I remember when my sister came up from the south and we went sightseeing in Rotorua. We met you at the hot pools. You were cooking lunch, I think.' The woman shifted uneasily. 'So tell me, have you moved to Auckland?'

'No,' the woman said, casting her eyes downwards. 'If I could just see Mr Batten for a minute.'

'Fred. My husband. Oh, do come in, I'm sure he'd love to see you.'

But Fred was already at the door. 'Nell,' he said, in an urgent voice, 'I'll take care of this.' The child was gazing at his face.

The woman said, 'Mr Batten. I'm sorry. Times aren't so good for me.'

'I'm sure the little one must be a great penny diver,' Nellie said. She was referring to the Maori children who dived off a bridge into a thermal river, when tourists threw them money, filling their cheeks until they bulged. 'Fred, I've invited our guests in.'

But Fred was knotting a scarf around his neck, grabbing his hat, as he pushed the woman away from the door and closed it behind them. Jean heard them talking on the pathway outside, then the gate clicked shut, as all three of them made their way down the street. This time, Fred wasn't away long. When he came back he sank wearily onto the tattered green chair that had seen so many homes since Nellie had bought it, elegant and new, in Rotorua.

'Nell, Nell,' he said.

'Nell, nothing. You didn't tell me there was a child.'

'I don't know whether it's mine.'

'Oh, don't you just. Well, it *looks* like yours.'

'I don't know. Believe me. I didn't know.'

'I *saw* you with her. On one of your walks. I might have known you'd slept with her. You fornicated with her, Fred. We can agree on that, can't we? We left Rotorua because of the women. There was the patient who spread her legs for you when you'd finished filling her teeth, in the dental chair. And now there's this one. I'm sorry, I get them mixed up, there are so many. It's a disease, Fred, that's what you have, an illness that means you can't keep your trousers buttoned up. Whoops, another one who's willing.'

Fred raised a hand to strike her. 'Stop it, stop your wicked, dirty mouth.'

Jean put her hands over her ears and began to scream.

'Nellie, listen, I had no idea the woman had a child. I have no idea whose it is.'

'Oh no.' Nellie lifted a wicker chair over her head, and smashed it on the floor so that one of the legs broke. 'And how many have you left behind in France, Fred? Eh? Tell me that.'

Fred put his hands over his face, tears leaking between his fingers. 'I don't know,' he said, his voice broken.

'Well, you can get out. You can leave, Fred.'

He appeared to pull himself together. Jean had crouched down in a corner of the room. 'Don't worry,' he said. 'I'm off. You're mad, Ellen. Has anyone ever told you that?'

Nellie picked up a dirty dish from the table, where they

had been eating not half an hour before, flinging it at him so that it hit the wall above his head and shattered, gravy trickling down. This was followed immediately by the cruet set, the pepper pot breaking a window, splinters of glass flying into the room. Jean put her arms around her head.

Fred was standing, gripping his wife's wrist. 'For the child's sake, stop. For Jeannie, our little Mit. Don't do it any more.'

Nell let her hands go limp. 'Just go, Fred.'

'So that's it, Ellen? You want a divorce.'

Nellie looked at him in astonishment, stopped in her tracks for the moment. 'Don't be ridiculous, Fred. Of course I don't want a divorce. I just want you to go away.'

Before the night was over, Fred was packing a suitcase. First his trousers, folded neatly on the bottom, then the white coats he wore to his practice, his belts and ties and cufflinks, and lastly his shirts. Jean had crawled along the floor, as if standing up might invite some further wrath from her mother. Now she threw herself at the suitcase, dragging out his shirts. 'Don't go. Dad, please don't leave us.'

He knelt down beside her and touched her cheek with the back of his hand. 'I have to,' he said. 'It's my fault. Don't be sad. I'll see you very soon. I'll see you often.'

'You can take your sons with you,' Nellie said. 'I don't want them back here.' Harold wasn't living with them, so she really meant John.

'Don't blame them for this,' Fred said. 'They haven't done anything.'

'I looked after them in the war. The war you didn't need to go to. I had to deal with those big boys on my own and all the trouble they caused. It's your turn now, Fred.' While he was packing, she went to John's room and began filling another suitcase with his clothes.

John arrived home shortly after this, and seemed to take in what was happening at a glance, as if it were not altogether a surprise. Or that was until he found his mother in his room, going about her work, clearing his wardrobe.

'I didn't ask for this,' he said, and all of a sudden he wasn't adult at all, his face puckering as if he were about to cry.

'I don't care what you asked for,' Nellie said. 'You haven't had a good word for me in a long time, and I tell you I won't take it any more.'

'But I don't even get on with Father,' John said.

'Well, you'd better start, because that's who you've got now.' She was bent on one knee on the suitcase, pulling it together with a leather strap.

'Where will we go tonight?'

'Tonight? That's not for me to worry about. Just pick up your books and get going.'

Seeing Jean sobbing in the corner of the front room, John came over and knelt beside her. 'Jean, it won't be for long. They'll get back together, you'll see.' When her convulsive sobs didn't stop he put both arms around her.

'I'm sorry, I didn't mean to be rough on you. We've had good times, you and me. We'll stick together.' Jean's breath caught in her throat as she tried to stifle her crying. She put her head on his shoulder. 'You're just a little kid still. There are some things I can't explain to you right now. Perhaps you'll understand some day. You'll always be my little sister. Here, take my hankie. All right? All right now, you hold on tight to that, and I'll see you soon.' He stood awkwardly beside her.

'What if Harold comes back?' she whispered.

He paused, ruffling her hair, an unhappy expression crossing his face.

'He'll be my problem, I guess. Anyway, our mother won't let him come back.'

By then it was nearly eleven o'clock. Fred pointed out that they wouldn't get into a hotel now, the doors would be all shut. Nellie reminded him that he had his surgery rooms: why didn't he and John just go there and sleep on the floor.

Chapter 5

When it came down to it, it was Nellie who left Fred. The night after their quarrel, Fred used his key to return. He was carrying the suitcase he had packed the night before. 'This is where I live, and I pay the rent,' he told Nellie. 'You might as well get used to it. John will be back later this evening.'

Nellie had been weeping all through the night and looked at him now with haggard eyes. 'Ellen, stop this. I'm not shifting anywhere.'

She straightened herself up. 'I might have known,' she said. 'You want it all, don't you? The women and us. I'm not going to stand for it.' But she must have known this would happen because, even as she had wept, she had packed bags for herself and Jean. 'We're the ones who're leaving.'

'Good luck,' he said. 'Don't expect me to pay two rents. And don't think I'll leave our daughter living on the streets.'

Nellie held the big bag that had stayed in the back of her wardrobe since Fred came home. 'She won't,' she said. 'I can promise you that. My daughter.'

'Mother,' Jean said, but Nellie had her by the arm and

was marching her out the door. That night they slept in their new accommodation — one room, a tiny kitchen and a shared bathroom, above a shop in Parnell. Nellie paid over a month's rent in advance. 'We've made out on our own before,' she said breezily to Jean, as if recovered from the trauma of the night. 'The war was a good training ground. Life's one long battle, it seems, but we're prepared, you and I.'

In the little room that night, Jean lay awake in the double bed, Nellie's body rising and falling beside her as she slept, exhausted beyond reason. She reached out and touched her mother's arm, but she didn't respond. In the kitchenette, gas hissed in the pipes. Through the wall a woman's voice rose in an odd shriek. A man's voice spoke and there was laughter, and then the woman made yipping noises as if she were happy and ended with another shriek. Out on the street men sang, swore, much as they had done on the nights when Nellie blockaded the doors while Fred was away. Only then there had been John. Jean thought that they might not be safe in this room. She vowed to herself that she would stay awake every night and keep watch over her mother.

As time wore on, and nothing changed, a terrible dullness, like pain, descended on her. If Nellie noticed she didn't say anything about it, for they had both sunk into listless bouts of silence. One day, Nellie said, as if coming out of a reverie, 'I did love him, you know.' She wasn't expecting an answer, and Jean had none to offer. She felt hollowed out, as if there was no flesh behind her sleepless eyes. Her mouth was dry and seemed to prickle. In the night, as she lay watching her mother's solid, unmoving sleep, she thought there were ants crawling across her skin, but when she shone her torch under the blankets there was nothing there.

Nellie wasn't really prepared for battle. The bag of money emptied quickly. Jean hadn't been to school since they left Fred. The second month was nearly at an end, when Fred appeared at the door one day and demanded to be let in. On seeing Jean, he said to Nellie, 'She needs to be out of this. I'm taking her away.'

'You can't do that.' Nellie's voice was thick, the flat dirty, with dishes piled up around the sink, the floor not swept. There was a stain of egg yolk on her blouse.

'You're coming with me, young lady,' Fred said.

'I can't leave Mother,' Jean said. 'I can't.'

'You will,' he said, and before long he and Jean were heading for a tram, then down Queen Street to the ferry terminal. Jean had an image of her mother's face, the beauty washed out of it, not seeming to resist her being taken away. Exits and entrances, like one of John's school plays. Before long Jean and Fred had boarded a ferry that would take them across the harbour and dispatch them at Birkenhead. 'You need some sea air,' he told Jean. 'This is where people come for their holidays.'

'I don't want a holiday.'

'Yes, you do.' He had said little to her as they crossed the water, his big jaw set at a resolute angle. They boarded a bus that drove them on past little shacks and baches painted in different bright colours, and out into countryside that gave way to an expanse of strawberry fields. They were filled with long rows of planted mounds, and even from the bus window, Jean could see the blush of reddening fruit. The house where Fred took his daughter belonged to a strawberry grower and his wife, a comfortable place with heavy armchairs covered with fawn moquette and a piano in the front room, a kauri dining table that seated eight, feather pillows on the beds. In the garden there was an apple tree, and cape gooseberries. A track led to a still, green inlet of the sea. Fred told the couple that his daughter was an invalid who needed fresh milk and red meat, and kindness. The man was a wiry fellow with quick eyes and a slight hunch from bending, impatient to get back to his work. His wife, Belle, into whose care Fred was placing Jean, commented on how pale and thin the child looked, while at the same time admiring the cut of her blue linen dress, her hand reaching out to finger the crocheted white collar, an action Jean disliked. She stepped away.

Belle seemed an unlikely name for her new guardian. She was a tall, thin woman, her greying fair hair blunt cut beneath her ears, her dress plain and dark. But she had expressive, large-knuckled hands that gestured as she talked, spreading palm up, the pads of her fingertips like odd bleached little moons, clicking finger and thumb when she wanted to make a point. Later, Jean understood that her hands were roughened from her work in the fields. Belle and her husband had children of their own.

Fred said that when Jean was well again, it would be advisable for her to go to the school with them. In the meantime, if it were no trouble to them, she could read books all day long, or just sit in the sun.

When her father left, Jean's sense of abandonment all but swallowed her up. What could her parents be thinking, leaving her alone among strangers? What demons had brought them to this? She reminded herself that she was British. The strawberry growers' children arrived home from school, a girl younger than her, and a boy about the same age. They looked at her with little curiosity. The girl said, 'The last girl who came had some marbles. What have you got?'

'Nothing,' said Jean.

'Didn't they give you sweets to bring?' the boy said.

'I came in a hurry,' Jean said. 'My parents had to leave on a sudden trip to London. The ship's leaving tonight.'

'So, you'll be here for a while by the sound of it,' said the boy.

'Probably not. Soon I'll go to my aunt's place. No, I don't think I'll be here for long at all.'

'Liar,' he said, and laughed.

He and his sister left her alone after that, perhaps instructed by their mother to let her be. They seldom included her in their conversation even when they gathered for meals around the long table, as if they were used to children like her, though their parents made occasional desultory attempts to talk to her. Belle sometimes sat back with a worried frown, watching her. Jean averted her eyes, happy to maintain the cloak of invisibility she believed she had acquired.

The children left each morning, and when they had gone Jean came out from her room and walked in the garden, and usually down the track to the sea, while Belle pegged out lines of washing, the socks and shorts and towels, with the underwear pinned discreetly behind the crisp white sheets, waxed her kitchen floor, and peeled the potatoes for the evening meal. Once or twice she invited Jean to help with some small task, but Jean brushed this aside, too, as if she hadn't heard correctly. Belle merely shrugged and resumed what she was doing. Jean sensed an expectation that she would 'come out of herself' sooner or later, but she had no intention of doing any such thing. At the edge of the sea, she skipped stones on the green water, watching the gulls wheeling in flight, the wading birds busy when the tide was low. The sea, on windless days, was covered with the reflected shadows of clouds. She thought how easy it would be to walk out onto them, as if the water might somehow be solid beneath them, but another self, a person who was old enough to know better, told her not to do this. Some mornings she saw a flying boat pass over her, always on the same route, and wondered if it was the one she had seen with her mother and brothers. On one of these excursions she resolved to write to John and ask him how his plans for fame were coming along. In spite of herself, she began to sleep all night. A morning arrived when she woke up and the cloud seemed to have shifted. She brushed herself to get rid of the ants, but they had disappeared of their own accord.

As if she saw the change in her, Belle said casually, 'Well, you must be ready to go to school now.'

'Why ever should I do that?' Jean said. 'It's nearly the end of the year.'

'That's not the point. You need to get into a routine again.'

'I've no intention of going to school.' Jean stood as tall as she could, and stared at Belle with defiance.

'Your father thought it for the best.'

'That's what my father said to you. He didn't say it to me.'

'Jean, little girls don't talk like that.'

'I'm your guest. You shouldn't speak to me like that.'

Belle's mouth dropped open, soundless for a moment. She looked as if she were going to say something and decided against it.

The day was unusually grey, a damp drizzly morning that sent Jean hurrying inside in the afternoon. For a while she lay on her bed and read. Her reflection in the oval mirror on her dressing table stared back at her. Her dark hair was long and thick and curly, her teeth white and even. She sat up and looked at herself more closely. Her chest had grown. Breasts. What grown women had. When she smiled at herself, she liked what she saw. This smile reminded her of her mother. I am like my mother, she said to herself. Not like my father. Next time Belle called her a child and invoked Fred, she would tell her what she truly thought of her.

In the front room, someone was playing the piano. Jean tried to ignore the music, but there was something insistent about it that made her open her door. Down the passage, she could see into the room where Belle was quietly playing a slow melody, humming to herself.

Belle paused. 'You can join me if you want,' she called.

Jean stood still.

'It doesn't matter about school,' Belle said, in a voice loud enough to carry.

Jean walked towards her. 'To tell you the truth, I don't really care,' Belle said. 'You don't belong to me. I don't have to worry whether you pass exams or not.'

'You were playing Debussy,' Jean said.

'How did you know that?' Belle asked, startled.

'I just do know. Modern, my mother used to say it was rather modern.'

'I see. Can you play the piano?'

'Not really. My parents had one before the war, but not now.'

'Perhaps you could pick up a tune. Do you want me to show you what to do?'

Jean seated herself in front of the piano and ran down some scales. Belle murmured to herself, 'Hmm, I see. Can you do "Chopsticks"?'

'Yes, but my mother called it "The Flea Waltz".'

'Do you want to try a duet with me?' Belle asked.

So they played together and Jean laughed with excitement as they skipped around the notes.

'There now, that was fun,' Belle cried.

Without speaking, Jean began fingering the keys again, the swelling throb of Chopin's 'Raindrop Prelude'.

She didn't know much of it, but what she played was enough to make Belle sit up very straight. 'Prelude number fifteen. I wish my daughter could play like that. Who taught you all this?'

'My mother. My father. I don't remember. It was ages ago, when I was little.' She did remember, of course, her mother on the piano stool beside her, smelling of soap and freshly made bread, a mother who didn't seem to exist any more.

'You've got a gift,' Belle said. 'Lots of kids can play "Chopsticks", but not many can play a Chopin prelude unless they've had lessons. Not even a little bit of one. Perhaps you could be a pianist when you grow up.'

'Can you be famous if you play the piano?' Jean asked.

'You certainly can. Do you want to be famous?'

Yes, Jean replied, that was what she wanted more than anything else. If she were famous, she explained, nobody would be horrible, people would have to be nice all the time.

'Are people horrible to you?' Belle asked with care.

'No,' Jean said swiftly.

'Your brothers?'

Jean gave her a blank stare. 'What brothers?' she said, as if Belle had been rude. 'I'm just going to be famous, that's all.'

Belle laughed. 'Oh well, I hope so. Perhaps you'll marry a famous man and get a title.'

'No, I won't,' Jean said. 'I don't intend to get married. I'm never going to get married.'

'But why ever not?' Belle asked.

'People who are married say cruel things.'

Belle said, 'But I'm married. My husband and I are very nice to each other. Most of the time anyway.' She laughed then, amused at herself. 'Life's never perfect, Jean.'

Jean continued to look past her. It was true, some hardness had begun to grow inside her, a resolve to be perfect, whatever Belle said to the contrary. There had to be a way out of the turmoil she had left behind in Auckland. When she had come to Birkdale the depth of her misery seemed bottomless, but it mattered less than at the beginning. She supposed she had moved on into some other state.

What passed for a guarded friendship was developing between her and the gaunt Belle. One of Belle's many tasks was to drive a rickety flat-bed truck to the sawmiller's yard to collect wooden boxes in preparation for the fruit-picking season. Jean admired Belle's ability to guide the truck over potholes and narrow roads, and back into the yard, as skilful as any of the men in their pick-ups. She helped load and stack the boxes, her strength surprising both of them. On the way back to the farm, Belle would pull over at Verran's store, and buy ice creams. As they sat on the truck's running board, the flying boat Jean had seen earlier passed over head again, while the ice cream melted over their fingers in the warm morning air.

'That's the mail plane to Dargaville,' Belle said.

'I've been in one of those planes,' Jean told her.

'For a ride?'

'No, but some day I'll fly. I know I will.'

'You're going to be busy,' Belle laughed. 'Being a famous concert pianist, and flying planes. What else will you think of?'

As spring went by, and summer's heat stroked the house, it became harder to recall her parents' faces. Sometimes, just before the fast, sudden sleep that overtook her nowadays, she saw her mother's eyes, like a cat's, glowing in the dark. She tried not to see them. Whatever she did must now be directed towards being the best, somebody who stood out, not just lost among strangers.

The first harvest of strawberries was gathered. The fields were now filled with people bent over the mounds, their hands flying in incessant rhythm, their heads covered with straw hats as they picked. At the end of the day, when the main meal was cleared away, Belle placed bowls of the scarlet fruit in the centre of the table, still aromatic with the warmth of the sun, along with jugs of cream. The voluptuous scent of hot strawberry jam filled the house. Strawberry stew, Jean said, the first time Belle made it, and everyone laughed, even the brother and sister she so studiously ignored. Around the table in the evenings, talk was turning towards Christmas, causing Jean unease, as if the spell she was under was about to be broken. Christmas meant long summer holidays, and the children here at the house all the time. Jean thought,

I should do something to save myself. She sat down that evening and wrote to her mother.

Dear Mother,
    I have been British every day since my father brought me here. It's not so bad and the countryside is pretty. But I am not with you and I worry that you are on your own. Perhaps you need me to look after you. I have learned to be useful since I came here.
    Your loving daughter
    Jane (Jean) Gardner Batten

Not long after this, Nellie did come and take her away. Her appearance in Belle's kitchen was regal, the Nellie of old. She wore a dark hat with a huge round brim swept back from her forehead, like a tricorne. The collar of her jacket was edged with fox fur, her grey dress with its sweeping skirt cut low over her bosom, amber beads at her throat. Her famous winged eyebrows swept upwards as she took in her surroundings. She clasped Jean to her. 'I'll never let you go again,' she said.

She barely acknowledged Belle, as Jean's belongings were gathered together, and turned down the offered cup of tea.

'Your daughter has a talent for music,' Belle said, her voice tentative.

'But of course, she comes from a very musical family. My husband and I both play instruments. I've been on the stage a good deal myself, you know.'

'It would be nice if she could have some lessons,' Belle went on, determined to make her point.

'Well of course she'll have lessons,' Nellie said, impatient now. 'She's enrolled at Ladies College in Remuera, starting next term. She'll have the best of everything — music, dance, foreign languages, etiquette.'

They left with barely a goodbye to Belle, Nellie not wishing to prolong the conversation, a certain haughtiness in her demeanour, as if Belle had trespassed, while Jean, sensing the atmosphere, was unwilling to upset her mother so soon after their reunion. She would have liked to run back and given Belle a hug, not that they were in the habit of touching each other.

As they crossed the harbour, Jean said, 'Did John get my letter?' She hadn't dared to ask about her father, although when Nellie had referred to Fred as her husband in the conversation with Belle, her hopes had soared.

'Letter? Oh, I shouldn't think so. John has gone.'

This was how Jean learned that John was no longer in Auckland. Harold had reappeared but had been vague about his whereabouts. He had been working down south, building bridges, he told his father, who at some stage had passed this information on to Nellie. No, of course he hadn't been in Australia, and yes, he saw that stupid thing in the newspaper because the man he was working for had told him about it, and to be honest, he could have wished for any name except Batten. He'd taken to calling himself Fred; he might as well get some benefit from the connection. In fact, he was going to adopt that name for good, seeing that it was his first given name anyway. Of course, Nellie still referred to him as Harold, which, she imagined, the family always would.

Fred did tell her, over tea and cakes when they had met for what she described as a 'civilised conversation', that he had been worried by Harold's apparent envy of the plan to blow up ships. It was something he might have done if he'd thought about it, but anyway, it wasn't all bad because there'd been plenty of explosives used on the jobs he did, blasting rocks along riverbanks in preparation for bridge building. Fred had said that, really, he had no idea if a word of it was the truth. Not long after Jean had left Auckland for Birkdale, Fred had presented both his sons with fifty gold sovereigns and told them to go and find their fortunes in Australia. There was, he said, so little work to be had in New Zealand, they might as well go. For Jean, Harold had lost his substance, turned into a shadowy figure who had come and gone for years now. His presence wasn't one she thought she would miss. But the disappearance of John shook her.

'Well,' Nellie said, as she recounted all this to her daughter, 'I said he wouldn't be able to manage those boys. Now he knows what I had to put up with. At least John came and said goodbye.'

Nellie and Jean had Christmas dinner at a hotel where they were staying, just the two of them eating roast poultry and plum pudding. Jean was overtaken with longing for her father, but knew better than to ask further. He had found himself quite a fancy flat, her mother said. Trust him to fall on his feet, he always did. But over dinner, Nellie seemed in high spirits. They would shortly be moving to a house in Remuera, then Jean would start at her new school. In the meantime, she declared gaily, they would go to the races together and have a flutter or two.

In the weekends that followed, they travelled often by train to the Ellerslie racecourse, where the crowds of people, mostly men, seemed immense. Nellie, in her finery, knew her way to the ticket window, a list of horses' names and numbers clutched in her hand. She was familiar with foreign-sounding terms like quinellas and trifectas. It wasn't clear how Nellie picked horses, but she often backed winners. A horse with a good eye and nice shoulders, she would say in passing. 'A man I knew in Rotorua gave me some tips. Do you remember, Jean, the white horse we rode? Wasn't it handsome?' There were times when Jean was almost overcome, caught in a claustrophobic crush between the bodies of men leaning towards the fence in unison, their arms raised, voices hoarse, not seeing her, the rough tweed of their jackets against her face. They roared and waved their hats in the air, shouting and swearing as the horses thundered past. Nellie watched more quietly, but her cheeks were pink with excitement. Sometimes, when she was flushed with a win, she would hand Jean some money and tell her how to place a bet. On her first bet, Jean won ten shillings while her mother lost roughly the same. 'You needn't tell your father about this,' she said.

This at least was news. It seemed she was going to see Fred again.

Chapter 6

Fred turned up the day Jean started at Ladies College, to escort her and Nellie to the parent welcome. This new school for Jean stood in formal gardens with sweeping lawns as crisp as ironed sheets. The main building featured an elegant crenellated square tower.

'There are only fifty girls enrolled at the school,' Nellie said proudly, adding for Fred's benefit, in case she hadn't already explained, that there were seven teachers and eight visiting professors. Five of the professors specialised in music. The prospectus declared that the school catered for the new requirements of women, not just in home life, but in business and industries and the arts. Women had new privileges as citizens. Since women had won the right to vote, Nellie explained to Jean, it was easier to choose their own vocations, too. She sounded wistful.

Months had passed since Fred and Jean had seen each other. Nellie insisted that Fred was not fit company for his daughter. It had been him who had wrenched Jean from her arms and left her in her time of need. How could she trust him not to kidnap her again? Not that anyone observing them would have guessed this state of affairs, so convincingly did he play the role of devoted father, not to mention that of attentive husband. Dressed in his suit, a white handkerchief in his breast pocket and his gold watch chain over his chest, he ambled along the white-pebbled paths, Nellie on one arm and Jean on the other. The three of them posed together in the gardens for a photograph. Nellie spread a blanket for them on the grass in front of a stand of palm trees, edged with begonias. She and Jean sat down, while Fred stretched alongside, pipe in his mouth, his face level with his daughter's shoulder. He placed his trilby on the ground near Jean's wide-brimmed Panama.

'Perfect,' the photographer announced, emerging from under the dark cloth over his tripod. 'This is a picture for the record books.'

'So, there we are,' Nellie said, when the man had retreated. 'That's us, the perfect family.' The sarcasm simmered close to the surface.

'That's not what you said when you took me to court,' Fred said, without taking his pipe out of his mouth. Nellie put a finger to her lips.

'Three pounds a week, Fred, it's useful.' Jean sank her head onto her knees, to hide her face from them, her hair escaping in tendrils from the ribbons holding it on either side of the straight, pearl-white centre parting. 'Well,' Nellie continued, briskly, 'here comes the headmistress. Stand up, Jean.'

Jean looked up. Mrs Sarah Jones, handsome in a way that was almost a match for Nellie, stood looking at the group as they scrambled to their feet. 'All well, Mr and Mrs Batten?'

As he shook hands, Fred said, 'Our Jean has a delicate constitution.'

'Not at all,' Nellie said. 'She's a very strong girl for her age. You've seen her reports. What Jean lacks in size, she makes up for in her natural abilities.'

Sarah Jones looked from one to the other, her eyebrows slightly raised. 'I'm sure Miss Batten will fit in very well with our young ladies,' she said, after a short silence. She clapped her hands at two girls who had strayed onto the smooth green. 'Ladies,' she called, 'paths are where we walk, not on the grass.' Turning to the Battens, she said, 'We always address our students as ladies, you see. Ladies are ladies and gentlemen are gentlemen. Not that they will meet any young gentlemen while in my care. Miss Batten has brothers, I believe?'

'John,' Nellie said swiftly.

'Frederick,' Fred said in the same breath.

Sarah Jones's eyebrows flickered again, as if she had remembered something.

'Two brothers then? John and Frederick?'

'Both Jean's brothers are overseas,' Nellie said.

'Yes, I see. Well, there are great opportunities for young men abroad. So there are the two?'

'One of them is studying for the theatre,' Fred said, with unexpected authority. 'Our other boy is trying his hand at farming in Australia. We're proud of all our children.'

'Of course.' The principal's face was smooth. She looked Jean over again with a calculating eye. 'Young Jean has the figure of a dancer. We will make something of her, I promise.'

Afterwards, Fred returned to his flat, Jean and Nellie to their newly rented home. It was a basement flat in the house of a milliner, not far from the school, but it was a good address. Then, out of the blue, Fred bought Jean a piano, brand-new and stylish with square plain pillars and a very good tone. Jean could practise in earnest and Nellie could play again. She and the milliner had become instant friends. Nellie was an ideal model for her landlady to experiment on; already her hats were more varied and flamboyant.

Nellie decided that, after all, there was no harm in Jean spending some Saturday afternoons with Fred. These were the days when she dressed with particular care and, carrying the heavy purse over her arm, set off on private expeditions. Some evenings she would come home looking elated, and other times she could barely conceal her despondency, screwing up tote tickets with thinly disguised rage. But she had other preoccupations, too; several evenings a week she went off to work. There were a dozen or more picture theatres in the city, and all of them were crying out for accompanists.

'There,' she exclaimed with satisfaction, one afternoon, when Jean came home from school. 'Thank goodness I kept something up my sleeve. You can see the value of learning the piano. I have a real job.'

Jean's piano did double duty for them both, for while Jean was at school Nellie improvised and practised a repertoire that suited the dramatic needs of the movies she would accompany. While some of the films came with their own scores, which Nellie was obliged to learn, she was taking an interest in Wagnerian music, understanding the value of leitmotif, recurring melodies that could be associated with a certain character in the film, or a place, or an emotion, subtle hints to audiences following the comic twists and turns of Charlie Chaplin or Rudolph Valentino's burning loves and hates. Some evenings, Jean would stay home alone and study; on other nights, she watched a film while her mother played. She studied stars like Lilian Gish in *Broken Blossoms*, and the new Swedish actress Greta Garbo, admiring their poise, the *look* of them, clear-eyed and delicate, the smoothness of their complexions, the way they carried themselves, the tilt of their heads. In Garbo, she sensed some extra quality, a reserve that suggested more than was at first apparent on the screen, an intensity that shimmered beneath the surface, something that might have passed for pain.

On Sundays, Nellie had still another interest. She began to play the piano at Golden Lights, the little spiritualist church in McKelvie Street, where she hoped to find the voice of her baby who had died. So far she had not heard from him, but she believed it might still happen. Somewhere, Nellie thought, her child might have continued to develop a mind beyond this life. It was, she explained to Jean, not so far removed from Christianity, just a little more free in its expression. And what she liked, in particular, was that women got to stand up and speak.

'We do believe in God, the Infinite Intelligence,' she said. 'But we know that God listens to the voices of women as well as those of men.'

She didn't invite Jean to the church, and Jean guessed that if she did and was found out, Fred's three pounds a week might quickly be withdrawn. It was, Nellie said, a simple plain little place, not showy like the big churches, but perhaps for the moment Jean should focus on her religious curriculum at school. 'You don't need to tell your teachers about this,' she said. 'Or about the movies.'

Jean had no intention of doing so. She knew that her teachers would have disapproved of the way she and her mother spent their time. If anything, this double life inspired her to work harder at school. Literature was easy. From the beginning she was in thrall to the poets. *Glory be to God for dappled things* ... Gerard Manley Hopkins. *The Assyrian came down like the wolf on the fold / And his cohorts were gleaming in silver and gold* ... Lord Byron. She hugged that one to her heart. Not bad choices, her teacher said, although, of course, Hopkins was a Roman Catholic and Byron a hedonist, but she should judge the text, not the man.

As Sarah Jones had predicted, Jean was learning to dance, as well as to play the piano, and also to speak like any English lady. Her elocution lessons were going so well that she was frequently asked to do the daily reading at school assembly. When she read a psalm, she felt her mouth releasing a volley of perfect vowels. Her music teacher said she had the making of a great concert pianist; the dance teacher wondered aloud if Jean should consider going to England to train at the Royal School of Ballet. The shorthand and typing teacher, a young man with a thin moustache, said she would make an excellent secretary for any man, and reddened when she said that women might require secretaries in the future, too. Her coach in speech and drama told her mother that Jean not only had an excellent accent, stripped of any unpleasant New Zealand vowels, but a remarkable beauty which should stand her in good stead, should she decide to go on the stage, not that that was quite what was expected of the pupils of Ladies College, but of course times were changing.

Her prizes accumulated: top in scripture, English literature, history and botany, and special prizes in music. Half the girls in Jean's class were in love with the young curate who taught scripture, but it was in Jean that he seemed to find the most spiritual qualities. This was the way he put it. He gazed at her like a man who needed meat. He feels very spiritual about you, someone said at lunch, and laughed, which made Jean blanch. She thought her mother's activities were a secret, but it had been a joke, not freighted with meaning. Life, on the whole, had a glittering quality. It seemed she could do anything she wanted. On days when parents were invited to the school, Jean's classmates waited for Nellie to arrive, eager to see what she was wearing, always something more vibrant and interesting than the other mothers, a frill tucked into some unexpected place, an impossibly large ostrich feather on her hat. Jean didn't know whether to be embarrassed or pleased. Nellie was the only mother who wore lipstick. Fred didn't appear at school again.

Once or twice, Nellie said glumly that there was talk of films getting sound, and characters talking. Of course, she added, she was only playing for pin money, their clothing allowance. She didn't know what they would do if the money ran out. Go around looking like gypsies, she supposed. Meanwhile, she sat, magisterial, before pianos in darkened theatres, dressed in dramatic dark skirts, a fur stole around her shoulders. Women in the audiences who had taken to slim-lined dresses with revers and box-pleated skirts, long beads and cloche hats looked at her with curious gazes.

While Nellie worried about the death of silent movies, Jean began to wonder how much more Ladies College could offer. There were glimpses of the future: a debutantes' presentation ball, marriage to the right kind of man. But who would present her and, more than that, who would marry her? If anyone suitable turned up, he need only peel the first layer off the onion to see what lay inside the Batten family's lives.

And, although for a time she had friends, they were not friends she invited home. There was no real home for them to visit. Nellie had fallen out with the milliner and they had moved on, to another, cheaper place. It took four men to shift the piano. Jean visited girls whose parents had houses with gardens and tennis courts, and maids who served dinner in covered dishes made of silver.

When the invitations were not returned, the friendships began to drift away.

Fred seemed to guess this, even though he stayed away from the school. He surprised Jean, the year she turned fifteen, by offering outings to the beaches for Jean and the girls whose friendships had survived. That summer, the last before she left Ladies College, she could invite the Hermiones and Winifreds, the Annabels and Doras, on excursions. Fred's sister and her husband, who had come to live nearby, had a yacht, and at weekends Fred and his brother-in-law sailed them all across the shining harbour, stopping at small secluded bays to sunbathe and eat and drink. The sun blazed down. While the men smoked and drank beer from heavy brown bottles, the girls rubbed Helena Rubinstein's Sunbathing Oil on each other, swam and larked about, building sandcastles like children, although most of their talk as they burrowed and tunnelled was about boys they knew, about kisses snatched at the end of gardens during their parents' weekend parties, about what it must be like to lie in bed with a man. Fred, bare-chested in his swimming trunks, made jokes, talked to the girls as if they were grown-ups. Jean had never loved him more nor hated him so much.

There was a day when the sea was as blue as gentians and warm as a tub of bath water, the sky bleached with spare white light. The sand was toast beneath their feet.

They photographed each other, taking it in turns so that everyone got in one of the pictures, the girls and the man posing in crocodile formation on rocks in a bay where they had anchored. The girls' bathing suits showed their long golden legs and bare backs. In one photograph, Jean sat at the front, hands on her hips as if preparing to dance, the other girls behind her, the two brothers, her father and uncle, at the back. Something was happening behind her, she wasn't sure what it was, but the air was charged, as if the other girls were aware of something she was not. When the picture was taken, she turned to see her father with his hands still resting on the hips of a girl. He saw that she saw and didn't move. The girl looked back at her, a smile hovering in the corner of her mouth. Everyone but the girl and her father stood and ran down the beach. Fred lifted his face towards the sun, arching his chest muscles, his penis tilting languidly in his bathing trunks. The girl got up and followed the others. All of this happened in the space of seconds, yet when her friend walked away Jean found herself staring at her father as if she had seen him for the first time. She thought, he knows this girl better than the rest. It made her shiver in the heat.

An image rose in front of her, seemingly from nowhere, but it was perfectly clear. The family was at the bath house in Rotorua. It was a Sunday night, and the children had gone on ahead to change. She must have forgotten something, a towel perhaps. Or it could have been that her parents had stayed a long time in the tub and she was looking for them. When she returned, her mother had released her breasts from her costume. They floated like two milky cradles in the water, their nipples upturned and rosy. Fred was behind her, his knees gripping her hips, hands caressing her. Then they had seen her. Fred had sworn and the two of them, in some guilty way, had jumped from the water, her mother covering herself as she did so.

As the launch sped over the water on the return journey from the bay, a turbulence of waves rocked the boat from side to side, the girls shouting with laughter, the men more subdued now, looking their age again.

The next time a boating trip was proposed, Jean turned it down.

Fred shrugged, letting his disappointment show. After a while, she thought she must have imagined what she had seen. Her mind was playing tricks on her. Too many scripture lessons. Too many things not understood, half-remembered. Too much already that she would like to forget if she could.

By then it was too late to change her mind. Fred didn't offer to take the girls sailing again.

Chapter 7

The bewildering cloud of darkness reappeared. As before, it was like fog, something she couldn't brush away. She was aware of a spreading silence within herself. At night she wrote lists in a notebook of her defects. She was too fat, her breasts were too large, even though they were barely evident, her hair she described as messy and had it cut short. When Fred next saw her he was aghast, as if she had had an amputation. This disapproval gave her an odd sense of pleasure.

None of it mattered, she said, when the subject of the new school year arose, because she had decided to leave.

'Did your mother put you up to this?' Fred asked.

This was more or less what Nellie had asked in reverse order. Had Fred put her up to it? Had he said that he didn't have enough money to keep her at school, and if so why hadn't he talked to her about it?

But Jean said, to both of them, no, it wasn't any of those things, and she didn't know exactly why. If they would just leave her alone she would get a job as a secretary. Fred asked her then, would she like to go back and stay with Belle.

'That's what you'd like, wouldn't you?' Jean snapped. 'Get rid of me, just like the boys.'

'Don't tempt me,' Fred said. 'After the money I've spent.'

'You know,' Jean said, 'you and my mother, that's all you can think of, isn't it. You're as bad as each other.'

'Have it your way,' he said, wearying of her. 'Get a job. Find out what it's like to earn money.'

There was something appealing about the idea of going back to Belle, of simply fading into the backwater of Birkdale, of being soothed and fed and reassured. But it occurred to her that now that she was, as she styled herself, an adult old enough to leave school, she might not get away with this. Besides, she sensed in her mother some vulnerability that hadn't existed before. Her mother's visits to the races had become more furtive. Perhaps Nellie's luck had run out. Jean often wondered where John was, if he might ever come home. Her mother said he was learning to be an actor, so she supposed he must be following in her footsteps, but she wished he would *consult* her about this, because there was much that she could tell him about the profession.

Harold had already returned to New Zealand with an Australian wife, a woman called Alma. With the help of Fred's war pension, they had bought a piece of land up north near some caves. The question of Harold seemed to be settled.

Nellie and Jean moved again, the beginning of a succession of boarding houses, each one a little shabbier than its predecessor. As they moved, the number of their possessions grew steadily smaller, making it easier to up sticks and leave. The tall vases, the rugs and the pictures Jean dimly remembered had been sold long before. The chairs and tables that had once furnished the family homes had gone to Fred's flat. Nellie did carry clean sets of bed linen in her suitcase, and her own egg-beater, but little more, except for a hat-box. They must keep up appearances, she told Jean. No matter where we live, we must dress as if success is just around the corner. Jean lay in the cramped bedrooms they now inhabited, overcome with the desire to sleep, as in the bad time when she was younger. The triumphs of school days seemed far away. Nellie wanted her to see a doctor but she said that she didn't need one and would Nellie please *please* please leave her alone. Nellie didn't, of course. At nights, when she came home from the theatre exhausted, she sat by Jean's bed, while her daughter pretended to be asleep because, having dozed all day, she couldn't rest at night.

In the spring of 1926, the dancer Anna Pavlova came to town with her company. Nellie queued for five hours in order to buy tickets in the gods at His Majesty's Theatre for sixpence apiece. Together they watched Pavlova dance her famous Dying Swan role. For an evening it seemed to Jean that it was possible to suspend belief, to enter another world. The words *gossamer* and *fragile as a butterfly*

would shimmer through the newspaper reviews.

'Did you see?' Jean said, turning to her mother. 'She *flew.*' The crowd was stamping and roaring, flowers raining on the stage, a wild dark stain of red roses spreading across the boards. Pavlova came back time and again to take curtain calls. She picked up handfuls of petals and threw them back into the crowd. We love you, the audience shouted. And then they simply chanted, 'Pavlova, Pavlova, Pav-*lo-va*', the longing for the magic to stay almost unbearable.

'You could do that,' Nellie said, as they pushed their way through the crowded streets, back to their lodgings. 'Your teacher used to say you were a wonderful dancer.'

'Oh, Mother,' Jean said, tired, and suddenly cross. 'Of course I couldn't.'

'Pavlova wasn't perfect when she began dancing. It took her a long time to find her feet, in a manner of speaking. I'm not going to let it rest there. You enjoyed yourself tonight. I saw that.'

One day soon afterwards, when Nellie left to do what she termed some business, Jean got up and walked to the wharves at the end of Queen Street. She looked at the sea, wondering if it would be such a bad thing after all just to keep walking over the edge of the wharf and let the water wash over her. She thought then that this was some form of madness, that it was not the first time it had happened, and that she must save herself. She shook herself, as if to rid herself of the unnameable dread that had filled every waking moment for months.

As she retraced her steps to the boarding house, Jean

looked for signs in the windows, advertising for staff. She came to what she was looking for, a notice for a lady secretary to a gentleman accountant, thirty shillings a week, must have shorthand and typing skills and be well spoken. Nellie was still out when Jean got back to their room. She washed her face and changed her clothes, before setting off to apply for the job. On meeting her, the gentleman accountant threw up his hands and said that he had given up hope of finding the right cultivated sort of young woman. A portly man, he had sleek grey jowls and pale plump fingers. He was eating gingernuts that crunched as he chewed and fell in crumbs on his waistcoat. Her lovely diction was admirable, he declared, waving her in the direction of the plate of biscuits, and the job was hers to start the very next Monday if she wished. He would be happy to give her a week's pay in advance. After some hesitation, Jean said that that wouldn't be necessary. She would, she said, like to talk it over with her mother first. All the same, she felt light-headed with relief. The problem seemed solved, like a skein of wool that she had suddenly untangled. It was possible to save herself.

But, as it turned out, Nellie had a new plan. At the Majestic, some nights earlier, she had met a woman who would be the perfect dance teacher for Jean. Her troupe had provided a Russian dance as an opening to the new Rudolph Valentino movie.

Valeska's interpretation had been dramatic, quite passionate in fact, and Nellie knew she would liven things up for Jean. 'Darling, you need livening up,' she interrupted, when Jean began to tell her about the job. 'I've been to see her. Now tomorrow, you'll go and meet her. I couldn't face her at the theatre if you didn't go, not now.'

Valeska, a fair, solid woman, past her own dancing best, wore a fitting dress with black lace sleeves. 'I danced with Diaghilev's company in Europe, you know, as of course did Pavlova,' she said when she and Jean met. 'Now Pavlova is supreme, there is nobody in the world who can surpass or even touch Pavlova, but you will learn from me to dance as nearly as possible like her. At the same time, you will learn, too, a variety of styles. Fancy dancing of every kind, jazz, tap and circus dancing, too. You never know what sort of a show you might be called on to perform. Ballroom, too, of course. Young ladies and gentlemen are expected to waltz these days. You will know, of course, a young lady like yourself, how to waltz and foxtrot?'

'I do know how to waltz, although I've never danced with a man,' Jean said.

'Ah well, it's time you did. You can show the young chaps how to lead, before they lead you. And I hear you're talented on the piano?'

'People have been very kind in their comments,' Jean said. Although her words were modest, she was aware of how confident she sounded.

'A concert pianist in the making, I hear.'

'So they say.'

'I see, Miss Batten. And do you say so?'

'I can play whatever I'm called on to perform.'

'Excellent. Then you can play as an accompanist to my classes, it'll save you your tuition fees. You need somewhere to store your piano?'

Jean saw that it had all been arranged. Valeska had not been in business long. A spare piano would be useful and she would be useful to the teacher. Still, she felt anticipation flood through her. The office job looked less attractive than it had. Less famous. She had envied the roses pelting the stage around Pavlova.

Nellie had been busy indeed. As well as Madame Valeska, she had been to see a music teacher named Alice Law, who had also agreed to take Jean as a private pupil. Noted for her talent, she had once taught at Ladies College before studying in England. The music teacher at the college had persuaded her that Jean was a special case, that it would be a tragedy if she were lost to the world of music. The fees Nellie had negotiated were modest.

Nellie won, of course. Jean didn't take the office job, even though thirty shillings a week might have elevated their existence. Most days, Nellie and Jean lived on milkshakes that Nellie made in the communal kitchens of the houses where they lived, a cup of milk and an egg beaten together, raw fruit that farmers were sending to town when they had a surplus, a steak dinner twice a week at what Nellie called a 'greasy spoon' in Queen Street. It cost them two shillings and sixpence each. Ten shillings a week all up. Real money. The steaks were Jean's favourite food. 'When I get rich, I'll eat rump steak every day,' Jean said, which meant that Nellie somehow found the money for the treat, although some weeks it was a struggle. 'Madame will provide you with an extra apple each day,' Nellie said. 'You need more fruit in your diet.'

There was no way to argue with her mother. The portly accountant was irritated when Jean turned the job down, then suddenly appeared wistful, his fingers threading and flexing, as if they itched to be otherwise occupied. Jean felt released when she left his office, relieved that her mother had devised an alternative. At least, she told herself, she had done something. It was a start.

In this way, her new life began. Alice Law was said to have once been so beautiful that girls at the college used to swoon and bring her flowers and bonbons. She did have a softly curved mouth that became expressive when she played, but otherwise she was plump with round spectacles and tight finger waves in her hair. In her private city studio, Jean was the centre of her attention, and for a time the music seemed enough. Miss Law said she had ability beyond her years, the very best, not that she wanted to give her students swollen heads, but they did have to believe in themselves.

As for the dancing classes, with Madame Valeska, Nellie said she must work hard and look out for herself: she was there only to dance. She should focus on the classical side of things and not get carried away with fancy dance, which was merely an entertainment for those with nothing better to do. On no account was she to let young men take liberties in the ballroom dancing classes. They would try, she said, it was what young men did. As it happened, they were already seeking Jean out, begging her to partner them. When she obliged, allowing their rubbery hands to clasp her around the waist, she tried to remember to hold them away when their hot breath came too close to her cheek. One kissed her ear beneath her hair, and she thought that, after all, this was not so bad. Another copied a poem from a book: *How do I love thee? Let me count the ways.* She liked this even more and put the poem inside her music book.

Nellie found the folded slip of paper and took matters into her own hands. She took Jean to see *Damaged Goods*, a movie which had somehow got past the censors and was causing a scandal and letters to the newspapers. The story concerned a young couple who contracted syphilis when the husband slept with a 'girl of the streets' ('They're called prostitutes,' Nellie hissed in Jean's ear), a fake doctor and miserable deaths for all concerned.

'Let that be a warning to you, my girl,' Nellie said when they left the theatre. 'And make sure you don't ever sit right down on the seat of a public toilet. You understand?'

When Fred discovered that Nellie had taken Jean to see the film, he was so enraged that he came to the boarding house to berate her. 'How could you?' he asked.

'Easily,' Nellie said. 'She needs to be saved from depraved men. She needs to know what she might let herself in for.'

'You want to put her off men,' Fred said. 'That's it, isn't it?'

'Men like you, perhaps,' Nellie said.

Nellie was considering taking Fred to court again to enforce him to pay more maintenance to her and Jean. Nellie said three pounds was not enough and, all things being equal and considering what Fred had put her through, he could afford to be more generous. But things weren't equal. Jean could see this. Besides, it cost money to go to court.

Whatever happened, Fred said, Jean must keep up with her piano lessons, as well as this dancing business. This was something he was willing to subsidise, in order that she might prepare herself for her exams. He still hoped, he said, that Jean would become a concert pianist. It was his dream, he told his daughter, just as once he had had dreams that were nothing to do with teeth and divorce.

Jean had been steeling herself to ask her father something. 'All right, but could I do something jolly?' she asked boldly.

Fred looked at her, a hint of the old indulgence in his eyes. 'So what would you like, Mit? What's the treat?'

She had read in the newspapers about the return of Malcolm MacGregor, the man they called Mad Mac when she was a child, the daredevil pilot who had become respectable since the war, although still daring in his ways. He had returned a decorated hero, and tried to settle down as a farmer, but all he wanted to do was fly. Now he had opened a small airline where he charged people for joy rides in a Gipsy Moth aeroplane. Photographs showed not the wild-looking youth who had gone off to war but, rather, a sombre man with a clipped moustache.

'Well.' She hesitated. 'I want to go for a ride in Malcolm MacGregor's plane. Oh, please, Dad, that would be a real treat. Say that I can go, won't you?'

Fred looked from Nellie to Jean with disgust. 'You see what you're doing to her? You're putting more mad ideas in her head than you anticipated. Stop doing this to my daughter, Ellen.' He used her given name when she most angered him.

Nellie looked at him with defiance, but Fred would have none of it.

'I'm not paying for it,' he said, 'and that's that. That man's flying over the city in a plane painted brown, advertising chocolate. The chocolate plane. Is that what you want? Pay attention to your music, Jean, that's my advice to you.'

Chapter 8

Alice Law's praise of Jean's progress in music continued to be fulsome. She didn't need to be told to sit up straight, or be chastised for not practising her scales and arpeggios. She followed the clicking of the metronome hour after hour without complaint. 'Good, Jean, good. Perfection doesn't come in a day, but if you can accept the discipline it will come.'

This approval was enough to send Jean to Madame Valeska's studio every day to practise on her own piano, which now lived there. The studio had a high ceiling, and stained-glass windows that cast showers of blue and pink light across the bare golden-red surface of the floor. Valeska's real name was Doris Scott, somebody whispered. She was married to a man with huge biceps called Len Wilson, who had been a weightlifter and taught the students acrobatic dancing.

The girl who told Jean Madame's other more prosaic name was called Freda Stark. Every day before they began lessons, the students were expected to skip for thirty minutes. Jean and Freda skipped side by side, the fastest there, and before they realised what they were doing began trying to out do each other. Freda never seemed out of breath. She could do a hundred and fifty skips a minute and Awesome Annies and Toads, then she invited Jean to be part of Double Dutch. Their feet moved faster and faster. Freda sang:

> *Lizzie Borden took an axe*
> *And gave her mother forty whacks,*
> *When she saw what she had done,*
> *She gave her father forty-one.*

This became their daily ritual, single skipping, doubles, chanting rhymes together. It was a long time since Jean had had friends — they weren't to be trusted, she'd decided — but Freda Stark was different from the girls at school. She was under five feet tall, as slender as a heron and as quick in her movements. Her hair gleamed in a copper-coloured bob, her saucy grey eyes rimmed with black kohl, lips shining with Vaseline. A shameless girl, Nellie said when she met her. Besides, her father was in trade: he mended shoes for a living. His shop was in the same street, so the girls walked to and from Madame Valeska's together.

Freda had been born up north — in a little village in a green valley, was how she described it, with the sea not far away and mangrove swamps and kingfishers. She excelled at tap and jazz, and acrobatic ballet, which she performed with the muscular Len Wilson. He lifted her high above his head, as if she were made of down. Her mother made her costumes, beaded and sequined, that skimmed her hips, shimmering round her knees as she slammed her way through one Charleston after another. As long as she could remember, Freda said, she had danced. Her father was a dancer, too, and on Saturdays, when his shop was closed, he tap-danced in shows at Fuller's, where there were jugglers and acrobats, trapeze artists, singers and comedians. That was until the theatre burned down one fiery scorching night. Nellie said grudgingly that she supposed they were all in the entertainment business in one way or another, but it wasn't something she'd want Jean mixed up in.

When she was still a small child, after the family had moved south, Freda had shocked the neighbours when she ran outside and danced naked. 'I love the feeling of the air on my body,' she told Jean. 'That's how dance should be performed. Don't look so *worried*, there'll come a time when it's what people do. I'll do it, and they'll throw flowers at my feet. Like Pavlova.'

Nellie said to Freda, when the pair set out to the studio together, 'You'll look after her, won't you? Hold Jean's hand when you're going on the trams.'

Freda laughed when they were out on the street. 'You're not a baby, Jean. Doesn't she realise I'm six months younger than you? Come on, I'll race you.' They ran all the way down to Albert Park beneath the university and threw themselves under the trees, lying in dappled shade while Freda lit two cigarettes and passed one to Jean. When the smoke curled up between them, Freda said, 'Why does she look down on me? You and she are having a harder time than my family. You don't even have a house any more.'

'We will,' Jean said, stubbing out her cigarette on the grass. She pushed her hair behind her ear. 'When I'm famous.'

'That's all very well, but how long will that take? Look, don't take it to heart, it's just that your mother's got all these ideas about suffragettes and emancipation and the theatre and keeping yourself pure, but she doesn't have a clue about working people. She spends all her time wanting to be better than them, but you're living on the bones of your backsides just like any of the poor. And she depends on someone like me to look after you.'

'My mother's just my mother. You don't understand her.'

'I don't understand the Queen of England either. Oh come on, Jean, stop looking all stony-eyed.'

'Well, if you're going to go political on me.'

'Anyway, the Queen of England isn't really the queen.' Freda screwed up her eyes against the smoke from her cigarette. The sun played through the branches above them. A group of university students, all young men, walked past them, one of them whistling in their direction.

Jean pretended not to see them, although Freda returned their gaze. She stretched her lithe body, arching her shoulders back.

'Of course she's the queen,' Jean said.

'No she's not, because the King was married in secret to someone else before he married her. And anyway, she might be called Mary now, but they all called her May.'

'Freda, that's lies. What a terrible thing to say.'

'Haven't you ever heard that story?'

'People say all sorts of things about royalty. They proved it wasn't true. Someone was trying to blackmail the King.'

'Oh, so you have heard the story?'

'It was propaganda. The man who said that went to jail for lying about the King.'

'Oh, I forget that you've been to a smart school, Jean. Say, have you got a brother called Harold?'

Jean dusted herself and got to her feet. 'We'll be late for class.'

Freda leapt to her feet in one smooth action, her hands not touching the ground. 'So have you?'

'One of my brothers gets called that sometimes, but his first name is Frederick, the same as our father.'

Freda laid her hand on Jean's arm. 'You're beautiful, did you know that? The most perfect-looking girl in the world.' She slipped her arm through Jean's, stroking the inside of her elbow. 'I'll bet boys are after you.'

'I don't go with boys,' Jean said.

'Why ever not?' Freda laughed. 'You should.'

'I wouldn't know what to do,' Jean said, feeling herself redden.

'I could show you,' Freda said.

'How could you? You're not a boy.' Jean inhaled the scent of canna lilies that glowed orange and red on a bank above the park, and nearer, Freda's spicy smell,

106

which made her think of nutmeg. They were so close the hairs on their arms touched.

'Oh Jean, don't be silly,' Freda cried, mocking her, 'of course I'm not a boy, but I could show you a thing or two. You want to have fun, Jean. You're a deep one, I don't know what to make of you.'

They had left the park, walked on down the steep little hill towards Queen Street. A huge new theatre was being built, the Civic. It would be more like a palace than a theatre, the architects said.

'I want—' Jean said, vehement, and stopped, suddenly sad.

'What do you want, Jean?' Freda asked quietly.

'I don't know. I just don't. Am I supposed to be a dancer or a pianist or what? What do you want?'

'I want to dance.'

'Well, there you are, Freda. At least you know.'

'I want to fall in love,' Freda said. 'That, too.'

She suggested then that they should go to the Regent tearooms, and get a teacup reading from Madame X, as it was free between two-thirty and five, and why not just forget rehearsal for today? Madame X, self-styled after a movie of the same name, was a woman of perhaps fifty, her yellow curls touching her ample shoulders, wearing a coloured headscarf and a pink blouse with a dagger embroidered on the sleeve. She shook her finger at Freda and Jean. 'I know you two are out on the town. You're dancing girls, aren't you?'

All the same she picked up their bone china teacups

and peered inside them, first Freda's and then Jean's. She wrinkled her nose as if she had seen something distasteful.

'What is it?' Freda asked, wide-eyed.

'Oh there's nothing much there,' Madame X said.

'Yes, there is,' Jean said. 'Or do you just make it up? Any old tosh?'

Freda dug her elbow into Jean's ribs and giggled.

Madame X slammed down the cups and glared at them. 'You want to know? Very well. In yours, Miss,' and here she looked at Freda, picking up her cup again, 'I see something very dark.'

'What is this dark thing?'

'I've got no idea.' The woman looked so agitated that Freda stopped laughing. Madame X put down the cup, her hands trembling. 'You will go into the underworld for a time.' They were all quiet then.

'Will I stay there?' Freda asked.

'For a time, I said, for a time.'

'I think I've had enough of this,' said Freda.

'As for you,' Madame X continued, taking up Jean's cup again, 'it's strange. I see nothing at all.'

'Am I dead?'

'No, I don't believe you are. There's just nothing. Only space. You're somewhere in it. I can't tell where.'

Nellie found out that Jean hadn't been to class, having stopped by Madame Valeska's that afternoon in order to walk her daughter back to the boarding house. 'That girl is a bad influence, Jean,' she said. 'I'd rather you kept away from her.'

It was, of course, impossible to avoid Freda, and Jean didn't want to anyway, but she met her in more surreptitious ways, coming out to the street early when her friend was due to call for her. If Freda noticed, she said no more about it, or about Nellie.

Graduation photographs of the girls Jean had gone to school with began to appear in the *Weekly News*. They wore puffy white dresses, confections of organdy and lace. Winifred and Annabel one day. Phyllis, Clarice and a Miss Betsy Biss another, which made Jean laugh. 'They sound like a nursery rhyme,' she said to Freda.

'Are they really virgins?' Freda asked, looking over her shoulder.

'How would I know?'

'I only asked.'

It didn't bear thinking about. Jean did wonder how many of the girls had blue toes at the end of their first ball. She had coached a few of their partners through painful steps in preparation for dancing with them. Valeska had offered her an extra five shillings a week to help some of the difficult cases. She could hardly do pointes for days after these sessions. 'I reckon they owe us dirt money,' Jean said, tossing aside the newspaper.

Something changed in Alice Law's attitude. At the last recital, there had been what her teacher described in unfriendly tones as 'an *incident*, a thing that should not have occurred'.

It had begun when the teacher was planning who would play solos. 'Now, Jean, we all know that when you play it's wonderful, but you've performed at the last two recitals. I think it only fair that you take a back seat this time.'

'But people expect me to play Chopin,' Jean said. The 'Raindrop Prelude' had become a central element of her performance work.

'They expect a recital that represents the abilities of all my students, Miss Batten.'

When Jean told Nellie, her mother exclaimed over it. 'People will think your work has slipped.'

'I tried to tell her that.'

'Is it about me?' Nellie said, her face hot. 'Does she think that what I play is a bad influence? Just because it's popular.'

Alice Law was unmoved when Jean made a second plea for a better place on the programme. 'Not this time, Jean. Now please don't make any more trouble about this.'

But trouble was what Jean had in mind. On the evening of the recital, when the chosen girl started to play, Jean was possessed by a flash of rage. She walked to the stage and sat down on the edge, as close as she could get to the piano.

After a nervous glance in Jean's direction, the girl played on, her notes faltering. Alice Law told Jean coldly afterwards that if she didn't behave herself she would suspend her tuition. Jean apologised. 'I don't know what possessed me, Miss Law,' she said. But she did know: she had to be the best. It was the only way out, or so it seemed. Otherwise she would be coaching rich boys to dance with rich girls for eternity. Besides, she was caught in the middle. Valeska's studio was home to her piano. She couldn't have one without the other.

Then dashing American Charles Lindbergh flew solo across the Atlantic in a monoplane he called the *Spirit of St Louis*. It was 1927, and the world stopped to applaud. Jean found herself at the news stand each morning, breathless to learn more about the aviator. Here was something more important than arpeggios or pirouettes.

Spurred on by this exploit, two New Zealanders, George Hood and John Moncrieff, decided to try their luck by flying across the Tasman from Australia to New Zealand. Both of them had flown in the war, and Hood had lost half his lower right leg in a crash. Now he earned his living driving taxis. In a photograph taken the day before the flight, in January 1928, he was a balding solid man, looking older than motor mechanic Moncrieff, intense and handsome with a tanned complexion. Jean and Nellie sat transfixed by a battered Radiola in what their landlady described as her sitting room, in order to follow the flight, then rushed out to buy the morning newspapers.

Hood and Moncrieff had disappeared. Their radio signals continued for twelve hours after they departed from Australia, but they left no trace of where they had been swallowed up, either in the deep sea or the mountain passes of the South Island. The wives of the two lost airmen were photographed, dressed in cloche hats and fur stoles, with corsages pinned to their breasts. Hood's wife wore her hat pulled down so that it shadowed her eyes; her mouth was set in a stoic line. Moncrieff's wife was pouting a little, her lips parted, as if to make a good impression for the photographer. Feathers jutted from her hat around the ears. 'She doesn't understand yet,' Nellie said. 'They're not going to come back.'

'Of course she understands,' Jean said. 'They would have known the risk their husbands were taking. You can't afford to be afraid if you're going to fly. They wouldn't be married to women who wept every time they left the ground.'

Nellie said she supposed Jean was right, but she still thought the Moncrieff woman was in shock.

'The fools,' Fred said, when Jean spoke to him next. 'They should have known they'd land up in the drink.'

Just a month later, an Australian called Bert Hinkler flew a tiny biplane from England to Australia. No flying suit for him: he wore a double-breasted suit and tie. The journey took him fifteen days, with landings to refuel and sleep briefly along the way. 'It's possible, Mother,' Jean breathed. 'People really can fly across the world.'

One day soon after this, Alice Law looked at Jean, bent over the piano, with a worried frown.

'Jean, stop,' she commanded.

When Jean lifted her head, Alice said in a quiet voice, 'You play each note to perfection. I would trade you for a dozen pupils who played half as well.' She might have added, and paid twice as much. 'What is it? Where's the passion gone?'

'You're mistaken. I'm just a little tired.'

'It takes more than talent and energy to be a great pianist,' her teacher said. 'The search for perfection brings its own problems.'

Jean turned back to the piano, her hands rising and falling adroitly in a show of exuberance. Alice watched her and sighed.

Jean turned towards her. 'What problems?'

'There's such a sense of loss if you fail.'

'You're talking about the concert? I'm sorry, I shouldn't have done that.'

'It should be enough to seek perfection for the music's own sake, not just for an audience. You didn't play at the concert and now the music means less to you.'

'So it was a test?'

'If you like.'

'And I failed it?'

'You're still a fine pianist, Jean. You could have the world at your feet if you wanted it badly enough.'

'I'll pass my exams, won't I?'

'Oh, the examinations? I'm sure you will.' Alice pushed

a damp grey curl behind her ear. 'Just think about what you really want.'

When Jean got home she said to Nellie, 'I want to fly to Australia faster than Bert Hinkler. I know if I learned to fly that I could do it.'

And then, as if all that were not enough, Charles Kingsford Smith did fly across the Tasman Sea, with a crew of three men in a plane called the *Southern Cross*. When he landed in Auckland, thirty thousand people waited to greet him.

The flight of the stars, the newspapers exulted.

Chapter 9

When Fred arrived to take Jean to dinner, Nellie had gone out. If she could avoid seeing her husband, she did. Nearly seven years had passed since they began living apart. Although Fred was thickening in middle age, his suit buttons tightening, his dentist's hands remained delicate in their appearance, fingernails perfectly trimmed and manicured. He had continued to live in the block of Auckland flats called Courtville, next door to a vacant section where wild fennel bloomed in summer and loquats hung heavy on the trees. Nellie spoke sharply of his situation in comparison with theirs, wondering aloud how he could afford such luxury, while they lived in squalor. Sometimes, just for peace, Jean reminded her that Fred had to share a kitchen and bathroom, just as they did. Nonetheless, Fred had endeared himself to his landlady and appeared to be living a comfortable life. He told his wife and daughter there was nothing more he could do. Times were hard, people weren't paying to have their teeth done. Or they would come to him in agony with a toothache and he couldn't bear to turn them away, even though they couldn't pay. Nellie couldn't have it all ways: an education for their daughter plus a smart address.

And after all, it was she who had left him, and not the other way around. This, Nellie said, was a sophistry. What else could she have done?

On this particular evening, in order to avoid him, she had taken herself off to the Temple of Higher Thought where, she maintained, reason prevailed. She had forsaken the spiritualist church, disenchanted by séances that she had decided were rigged. There was no sign of her missing son, nor did she expect any longer to find him in this life. The red-brick temple with its arched door stood in the centre of the city. When she wasn't at the theatre, Nellie took herself there for solace and contemplation. It offered, she said, the opportunity for people to study the principles of religion and the mysteries of the universe, without dogma or prejudice, and to learn how to solve their own problems. You wouldn't catch her having hysterics, or taking Veronal, so beloved by society women, to calm her nerves. Logic and careful planning would see her through in the end, just wait and see.

One of Fred's patients, once well-to-do but now down on her luck, had given him tickets for a dinner in honour of Charles Kingsford Smith, traded for his treatment of her abscessed tooth.

Jean met Fred in the entrance to the latest boarding house in Symonds Street, surrounded by ancient smells, the stale rush of stew, unaired blankets in rooms with full chamber pots, windows covered with brown paper to stop passers-by from looking in. She was wearing a white silk sleeveless dress that fell in graceful gathers from her waist and swirled around her knees. Her mane of hair, so like his, was parted neatly on the side.

'I couldn't have asked for a better-looking date. I like the outfit.'

'I wear it to play at the dances. It's something I designed myself. I admire simplicity.'

A woman on the stairs, wearing a cardigan with holes in the elbows, asked for the price of a wad of tobacco, her voice shrill. 'You could spare it,' she shouted, 'even if Miss La-di-dah here won't part with a penny.' She spat a stream of rotten phlegm at their feet. Fred pulled a packet of cigarettes from his pocket and passed the woman two, as he stood, still appraising his daughter.

'Why did you do that?' she said, when they were outside in the fresh evening air. It was September, the oak trees overhead green with the new tender light of spring leaves, the salt-laden breeze from the sea dispersing the smell of the old building they had left behind.

'She'll be nicer to you now,' Fred said, 'you'll see. You want to remember that, girl, it pays to give a little now and then.'

'You have to have something first,' she answered.

'That's enough,' her father said, tucking her hand under his arm. 'I'm taking you somewhere, aren't I? This is what you wanted. You've been talking about aviators and flying machines for as long as I can remember.'

The dinner was held in the dining room of the Grand Hotel. Jean shivered with pleasure as they entered. She had often walked past the ornate frontage on her way to music lessons, longing to enter, and the interior was as beautiful as she had imagined. Near the entrance was a spiral staircase, and alongside the lower steps, a Victorian open-shaft lift with an iron grille, designed, her father told her, to resemble a smart French hotel. Alongside the grille was a black oak board bearing the words *A Message Awaits* engraved in gold lettering. The pigeon-holes where messages awaited were also embossed in gold. There were potted palms and large chandeliers, and to Jean it seemed as if she were in a dream. The doorman looked at the reception card Fred handed him, bowed and directed them to the dining room, where a waiter led them to their seats. The tables were an ocean of white linen and silver. Jean felt she would choke if she so much as breathed.

They were barely seated, when Kingsford Smith himself was there, taking his place at the next table. The aviator was small in stature, slim and fair, with a long hawk-shaped nose. He looked over at the Battens, his smile revealing widely spaced teeth, but he seemed to Jean older than his age. He was just thirty-one, but already he had served in a war, shot down German planes, had half his left foot blown off and had a Military Cross pinned on his chest by King George V. Not that he gloried in war. It was a massacre, he said, a horrible thing to look back on, not something he remembered with pride. All that had happened before he turned twenty. Now he held records: for an around Australia flight, the first Pacific Ocean flight, the first non-stop flight across Australia, and this latest, the first Tasman Sea crossing.

There was nothing quiet about Kingsford Smith, who was already in animated conversation with fellow guests at his table. He carried himself with jauntiness, reminding Jean that since his feats in the war he had also been a flying stuntman in Hollywood. Anything to raise the cash, he'd told reporters. The three companions who had flown with him on the historic flight across the Tasman were dotted around at other tables, but it was Smithy who was the centre of attention. When Jean came to describe the evening to her mother, she couldn't remember what she had eaten, just that after the main course, before dessert was served, the famous pilot had stood and spoken of the flight, the way the wild Tasman Sea had lived up to its reputation, with torrents of rain whipping at the sides of the plane, and fifty-mile-an-hour gusts of wind hitting the *Southern Cross* side on, spinning her about. Ice had formed on the wing tips, weighing the plane down. He remembered then, he said, the New Zealanders who had already lost their lives trying to fly the Tasman, and it made him humble that he and his crew had made it, when they did not. He called for a toast in memory of Moncrieff and Hood, and asked the guests to make it in silence. They should never forget, he said, that flying was a great adventure, but also a risk. And then he was away again, recalling how they had outflown the storm, suddenly finding themselves in sunshine, with Christchurch lying beneath them.

As he spoke, radiant points of light showered on him from the chandeliers, so that he seemed larger than life and bathed in a golden aura. Jean felt she had reached a point in her life from which there was no turning back.

Later, she told Nellie that they might have had trifle, because her head was spinning from its sherry, but really she couldn't remember much else, except that Kingsford Smith had walked over to her table and asked her name.

When she told him that she was Jean Gardner Batten, he turned to Fred and said, 'She's a good-looking sheila, this daughter of yours.'

'She's clever, too,' Fred said, pride in his voice. 'She's going to be a concert pianist.'

'Actually,' Jean said, 'I'm going to learn to fly.'

Smithy looked at Fred and laughed. 'I reckon your little girl's got ideas of her own. Flying, eh?' He rapped on the table, calling people to attention again. 'Raise your glasses,' he said. 'This young lady is going to learn to fly. Let's drink to it.'

Around her, people laughed and cheered and threw down another glass of port, for the wheels on the party were now well oiled.

'Dad, let's go,' Jean said.

Outside the hotel, Fred said, 'Why did you say that?'

'Because it's what I want to do. They didn't need to laugh.'

'Don't be silly, dear,' Fred said. 'Girls don't fly.'

But Jean knew there were women who flew aeroplanes and so would she.

'I expect they're very like men in their ways then,' Fred said. 'You're having one of your moods, my dear. You know you must stay calm.'

'I am calm. Don't say I'm not calm, Father. I tell you, there are women who fly.'

'Name one,' he said.

'Millicent Bryant, the Australian. Like Smithy.'

'Oh, yes, and look what happened to her. She's dead.'

'Not from flying.'

But there was no point in arguing with Fred. Millicent Bryant had died in a ferry accident the year before, and the story had been carried in the newspapers, but this all seemed beside the point. Fred set his pipe between his teeth, and put his hands in his pockets, as if he had said all he needed.

They didn't break their silence as they made their way back to the boarding house. The atmosphere between them had grown hostile. It was all Jean could do to thank her father for taking her to the dinner. Afterwards she thought she had been unkind to him, and this would come back to haunt her, because, after that, their meetings always ended in disagreement. Nellie was her only friend in the family. She supposed John was still her friend, but he didn't write.

He had appeared in his first Hollywood movies: a walk-on role in *Backstage*, the persuasive lover Jimmy Garret in *The Chorus Kid*, playing opposite Thelma Hill, known as 'the Mah-jong Bathing Beauty' for the patterns on the swimming costume she wore. A part of Nellie disapproved. As she'd reminded Jean more than once, she understood all too well the way men fell for women who flaunted their charms. There's more to talent than flesh, she said. On the other hand, she was pleased that John was making a name for himself as an actor. And money, too. Jean thought, in secret, that it must be nice for Thelma Hill to fall into her brother's arms for all the world to see, not that she would have wanted to herself, but she missed him. She missed the way they used to talk beneath the pepper tree in the garden, when times were better. He had asked her one day what she wanted to be when she grew up. 'Famous,' she had replied, 'that's what I want.' And he had said that, yes, that that was what he wanted, too. She hadn't seen *The Chorus Kid* yet, just a picture of Thelma Hill. She wasn't all that pretty, and she didn't look especially clever, but Jean could see the proportions of her bust. She had written to John to ask him if he'd met Greta Garbo, but he hadn't replied.

'Father disapproves of me wanting to fly,' Jean said to Nellie in the dark that night. They were lying on twin beds, pushed close together with just room enough for a wardrobe in the corner that didn't fit all their clothes. The landlady had used Lysol to clean up some mess in the passageway, and the acrid smell burned their nostrils as they fought for sleep.

'Does he just?'

'I'm not sure that I want to be a concert pianist after

all,' Jean said. 'In fact, I'm not sure that I ever wanted to be. It was his idea.'

'I want you to fly,' Nellie said in a fierce voice. On the other side of the wall beside their heads, someone banged their fist, calling out for them to shut up, and couldn't a man get a good night's sleep.

'I'll get you out of here, dear, just wait. I will,' Nellie said in a whisper no less passionate.

Chapter 10

Just how Nellie intended to get Jean out of the boarding house and make an aviator out of her was unclear, nor was it in the weeks that followed the meeting with Kingsford Smith. Shame of one kind or another had brought them low, but they were not on their own.

In spite of the lavish dinners the rich could still afford, the slump, as they called it, was biting hard. The grey faces of the unemployed began to haunt the streets of Auckland. The normal things of life were slipping away — the chance for jobs, even the hope of getting married. Men could no longer afford to support their families. Nobody trusted the banks any more. If they go under, people said, we'll lose everything. We'll wake up in the morning and our last sixpence will have disappeared.

All the same, Jean wondered if her mother might have something up her sleeve. In the weeks that followed the momentous dinner, they returned over and over again to the subject of Jean learning to fly. The unspoken matter was that of Fred's opposition. Jean supposed he might have grounds for cutting off their allowance, let alone providing money for lessons. But Nellie was writing mysterious letters and posting them off. She was studying the newspapers, too, and talking to the tobacconist at the corner. Hot tips, some insider information perhaps. He was a man who followed the horses.

Jean still saw Fred from time to time. They were visits he expected of her, and, in spite of herself, she still felt herself drawn to him. Love, she supposed, was what children should feel for their parents, though what she felt for Fred didn't resemble how she felt about Nellie. There was something complicated about it. She remembered blue days by the lake when she was a child, the nights when it was all right for him to tuck her into bed, the contours of his knees when she sat in his lap. On one of her visits, she brought up the subject of flying once again.

'What have you got against it?' she asked him.

Fred ran his hands through his hair. 'Haven't I told you,' he snapped. 'Flying is men's business. It's too dangerous by far. Remember how I told you about the planes falling out of the sky when I was in France. Besides, there was talk there of prostitutes taking up the job. There was a Frenchwoman who was straight out of a brothel when she found herself a rich man with an aeroplane. The fool married her.'

'Marthe Richard,' Jean said. 'She set a record. I read about it.'

'And her poor sod of a husband was killed in the war. Then she married a spy. Is that the kind of person you want to be?'

Jean was silent then. Her mother would call this dirty talk. Her father was agitated, his eyes narrow. After a while he went along the passageway to the kitchen he shared with other tenants on his landing, and came back with tea and some toast spread with home-made blackberry jam. A treat, he said.

That morning, before Jean had gone out, Nellie had put on a stylish hat and picked up the big bag. 'I'm gone for the day.' When she returned, her face was lit with a small, understated smile of triumph.

'We're going to Australia,' she said.

Nellie had decided that if Charles Kingsford Smith could teach Jean to fly, all would be well. She had written to him, on the strength of the meeting the year before. She knew, Nellie said, as if she understood more about him than Jean, that he was a happy-go-lucky man, keen to offer flights to people. 'You'll see, when he meets you on your own, away from all those people, he'll see how smart you are, how much you really want to fly. Aren't you pleased?' Nellie's eyes glowed with excitement.

'I'd never have asked him,' Jean said. She was over-awed that her mother had had the nerve to do this.

'No, of course you wouldn't. But I have.' Nellie produced tickets from her bag. 'We're booked on a steamer that leaves tomorrow, and a week from now you'll go for a flight in the *Southern Cross*. What d'you say to that?'

'I'm so happy.' Jean was caught up in the contagious warmth of her mother's excitement. 'I'm the luckiest girl.'

When Kingsford Smith saw her, he scratched his head, a roll-your-own behind his ear, and grinned, appearing to remember her. 'I don't know what to make of you. You've got a mind of your own, I'll give you that.'

They had gone to the aerodrome of the Royal Australian Air Force near Sydney at eight that morning. Nellie and Jean's ship had berthed the night before, but neither of them had slept well in their hotel, afraid they would wake too late. 'I want to fly,' Jean said to the pilot. This time she didn't feel shy. On the journey over she had sat on the ship's deck and looked at the sea and the sky, and it seemed as if they were sailing to her destiny. She had dressed with care for this adventure, in a blue knee-length coat with a pleated skirt that would allow her to move easily as she climbed into the plane, a plain cloche hat that fitted snugly over the tops of her ears, and flat sensible shoes.

'Well, we'll take the old bus up for a spin, eh?' Smithy took the cigarette from behind his ear and pointed to where the *Southern Cross* stood on the tarmac.

'Just you and me?'

'You scared of me, eh?' He chuckled at himself. 'I can't do much while I'm flying a plane.'

'I didn't mean that.' Jean blushed.

'Don't worry, my mate here's coming along with us.' Then she recognised Charles Ulm, who had also been at the dinner in Auckland. He had been Kingsford Smith's companion when he set his records. His black hair was tangled with wild curls, his complexion olive. He made flourishes and gestures with his hands, in a way that reminded her of her brother John, only more instinctively sexual. His voice held a faint exotic trace of an accent.

'Is Maman coming with us?' Ulm asked.

Jean shook her head. She and Nellie had already decided that she would make the flight alone, lest it be thought that Jean lacked courage. Her mother was ensconced in the clubhouse, watching through binoculars. 'You're French?' she said.

'My father,' he said. 'An artist who ended up in Australia.'

'Take your eyes off her,' Kingsford Smith said. 'He's trouble with women, I can tell you.'

'You play the piano and dance as well?' Ulm said.

'Who told you that?' She had asked her mother not to tell the men what she did in New Zealand: she did not want to seem unsuited for flying.

'We did our homework,' Kingsford Smith interrupted, and that was all either of them would say. 'Mind you, I can't blame my mate here.' He offered her a hand up, still grinning. 'The best-looking skirt we've had in the old girl.'

'I expect you say that to all the girls who fly with you,' she said lightly, surprised at herself, yet not wanting to prolong the banter. She remembered Kingsford Smith's appraising look at the dinner in Auckland. She was flattered that he had remembered her, but all she wanted was for the plane to lift off, to carry her into the sky.

'You get to sit up front with me.' Smithy laughed, and

touched her back lightly as she settled in beside him.

As the plane hurtled along the runway, she was overtaken by delirious joy. And then they were airborne, banking away over the city and heading north, climbing higher and higher, and before long the Blue Mountains lay beneath them in the glittering air. Whatever else had occurred in her life until now became insignificant. The sense of speed and of power almost overwhelmed her. Everything that had been dull and ugly ceased to exist. She cried out aloud at this sensation of flight, her face rapt with pleasure. The plane swooped down towards the mountains, the blue gum trees filled with coruscating silver light, and she glimpsed the floor of the world through their leafy branches, before the plane banked and rose again through the sky, seeming to ride the edge of a cloud. 'This is it,' Jean shouted above the roar. 'This is what I have to do.'

When they were back on the ground, she turned to Kingsford Smith and said, 'Will you teach me to fly?'

He scratched his head again and lit the cigarette that had stayed in position throughout their flight. 'I dunno about that. Look at you, you're just a slip of a girl. We've got a lot on, some big trips planned. You serious about this?'

'Never more serious in my life. I know how to use a compass.'

As if sensing that his friend was going to make a commitment he might regret, Ulm said, 'You're too pretty for this game. If you've got a gift for music you should make use of it. I can see you in a concert hall. All you'd have to do is smile and you'd be a star.'

'I don't see that my looks have got anything to do with it,' Jean said hotly. She felt a tension in herself as he looked at her.

'If music be the food of love, play on,' he said.

'*Twelfth Night*. Act one. Opening line.' She understood that she could have him if she wanted. For what, she wasn't sure, but he was there for the taking.

'Quick,' he said, impressed. 'This one's got flavour, Smithy.'

But Kingsford Smith hesitated. 'You say you know how to use a compass, eh? Get yourself some flying lessons. There's a flying school in Auckland. Come back at the end of the year and let me know how you're getting on.'

'So that's your advice,' Jean said, downcast.

'Yeah, well, a couple of things. If you do take up flying, don't ever fly at night, you won't be able to get your bearings. And don't go after men's records. Blokes make the records.'

Ulm took her by the shoulders and kissed her on either cheek before they parted, holding her a moment longer than was necessary. Kingsford Smith said, 'See you, kid.'

Jean hoped that the backing of her hero would soften her father's heart, but within weeks of her return to New Zealand, Australia was rocked by a scandal involving Kingsford Smith and Ulm. The pilot and his crew set off at the end of March to fly from Sydney to England to arrange for the purchase of more planes. Kingsford Smith was at the controls when the *Southern Cross* was forced to make an emergency landing on a desolate mudflat near the mouth of the Glenelg River in Western Australia. They were lost for a fortnight, during which time the crew lived on a diet of coffee and brandy. Two airmen, Keith Anderson and Bobby Hitchcock, who had joined the ensuing search, crashed and died in the desert from heat and thirst.

It turned out that, at the beginning of the 1928 endeavour, when Kingsford Smith and Ulm made the flight from the United States, these two men had been part of the original crew, but they had fallen out. Anderson sued his former friend for breach of promise, bitter because he had not shared the glory of the epic flight. Kingsford Smith had made an out-of-court settlement for one thousand pounds, with which Anderson and Hitchcock had bought a small touring plane, intended for sightseeing. It was this they used to look for Kingsford Smith and Ulm.

The *Southern Cross* crew were accused of staging a forced landing as part of a publicity flight that had gone wrong, and, as quick as an ocean wind, the saint turned sinner in the eyes of the public. Anderson and Hitchcock had sacrificed their lives for the sake of a cheap stunt. Or so it was now said. An inquiry was called for. Again, tabloid headlines stared back at Jean on street corners, dubbing the scandal the *Coffee Royal* incident. The affair raged all year as Kingsford Smith faced his inquisitors.

'Where did you go?' Freda quizzed Jean, after her return to Auckland.

'Australia,' Jean replied shortly.

'Quite a holiday.'

'My mother had a windfall.'

'Oh well.' Freda put her chin in one hand, her eyes narrowed. 'As a matter of fact, Jean, I'm going to Australia next week, too.' Her voice was flat. They were sitting in Milne and Choyce's having tea. Jean hadn't been keen to have this conversation. If word got about that she had been flying, Fred would be furious, as would Alice Law.

Besides, she and Freda seemed to have drifted apart. It was hard to put her finger on what was wrong — perhaps her interest in aeroplanes rather than dance? But Freda had pressed the invitation, as they changed into their street clothes at Madame Valeska's: 'Please Jean, I do need to talk to you.' Her face was pale and set.

Freda had money, as she usually did, and had ordered tea, a plate of sandwiches and a cream puff each.

'We'll get fat,' Jean said, then watched in astonishment as Freda's eyes filled. 'Only joking, you're skinny as can be.'

Freda was devouring the food as if it were her last meal. Cream and jam glistened on her lip. Even so, Jean couldn't help noticing the beautiful curve of eyebrows, how perfectly she had applied her make-up. 'You're not to tell anyone? Jean, you promise.'

'What's not to tell?'

'I thought you might pick it. I'm in the family way. Jean, don't look at me like that.'

Jean reached out across the table and gripped her

friend's hands in hers until Freda pulled them away. 'Don't,' she said. 'People will stare at us.'

Something had happened that Jean couldn't imagine. Sex, the longing and desire that people had for each other, none of it seemed to have done much good to anybody she knew. It didn't make sense to her. A dull ache of shame flooded through her, as if she were guilty of some nameless misdemeanour. When Freda had teased her and egged her on to try out the forbidden, she had thought it a joke. But Freda did know.

'Who's the father?' she asked at last.

'You sound just like my mother. "Oh, the shame of it." I've been hearing that for days. Well, I should be relieved it's not your mother, she'd be kicking up a worse stink if it were you. Look, it doesn't matter who the father is.'

'You're not going to tell me?'

'Of course not. I'm not telling anybody.'

'I don't understand. Are you getting married in Australia?'

Freda said, 'I'm getting things fixed up over there. I'm not going to have the baby. I thought perhaps, well, I thought maybe that's why you'd been to Australia.'

'Is that why you wanted to talk to me?'

Freda gestured helplessly. 'Well, you could have told me what they did to you.'

Jean stood up shakily, brushing crumbs from her skirt. 'As if you would thin ...' She stopped, put her hand over her mouth.

'Well, it seemed surprising. No, of course I wouldn't

133

think it of you.' After a moment in which they stared at each other, as if they had never been friends, Freda said, 'Goodbye, Jean.'

'You'll come back?'

'I don't know. I might die there, mightn't I?'

'I think you're being dramatic.' Jean was aware how cold she sounded. It wasn't how the words were meant to come out, but they did. She walked away as quickly as she could.

Months dragged past while Kingsford Smith and his witnesses were interrogated before the Air Inquiry Committee. In the end he was exonerated, and Jean awaited the outcome with dwindling hope for her own chances. When the outcry, for and against, began to subside she approached Fred again, hoping he would relent and pay for her flying lessons.

'Don't you understand the meaning of the word no?' he said. 'Look at this thing in Australia. Death and disgrace. If I'd known your mother was taking you to see Kingsford Smith I'd have put a stop to it, I can tell you.'

'You introduced me to him.'

'The bigger fool me. I didn't know what a shyster he was.'

'He was cleared. He wouldn't do a thing like that.'

'That's enough, Jean.' He sounded weary of her. 'Get

back to work on your music. You're not paying attention to what's important.'

'Well …' She hesitated.

'Well what?'

'If I'm going to be a concert pianist, perhaps I need more experience. I've gone as far as I can with Miss Law. I really need to go to England.'

'That's a nice idea. A good dream. A better sort of dream. Not something I can afford.'

'I can see that, Dad,' she said. 'I've been wondering if perhaps I should sell the piano. It would pay for our fares. Mother would have to come with me, of course. I wouldn't know where to start without her.'

Chapter 11

Jean came to the caves, near Waipu, in the heat of summer before leaving New Zealand. This was where Harold now lived, high on a hill, along a dirt road winding through bush. He collected her from a bus that travelled north out of Auckland, over a mountainous pass opening onto far-flung islands lying in an indigo sea. The small town consisted of a straggle of low buildings along either side of the main road. Harold was dressed in ragged overalls, the bib done up in a loose knot over a checked shirt, the hair touching his collar as dark as Jean remembered it, teeth gleaming in his tanned face. He led her to a flat-deck truck, its tyres bare to the tread, not unlike Belle's vehicle at Birkdale. They set off, Harold blaring his horn at hens that strayed into his path. He pointed out landmarks — the store at the crossroads, a high, bare house standing back from the road. A tall, slender woman dressed from neck to ankle in black, hair scraped up into a severe bun, was sweeping the verandah. 'They reckon she's a witch,' Harold said. 'Never talks to anyone.' Further on, as they moved inland, they passed low-lying farmland, and a river that coiled its way through paddocks of grass and late buttercups. Trees pressed in against the speeding vehicle; it bounced from side to side, leaves whipping the windscreen, stones flying through the air and smacking the glass as they approached another curve. This road led to underground caverns, and fields of limestone rocks with scant blades of grass between them.

The house where Harold lived with his wife, Alma, and their children overlooked a limestone quarry that Harold had developed. This was what he farmed — rocks. Grey-blue rocks that he blasted from the reluctant earth, setting detonators among the gullies. He and his men ran lines of cordite to the gunpowder that would explode and bring slabs of the limestone crashing down. Harold's love of explosions had come into its own. The sound of the detonations shook the air as the truck approached the farmhouse, the lime crusher silhouetted against the sky rattled and echoed around the canyons, the engine was a continuous whine, as the clouds of pale dust swept towards them. To Jean it looked like a scene from a hell. Her brother's darkened face gleamed with an unholy joy, laughter on his lips as he took in her astonishment.

She turned to him, and something about his glee was contagious. 'Harold,' she breathed, 'this is amazing, the most wonderful place.'

'I reckoned you'd like it.'

'It's so dangerous.'

'Yes,' he said simply. 'A man could die up here in the wink of an eye. Or a sheila.'

His accent had roughened, his vowels mirroring his wife's Australian twang. Going by a photograph on the mantelpiece of their wedding day, Alma had been a slim, pretty girl then. Broken Hill, she came from, hard mining country. It wasn't as if she hadn't seen it all before. But already she was weathering into motherhood, her waist spreading beneath her apron, her hands raw from boiling napkins in the copper, an art Jean would soon learn. As Jean came to know her she would notice an anxious shadow lurking in her expression that never seemed to entirely disappear.

The house was square, three bedrooms, a kitchen that also served as a sitting room, a lean-to where the copper and a tin bath were sheltered and a verandah — more a shelf where Harold could stand and keep an eye on the quarry than a place to sit and contemplate.

'You don't mind sharing with one of the kids,' Alma said, more as a statement than a question, as she introduced the children who clung to her knees. There was another one in a cot. She eyed Jean's canvas bag with some suspicion. 'We're not fancy here,' she said. 'We kill our own beef, there's ripe plums on the tree if fruit's what takes your fancy. And we share our bath water. No sneaking water. You can go down the road to the river if you want your own bath.'

'I understand.' Jean knew she was being tested to see how much she would accept without demurring, to see whether Harold should turn the truck around and take her back down the winding road.

'She talks flash,' Alma said to her husband. 'She sounds like a Pommie.'

Jean smiled at her. 'I like it here. I've brought licorice all-sorts for the kids. And some cigarettes.'

Alma's face softened. 'Ah, those won't go amiss. I hear you play the piano.'

'That's right,' Jean agreed.

'The folk down the road say you can tickle the ivories there if you want while you're here,' Alma said. 'There's a lot of Scots people round here. Most of them came via Nova Scotia. They had hard times. Then there's the ones that followed their families out from the old country. They keep themselves to themselves until you get to know them. But they all like their music. They'll take to you if you're any good.'

Her voice was drowned out by another reverberating roar. 'Work to do,' Harold said. 'Morning until night. I'll bet our mother wouldn't have let you come up if she'd known what goes on here.' His face cracked into another strange gleeful smile.

'You're right,' Jean said. 'Mother wasn't so keen.'

He looked at her curiously. 'So why did she send you?'

Jean busied herself with picking up her coat and bag as if to put them away. 'She had some business to do with our father. It was his idea that I come.'

'That figures. Tearing strips off each other as usual. So how is the old lady then?'

'Don't talk about our mother like that.' Jean felt she was always defending one or other of her parents.

They left it there. Jean helped Alma around the house, wiping the children's snotty noses, rinsing out their handkerchiefs before she put them in the tub, scrubbing grass stains from their shorts. The food was as Alma had described it: meat with threads of yellow fat from beef cattle they killed on the farm, potatoes that were surprisingly sweet, fresh from the ground. It pleased Alma that the children followed Jean on her walks. These children were her nephews, her flesh and blood, not like the children at Birkdale that she had ignored. She taught them how to make whistles with blades of grass, stretching the blade between thumb and forefinger and blowing on them, the way Fred had shown her when she was a child, and to do cat's cradle.

This was how the summer passed, among the threadbare rocks, with occasional trips to the township and calls on the neighbours. On the far side of the town, the people took their religion with great seriousness. Harold and Alma didn't visit there. Along the Caves road there was a mixture of families who drank beer and smoked and swore. Someone, although she couldn't be sure who, because nobody ever said, had a whisky still: moonshine. The people spoke a mixture of English and half-remembered Gaelic, and late at night they sang. She didn't understand the songs and didn't offer to play their pianos. After one of these nights, they would drive back up the hill, Harold and Alma in the front, Jean and the children on the tray of the truck. Later, when she heard Harold's rough shouts of lovemaking, Jean would roll over and put her fingers in her ears.

It wasn't until she was invited to the McLeans' house, in

the area known as North River, that she had the opportunity to play. This was a family known for its industry. Their daughter, Kathleen, was a quiet young woman, a little older than Jean, although she had vivacious, dark eyes in a tanned face, her body fine-boned and sinewy from working around the farm. She could have been a dancer, too, the way she carried herself.

'Why don't you stay the night?' she said, late one afternoon. 'We could play cards and have a bit of a singalong.' Jean was caught up in Kathleen's enthusiasm. Besides, it was a long walk back to the caves at this hour.

After the meal, the family gathered around the piano. Jean played some Chopin to polite applause, then Kathleen and her parents took it in turns to play the piano and sing old songs from Scotland. They didn't stay up late; there were cows to milk in the morning. Kathleen dropped into a deep sleep the moment her head hit the pillow. Jean lay under her eiderdown and listened to the even breathing in the other bed, and to the rustle of the North River night, to the sound of moreporks calling and pukeko in the swamp near the river. This was friendship of a different kind to any she had experienced, warm-hearted and uncomplicated. She soon fell into a pattern of practising at the McLeans' place, and staying overnight. On one of these visits she and Kathleen rode along North River Road towards the little township.

As they came near to the house where the woman in ̲lived, Kathleen reined in her horse. 'This is my ̲s place,' she said. 'We're going to collect some butter. She's famous for her butter.'

'You mean the witch?' Jean saw at once, by the look on her friend's face, that she had said the wrong thing.

'Kitty's no witch,' Kathleen said. 'She simply prefers her own company. What's the harm in that? You wait until you taste her lemonade.'

When they arrived at the house, Kitty immediately came out on to the verandah, her face lighting up with pleasure at the sight of her niece, as she gestured for them to sit down.

'You'll have to speak up,' Kathleen said. 'My aunt is a little deaf.'

Jean found herself tongue-tied with embarrassment, having spoken as she had.

'Jean wants to know why you live by yourself,' Kathleen said, laughing at her friend's red face.

'Aha, everyone wants to know that. What did you say your name was, girlie?' She put her hand behind her ear.

'Jean Batten,' Jean shouted.

'No need to shout. I'm not in the habit of discussing my affairs with outsiders.'

Jean dropped her head.

The woman's voice softened. 'You've got a bonnie face, lass. It's like this, you see.' She paused to gather her thoughts. 'When my parents died, Kathleen's grandparents, you understand, I wasn't of a mind to leave. I missed them a lot. I still do. We came from Gairloch Scotland. You could say I never really got used ways of people here.'

'Thank you.' Jean felt that she was being honoured, despite the woman's strangeness, or perhaps it was just reserve. The lemonade Kitty had given them was very good indeed, cool and freshly made.

'You see,' Kitty continued, 'the months passed and then the years. I like the sea out there, and that big macrocarpa outside my bedroom window. I used to be able to hear it scratching at the window, but I can't now. Still, I know it's there.'

When Kathleen had collected the butter, Kitty withdrew soundlessly, without bidding them goodbye, almost as if they hadn't been there at all.

Kathleen said quietly, as they rode on together, 'In a funny sort of way, she's my inspiration. I want to get married some day, but not until I've done my nursing training. When I look at her, I know it's possible to be happy without rushing off and marrying the first person you meet.'

'But she's never married anyone,' Jean protested.

'I guess she just didn't meet the right person. I'll know when I do.'

One day, not long before Jean was due to leave, the children took her to see the mouth of the caves, picking their way through boulders, the bush hacked away around them. They weren't allowed to go into the caves, they told her, just to show her where they were. In the side of the hill, the first cave arched over a shallow riverbed. To the children it was just a hole in the ground, and soon they ran off, chasing a rabbit with a stick. When they were out of sight, Jean moved closer into the mouth of the cave. An unearthly stillness surrounded her. The interior was like a magnet, a darkness she wanted to enter. She shivered. Beside the river ran a ledge of rock. She crawled down the bank and stepped onto the ledge.

Harold's face appeared above her. 'I told the kids not to go in there,' he said.

'I'm not one of the kids.'

'You're not to go in.' He stood silhouetted against the sky, menacing above her. She drew a deep breath. Harold had got the better of her when she was a child but she decided on an impulse that it wasn't going to happen now.

'I'll do what I like,' she retorted.

'Christ, wait for me then. I'll get a light from the truck.'

He came back in a few minutes, a torch in his hand. 'You know you're going to get wet through.'

'I don't care. I need to go in there.'

So they knelt and crawled their way into the cave, and in a short while they came to a place where they could stand. In the total silence inside the earth, the darkness was lit by the glow worms' million stabs of light, creating an eerie iridescence, the stalactites shedding a milky glow. They stood beside each other, brother and sister, almost touching, neither of them speaking. Harold's breath was short in his chest.

'I could die in a place like this,' Jean said at last. 'A field of stars, that's what it is.'

'You talk too much,' was all he said. After a time they left the caves and emerged, back on the surface, blinking in the blinding light of day.

'Show me how you blow things up,' Jean said. Her cotton dress was steaming around her knees, drying out under the sun.

This time Harold didn't seem surprised, as if he expected her to ask this of him. At the quarry he showed her how the ground was dug out, the detonator put in place, the cordite fuse lit to snake its way through the grass until the gelignite was set alight.

'Let me do it,' she said.

When the canyon resounded with the blast she'd made, she looked at him with blazing eyes. 'That was marvellous,' she said.

'You're crazy,' he said, his tone quiet.

'But you are, too. Mother says so. Mad as a snake, I heard her tell Dad that.'

'We're two of a kind then,' he said. 'Only you're not supposed to be crazy, you're the concert pianist. Why are you really here?'

They were alone in the quarry, while down the hill the men boiled their billy for a brew of tea.

'Mother's selling my piano to raise enough money for us to go to England. Dad's not so keen on it. He did pay for it. But, you know, I'm going to the Royal Conservatory of

145

Music, so he can't really complain. That's what he wanted me to do.'

'But you're not going to do that, are you?'

She hesitated a moment too long. 'I want to fly aeroplanes,' she said. 'I'm not going to learn music any more.'

'Flying, eh? You rotten little cow. You're telling lies to the poor old sod.' He seemed half-serious, half-amused. 'I suppose our mother put you up to this?'

'Why do you talk about Mother the way you do?'

He shouted with laughter at this. 'You don't know? I'm the cause of all her troubles. The old man put her in the family way. She had to marry him.'

Jean turned towards him, horrified. In the family way. Like Freda. Like Alma with him. 'I don't believe you. Mother's not like that.'

'Please yourself. Ask her. The great dramatic actress strutting the theatre boards and turning people's heads wherever she went, up the duff. You'll find out the truth some day. And what did she get out of it? She got me. The mad son.'

'I was joking. About you being mad.'

'But she wasn't.' His voice was filled with an old, weary sadness.

'You won't tell Dad, will you? About the flying.'

'What's it worth?' Her back was against a rock face. He had moved close to her again, putting his hands on either side of her body, creating a barrier she couldn't pass.

'Harold, what are you doing?'

His voice was hoarse and thick. 'I like you, Jean.'

'Of course.' She tried to move away. 'I'm your sister.'

'You used to play mothers and fathers with little brother. Our brother the Fairy Queen.'

'No. We dressed up, that was all.' He held her against the rock with one arm, his other hand fumbling at her skirt. 'No, Harold, please. Don't do this to me.'

His breath was hot against her mouth, his saliva acid as if he had inhaled the explosives they had been detonating.

Then, when she had begun to fall beneath his weight, his body convulsed and arced backwards, spittle flying from the corners of his mouth. His eyes rolled upward in his head and he fell.

She picked herself up and stepped away, watching with fascinated horror as his seizure abated. He was sitting on the ground, his face suffused with a plum-coloured glow. 'That was a cracker,' he said. 'Lucky that one didn't blow us right off the planet. You all right?' He stretched out his hand for her to haul him to his feet, as if nothing unusual had passed between them. It was impossible to tell whether he believed that an explosion had caused him to fall, or his own failing, the ailment she suddenly understood. Somehow she felt safe from him now, that this wouldn't happen again.

When they returned to the house, Alma looked both of them up and down. Perhaps she imagined it, but Jean thought her eyes were searching for tell-tale signs of misdoing, as if she had been expecting all along that Harold would try to seduce her. She found herself smoothing her skirt, crumpled and dirty from the excursion into the cave.

'I've been a bit crook,' Harold said.

'Ah.' Alma turned her attention to him and nodded in a knowing way, as if satisfied all was well. 'You'd better have a lie down,' she said to her husband. 'There's a letter there for you,' she told Jean.

The letter was from Nellie: Jean was to hurry back to Auckland. Her mother had tickets on a ship leaving for Sydney in three days. From there they would join the liner *Oriana* and sail for England.

In the evening, Harold took a battered book from a shelf in the kitchen. It was the old atlas that he and John used to pore over with Jean. He opened it and his finger traced a route from London across the world. Paris. Cyprus. Damascus. He murmured the words, caressing them. Babylon. 'Do you know how Nebuchadnezzar built Babylon?' she asked, hoping to impress him.

He answered immediately, explaining how cylinders and tablets had been unearthed that told in the king's own words how he had constructed the city, and his palace with its hanging gardens. Nebuchadnezzar and the bath house.

'You remember the bath house when we were kids, Jean?' he said.

She lied to him, saying that she didn't, she was too young to remember. She knew he didn't believe her.

When Harold took her to the bus the next morning, they stood on the side of the road. Summer had slunk behind a cloud, and the day had turned dull. They heard the bus approaching before it turned the corner. He took her by the shoulders. 'You're the only sister I've got.' He released her and tapped his forehead with his finger. 'I'll get old and you'll still be up here. You remember that when you go flying off in the sky.'

Chapter 12

After their arrival in London, Jean and Nellie researched flying clubs. They decided, or rather Nellie did, that the London Aeroplane Club would be the most suitable to approach for Jean's flying lessons. It was subsidised by the Air Ministry, which meant it was cheaper than others they looked at. The ministry was keen to train top pilots in case there was another war. Still, it was two pounds and ten shillings an hour for dual control instruction and one pound ten an hour to hire a plane for a solo flight. 'How many lessons do you think I'll need?' Jean asked. 'Oh, six or eight, I'd say,' Nellie said, with an airiness that belied her anxiety.

She had calculated many times on small notepads just how far her money would stretch. This was a time when a man was fortunate to earn five pounds a week. Fred was sending her an extra two pounds a week for Jean's music lessons, over and above the regular three pounds. Jean gritted her teeth and expressed the hope that she would learn to fly very quickly. 'Deep breaths, Jean,' Nellie said. 'It doesn't pay to think about it.' Whether she was talking about the speed with which Jean could learn or their duplicity in regard to Fred's allowance wasn't clear.

The Royal College of Music was a forbidden topic of conversation.

The London Aeroplane Club had another thing in its favour: it welcomed women pilots. Some of them had already become famous. The exploits of Lady Sophie Mary Heath particularly dazzled Nellie. This woman had challenged an international requirement that women could not fly commercial flights because menstruation impaired their capabilities, and she'd won. Trust the Irish, Nellie said. The club was based at Stag Lane aerodrome, which lay among farmland, some ten miles from central London. It was the base for Sir Geoffrey de Havilland's famous aircraft company: he had been building Gipsy Moths there for the past five years. The skyline was dominated by the company's hangars and engineering workshops.

As flying fields went, Jean already knew that Stag Lane had a reputation for being difficult. It sloped steeply from the road, forming a depression like a shallow basin. From the clubhouse, you couldn't see an aeroplane landing because it was completely hidden in the dip. In winter, the whole field became waterlogged.

As she and Nellie approached on foot, dressed in tweed suits and good brogues, luxuries purchased in Oxford Street, Jean looked around and shivered. 'I suppose if I can fly off this aerodrome I can fly off any,' she said.

'You'll need to if you're going to fly across the world,' Nellie said. 'Come on, we haven't come all this way for you to get your tail down now.' For today's journey, all

they'd had to do was catch the underground train in central London and alight at Burnt Oak Station at the end of Edgware Road, the old Roman highway. It seemed almost too simple. A stone church slumbered between red brick houses with paling fences, quiet and suburban. Like Sunday afternoon in Auckland. But it was spring and oak leaves were unfurling. Daffodils shone in small gardens.

As they neared the flying field, they were startled to see the Prince of Wales striding around the perimeter. He wore a top hat, a high white collar, a bow tie and a jacket with satin lapels; a trailing silk scarf was thrown around his shoulders. His long, fair face was flushed with annoyance. The tremendous roar of several engines on test beds filled the air with a high metallic whine.

He shouted to an engineer dressed in overalls, 'Why can't that noise be contained in a soundproof room?'

The man turned, looked the Prince up and down and shouted back at him, 'How would you like to be cooped up in this noise for two hours in a closed room?'

The Prince looked momentarily stunned. 'My dear chap, I see what you mean. So sorry.'

A second engineer, who had watched this exchange, now hurried to the first man, and spoke to him in an urgent way. It was clear that, despite the clothes and the top hat, His Highness had not been recognised. The man put his face to his hand and ducked his head.

'No cause, it's my fault.' The Prince turned to make a

hasty retreat, nearly bumping into the two women. 'Ladies,' he said, sweeping off his hat to reveal an immaculate parting. 'Forgive me, I've had a wretched morning. I stayed out hunting longer than I meant to and now I'm running late for an important event. You understand how it is. I've brought my plane in for some work. Can't find my fellow at Hendon, he'll be hearing from me. Taken the afternoon off, by the look of things. We know each other, don't we?' he said to Nellie. 'Where was it? You'll have to remind me.' He glanced with undisguised curiosity at their feet, their shoes muddy from tramping across the damp field.

'It must have been in New Zealand,' Nellie replied, her voice as smooth as whipped cream.

'Ah, New Zealand, my goodness, that was a long time ago.' He looked as if he were about to ask more, his eyes intent and admiring as they rested on Nellie, but he was distracted by the appearance of a blue and silver DH 60M Gipsy Moth being wheeled out onto the airstrip.

The Prince inclined his head, replacing his hat as if it were a crown. 'We must talk more about New Zealand the next time we meet.' He walked over to his aeroplane, took off his hat again and exchanged it for a flying helmet. Within minutes he had risen into the sky.

'He liked you,' Jean said, later that night, when they were going over the events of the day. 'The Prince is said to like the company of older women.'

'Jean!' Nellie's tone was scandalised but suddenly it

seemed like the funniest thing, an auspicious start, that had them bursting into laughter every time they thought about it.

Outside the hangars where Jean and Nellie had met the Prince, stood a whole row of Gipsy Moths, all painted yellow. These were biplanes, flimsy to the casual observer, with plywood-encased fuselages, and fabric covering the rest of their surfaces. Jean was aware of the plane's design and the way the wings could be detached and folded away, making space in hangars to store several at a time.

Alongside the Moths, to Jean's astonishment, a glamorous woman in a striking black and white ensemble, including a huge Eskimo hood made from expensive-looking furs, was posing against a monoplane painted to match her outfit. Her face was very pale and her straight black hair was worn like a helmet on her head. A photographer was taking stills, and a retinue of men in suits scurried around calling out instructions.

'I know her,' Jean breathed.

'Keep walking,' Nellie instructed.

The clubhouse was a modest hut on the far fringe of the aerodrome. They were expected — Jean had written in advance enquiring about membership — and a secretary came out to greet them. Around a fire blazing at the far end of the room stood a group of people, all casually handsome at first glance, the jackets of their flying suits unbuttoned, goggles sitting on top of their heads. There was laughter and blue smoke from cigarettes and pipes.

The pipe smoke reminded Jean suddenly of Fred, far away, and not knowing where they were. Nellie caught her eye, as if she, too, had thought of her husband. 'Somebody just walked over my grave,' she said.

The club secretary looked startled, then handed Jean a form to fill in.

'You're under twenty-one,' the secretary said, when he looked through her answers. 'You have to get your parents' consent to fly.'

'Both my parents?' Jean asked in alarm.

'One will be enough.'

Nellie stepped forward. 'I am Miss Batten's mother,' she announced. 'I take it you'll accept the maternal signature.'

The secretary looked amused. 'Yes, of course, Mrs Batten. Just put your name here.'

'You're not related to the film star of the same name, by any chance?' he asked. Nellie reddened and agreed that yes, John Batten was indeed her son.

'He was tremendous in *Under the Greenwood Tree*. Loved that picture. You must be very proud of him.' Nellie didn't tell the secretary that they hadn't yet seen the film. Instead, she handed over six guineas, three for the entrance fee to the club, and three for a year's subscription.

But Jean was emboldened to ask if Louise Brooks, whom she believed she had seen on her way over to the clubhouse, was one of the other students.

The secretary laughed. 'Not everyone who comes here wants to fly. The film stars come along to be seen doing adventurous things. They just have their pictures taken.

The people who come to fly are in this room. You should meet some of them. There's Miss Amy Johnson over there — she'll take you under her wing.' He chuckled. 'She's a true aviator, a star in the making. She's planning to fly to Australia next month. If she does she'll be the first woman to make it.'

Jean froze. A plain woman, she decided, with a large nose, and an overlong upper lip.

Nellie nudged her. 'She's just a typist,' she whispered.

'*Mother*,' Jean hissed. 'I think we should go now.'

The secretary had already handed her an appointment time for her first lesson the following morning. Her instructor would be Herbert Travers, a wartime flying ace. He was the best. He'd trained Miss Johnson, and that was some recommendation.

When they were outside, Jean said, 'But what if Amy Johnson flies to Australia before I do?'

'Then you'll have to fly faster,' her mother said. 'She'll probably crash anyway, she doesn't look very clever.'

Just one afternoon, and already their heads were reeling. The Prince. The film star. The rivals. Nellie was calculating again, working out how much of her savings would have to go on better outfits for Jean. A good flying suit was an obvious necessity. Her hands were itching to get her notebook out.

They had, of course, seen John on their arrival in London even though they hadn't seen his new movie. Jean had been taken aback by his beauty, as if he were a stranger. It was a graceful, muscular beauty, utterly natural and seemingly without guile, his body light and free, as if it completely belonged to him. He seemed to have grown taller, his eyes intense and glowing, his mouth curved in a deep, expressive line. By now he had appeared in five films and was making his sixth, with another one in the pipeline. *The Greenwood Tree* was putting him back on his feet, he said. He was living in St John's Wood, a small flat above a fish shop, the thin blue smell of the unsold merchandise wafting up the stairs in late afternoon before it was sluiced down. There was something familiar about the way the flat was furnished, elegant in its simplicity. A chintz-covered chair, light curtains at the window, dashes of colour in unexpected places. A hyacinth in a dark pot on a tall stand in the entranceway. A room Nellie might have furnished long ago, in their Rotorua days.

Hollywood had been great, John said, a tremendous place to have fun. He'd made a lot of money and lost the lot. 'Dud investments, the Wall Street crash,' he said. 'You'd know about the slump back home, wouldn't you?'

'Back home,' Nellie said, marvelling. 'Oh, you've got no idea. Things are bad. Well, John, we hope to make our home here if Jean passes her exams.'

'Dad wrote and said you'd been doing well with your music. You'll be my famous kid sister. You always said you'd be famous.'

'I'm going to have to work hard to catch you up,' Jean said, not giving anything away.

'I'm sorry, I haven't got much space,' John said. 'I should offer you a bed, but I've only got the one.' He gestured to a day bed covered with a deep red spread, in an alcove off the main room.

'No need,' Nellie said. 'We've taken rooms just off Oxford Street, in the heart of the city.'

John whistled. 'Nice address.'

'It'll probably be temporary,' Nellie said quickly. 'But for now it's very handy to everything.' The rooms were up five flights of stairs, and very cold, but she didn't mention these details. John looked relieved. Jean guessed that they weren't meant to stay anyway, that if they did his delight in their welcome might soon be exhausted.

They began to take their leave with promises to see each other again soon. John was in rehearsals all day, and shooting was due to begin the following week, but he insisted they must come for dinner at the weekend. A young friend would be coming, a chap called Rex Harrison who'd done some theatre work, but it was his first film, he needed some coaching. They wouldn't be in the way. Rex was a barrel of laughs. John promised fish, the best money could buy, but he'd get a discount for putting up with the smell. The three of them laughed: dutiful, affectionate, reunited.

'By the way, are you seeing anyone?' Nellie asked. In the silence that followed, she said, a trifle too sharply, 'A woman. Some actress or another?'

158

'No, Mother, I'm not seeing a woman.'

As if to hasten their departure, he insisted on walking them to the train station. Outside, a fog had settled over the houses, clinging to their hair, seeping under their collars. There was a flower seller's kiosk on the way to the platform. By way of a peace offering, he stopped and bought Nellie a bunch of freesias, lemony and delicate.

'You shouldn't have,' Nellie said, her face flushed, but pleased all the same.

John kissed Jean on the cheek. 'You're gorgeous,' he said. 'Do you know what a stunning girl you really are? I bet you don't, but you'll find out soon.'

On the Saturday morning, Nellie had sent a note to say that she was indisposed and was truly sorry that they wouldn't be able to come for dinner. Perhaps they could meet for a cup of tea some time. 'Don't worry, darling,' she said to Jean. 'I know how much you want to see him, but he needs to get used to the idea of you flying when the time is right.' Her voice was tinged with regret. 'We can't really fib away to him all the time. Besides, you can see how busy he is.'

The morning following her enrolment at Stag Lane, Jean made her way back to the aerodrome. Nellie wanted to come, but this time Jean said that she could do this on her own. Besides, she reminded her, only one of them had membership of the club. There were all those shops for Nellie to look at in Oxford Street, and she would need weeks to see everything in the British Museum.

Herbert Travers was waiting for her, a tall man, dressed in tweeds and plus-fours, his collar and tie immaculate. She wasn't sure how old he was, perhaps in his late thirties, going by his war record, although he looked older, fair and already going bald. She would begin her lessons in a Cirrus Moth, which was much the same as a Gipsy Moth.

'The first lesson,' he said, after they had shaken hands, 'is to discover what the inside of the cockpit of a Moth looks like. I'll see you in the morning.' With that she was dismissed.

Chapter 13

The fear that had been sitting at the bottom of Jean's stomach since she woke up threatened to overwhelm her as she climbed into the cockpit of a fuselage at the technical school. This was the moment she had been waiting for all her life, but now it had arrived she felt small and afraid. Worse than that, she felt as if she might throw up and disgrace herself.

'You're a dainty little girl,' Travers said, looking her over more closely than he had the day before. 'Do you think you're tough enough to be a flier?'

'Very tough,' Jean said, lifting her chin. 'How many pirouettes can you do in a row without falling over?'

He scratched his head and thought about this. 'You're a dancer?'

'I was. I sold my piano in order to come here.'

'From where?'

'New Zealand.'

'My word. A little ballet dancer all the way from New Zealand who has sold her piano in order to become an aviator.' She wondered if he were making fun of her. She had heard him addressed as 'Major' that morning by fliers on the field. His size and crisp manner were intimidating.

'Well, yes and no. I'm supposed to be in London to become a concert pianist.' It sounded silly, a little vain. She looked at her hands and wished that she was in Alice Law's studio practising scales, or along the road at Madame Valeska's pulling a tutu over her head in preparation for a recital. 'I've flown with Charles Kingsford Smith,' she said.

'Smithy, eh. Well, well. You'll know what all these controls are then?'

She shook her head. 'It was just the once, to get the feel of flying.'

'So did you learn *any*thing from him?'

'Not to fly at night.'

'Good advice.'

'He suggested I didn't try to beat men. But I'll make up my own mind about that.'

Travers looked impressed, and gave her a sudden grin. 'Well then, we should begin. Think of this as the barre. Isn't that where ballerinas go each day to warm up before they practise their routines? Yes?'

And she thought yes, indeed, this was the right place after all, and that he wasn't taking her down a peg, the way she'd imagined a moment before. This was where she would go day after day, to learn and remember, this tiny cocoon of the cockpit, greenish-grey inside, the control column between her knees, a polished wooden panel in front of her, on which were arranged a quartet of instruments: the engine revolution counter, the airspeed indicator, the altimeter and oil pressure gauges, and in the centre, above them, a small halfmoon-shaped glass tube of liquid with a bubble in it to indicate lateral stability during the flight.

He explained to her then how the controls surrounding the cockpit operated. The pedals at her feet controlled the rudder at the back of the plane, changing its direction. Had she ever sailed a boat? And when she said that she had, he exhaled a small grunt, indicating that he was pleased. This was the control column, or the joystick if she liked. Don't ask him why it was called that, he said, but it did two things. If she held it in the middle she would fly level. Push it forward and the plane descended. Pull it back and the plane climbed. That controlled the elevator on the back of the plane. Move it to the left and the plane rolled to the left. Move it to the right and the reverse.

Was she with him? Good, that was good.

On the back of the wings were the ailerons that controlled the rolling motion of the plane. The lever on the left was the throttle. 'On your first flight,' he told her, 'you will find that you're gently using all these controls together.'

'Like playing the piano?'

'Hmm, yes, perhaps, but you don't have the luxury of making mistakes, not once you're on your own. You've got me in the front to rescue you while I'm training you, but not when you go solo.'

He showed her the throttle on her left-hand side. She must always remember that the nut in the middle was finger tight. 'Move the throttle forward to increase the engine speed. The plane might start to climb and you mightn't want that, so you use the other wheel by the throttle to trim for level flight. If you want to climb or descend, gently use the throttle trim. Gently, always gently.'

That was the first lesson on the first day, taking her through the controls over and again until she could touch them with her eyes closed and tell him what they were. They still weren't airborne.

The next day they were. The weather that had threatened to close in with misty rain first thing in the morning had lifted and the air was clear. Travers was not a man to take risks, he told her. There are bold pilots, and old pilots, but there are no old, bold pilots. Favourite saying, she'd better get used to it.

She must also get used to going through a pre-flight check every time she left the ground.

'How will I remember all the checks?' Jean asked.

'Very good question. Here's a little phrase that might help you remember. "Too many flying instructors here."'

She looked at him in astonishment. 'Why on earth would I remember that? It sounds ridiculous.'

'Take the first letter from every word. Start with the letter "t". Throttle nut finger tight. Trim set for takeoff. Next, the letter "m", mixture control wired back. "F" is fuel sufficient for flight. You see this gauge? You'll learn over the next weeks to calculate how much fuel you need for a flight, and if you haven't enough, you may land anywhere but the place you intended. Perhaps in the sea, perhaps in the middle of a forest, or on a busy road. There's a strong chance you won't come out of the plane alive. There are plenty of bold pilots who don't. Do you still want to fly?'

'Yes.'

'I thought you'd say that.' He completed the rest of the checklist, and nodded towards the control panel. 'We should begin our flight, Miss Batten.'

They took to the air and she shouted with delight, her fingers dancing on the controls. 'Pay attention,' shouted Travers through the speaking tube that connected them. 'You're not here to have fun.' They were rising up in the sky, five hundred feet, a thousand, the world getting smaller beneath them, trees shrinking, houses tiny.

'Good, you're doing well. Now level her out, excellent.'

When they were back on the ground, he turned and nodded briefly. 'That's not bad for the first time up. I can make a flier out of you if you want it badly enough. It's over to you.'

'Of course I want it,' Jean said. 'As a matter of fact, I'm planning to fly from here to New Zealand.'

'Oh, I see.' He laughed. 'You're quite something, aren't you?'

In the mornings, she would line up with other students outside his tiny office near the field, sitting on a wooden bench, waiting for her turn to fly with him. The rule was that they turned up rain or fine, because the weather could change. If there was no visibility, he cancelled their flights. In the evenings, she went to classes in the school to study aerodynamics, compass swinging, rigging … She enrolled for them all, essential or not.

Nellie shifted them out of the rooms in James Street to others near the aerodrome — cheaper, deal furniture, rough horsehair mattresses, discoloured lace anti-macassars on the backs of stiff chairs. She began what had become a ritual each time they moved, scrubbing every inch of the rooms they were to inhabit. It was goodbye to Piccadilly Circus, the parks and museums, the glowing shop windows they had lingered in front of in the afternoons. But Jean could walk to and from her flying instruction and evening classes. By now both Jean and Nellie had realised that six or eight flying hours might be optimistic. The hours, at best, took a long time to accumulate, while Nellie's funds slipped away. Sometimes Jean could fly for only an hour or so a week. Nellie's pencil and pad were busy all the time, saving a penny here, a shilling there.

Amy Johnson, true to her word, had flown to Australia. She had set off from Croydon airfield on the fifth of May and landed in Darwin on the twenty-fourth. Her intention had been to break Bert Hinkler's record of sixteen days, but that hadn't happened. All the same, she was the first woman to make this solo flight, and now she was an instant heroine, the toast of Britain.

'So where did she get the money?' Nellie fretted, as the tributes poured in. Jean said she had heard at the club that Amy's father had raised the money to buy a plane with sponsorship from Viscount Wakefield, who headed

Castrol Oil. Amy's plane had cost her six hundred pounds.

'Well, at least her father helped,' Nellie said, her voice sour. They had met up with Fred's sister Ida, who was visiting London at the same time. Ida, who had means, took them out to dinner in a restaurant.

'So why haven't you seen more of John?' Ida asked. She had Fred's licorice eyes, without the warmth. 'He seems quite put out that you've hardly seen him. It doesn't seem natural.'

Nellie flushed and looked away.

'Well, Ellen? Surely I have a right to know. He's flesh and blood to both of us.'

'Ida, can you keep a secret? Please. It's very important.'

Ida glanced at Jean. 'She's not in some kind of trouble?'

'No . . . well, she would be if Fred found out. You see, Jean's not studying music.'

Ida put down a spoonful of blancmange in her plate with a clatter. 'What on earth is she doing here, then?'

'Learning to fly.'

'Oh, my Lord. You don't say so. Fred was always afraid she'd get up to something like that.'

'Please,' Jean exclaimed. 'It's not Mother's fault. She knew I'd find a way, and she's just helped me, that's all.'

Ida was wiping her mouth with furious swipes of her linen napkin.

'So you see,' Nellie said, 'it wouldn't be fair to John if he had to keep a secret from his father. We just thought it better not to tell him. We've tried to keep everything to ourselves. We have all our mail addressed care of Thomas

Cook in Berkeley Street, so nobody can track us down.'

'It's preposterous,' Ida said.

'You promised,' Nellie said, her tone righteous.

'I did not,' Ida said.

'But of course you did, or I wouldn't have told you,' Nellie said. 'You know you did, Ida.'

Ida looked from one to the other, her lips pursed like a coin bag, as she waved for their bill.

'It's just not fair,' she said, as they parted, 'not to John or to Fred.' She was pulling on her kid gloves. 'I never have worked out why you and Fred don't live together,' she said. 'You do know it's caused unhappiness in our family, Ellen. A good husband like Fred.'

Afterwards, Nellie had lain awake and worried as to whether she could trust Ida or not.

'I shouldn't have told her about the flying lessons,' Nellie said. 'I'm a fool. Or perhaps I should have told her what antics her brother gets up to. That would have fixed her.'

'It wouldn't, Mother,' Jean said. 'She wouldn't have believed you.'

This hadn't contributed to Nellie's peace of mind. 'How come this Miss Johnson won favours from Lord Wakefield?'

Jean didn't know. She never stayed long at the clubhouse. Sometimes she stood at the edge of the crowd and heard snippets of information. She was there the night everyone raised a toast to Johnnie, their very own girl. One thing she learned was that Amy Johnson had been a skilled engineer before setting off on her flight. It was when she became the first woman to qualify as an engineer that she had caught Wakefield's eye.

Jean decided to take a leaf from Amy's book, and enrolled in more classes at the technical school, taking a course in the general maintenance of aircraft and engines. Here she learned the importance of inspecting the aircraft and the engine before each and every flight, and how to correct malfunctions. When the aeroplanes were wheeled out of the hangars and the propellers swung each morning, she felt alert to the throb of the engines, listening intently for the smallest miss or murmur. She surprised herself at the pleasure she took in getting her hands and overalls covered with engine grease. One morning, she was bent over a crankshaft, her hands thick with oil, when a tall, loose-limbed figure loomed above her, watching what she was doing. 'Miss Batten? You're doing well, young lady.' Jean instinctively tried to wipe her palms on her overalls, in order to shake hands.

'Don't worry,' he said, and laughed. 'Just stick with what you're doing. I'm de Havilland, by the way, I've heard good things about you.' He had a slight hesitancy in his manner and a reputation for shyness in spite of his status. Jean thought his eyes generous in their expression. He bent down to run a finger along the crankshaft, nodding his head. 'Yes, that's all right.' He squatted on his heels, looking like an oversized school boy. 'You know, I used to make model aeroplanes when I was a youngster. I didn't really believe people would fly in the planes I made. Not then.

Keep up the good work, young lady.' And then he sprang lightly to his feet and made his way to the next student.

'Geoffrey Just-Call-Me-God de Havilland,' her instructor said, when he'd gone, but there was admiration in his voice. Praise from the great man wasn't offered lightly.

'De Havilland's all very well,' Nellie said, when Jean recounted the meeting, 'but you need to meet Viscount Wakefield.'

Despite the small snippets of praise coming her way, this was beyond Jean's current reckoning. So many people at Stag Lane were so famous, so self-confident. So rich and so well dressed. Nobody said the word 'colonial', but that was how she saw herself. When she opened her mouth she didn't sound nearly as eloquent as she thought she had back in Auckland.

Amy returned later in the summer, radiant with success, mobbed by her fellow club members. She had assumed a new aura of glamour. Her eyebrows were plucked finely, her hair floated stylishly in a long bob. Men flocked around her, offering her drinks, cigarettes, opening doors, as if they could absorb her success. Jean would have liked to speak to her, but when she approached there was always someone else there ahead of her. And, somehow, she felt her voice stuck in the back of her throat before she even tried to open her mouth.

Amy was honoured by the King. When she returned from Buckingham Palace on the afternoon of the ceremony, the new medal on her breast, there were more rounds of drinks and applause. 'Johnnie, Johnnie,' everyone shouted, the swirl of noise rising like the shriek of seagulls. Jean, standing outside the circle, her flying helmet in her hand, felt as if she were standing at the edge of the water back home, a child with no particular direction. She turned and walked out of the clubhouse.

The summer passed, months of heat and work. Jean had watched the oak leaves round Edgware Road turn from pale sprigs to dark green canopies, and now autumn was upon them, the leaves beginning to fall. Late one afternoon, she and Travers were doing circuits and landings on Stag Lane, gliding in without using the engine and putting the Moth down in a three-point landing. The two wheels and the tail-skid touched the ground gently at the same moment, the plane coming to rest in a climbing position. It was a manoeuvre that required practice and skill. If the speed was too high when the control column was pulled back on approach, the Moth would stall; if it were too low, it would land on two wheels and hurtle down the runway. The aircraft had no brakes to slow it down. If either seemed about to happen, Travers pressed the engine throttle forward to avoid a catastrophe, and round she would go again.

That afternoon, she had completed the final three-point landing of the day and begun to taxi towards the hangar.

Travers' voice carried down the tube to the earphones on her leather flying helmet. 'Wait, Miss Batten,' he said. 'Stop the plane.' He began to climb out of the front cockpit, the dual control column under his arm.

'Over to you,' he shouted. 'She's all yours.'

She watched as he walked away, without seeming to look back. There was an unnatural stillness in the air, punctuated only by the staccato note of the propeller turning over. Everyone had gone, the doors of the factory were closed. From the nearby fields a light evening mist was advancing slowly, like a sluggish, milky tide.

Jean taxied the Moth back to the edge of the aerodrome, and turned it into the wind. For a moment, she sat quite still, taking in this moment that would never happen again, her very first solo flight. She reached out her gloved hand and gave the engine full throttle. The Moth taxied forward, gaining speed, and the tail rose. She eased the joystick back. After a very short run she was airborne. This time there was nobody to hear her shout of exhilaration. The sound of her voice was carried away, but inside she felt a joy so intense she could hardly breathe. Three words flashed through her mind: *Never look back*.

As she banked the Moth in a left-hand turn, circling the aerodrome in preparation for landing, she looked over the side of the cockpit to the landscape beyond. In the twilight she could see the silver outline of the R101, the airship being built at the Cardington base, to the north of Stag Lane. The huge craft, moving through the descending mist, appeared as a great whale swimming in a calm sea.

Travers was waiting for her on the ground. For a moment his hand rested lightly on her shoulder. 'Very good, Miss Batten. If I may say so, a quality performance.'

Chapter 14

The crash couldn't have come at a worse time. Nellie's cash was down to twenty pounds. How many more solo flights would Jean need, she wondered, before she got her A licence?

'Another two flights,' Jean reassured her. 'Not long now, darling.'

She and Nellie had taken to calling each other darling with a tenderness that had grown between them since their arrival in London. At least three young men at the club had now invited Jean for outings, to go to town, see a film, have a drink perhaps. People were at last beginning to notice her silent presence. There were moments when she was tempted. But when she thought about Nellie, alone in their rented room near quiet Edgware Road, counting their pennies, it seemed unfair. Besides, she had never gone out with a young man. At Madame Valeska's, she had put what she called a professional distance between her and those who mooned around her. Pity poor Freda, who hadn't had that sense. She wondered now and then what had become of her friend. And those offering the invitations were mere boys, eighteen or so. If she wanted to be seen with a man, he needed to have a little maturity, she told her mother, who agreed. 'You're not to waste your time with beginners, darling,' she said. They'd had a thin soup and some green beans for dinner, and an extra cup of tea for warmth, when this discussion took place. The time had come for some change in their situation, and only Jean's licence could make a difference.

But just when the licence seemed within her grasp, she flew too low as she was coming in to land. The plane's undercarriage clipped and caught on a low boundary fence, tipping the machine on its nose. She pitched forward, her head connecting with the compass, before releasing her straps and tumbling onto the ground. Jean made a little mewing sound, crouched on hands and knees on the grassy field. It was hard to imagine worse humiliation. Around her gathered a group of fliers, concerned at first that she was safe, then laughing when they saw her plight. Among them was one of her admirers. With a small shriek she threw herself into his arms, sobbing wildly.

Travers came to lead her away. 'A bit bold today, were we, Jean?'

'Will I have to pay for the damage?'

'You got lucky, not a mark on the plane. You came off worse. Come on, dry up those tears.'

'I'm sorry. I'm British. I shouldn't cry.'

'British?' He looked at her and laughed. 'You shouldn't have got over-confident. You're going to have a cup of tea, and then you're going to get up in another plane. You understand?'

She nodded. 'So will I have to pay for the extra time?'

He regarded her with deeper concern, appeared about to say something, then led her in silence to the clubhouse. Inside, he drew her close to the fire, took her hands and rubbed them between his. 'You're very cold, you're in shock,' he said. At the bar he ordered hot milk with a dash of brandy and two egg sandwiches. When she had eaten, he told her that when his students did something reckless or foolish, there was a price to pay. He couldn't make an exception of her. What she had done was serious, she must understand. 'In a few minutes you'll be in the air again, repeating today's exercise. You'll have to pay for your time, all right?'

'I'll have to go home and ask Mother,' Jean said.

'No, you won't,' he said, his voice gentle. 'I've already cancelled the payment on your first flight.'

This kindness, so unexpected and generous, restored her. In the air, she said it to herself, the mantra, the words she had promised herself: *Never look back never look back.* All the same, she stayed away from the clubhouse for the next few days, preferring to leave the field as soon as she had flown.

She mightn't have gone back at all, had another woman, a very distinguished woman, not had a spectacular mishap the same week. The Duchess of Bedford had set a record, years before, flying to Cape Town in a Fokker F.VII with an accompanying pilot. A picture of her hung in the clubhouse, taken when she was young, wearing a sweeping gown, cut low at the neck, masses of hair piled up on top of her head with a tiara perched above

— a romantic-looking figure. Now she was plump and elderly, her face weatherbeaten. She saw no reason why she couldn't fly to Cape Town alone in a Gipsy Moth, but first she had to learn to fly one. If that young Johnnie woman could fly to Australia, she saw no reason why she couldn't make such a journey, she told everyone. It wasn't as if she didn't know the way. Setting records was one thing, she remarked, but they were something of a Pyrrhic victory if somebody else did the work.

Reporters gathered around the Duchess's red and gold Moth as she prepared to leave. She climbed into the cockpit and taxied across the aerodrome, giving waves and salutes. Rain had been falling in the night and the ground was sticky underfoot. Before she got to the boundary fence, she was stuck deep in mud, did a ground loop and was left hanging upside down from her safety belt. Jean watched in horror as the crowd surged forward to help. She could break her neck if she falls, someone muttered beside her. The Duchess did fall, without breaking her neck, but letting forth a stream of invective. Her face was puce, as she staggered to her feet. 'Go to buggery hell,' she shrieked, kicking the plane. 'Bastard thing.' The reporters scuttled away, pocketing their notebooks.

Jean knew how the Duchess felt. But when she had fallen out of the plane, she had been wearing thick flying trousers. The Duchess, on the other hand, was wearing a skirt and thick red bloomers, revealed for all to see.

Jean made a mental note. Never wear clothes that will reveal one's private affairs to the world. Never use bad language in a public place. These were things she didn't need her mother to teach her. She would, she decided, prefer to look like a film star, who also happened to fly planes. Surely, she could do both. If possible, she would like to avoid being gossiped about as well. The ground staff loved to pass on rumours to their favourites, and she could tell she was becoming one of them. She always said 'please' and 'thank you', words often overlooked by her fellow fliers.

The awful news that the R101 had crashed in France on its first overseas flight, killing forty-eight passengers, had cast a pall over everyone. When Jean did go back to the clubhouse, it was not to relive the Duchess's misfortune, but to join in a long minute of silence for those lost. They reminded each other of the perils of the air, and the dangers they faced when they trusted it to hold them aloft. For the first time Jean felt close to her fellow fliers. Her own scrape with the fence seemed risible.

The Prince of Wales was still turning up at Stag Lane, usually in his Bentley, despite his father commanding him not to go solo again until his flying improved, to take his princely duties more seriously, and not to place his life at risk. The young women who worked in the fabric and glue factories came streaming out to see him every time he turned up, until their forewomen sent them back to work. He basked in these impromptu welcomes.

A hapless group captain, a man by the name of Fielden, had been charged with the responsibility of keeping the wilful Prince safe and not letting him fly alone. One morning, when the pair was practising circuits and bumps, and as the royal Moth was about to take off, the Prince looked appealingly at Fielden and said, 'Bother, I've left my handkerchief in the clubhouse.'

'I'll nip in and get it for you, sir,' Fielden said, knowing he must oblige. He jumped down from the plane and ran inside. The Prince opened up the throttle, took off, made a circuit, then landed. Fielden leaned against the clubhouse, his face pale.

Jean, who witnessed this incident, found herself laughing out loud as the captain made his way back to the centre of the field, waving his arms.

'Good Lord, how do you punish a Prince?' said a man in a flying suit, who was standing nearby. He was sleek in his appearance, well built, tall enough to look imposing as he stood by Jean, his head thrown back with a merriment that matched hers. 'Hey,' he said, looking down at her, 'I've seen you around. What's your name?'

When she told him, he held out his hand. 'Victor Dorée, pleased to make your acquaintance.' His eyes seemed friendly, his hair combed back from his forehead. Handsome, she described him to Nellie later that night.

'You look like a girl who enjoys mischief,' he said, as they appraised one another.

'Absolutely not. I'm the least mischievous person you could ever meet.'

'I don't believe you. Have a drink with me at the club later on?'

'I'm a strictly lemonade kind of girl,' Jean said, her voice demure.

'Never mind, lemonade it is. Five o'clock. I'll see you there.'

In the clubhouse, the Prince was downing drinks with Fielden and a friend. Because he was the Prince, it was impossible to refuse to join him in each round. The men were getting louder and more raucous by the moment.

'Bit hard to find a quiet spot,' Victor said.

'Are you a student?' Jean asked. 'I haven't seen you before.'

He looked amused. 'I keep my plane here in a hangar. I'm a lucky chap. My mother bought it for me for my birthday. We live across the road. You live near here?'

She explained that for the moment she did, although she came from New Zealand.

'New Zealand. I meant to go there, just didn't get round to it. I learned to fly in Australia, 1928. Great place. Suppose you've been to Australia?'

The Prince was now the worse for wear. Fielden came over and spoke in Victor's ear. Victor shrugged and gestured towards Jean. 'We're a bit busy here,' he said.

'Just five minutes, give me a hand, and don't make a fuss. You know the drill.'

Victor signalled for Jean to stay where she was, but she couldn't resist moving closer. Victor and Fielden were each taking the Prince by an arm, supporting him as he hobbled towards the door. Outside stood a laundry van bearing the royal insignia. The Prince was heaved inside, his shoe flying through the air.

'Pick it up, Jean,' Victor called. 'Quickly now.' The door of the van slammed shut, and the vehicle took off at speed.

'You weren't supposed to see that,' he said. 'Curiosity killed the cat.'

'What's the penalty?'

'For throwing His Royal Highness's shoe into the pillow slips? The Tower, I wouldn't be surprised.'

'What will they do with him?'

'Drop him off at the back door of Buckingham Palace. Hey, what about we go up town and have a meal? Come on, don't look so worried. I'm not Bluebeard.'

'It's just that tomorrow I'm going for my licence, first thing. I have to get it, Victor. I won't get a second chance.' It felt easy and natural to talk to him, even though she wasn't ready to tell him all about her life. His eyes rested on her.

'Well then, we can celebrate tomorrow night.'

'Perhaps. My mother, well, if I do succeed I think I'd like to spend the evening with her. It's been quite lonely for her over here, waiting for me to get this licence.'

'Bring your mother with you.'

'Really?'

'Yes. C'mon, I'll give you a lift home, show you where I live.' In his car, she settled back into the seat beside him. The leather smelled new, gamey and rich. He slowed down to show her his house, what could be seen from the road, sumptuous and stylish. It sat in what she would later learn were ten acres of gardens and orchards. As if reading her thoughts, he said, 'My old man's in the linen trade.' He eased the car into gear. 'I've got four brothers. Some of us still live at home.' He laughed. 'I'm not ready to cook for myself yet.'

'I can walk from here,' Jean said. Already she was opening the car door. 'Please, stop.'

Taken aback by her distress, he shifted his hand from the gearstick onto hers, holding it lightly for a moment. 'All right then. I didn't mean to frighten you.'

'Don't follow me. Promise.'

'I promise. But don't forget tomorrow night. The offer's open. Your mother, too.'

He sat there with the car idling, while she walked away. She knew he wanted to follow, but thought him a man of his word. If he glimpsed the rooming house she and Nellie occupied, she felt she might never see him again.

5 December 1930. A hint of snow in the air. The sky lowering itself towards the aerodrome. The trees in the fields black in the sour landscape. Mud ankle-deep at the edge of the airstrip. The roaring test engines, which she'd got so used to she didn't hear them, that day sounded like beasts inside the factories.

At the end of the test the examiner saying, 'Well done. You've passed, Miss Batten.'

Her mother standing outside the clubhouse, a scarf wrapped around her face to keep out the perishing sharpness of the cold. Jean's joy, as she flew into Nellie's arms.

She danced up and down on the spot. 'Mother, I've done it! I've passed.'

Nellie's voice was unexpectedly wan. 'I'm so proud of you, darling. Come away, we have to hurry.'

'But Mother,' Jean cried, for the first time wanting to boast about her achievements, 'I've got people to see.' She meant Victor, of course. He would be waiting for her, might even have watched her victorious flight. Travers had already given her a warm handshake, and what passed for a kiss on her cheek, brushing her with his moustache. He would be ordering her hot cocoa right now. And the Duchess, who was not really as formidable as she looked, especially since her tumble and the aborted trip to South Africa, would be there. And Amy Johnson, and today Jean would say hello to her in a bright, one-of-us kind of voice.

'Your father's found out what you're doing. We have to pack up and leave here.' Nellie had begun to stride away, back towards Edgware Road.

'I don't care if he knows,' Jean said, trotting at her heels. 'I've got my licence, Mother. It doesn't matter.'

'He's cut off your allowance, Jean.' Nellie waved a letter in the air. 'We have no money. Do you understand?'

They decided it must have been Ida who had told Fred. Spiteful, Nellie said. She always was a woman drenched in vinegar, they should never have trusted her. And thank goodness they hadn't told John, so they didn't have him to blame. There were two return tickets to New Zealand in Fred's letter. The ship was sailing at the weekend.

Jean said she would do something, go to the High Commission, ask them to help her, anything but return home now. Nellie shook her head. 'Face reality, Jean,' she said. 'Don't you think it's a bitter enough pill for me?' They spent the evening packing up their few belongings. The point of seeing Victor Dorée was lost. The memory of his easy laugh, the warmth of his hand on hers, lingered as Jean tossed and turned. There really wasn't any help for them, whichever way you looked at it.

Chapter 15

It was freezing in Quetta, Frank Norton told Jean. The city was high in the Indian mountains of Baluchistan, almost cut off from the rest of the country, except for bone-crusher metal roads, and a modest airstrip operated by the Royal Air Force's 31 Squadron. Right now it was midwinter up there, with the snow waist deep some days. You wouldn't think it in a country that got so hot. Frank had joined the SS *Rotorua* at Bombay on his way home to visit his family in New Zealand whom he hadn't seen for years. He'd worked in a shop when he was younger and saved his fare to England so he could join the RAF. Already the sun had tanned his face to a leathery texture. His hair had begun to recede, making him appear older than his twenty-nine years.

Nellie had fallen into conversation with Frank on deck and introduced him that evening to her daughter. 'He's a flying officer,' she said. 'I've suggested we could have dinner together. You could talk about flying.' The three of them met in the second-class dining room. The roast lamb and potatoes, with gravy and tinned peas, reminded them just how few weeks were left before landfall at home, something Jean was dreading.

Frank appeared to have an easy warmth about him. He flew Bristol Fighters, and that was enough to hold her attention. Nellie drifted off to join a group of women playing mah-jong, apparently not bothered that Jean was left unchaperoned. Later, she would say, with a small gulp of distaste, that it had never occurred to her that an attraction might develop. Frank wore such a badly fitting set of dentures, a subject on which she was something of an authority.

Jean and Frank talked about engine maintenance, and weather patterns, and how to maintain height if hit by a storm. Then Jean asked him about local conditions in Baluchistan, as she would be flying over the area when she flew from England to Australia.

Frank looked at her in astonishment. 'You're serious? How old are you?'

'Twenty-one.'

'Really? Most girls your age are settling down.'

'I'm not settling anywhere until I've done what I've set out to do. And when I've done that trip, I'm going to fly to New Zealand.'

Frank roared with laughter, slapping his thigh. 'In a Gipsy Moth? That's priceless. You any idea what the weather's like over the Tasman?'

'Well, of course I have. You think I'm totally ignorant? The hard part's finding the money.'

'Have you got a plane?'

'Not yet. But I'm sure it's just a matter of convincing someone that it's worth sponsoring me. I did go and see someone at the high commission in London. They weren't very helpful. You'd think public officials would be a little more far-sighted. They were rather a stuffy lot.'

'The bar'll be closing soon,' Frank said. 'How about we get a nightcap?'

'I don't drink alcohol.'

'Oh, well, you'll have to get used to me. I do.'

'Mr Norton, there is no requirement for me to get used to you.'

He stumbled for words, his expression crestfallen. 'I beg your pardon, Miss Batten. I hoped we might spend time together on this voyage. If you'll forgive me asking, are you by any chance engaged?'

'I thought I'd made that pretty clear. No, I'm not.'

'We dock in Colombo tomorrow. I'd be honoured if you would allow me to escort you round some of the sights.'

'Why, Mother and I would be delighted, I'm sure.' Jean held out her hand and wished him goodnight.

'Time for that nightcap, I suppose,' he said, his expression wistful.

In the morning he met them at breakfast, his face flushed but eager. Jean and Nellie had walked around the deck several times and observed Ceylon appear on the horizon, the ship berth, the noise and apparent chaos of the dockworkers. Jean had on the white silk dress she had first worn at Madame Valeska's dancing school, and the night she met Kingsford Smith.

'Mother, wherever did you find this old thing?' Jean said. 'I thought you'd thrown it out.'

'Waste not, want not. You look beautiful. It's just right for the tropics.'

Frank stammered when he saw her. He had, he explained, been arranging rickshaw transport for the day. They could go wherever they wished. Then Nellie, all of a sudden, decided that she was going to spend the morning with her newfound mah-jong friends. She would meet them at lunchtime.

In this way, Jean and Frank came to spend the morning in the marketplace among brilliant sarongs, the mingled scents of cinnamon, fragrant teas made from dark-leaved camellia, and freshly picked orchids. They wandered past the domes and minarets of the city, peacocks scattering at their feet, butterflies catching in their hair. 'I'd like to ride an elephant,' Jean said. 'One of those dark, wild-looking ones.'

'Then why don't we do it?' Frank said.

When they put the idea to Nellie, who was eating cucumber sandwiches and sipping tea with her friends on a shady verandah, she waved them off with a dismissive gesture. 'Me, ride an elephant? My dears, I'm here to relax. Just go. Remember the ship sails at eight.'

Jean found the elephant easy to ride although its keeper warned of its savage eye. Frank said it was worse than a Bristol in a high wind. He would have a sore beg your pardon for a week. His breath held a stagnant earthy odour, close to her ear, as they bumped along, perched in the canopied seat above the elephant's head. The animal thrashed its trunk in Frank's direction when they dismounted. The keeper, a man dressed in only a loin-cloth and a turban, motioned him away. 'Run,' he cried. 'Go, you go quickly.'

They retired to a teahouse, where Frank ordered a cold beer. 'Thirsty work,' he said, taking a long swallow and emptying his glass. Jean sipped lemonade and watched while he ordered a second beer. 'We should go back to the ship,' she said.

'Soon,' he said. They were alone in the teahouse, mosquito nets creating a gauzy film between them and the bright trees beyond. Dusk was approaching, the sky full of primrose light. Frank said, 'This has been the best day of my life.'

Jean agreed that certainly it had been very nice, she'd had some new experiences and it had all been great fun. A warning voice in her head told her that the conversation should go no further.

'So you haven't got a boyfriend?' Frank asked. Then before she could answer, he grabbed her right hand, holding it tightly to his chest. 'Feel my heart,' he said. 'We're meant for each other, you and me. We don't have to get married straightaway. I can wait.'

Jean burst out laughing. 'Are you proposing to me?'

His face flushed. 'What do you think I'm doing?'

'It's the heat. You've had too many beers. Come on, Frank, let me go.'

In the morning, after the ship sailed, Frank came to see her as she sat reading on the deck. Nellie reclined nearby, reading English newspapers she had picked up in port the day before. 'I've come to apologise,' he said, addressing Jean. 'I can't bear that I shouldn't see you for the rest of the journey.'

'We'll see,' Jean said. 'Thank you anyway.' She felt cool and in control of herself.

'I should have thought. I expect you do have a boyfriend anyway. You didn't say.'

She looked away from him. Was Victor Dorée her boyfriend? She thought not.

'Dinner tonight?' he asked, after an excruciating pause.

'Tomorrow, perhaps.'

'What was all that about?' Nellie asked. Jean hadn't told her about the proposal.

'That man drinks too much,' Jean said.

'He hasn't made a pass at you, surely? He's old enough to be your father.'

'He's twenty-nine.'

'I thought he was older. Well, you know how it is, men go a bit crazy when they've been out East for a while. Do you want me to speak to him?'

'No,' Jean said. 'It would be embarrassing. I'm sure it'll be all right.' There were more ports to explore, more dinners, more conversations about flying to be had. She was impressed with what Frank knew, the way he could describe the areas she planned to fly across. For his part, if he continued to drink on the journey, he was careful not to do so when he was near her. Some mornings she saw that he was flushed and tired but she said nothing. On the last night before their arrival in Auckland there was a dinner and dance. Nellie washed and dried Jean's white silk dress. Other people dressed up, but Jean didn't need to: she caught the eye of everyone at the party just as she was. Frank was dressed in his dining-out mess uniform, a single-breasted blue-grey jacket, tapering to a point below the waist, over a matching waistcoat. His black shoes were spit polished.

'May I have the honour?' he said, bowing to Jean and offering his arm. It was a long time since she had danced, but when the music began she realised how much she had missed it. He was a better dancer than she expected. The other passengers applauded as they danced a tango in a circle that had cleared around them. 'I love you,' he said, close to her ear.

She didn't reply. She already knew this, and felt a passing sadness for him.

Nellie and her estranged husband did not meet in Auckland. A note from Fred greeted them at the ship when they disembarked. *I wish to see Jean immediately on her arrival*, it said.

Auckland was more down-at-heel than Jean remembered. Although it was summer, the parks looked neglected, shop windows were boarded up, and some had been smashed. An air of desolation hung over the street corners. A queue had formed outside a soup kitchen near the wharves.

Her father was waiting for her when she arrived at his flat, looking out the window with his back to the room. 'Why?' he said, without turning around. 'Why did you do it, Jean?'

'Because,' she began, and stopped. 'Dad, I bought you some tea in Ceylon. It's delicious.' This was not exactly true. Frank Norton had bought the tea, but she had chosen it for her father. She held out the package towards his back. 'Because,' she began again, 'it's all I can think of doing in my life. I might as well be dead if I don't fly.' He turned around, his face closed. When he saw her, his expression softened and he reached out his arms as if to embrace her. Jean hesitated, then took both his hands, touching them lightly.

His arms fell to his sides. 'I'm so afraid for you,' he said. She saw that he had tears in his eyes.

'I'm not going to stop,' she said. 'As a matter of fact, I want to get my commercial licence so I can fly for money.'

'Then you'll need good navigation skills. Wouldn't you agree?'

'Of course.'

'I've enrolled you at the navigation school at Richmond,' he said. 'I don't want you getting lost.'

Some would say, later, that Jean Batten appeared irrational during her four months in New Zealand, her belief in herself so monumental. She had got the idea, it was said, that the government would step in and fund her proposed flight from England to Australia. Did she really think her flying feats were so impressive that people would fall over themselves to finance her ambitions? She must surely have seen the state the country was in.

For she had hardly stepped off the ship when the Hawke's Bay earthquake struck and more than two hundred and fifty people died and Napier and Hastings were largely destroyed. The government, already stretched to breaking point by the desperate unemployed, was hardly in the mood to be impressed.

Others said that, being poor, Jean could only be expected to help herself. At the navigation school where her father had enrolled her, she was learning how to calculate position and distances, how to use dead reckoning, the art of combining visual reference points with maps, advancing a position based on the elapse of time travelled at certain speeds. She had enrolled, too, at the Auckland Aero Club and acquired an endorsement to her licence that allowed her to carry passengers. Her first passenger was her mother. They flew over the mangrove swamps along the edge of the sea, Nellie's eyes fixed on the white lines of surf, her breath held, in a rapture of delight. 'My first flight, darling. With you.'

Jean learned, too, the variety of aerial tricks and manoeuvres the Gipsy Moth was capable of — flying inverted, circling and looping, slow rolling. Free of Travers' watchful eye, she began to experiment, tossing the plane, twisting and weaving, flinging it against radiant autumn skies. On days when the weather changed she flew until curtains of rain all but obliterated her visibility, landing only at the last moment before her landmarks disappeared. When she performed, people on the ground gathered to watch and applaud. Frank Norton was always on hand when she landed, ecstatic with admiration. The crowd would disperse, leaving a path for them to walk between, as Frank escorted Jean to another restaurant, or a dinner or the cinema. He and her father had met, and it seemed that having a boyfriend, as Frank Norton was now perceived, and a pilot at that, had eased his anxiety. But the prospect of raising money to fly was as elusive as ever. Jean had been to see Madame Valeska. Freda Stark hadn't come back from Australia and Madame was concerned about her. She'd heard, she said, that Freda was doing well enough in Sydney, but she wasn't dancing at present. Valeska didn't mention the cause of her absence, but at least Jean knew that Freda was alive.

Frank's leave was nearly over. Soon he would return to Quetta. He suggested, one evening, that he and Jean marry before he left. She could join him as an air force wife on the base when he had settled back in and arranged married quarters. They had had dinner at a small hotel where, at Frank's request, candles had been lit at their table in an alcove off the dining room, overlooking the harbour. Very cosmopolitan, the manager said. It was hard to tell whether he was approving or derisive. As they entered the hotel a woman with three children holding the hem of her skirt stood at the side entrance, begging for leftover food. They stopped at the bar on the way into the dining room. Frank drank two whiskies in quick succession.

'You can't stay in New Zealand,' Frank said.

'I'm learning a lot. You've seen me. And I've stacked up the hours.'

'But it won't last forever. You don't have the money.'

She didn't answer for a while. Her father's largesse had extended only to the navigation school, and she could see that even if he wanted to, he couldn't afford more. Nellie was back at the racetrack, wearing ever more flamboyant hats, a sparkle in her eyes when things went well. As before, there were Saturdays when she returned looking despondent, but it never lasted for long. 'Madame Valeska's offered me a partnership in the business,' Jean said at last.

'Is that what you want?'

When she said no, of course it wasn't, he pressed his offer of marriage.

'But we hardly know each other,' Jean said.

'I'd be gentle with you,' he said.

'Don't.' Jean wiped her mouth, leaving a trail of lipstick

on the white napkin. Frank sometimes got away with a kiss on her cheek, but that was as far as it went. His lips held all the appeal and suction of a plunger. When he tried to kiss her mouth, her insides went rigid with distaste.

'I know you're young. And, you know, I like that, well, that you haven't been with other men.'

'You don't know that,' she said, tilting her chin.

'Yes, I do. I'd stake my life on it.'

She felt resentment flooding through her. The sex and turmoil of married women's lives was not what she wanted either. Frank had once described how he saved money to fly when he worked on a haberdashery counter, and the way people he served put their change in a jar on the counter, marked 'Frank's Flying Fund'. He'd escaped. His customers wanted him to fly. People wanted her to get married and be safe.

'I don't want to talk about any of this,' she said.

Frank had borrowed a family car for the evening. When the dinner was over and she was seated beside him he began to drive away from the city. 'Where are we going?'

'To look at the sea. Just the two of us, and some moonlight. I thought it would be nice.' They had driven for some miles in silence when he pulled up near an estuary. There was only a crescent moon, and away from the town, it had grown very dark. Close by, Jean could hear the lapping of waves. Frank placed a hand on her arm. 'It's time for me to teach you some things.'

'Things? What things?' Only she knew what he meant.

'I'll be careful. I won't let you get pregnant.'

After scrabbling frantically at the door handle, Jean threw open the door before jumping from the car. The sea was very close and she ran screaming towards it. Frank was a step behind her. When he caught her, he seized her wrists. 'Shut up,' he said. 'Stop it, Jean. I'm not going to try anything. I promise.'

She stood there in the shelter of his arms. 'I'm sorry,' she said. 'Frank, I can't.'

'I know,' he said. 'I'm sorry, too. I wouldn't force you. I've never done that to a woman.' He edged her back to the car.

'Why are you so scared of men?' he asked.

'Why do you drink all the time?'

He sat drumming his fingers on the steering wheel. 'I'll stop. It's just that I'm on holiday, you know?'

She sat in the car and sobbed then. 'It's useless here in New Zealand,' she said. 'I need to get back to England, to Stag Lane. Everyone here thinks I'm silly.' He was silent then. 'It's true, isn't it? Because I'm young and poor they think I'm arrogant to want so much. When everyone's so desperate, they want me to be the same. I have to find a way of doing it myself. Back there in London, people know what's possible.'

Only days before, she had fallen foul of one of her instructors. A storm was coming up and he had advised her not to fly. I can make my own decisions, she had retorted. She didn't know herself why she had spoken like that. It was just that she was certain that it was all right to fly. Then she had taken off and a squall had hit her side on, causing the plane to slip and slide through the cloudbank in driving rain. The instructor spoke to her about it the next day, citing the poor example she was setting for less experienced fliers. She had, after all, only thirty hours in her logbook and really, who did she think she was? Just because she had trained at Stag Lane didn't make her an expert. That had been the finish really.

'It's your lookout, girlie,' he'd said.

She had embroidered her earlier response — 'It's my business what I do' — and walked away. She wished, later, she could take it back but it had been said, and there was no going back on it. The Auckland Aero Club suddenly seemed seedy and lacking, the instructor an amateur. Word had come that Amy Johnson and a co-pilot had set new records, flying from London to Moscow, and from there across Siberia to Japan, in the fastest time ever.

Jean sat there in the car, with the sea beating beside them, wondering how on earth she could get back to London, but knowing that she must.

'If you go back, I'll join you in London when I'm finished this tour of duty next year,' Frank said. 'I'll be out of the air force then. You'll be older.' He sighed. 'I'm not holding my breath.'

John was between movies in 1931. This was a chance for him to come home and see the family. He had work lined up, he assured them, but the slump had hit the industry. He and Jean and Frank Norton and their father shared a Sunday lunch at the Courtville flat. Jean had invited Frank before the disastrous night out. She thought he wouldn't show up, but he did, as bold as if nothing had happened. John told them he would go straight into rehearsals for *The Wonderful Story* when he got back to England. Reggie Fogwood had it all lined up. It was a pretty grim story, about a paralysed farmer whose girlfriend goes off with his brother. Moore Marriott, the comedian, would be in it, but John had a miserable role. He told them a funny story about Marriott, for his father's benefit, about how the actor carried four sets of false teeth to alter his appearance. He imitated him, pulling his lips down to make himself look toothless. 'You're obsessed with teeth, you lot,' Frank said, out of thin air.

'What do you expect?' John said lazily. 'This family's made its money out of teeth.'

'Plenty of teeth, not much money,' his father said, laughing at his antics. They seemed on friendlier terms, as though the ten years that had passed had softened their differences. As if to catch up on that lost time, John had seen more of his father while he was in New Zealand than he had of Nellie. Besides, he noted, it wasn't exactly as if his mother had gone out of her way to see him in London. And as for Jean, she was a brat, he told her. It never occurred to him that she wasn't following her music

199

career over there. After his first surprise at learning the truth, he spoke to her rather as an indulgent older uncle might have done. They exchanged notes on Harold. John said his time in New Zealand was too short for him to get up north.

'The kids'll be growing up. Perhaps I'll go,' Jean murmured, not really meaning it.

Fred wasn't sure, but he thought there might be another baby on the way.

'Poor Alma,' Jean said. Fred and John looked away. She sensed they were in agreement.

'It's really time I was off,' Frank said. His ship was leaving the next day. He caught Jean's eye, signalling for her to follow him.

In the passageway he stood close, breathing heavily. If he just could stop breathing, she thought, perhaps she could get to like him better. The idea, unbidden, made her smile.

'Will you come to the ship to say goodbye?' he said. 'That, at least.'

'Yes,' she said. 'Thank you for everything. I've had a very nice time.'

'So that's it?'

'I'll wave to you in the morning.'

'Get in touch if there's anything I can do to help. Will you promise me that?'

She allowed him to kiss her cheek, and listened to the thud of his shoes on the stairs. When she couldn't hear him any longer, she returned to John and her father.

'He likes you,' Fred said, teasing her. 'I was waiting for him to ask for your hand.'

'I'm not going to marry him,' Jean said. 'Not for anything.'

'You could do worse,' her father said.

'I want best,' she answered. She pulled her lip down over her front teeth, the same gumless look John had imitated.

John said, when the laughter had died down, 'If you want to come back to London, I'll pay your fare. You can stay with me for a bit until you get yourself sorted out.'

Frank had already said he would pay for her fare. Although she now wanted desperately to return to London, she had refused, believing that if she accepted she would be beholden to him. She hoped that in the morning she would be waving farewell to Frank Norton for good.

'The offer's there, Jean,' John said. 'I wouldn't want to stay here either. No offence meant, Dad, but I couldn't live in Auckland now.' He ran his hand through his beautiful tousled hair. 'It would squeeze the oxygen out of me.'

'What about Mother?' Jean said.

'Do you think I'm made of money?' John said. His flat was definitely not big enough to accommodate more than one extra person. Really, it was over to her.

Chapter 16

Stag Lane. The mud underfoot, larks rising above, the hedgerows heavy with hawthorn berries. And, inside the clubhouse, cries of pleasure when she arrived, as if she had never been away. Of more importance, as if they had always known her. Amy Johnson walked over and said, 'Jean, where *have* you been?'

And the Duchess of Bedford came in, stamping her feet to dislodge the mud, shouting, 'Mud pies.' Then she caught sight of Jean. 'Well, hullo, I haven't seen you for days. I thought you must be sick. Where did you say you were?'

'New Zealand,' Jean said.

'Good heavens, what were you doing there? The place is full of savages, isn't it?'

'I grew up there. It's my homeland.'

'Really, how extraordinary.' The Duchess studied her as if she were some interesting new breed of person.

Herbert Travers was pleased to see her again, if taken aback with her new daring in the air. She needed another seventy hours in her logbook before she could gain a commercial pilot's licence, something Travers now seemed to take for granted, once he had got over the surprise of seeing her looping the plane. The important thing was that she was back in the clear, bright sky over England that summer. As well as the general flying and cross-country tests that counted towards her B licence, at the end of her hundred hours of flying, there would also be a solo night flight between Croydon and Lympne. This was the greatest challenge, but it still lay a long way ahead. Nor was her study for a commercial licence just about flying. There were more exams to pass in navigation and air legislature, in meteorology and the inspection of aircraft and engines. She began another engineering course. For months she spent each day in a hangar, dressed in overalls, alongside the regular mechanics. She learned how to banter, and how to wipe the grease off the tip of her nose with her elbow.

So everything had changed again, and she was happy, although there were people missing from her life. The absence of Nellie was painful. Every week her letters arrived, full of promises to take a ship to England, just as soon as she could afford it. There was always a pound enclosed. Jean looked carefully for Victor Dorée each time she went to the clubhouse, knowing it would not do to ask after him. She had had more time to study the entrance to his house in Orchard Road, had seen the name on the closed gates: Oakleigh. In the distance she could see a fountain, and formal gardens.

It was Amy who brought his name up in a conversation.

Had Jean met him, she wondered aloud.

'I just know he has his own Gipsy Moth,' Jean said, avoiding the question.

'Good Lord,' Amy said sighing. 'If only. It's the money, it's always the problem, isn't it?' Amy was born into a fishing family, poor as muck, was how she described it, but her dad had worked and gone without to help her get her first plane. She was a strange person, Jean thought, intense and febrile, needing everything around her to be perfect. This was something Jean understood; it just seemed that her new friend let her feelings show more easily. She knew that if she smiled she often got her way, but this was beyond Amy, who tensed and snapped if things weren't going her way.

Jean considered enquiring about Viscount Wakefield's money, but decided that might be bad form. Instead she asked about Victor's apparent wealth.

Amy laughed. Victor was one of five sons of a wealthy linen merchant. Jean decided not to confess that she already knew these details. If she had learned one thing from her mother's flutters — she had never liked to call them gambling — it was not to show your hand. A good tip was worth its weight in real gold, and you used it for yourself. Victor's family had a chauffeur, and servants, and a gardener, Amy told her. And, it seemed, the sons got pretty much whatever they liked. She'd heard Victor was flying somewhere overseas. 'It would be nice to get your foot through that door,' she remarked. 'Well, I thought you might have bumped into him.'

Jean decided her new friend was being too curious. 'I just wondered about a man who could afford his own aircraft,' she said.

'He's fairly attractive,' Amy said, picking at a cuticle and nipping it off with her teeth. 'Anyway, he's not here, so that's that. I expect he'd want to marry someone rich.'

'You're famous,' Jean said. 'That might help.'

'Hmm, you can't tell with those types, can you?' Amy said. 'They usually end up marrying some girl whose family's in *Tatler*. Anyway, he's younger than me. Men never marry older girls.'

Sir Alan Cobham brought his Flying Circus to Stag Lane just as Jean arrived back. Described as swashbuckling, like a man out of a movie, Cobham had deep-set eyes, a narrow moustache and a cleft chin. Using op pilots and a dozen or more planes, his circus toured the country, barnstorming and offering joy rides on specially cleared fields or airstrips. The whole country seemed taken up with the possibilities of flying.

'I could do that, you know,' Jean said to Amy. A plan was hatching in her head. Cobham wanted to employ more stunt pilots and was offering to trial those who believed they had the skills, so when a group of airmen lined up for test flights, Jean lined up with them. She was the only woman. Nobody said a word.

When her turn came to perform, she walked over to one of Cobham's Moths, climbed in, went through her checks and started the engine. The engineer who was conducting the trials, and seemed not to have been taking much notice of the candidates themselves until they were in the air, started towards the plane, waving his arms. She waved back to him, smiled and rose in the air. She looped and rolled, dived and inverted, all the tricks she had learned above Auckland. When she landed, there was clapping and cheering. As she waved and climbed out, the engineer stormed across the field towards her. 'We don't take women,' he said.

'Was there something wrong with my flying?'

'That's not the point.'

'But it *is* the point,' Jean said. 'Surely it's the *whole* point.'

By now, Cobham had joined his engineer. His eyes rested briefly on Jean with a certain admiration. 'You were good,' he said. 'But you can forget it. I wouldn't put a woman up there. You'll be married and having babies in next to no time.'

Jean walked away, aware that her hands were shaking.

Her voice was bitter as she recounted the day's events to John that evening. He was distracted, barely seeming to hear her. He was filming *Men Like These*, a submarine disaster film that required him to be waist deep in water for much of each day. He was cold and hungry in the evenings, waiting for her to cook dinner. Although there was always talk of movie stars around the clubroom, living with one was different. Her existence seemed suddenly to be collapsing into a half-life. She depended on John's goodwill and income to keep a roof over her head, but on his terms. There were times when she felt that he was irritated by her presence. Of late, he had been spending time with a young novelist called Madeleine Murat. Although she was only nineteen she had written a novel called *Sidestreet*, hailed by the critics as brave and compelling. It featured movie sets and film directors, homosexual men having complicated relationships with women, and a cynical critic to whom the main character becomes pregnant, although she really loves someone else. Jean wondered where she had done her research. She had only met Madeleine once, a restless, pretty girl who exclaimed a lot and made dramatic gestures with her hands. 'Are you in love with her?' Jean asked her brother. Love was on her mind a lot these days, both its absence, and too much of it.

John had been evasive. 'What's love?' he'd said. 'It's nice to be seen around town with a girl. She's famous, you know.'

'She talks a lot,' Jean said.

'Oh, come on,' he said. 'You don't like it that she's famous.'

'That's ridiculous, John,' she said, stung. 'Wait until I break Amy Johnson's record.'

He gave her a look bordering on condescension. 'It's been done,' he said. 'Why bother doing it again?'

'So I should be writing books about sex?' she said.

They were very close to a quarrel.

'Madeleine's breaking new ground,' he said. 'She's daring and fearless. The critics think so.'

Jean stormed out of the room, though that was barely out of sight, and threw herself on the bed. If this kept up, she supposed she would have to find somewhere else to live, although so far John hadn't brought Madeleine to the flat. She wondered if he were waiting for Jean to leave, so that he *could* bring her here.

Frank Norton wrote her a letter care of Stag Lane.

My darling beauty,

My life without you is so lonely. I can't tell you how much a fellow can want to be with a woman the way I want to be with you. I think of you every minute and strike the days off on the calendar until this time in Quetta is over. Baluchistan is a harsh and difficult place. There are no white girls here, but even if there were I wouldn't give any of them a sideways look. I know you have said there is nothing between us, but if we were together again I'm sure I could change your mind. Are you all right for money? I have nothing to spend mine on here. You must tell me if there is anything you need.

Always yours,

Frank

She screwed the letter up in disgust. As if she wanted his money. Early the following morning she got up while John was still asleep, and began preparing a pot of soup. He was sleeping deeply on the couch, his blanket pulled

up to his chin. For a moment, she saw the old childish John, his glee as they dressed up in their parents' clothes. She wanted to touch him in his sleep, like their mother did when they were children, brushing hair back from his face, settling a kiss on his forehead with the end of her finger. It seemed better not to disturb him.

She began to peel vegetables, but her movement at the little kitchen bench woke him anyway.

'What are you doing, Jean?'

'I thought I'd prepare dinner before I went out. I know you like it early.'

'Oh, do what you like. Don't you always?' He crawled out from under the blanket, his face grey.

'That bed's too short for you,' Jean said. 'Why don't I sleep there tonight?'

He seemed about to say something but thought better of it. She turned her back while he put on a dressing gown and collected some coins for the bathroom. When he left the room, she scrawled a note, telling him to turn the gas down on the stove when the soup was ready, and left for Stag Lane.

There was a party that night. One of the pilots was turning twenty-one and he ordered champagne for everyone. Nellie's familiar refrain about the dangers of alcohol stirred in Jean's brain. She didn't need much reminding, having seen the way Frank Norton behaved when he'd been drinking, but the idea of champagne was seductive, just this once. The bubbles looked pretty in the wide glasses. The young man, who was called Mostyn,

with a double-barrelled surname that Jean never could remember when she thought back to that night, insisted that she try a glass. Hadn't she drunk champagne when she turned twenty-one, that's if she were that old, though he could believe she mightn't be yet? 'Oh, I'm ancient,' she quipped, 'Twenty-two is as old as the grave.'

Someone said, on a sombre note, that they might as well drink up, because who knew when their turn would come. There had been an air accident up north just the week before and two people had died in the crash.

Mostyn said, 'Not on my birthday, please.' He filled Jean's glass to the brim. She sipped and the champagne seemed as light as lemonade, not harmful at all.

Charles Ulm was in town, reconnoitering for a flight he was planning the following year. He recognised Jean immediately, singling her out with kisses on each cheek. '*La belle femme* from New Zealand,' he cried. 'Well, little Jean Batten, you've made it all the way to Stag Lane.' He held her by the hand, pinning her to his side, while he told the crowd how she had tracked him and Smithy down for her first flight. 'I knew she was going to make it,' he said. 'You could tell from the look in her eye that there'd be no stopping her.' This attention served to draw her more into the circle. Ulm whispered into her ear, at one stage, 'Have you got yourself a boyfriend yet?'

By this time she had had three glasses of champagne. They rustled down her throat, giving her the illusion that she was drinking nothing but bubbles. She turned to him and bit his ear in a playful way. 'Charlie, if you weren't

married you'd be my very first, you naughty boy,' she said.

'Charlie, indeed,' he said.

There was dancing in the cramped little space near the fireplace, although there wasn't room for more than one or two couples at a time. She danced with Ulm, and felt her head floating free of her neck. 'I think I'm drunk,' she said. He held her close for a moment, his cheek resting on hers. 'May the first one know what treasure he reaps,' he said, and let her go.

Mostyn volunteered to escort her home. It was too far out of his way, she objected, and he would have to go on the train with her. This was all the more reason that someone should escort her, it was decided, as if by committee. She wasn't the only person who needed help to get home. Others sang as they lurched into the starry night. Charles Ulm watched Jean leave, blowing kisses off his hand.

'Goodnight, Charlie boy,' she called.

If she had been asked to describe him, Jean would remember Mostyn as a slight young man, fair, with a touch of ginger in his hair, and brown eyes, but then his image would blur. Nothing appeared clear, and as the train sped them towards London, the shape of things became even less distinct.

John was still up when Mostyn escorted Jean in. His eyes ran over the pair of them.

'She needs to lie down,' Mostyn said.

'I can see that. Jean, since when did I say you could bring people here in the middle of the night?'

'I'm sorry,' Mostyn said. 'I just brought her home.'

John looked at him properly then, his eyes resting on the visitor. The room went deathly quiet. Mostyn was looking back at John, deep colour flooding his cheeks. In spite of her confusion, Jean had a moment of startling clarity. There was something about the way John looked at Mostyn that reminded her of the way her father had looked at her friend, as he held the girl's waist that day at the beach when she was fifteen. There was longing in the expression, but something more than that. A reckless certainty that he could get what he wanted if he chose. This was the way John was looking at his unexpected visitor, and Mostyn wasn't turning away from her brother's gaze.

The two men walked out of the room, their footsteps echoing in the passage, then disappearing down the stairs. Jean lay down on the bed without taking off her clothes, her head spinning. She wondered, briefly, if people died from getting drunk. Then it was morning, and late at that.

John was nowhere to be seen, but his shaving brush stood drying on the windowsill, and a cup and saucer rinsed and left out on the bench. There was nothing to indicate how long he had been gone the previous night. Her head was still spinning but she had a vague memory of what had happened. She remembered her flash of intuition: John really didn't want her around any more.

She packed her suitcase, not leaving a note as she put her key on the bench and pulled the door behind her. At the post office along the street, she sent a telegram to Frank Norton. *Your offer of loan gratefully accepted. Could you manage twenty pounds? Love Jean.* She took out the word 'gratefully' because it was cheaper. After some reflection, she deleted the word 'love'.

In the afternoon, she pawned the watch that Nellie had given her for her twenty-first birthday. In the evening she found a room at Hendon, not far from Stag Lane. The rent for a week was a pound, leaving just three shillings in her purse. The view from the window was appealing — cottages with gardens, a bustling street — but the room was like so many that she had inhabited, with dust in the corners and thin grey blankets on a mattress that had slept many. This time she was alone.

The events of the night before were foggy. Had she imagined the look between the two men? John had had enough of her in his flat, that much was clear. But he was her brother and she determined to write him a note and tell him where she was. Sooner or later they would be friends again.

She gazed at her reflection in the mirror hanging above the dressing table. The paint behind it had begun to flake, making spots in the glass, giving her a pock-marked appearance. A woman with a pale, pretty face looked back at her, but the eyes were startled, as if she were seeing herself for the first time. A grown-up woman, with flaws, even if she hid them well from the rest of the world. And a person who, for the moment, was on her own, her splintered family nowhere to be seen.

A bank draft from Frank arrived within days, and she could eat again. She wrote to thank him in her round, perfect handwriting, which had begun to develop little flourishes, taking care not to be too effusive. Soon, she wrote to him, she would have her commercial licence, and would be able to start earning money. Well, she did still need some more hours, but he could trust her: this money would see her through a bad patch. Before long her mother would set out for England and, as he knew, once she arrived, all would be well. She did not write the fatal word 'love' at the end of this letter either. It was unsettling to receive a telegram shortly afterwards that said, *My darling, you must not go without anything. I worry about you. More money coming next week.*

Nellie was already on her way to England.

Frank's money continued to arrive, week by week.

Chapter 17

Victor Dorée had been selling silk and linen wares in Australia, the place where he first learned to fly. This was now one of his regular destinations. There was talk of him settling there and establishing a branch of the family business in Sydney. On his first night back in London he made his way to the clubhouse at Stag Lane.

On seeing Jean, he said, with a note of accusation, 'You disappeared. I looked everywhere for you.'

She explained the hurried trip back to New Zealand. A family crisis, now resolved, was how she put it. They would have dinner the very next evening, he declared. Nellie, reunited with Jean, and installed in the room at Hendon, was impressed.

Victor bought Jean a corsage, and drove her into the city to dine at a restaurant near the Ritz. He ordered oysters for their first course, and poached salmon with mousseline sauce and cucumbers, followed by roast duckling, at which point Jean cried, 'Enough. I couldn't possibly eat more than that.'

By candlelight, he coaxed her to tell him what she had been doing in the last year or more, apart from vanishing to New Zealand, how her flying was progressing, what she hoped to do next. He gave a low whistle when she told him that she was within hours of obtaining her B licence.

The white silk dress, worn for this special occasion, was fraying and bedraggled. 'You're finding things a bit tough, aren't you?' he said. 'I mean, financially?' She wondered if he had caught the whiff of cheap talcum powder. 'Forgive me,' he said, 'I don't mean to pry.'

'Is it that obvious?' she said.

'I don't know how you make ends meet,' he said. 'Flying's a pretty expensive pastime.'

'My mother's a remarkable woman,' Jean said. 'She's living here in London with me. She's had to sell property in New Zealand to pay for all this.'

'That makes you all the more special,' he said, full of admiration. 'Two determined women. You'd honour my family if you brought your mother to visit us.'

The drawing room at Oakleigh was long, with an ornate ceiling and fine furniture worn to a patina with care and the passage of years. The lampshades were made of embroidered silk, the rugs came from Persia, statues stood at intervals in alcoves. The filtered light gleamed through stained-glass windows above a Steinway piano standing at the end of the room.

'Do you happen to play?' Victor Dorée's mother asked, on Jean and Nellie's first visit. She carried herself with the pleasurable certainty of a woman who has successfully raised five sons. Her pepper-and-salt streaked hair was caught up in a loose soft style, small tendrils escaping round her face. The dress she wore that evening was made of a satiny fabric with elaborate pin tucks over her bosom, expensive yet slightly dowdy. 'I play, of course, and so do the boys, but they seem to grow out of it when they're older. Sometimes I wonder if any of them have retained a tune in their heads.'

Nellie said, 'But of course. Jean can play now if you would like.' Jean seated herself in front of the piano and immediately began to play her favourite Chopin prelude. Mrs Dorée's face lit up with pleasure. 'Exquisite,' she breathed. 'Mrs Batten, you have a very accomplished daughter. But I'm sure you know that.'

Jean continued, while Victor and his family — some of his brothers, like him, still lived at home — listened with rapt attention. They appeared bantering, cheerful young men, but they sat in deferential silence while Jean played.

'Why, you could be a concert pianist,' Mrs Dorée cried, clapping her hands.

'That was the intention. Jean is one of those young women who can do anything she sets her mind to,' Nellie said, her voice full of pride.

The pair of them slid into the life of the Dorée household as if they had always been part of it. Jean showed Victor the outside of the building she and her mother occupied. 'You'll forgive me if I don't ask you in,' she said, and he had understood.

'There's no need,' he said, 'when you can visit me. Besides, I wouldn't want you to live any further away from me. Closer still would be nice, but we'll have to wait until we're married.'

So there it was again. Marriage. This wasn't even a

proposal, rather an expectation, taken for granted. She looked at his closely shaven chin, his broad, seemingly kind face, caught the scent of his expensive cologne. She supposed it might be possible. She wasn't yet convinced that she loved him as much as he imagined, but surely it would happen in time.

Nellie had met Madeleine Murat and disapproved. She thought her a flighty, show-offy kind of girl. John, she told Jean, had mentioned the possibility of marriage, which Nellie thought outrageous. The girl had a dirty mind; it was clear she was hanging around the film studio at Elstree in order to gather material for more of her rubbish. She didn't know how he could entertain the idea of marrying her, although it was clear Madeleine had set her cap at him.

'He can't marry her,' Jean exclaimed.

'Oh well, I suppose there's nothing to stop him, except common sense,' Nellie said. 'Well, is there?'

'Not that I know of, darling,' Jean said, wondering who she was soothing, her mother or herself. If Nellie wondered at the silence between Jean and John, she didn't dwell on it. She could understand, perhaps, that Jean found the girl's company intolerable, and besides, they had their own friends now.

This business of marriage, Jean reflected. It happened to everyone sooner or later, or so it seemed. She thought she might be falling in love with Victor Dorée, but how could one be sure?

Amy Johnson had just married a man called Jim

Mollison. They had met on a commercial flight and agreed to marry within eight hours of setting eyes on each other, while the plane was still in the air. Jim had set a new record flying from Australia to England the year before. Earlier in the year he'd set an England to South Africa record.

The couple had appeared at the clubhouse soon after the wedding, Amy clinging to her new husband's side, a huge smile illuminating her face. The newspapers had run a story that morning dubbing them 'The Flying Sweethearts'.

'It won't last,' Nellie muttered darkly to Jean when this was related to her. 'That man's a known playboy. You mark my words, he'll be off as soon as a pretty woman looks at him. Amy's a fool. He's just after a famous wife.'

The marriage had hardly taken place when Amy set off to break Jim's record to South Africa. This was to become the pattern of their marriage, Jim setting a record, Amy breaking it. Jean and Victor dined out with the couple from time to time, but Jean could see it already, Jim falling more silent as Amy became more animated.

Later that year, her brother John married Madeleine Murat, in what Madeleine glowingly described to the newspapers after the event as a 'secret wedding'.

'My own son,' Nellie said, her eyes glazed with unshed tears, her British upper lip for once trembling, when she read about it. 'They only live a couple of miles away. Was I that bad a mother, that I didn't get asked to his wedding?'

'Darling,' Jean said, putting her arms around Nellie,

'you're the very best mother in the world.' It occurred to her that John would not have wanted her at the ceremony when the congregation was asked if there was any reason why these two people shouldn't marry. But then again, perhaps she was imagining something that wasn't there, and it was just Madeleine's flair for the dramatic that had prompted this public revelation of the 'secret' marriage. The couple would be going back to Hollywood soon, she said in one interview.

Frank Norton appeared one evening on the doorstep of the room in Hendon. Jean had supposed he would return to New Zealand when he finished his tour of duty in Quetta. In the back of her mind a nagging doubt persisted as she recalled, in bad moments, his promise to come to London, but she hadn't believed him. Or, worse, hadn't wanted to believe him. Now, when she saw him, she couldn't believe her failure to understand that he had meant it.

'Frank Norton,' Nellie said, 'what on earth are you doing here?' Frank stepped inside before she finished speaking and opened his arms, as if he expected Jean to walk straight into them. She held out her hand. 'It's very nice to see you, Mr Norton,' she said.

'Mr Norton — oh that's a good one. How English you sound, my darling girl.' He looked around them, at

Nellie's disapproving face, the cramped room. 'Come on,' he said, his voice full of urgency, 'I'll take you somewhere we can talk.'

This was a small pub across the road, low-beamed and heavy with cigarette smoke. He ordered drinks, a beer for himself, a lemonade for her.

'I'll have to get you out of that place,' he said. 'I should have sent more money.'

'It's been enough to help me with my flying,' she said. 'I do appreciate it. I hope to start repaying you soon.'

'No hurry,' he said easily. 'I'm flush. I've had my pay out from the air force. Five hundred quid. Enough to buy a house when we get back home.'

'Home?' she said.

'New Zealand.'

'Frank, London's my home. Don't you understand?'

He didn't, and there appeared to be no way of convincing him that she wanted to stay where she was. 'Frank, you don't know me,' she said, 'really, you don't. Once my mind's set on anything, it's useless to try to swerve me from my purpose, or take away my enthusiasm. I love it here. I'm going to finish what I set out to do.'

But he had bought a car, he told her, so that they could go touring around the countryside, up to Scotland perhaps. It was as if she hadn't spoken. They might as well see a bit before they settled down. And he'd joined the club at Stag Lane, so they could fly together.

'No,' she said. 'You can't do that.'

'Jean,' he said, 'stop this nonsense. I can join any club I

like. I want to spend as much time as I can with you from now on. We've been apart for too long. We're only staying here in England until you've got your licence and then we're going home, the way I said. You can earn some money back there. There's no reason why you can't keep flying until we start a family. I'll keep helping you out until you've finished.'

'I don't want us to get married,' Jean said, straining so hard to speak that she could hardly get the words out.

'Of course you do,' he said. 'Do you think I'd have been sending you all that money if you weren't going to marry me?'

'I'm going to fly to Australia,' she said, holding back angry tears.

On a murky night in November, Travers informed Jean that it was time for her to make the return night flight from Stag Lane to Croydon airfield, followed by the aerobatics test the following day. This was the final test for her commercial licence. She had been flying steadily in the weeks before, mounting up the final hours as fast as she could. Frank Norton paid for the use of an aeroplane each time she needed one. The faster she could obtain the licence, she now believed, the faster she could escape him. In the evenings, she no longer went to the clubhouse, lest Victor Dorée should appear. She and Nellie continued to dine once a week at Oakleigh, and some evenings she and Victor went in to the city. She did not want gossip about her, she told Frank icily when he invited her out. She had other friends, other commitments, it was not possible to spend every evening with him. There was something trusting about Frank that almost made her pity him. Pity, she thought, was very close to contempt.

But for the moment it seemed that she depended on him. If she failed the last test, she could not afford to sit it again.

As she made ready for the solo night flight, Travers came hurrying across to her, waving a small torch.

'You never know when you might need this,' he said.

Some fifteen minutes after her takeoff, the navigation lights failed. None of the instruments were luminous. She sat in the dark cockpit flashing the torch on the instrument panel, her fear mounting, as she tried to work out how to reach the ground. By now the plane had been reported over Biggin Hill without lights. A red beacon at Croydon appeared. Circling the aerodrome several times, she flashed the torch on and off and, at last, saw in the darkness beneath her a green rocket signal advising that she could land. Throttling back her engine, she glided onto the floodlit runway.

In the morning, she returned to Croydon to complete the final part of the test, a series of spins, seemingly easy after the events of the night before. Victor was at the airport to congratulate her. So, too, was Frank Norton.

She kissed each one on the cheek, as if both were mere acquaintances, and moved on. Neither man gave any indication of knowing the other.

The Dorées held a celebratory lunch for her the following Sunday. Already Nellie and Jean had enjoyed Sunday lunches when the married brothers came, bringing their wives, and this Sunday everyone was there. There was laughter, and toasts to Jean. Herbert Dorée sat at the head of the table, smiling around him with pleasure. The table was set with Wedgwood and crystal and silver. Servants glided silently in and out over the thick green carpet.

'So what next for our little Antipodean?' Victor's father asked.

'I still want to fly to Australia,' Jean said. 'I want to be the fastest person who ever flew there.' She laughed, as if half-joking. It was not the first time she had said this, but always lightly, as if speaking of the impossible.

'All Jean needs is an aeroplane,' Nellie said.

'Of course she does,' Victor said, turning to his mother. 'Mater, could you lend us the money? I'll be Jean's business partner. She'll make a fortune out of speaking tours, you know.'

His mother gave an indulgent smile. 'Well, you do have a plane dear,' she said, 'but I suppose you wouldn't want to be without it while Jean's away. Why not? Have you got a plane in mind?'

'I can speak to Fielden, the fellow who looks after the Prince of Wales,' Victor said. 'His Moth is up for sale.

The King's put a stop to his flying. I don't think he'll care much about the price.'

'That sounds perfect,' his mother said. 'Dear, do pass the vegetables to Mrs Batten.'

The cost of everything was worrying Frank. Jean had seen the way he turned his money over these days before he spent it. Sooner or later, she knew, it would run out. He wanted to think of himself as a man of means, like the people he was mixing with at Stag Lane, but it was temporary. There was only so much one could eat and drink and spend on restaurants, and petrol, and flowers, and still have change over from the five hundred pounds he had boasted of having when he arrived in London. Her flying lessons would have added up to just a fraction of this sum. Now that Jean had her licence he told her they should be thinking about booking a passage. He could book for all three of them, if that was what suited her and her mother.

She said again that she wasn't returning to New Zealand.

'Jean,' he said with exaggerated patience, 'of course you are. But you deserve a holiday first. I want you and me to go away together for a few days. Just the two of us.'

'Frank, I am not going. Not to New Zealand, not for a holiday. Forget it.'

A dark flash of anger crossed his face. 'Do your friends

at the club know how you pay for your lessons?' he said.

'Frank, you wouldn't tell them,' she said, her voice urgent. A cold hard knot of dislike tightened in her stomach. It had been there all along, only she hadn't seen it for what it was. And now she felt frightened of him as well.

His face had set in stubborn lines. There was nothing for it, she decided, but to motor to Wales with him as he had arranged. There, she would try to work out what to do next. In the mood that he was in, she thought it important not to surprise him. They had to do something alone, he insisted, something they could look back on when they were old, and tell the children about. Nellie, who had already been on one journey with them, didn't want to go. Driving in the back seat was not her style, and the man was such a bore, didn't Jean think so?

He had bought them new leather suitcases. The hotel he had booked them into was set far into the Welsh countryside. When they drew up outside, Frank took a ring from his pocket and thrust it on her finger. It was a plain band set with small stones, much as her mother had worn when she still lived with her father.

'Have you told them we're married?' Jean said.

'Yes, of course,' he said. While she tried to pull the ring off, he said, 'Jean, you have to leave it on. We mightn't be able to afford a honeymoon in New Zealand. This is it.'

They were the only ones in the dining room. A small fire spluttered in a grate, but Jean shivered and declared herself not hungry, picking at an indifferent meal of stew. Their conversation was desultory. Frank drank some wine, then retired to the bar for what he described as a quick nightcap. In the bedroom, she took off her clothes and lay down naked on the bed, so that he could see her unclothed, the small apples of her breasts tingling in the cool November damp of the room.

When he came in, he looked down at her, his face flushed. 'Corker titties,' he said.

She let him enter her without protest. He made whimpering expressions of gratitude when it was done, and again in the morning when he took her again. She felt neither pain nor pleasure, rather something like resignation. This, she supposed, was what whores did. It seemed futile to complain.

On the way back to London, he held her hand. She let it lie limp in his. He glanced sideways at her several times. Once or twice she thought she glimpsed regret in his profile, his eyes staring at the road straight ahead, as if wondering if what they had done was a mistake.

As they sat in the car, outside the room Nellie and Jean shared, she told him she had acquired a plane to fly to Australia.

His body stiffened in the seat beside her. 'I don't believe you. Who would buy you a plane?'

'A friend,' she said. 'You should go back to New Zealand.'

When he began to demur she said softly, 'You can't afford all those suitcases, Frank.'

Jean opened the car door and climbed out. She walked away without looking back.

Chapter 18

1933. It was a year when all kinds of things happened. It had hardly begun when Bert Hinkler died. The Australian Lone Eagle who had made the very first solo flight between England and Australia. The man who had been greeted by eighty thousand people in Sydney, singing 'Hinkler, Hinkler little star', and now there was a Tin Pan Alley song they called 'Hustling Hinkler'. You could dance a Hinkler foxtrot or a Hinkler quickstep. The man who had sat on the floor of Parliament in Australia. 'You know,' he had said in an interview that day, 'one day, people will fly by night and use the daylight for sightseeing.' And now he was dead. Hinkler had crashed in a remote part of the Italian countryside, near Florence. Jean remembered the way he had studied the ibis as they flew in order to understand the nature of flight, before he began his inventions. She shivered when she heard the news. Don't believe in omens, Nellie told her sternly. Those were for the superstitious.

Charles Kingsford Smith came to town on a brief visit, and gave her some of his maps. He and Charles Ulm, whom she had taken to calling Charlie whenever she saw him, both got in touch with her when they were in London. Jean felt she could confide in them. Victor had suggested that they keep their plans for her attempt on the record to themselves, but these were two men she trusted, and they seemed far away from the tight circles of London gossip. They had their own records to set, their business to pursue. She felt she was one of them now, someone they had put on her way. Smithy no longer told her not to try to break men's records. 'Go get 'em, girl,' he said, when he handed over the maps.

He took her to a pub where they drank to the memory of Bert. When she ordered lemonade, he demanded she try something stronger. 'I'll have champagne,' she said, daring herself to try again. As the bubbles surfaced she felt the spirit of Hinkler rising. 'To Bert,' they said, lifting their glasses.

With the help of Group Captain Fielden, Victor had purchased the promised plane from the royal flying unit. The logbook showed the DH60 M Gipsy Moth G-AALG registered jointly in the names of Jean Batten and Victor Dorée. The royal colours were a blue fuselage and silver wings, but a condition of the sale was that the colours be changed. Jean asked that the blue be changed to a lighter shade, with a fine white line running the length of the fuselage.

There were technical matters to be addressed, modifications to be made to the plane. Jean had routes to plan, visas for landing in different countries to arrange, and landing permissions and information about fuel supplies to obtain. In all she would pass through fourteen countries on her 10,500-mile journey.

The Moth's engine was gravity-fed from a standard tank in the wing. Victor had two extra tanks fitted. The larger, holding an extra twenty-seven gallons of fuel, was placed in the front cockpit and covered over, the second behind the rear pilot's seat. Victor had a hand pump installed so that the engine could be topped up in flight by pumping from the two new tanks. The flying range of the Gipsy Moth, normally two hundred and fifty miles, had thus been increased to eight hundred. There was very little space left for the pilot.

During the preparation of the Moth, a disagreement arose between Victor and Jean over the safety of the conrods, which had a record of being prone to metal fatigue where the serial number was stamped. Jean wanted the engine dismantled, and Nellie was all for it, but Victor insisted that the Prince's plane would not have been released without a complete overhaul. The costs were beginning to mount beyond his and his mother's budget. They agreed, half-heartedly on Jean's part, not to pursue the matter any further.

Now that the attempt on the record had become a reality, the need to keep the flight secret until the very last moment intensified. Jean was concerned that someone with a plane more prepared for a long-distance flight might set out ahead of her. Perhaps Amy Johnson, or

Mrs Mollison as she was now known. After three years, she was still the only woman to have flown to Australia, and seemed always ready for new attempts on records.

Jean had begun a regime of exercise. First thing every morning she swam in the baths, then stood in the park and skipped for twenty minutes, just the way she had at Madame Valeska's dancing school: *Lizzie Borden took an axe/and gave her mother forty whacks* ... Over and over. Far into each night, she spread plans on the floor. Nellie kept watch over her, all the while stitching and hemming garments. She turned coats, and trimmed hats, made delicate undergarments. Jean had a new white silk dress that Victor insisted on buying her at Harrods, but not an inch of the silk from the old one would be wasted, Nellie declared. Not that underwear was really a problem either. Victor carried suitcases of silk panties with him on his travels to Australia.

There came a moment when all the preparations were made. Nellie and Jean laid out everything Jean needed for the journey. She would go out to the plane wearing a long jacket with a fur collar, and a beret. You just never know, somebody might get wind of you going, Victor said, and she needed to look her best. Besides, the Dorée family were all planning to turn out. De Havilland, the only other person in on the secret, had intimated that he would like to come. She would change into her flying gear before she boarded the plane, a long leather flying coat, helmet and goggles. Victor had bought her a white helmet for when she reached the tropics, and a white flying suit. Jean wrapped up her belongings in a brown paper parcel, ready to take with her on the flight.

Victor did tell the press at the very last moment. He was, after all, a partner in the undertaking. Nellie had gone on ahead to Lympne airport, where aviators flying abroad had to clear Customs, while Jean collected her plane from Stag Lane. Victor had arranged for her to be driven there by his chauffeur, as befitted a star in the making. He sat in the front while Jean sat in the back, overtaken by bouts of terror. As they drove to Stag Lane, she saw bluebells in flower, washes of colour beneath the trees. She wished that Nellie was with her. The Dorée family was gathered, and Victor's father had arranged for a movie camera to record the event. Only the *Sunday Dispatch* had responded to Victor's press release. The reporter saw it as a scoop, interviewing Jean and eliciting from her the information that the flight had been planned in secrecy for months. De Havilland did turn up, boyish and excited that another of his planes was going to make the long journey to Australia. 'Did I ever tell you about my hobby?'

'You made model aeroplanes,' Jean said.

'Oh yes, there was that. But I collected butterflies and moths, too. That's why I call my planes Moths,' he said. 'And now I'm setting them free. Go well, Miss Batten.'

Jean stowed her parcel in a tiny compartment she had made behind the headrest in the rear cockpit. She leaned against Victor for a moment, sheltered by his arm, then it was time to go. Victor's own plane had been wheeled out and he followed her across the London sky to Kent.

He and Nellie and Jean stayed at a nearby hotel, each with a bedroom of their own. Jean found it hard to concentrate on conversation of any kind. Before long she crept up the stairs to her room. Victor followed her up to the bedroom door. He kissed her chastely on her forehead and wished her a good night's sleep. Victor had not asked Jean to his bedroom since they met, as if sensing her reserve. She was hardly settled before Nellie tapped on the door and allowed herself in, sitting down beside Jean on the bed.

'I'm scared, Mother,' Jean said in a small voice.

'I know.' Nellie's voice was trembling. 'Darling, we've had such good times together, haven't we?'

'We'll have more,' Jean said.

'Promise me you won't take any risks. I can't imagine my life without you.'

'I'll always come home to you, darling.'

'If you should change your mind about going,' Nellie said, 'you only have to say.'

'Of *course* I won't. It's all right, Mother.'

'You're right. Of course you won't. I'm just being selfish. You'll see it through. You and me together. Now go to sleep, my lovely daughter.'

Nellie sat holding Jean's hand until she felt the deep, even breathing that was so familiar to her in all the strange rooms the pair of them had inhabited.

The *Sunday Dispatch* reporter had made the most of his story. The headline read GIRL'S LONE FLIGHT — TO AUSTRALIA IN THE PRINCE'S OLD PLANE.

Underneath it was a picture of Jean looking glamorous, if a little uncertain, as she leaned against her plane. Although it was still early morning, more reporters had gathered as she made her way to the hangar. If she had been afraid the night before, the presence of this attention encouraged her to stand tall, and answer questions in a firm voice. There was no turning back. Victor got in on the act as well, telling one reporter how his fiancée Jean had lived so frugally, going without new clothes and nice cosmetics, a real rags-to-riches story, and soon she would show the whole world how fast she could fly. She winced a little at that. She was wearing a touch of the Chanel No. 5 he had bought her, but she wished he hadn't drawn attention to her past cheapness. Besides, she muttered to Nellie, when they found themselves alone for a moment, he hasn't actually proposed. Who says I'm his fiancée?

'He probably thinks he has,' Nellie said.

'You don't forget things like that.'

'Hush, you're nervous, you both are,' Nellie said in her most soothing tones.

Victor walked over to join them, and gave Jean a final embrace.

On 9 April at 6.30 a.m. Jean taxied out onto the airfield at Lympne. She rose into the air, circled the aerodrome once in salute, and set a compass course for France. Before long her vision was obscured by fog. She flew by instruments across the English Channel, climbing to an altitude of four thousand feet, high above the clouds, where the sun shone brilliantly. Near Paris, the fog cleared and the city lay beneath her. She drew a sharp intake of breath and flew low in order to catch a glimpse of the spring lilacs in bloom along the Champs-Elysées. Jean imagined their heady scent in the streets of Paris. Then the city was behind her, and a pastoral landscape unfolded.

She climbed again as she headed towards the mountains. At five thousand feet she was struck by the intensity of the cold, but the countryside she flew over was so beautiful that it seemed of little consequence. She crossed the mountains, passed over Lyons and down the Rhône Valley. The river threaded its way along the valley floor, appearing, from this height, to slither along like snail tracks. A wild sense of exhilaration now overtook her. Six hours had passed since she left Lympne and so comfortable was she with her flying, and with enough petrol to take her to Rome, she decided not to land. Instead, she set a direct course for Italy, four hundred miles away over the Gulf of Genoa.

This was the longest distance Jean had flown over water, and before long there was no land in sight. She flew on in a bright blue sky, with little wind, no sound except the purring of her engine. When it felt like lunchtime, she ate a leg of chicken, tossing the bone over the side. Pouring coffee without spilling it proved so difficult she drank directly from the Thermos. Even so, when she hit an air pocket, she was showered with liquid, and wondered if she had broken a tooth when it connected with the lip of the Thermos.

The clear sky was interrupted by a bank of cumulonimbus clouds, forcing her to fly low. Suddenly Corsica lay beneath her. The island, almost completely covered by snow, was surrounded by the deep blue of the Mediterranean. From above, its mountains looked like some strange and beautiful spectre risen from the sea. Many small islands lay beneath her now. She skirted the island of Elba with care, for it was forbidden to fly over it, since the Italian government used it for political prisoners. As she landed in Rome, she noted that ten hours had passed since she had left Lympne. She was greeted with the news that she was the first woman to fly non-stop solo from England. Already she had broken a record.

It was a quiet Sunday afternoon in Rome. She had come earlier than expected and nobody was available to fuel her plane. The gauge still showed enough petrol to take her on to Naples. The day was so beautiful, her spirits so high, that she decided to take to the air again. Her route now lay along the coast of Italy, the Appenines forming the country's backbone, rising in great heights against the skyline, white and then pink as sunset overtook them. The sea turned crimson and gold. Here and there, she saw tiny ruined cities, then strips of bone-white beaches with fishing smacks drawn up as evening closed in, and the fishermen's nets, like hairnets from this distance, hung out to dry. In the far distance, she saw a long line of smoke, and against the darkening sky she distinguished the outline of Mount Vesuvius. Smithy's words flashed before her: *Never fly at night.*

Darkness was almost upon her as she flew over Naples.

In the last of the twilight, she saw a cluster of lights and made out the aerodrome of Capodichino where she landed safely.

She sent a telegram to Victor. *First record fallen. Leaving at dawn for Syria.*

Chapter 19

Although it was late in the evening when she arrived in Naples, Jean now set to work on the plane's engine. Before she left England, she had worked out a daily routine of engine and aircraft maintenance that she resolved to keep at all costs. The Italian ground mechanics, apparently full of admiration for her day's flying, drained the oil for her, while she cleaned the petrol filter. She suggested they refuel and put new oil in the engine, so that she could start at dawn. Her plan was to fly to Aleppo in the north of Syria the following day, a journey of some thirteen hundred miles.

'Not possible,' the helpful mechanics indicated, shaking their heads sadly. While it was true that they were on duty, the petrol man had gone home early because it was Sunday. He always took the petrol key with him. No, they did not know where he lived, so sorry, signorina.

What was worse, the petrol man did not arrive until 8.30 the next morning. And no, they did not know his address. All of this discussion had taken place with signs, and gesticulations, and pointing at watches. Some Italian air force officers now appeared. One of them spoke some French, and he and Jean had a halting conversation.

He could, he was sure, track down the fuel agent's home address and persuade him to come in early in the morning. It was near midnight when Jean slid into bed at a small inn not far from the aerodrome. She set the clock for 4.30 a.m.

In the half-light of early morning she hailed a taxi outside the inn. She was already wearing her fur-lined flying suit and helmet and goggles.

'*Aeroporto*,' she said to the driver. He was a fierce-looking bandit of a man, complete with a heavy moustache, and a blue bandana tied around his head.

'*Aeroporto*,' he responded, smacking the steering wheel with the palm of his hand. '*Si, signorina, aeroporto.*'

Just to be sure, she had written down the directions. '*Si, si,*' he said, waving the piece of paper away. '*Aeroporto. Qui si va.*' Here we go, or so she understood.

Off they went, at speed across the cobbles, the taxi bumping and swaying. The ride was longer than she expected, and although she had not been able to see her surroundings the previous night as she was driven from the aerodrome, she had the distinct feeling that they were travelling in the wrong direction.

'Where are we going?' she shouted from the back seat.

'*Aeroporto. Non ti preoccupare!*' From which she took it that the driver had everything under control. Within a minute or so they had drawn up with a jolt at the end of a wharf.

'*Porto Napoli*,' the driver cried.

'No, no, no,' she cried. 'I do not want the Port of

Naples.' She flung open the door of the taxi and leapt out. At that moment two policemen walked past. '*Un momento, prego*,' she called, using most of the Italian she had absorbed in the last hours. She opened her hands imploringly, indicating the taxi driver who now stood looking sheepishly at the beautiful bay of Naples, which held no appeal for her at all at this moment. '*Aeroporto*,' she said, adding a wail to her voice.

The policemen looked at her, taking in the flying suit, and the piece of paper she was brandishing, and began to laugh. But when they spoke to the taxi driver, their voices were sharp. The driver took her to the aerodrome, without another word passing between them.

The air force officers she had met the night before were waiting for her, looking crestfallen. They hadn't been able to find the fuel officer. She would, after all, have to wait until 8.30. It was nine that morning before she left. Syria was beyond her reach before nightfall. Instead, she set a course across the Adriatic Sea, heading for Athens.

On the island of Corfu, she spotted a seaplane base, and flew down low over it. For an instant, she was back in Auckland, a child on the beach, demanding her turn to look inside the Walsh brothers' flying boats. She saw John and Harold racing ahead, their faces streaked by the sun. And now here she was, absolutely alone in the sky, in command of this plane, circling a seaplane base on the other side of the world and the mysteries of her brothers' lives lost to her. John, who had buried some secret in his marriage to Madeleine Murat; Harold married to Alma, blasting rocks out of hillsides, in whirling dust and half-light, the outsider, the wild card, the brother whom she still found it in her heart to love. For all his strange ways, she found it easier to think of Harold with a gentle heart than she did John.

She flew over the Corinth Canal. Soon, between the purple mountains that bound three sides of the city, she sighted the white marble buildings of Athens, the Parthenon gleaming high on the hill over the city, and, on the fringe of the city, the military aerodrome of Tatoi.

In darkness, at 3 a.m. the next day, she took to the air again, heading for Aleppo and, just as she had done on her first night flight, she used a torch to see the instruments, taking off holding the throttle lever and the torch in her left hand, while controlling the joystick with her right. She circled higher and higher in order to gain sufficient height to cross the mountains, and set off towards the obscure shadows over the Aegean Sea.

The night felt cold enough to strip the skin, but the sky was burning with stars, the moon coating her plane with ghostly rays. To the south a few lights still blinked from the heart of Athens. When they were behind her, and there was nothing but darkness all around, and the sea below, she was overwhelmed with such loneliness that it was like an arrow, as if the cold had turned to ice and was slicing through her with a peculiar pain that was not physical. Her only company was the blast of the four flames from the stub-exhaust pipes of her engine, and the purr of the engine itself. She was surrounded by cauldrons of stars and wastelands of blackness. Again she tried to summon the faces of her brothers, of her mother, and of the man, Victor, with whom she might be in love. The image of her father, with his small serial betrayals, was elusive. It was Nellie's face that stamped itself before her in the blistering chill of dawn light, and the dwindling of the stars.

It surprised her that she was not afraid of death, and she found herself wondering if Bert Hinkler had been fearful, whether he knew what lay ahead, and wanted to turn back. She thought of herself as a person who lived on the fringes, but here, over the austere land of Greece, she felt that she was reaching into the deep centre of herself, a lonely place indeed, but one that was, after all, without fear. This, perhaps, was what would keep her safe. To be afraid in a crisis was one thing, but the fear of death itself would never betray her. It occurred to her that it was loss that frightened her, although the loss of what exactly was amorphous, something she dimly understood.

On an island beneath her, someone must have heard her engine, and began signalling with a torch in Morse code. She tried to signal back a few letters in response. What language would her friend below be using? They wouldn't understand each other, perhaps, but it was enough. There were people down there, and the world was a real place, not just a dark canyon lit by unimaginable galaxies of distant planets. She felt her other self returning, a pilot on a mission, the excitement of the next destination.

Turkey, and the plane hit bumps, encountering a downdraught of huge intensity, dropping two thousand feet in seconds. Her Thermos and maps, some oranges and her sandwiches were hurled onto the cockpit floor, as gravity dragged her against the straps that held her in. Dangerously close to water, she gave the engine full throttle, then followed a steep climb over a range of mountains, one country after another seeming to dissolve behind her.

And there was Syria. She whooped, chanting aloud, *The Assyrian came down like the wolf on the fold* ... What would Lord Byron make of a woman, little older than he was when he wrote his poem, shouting his words five thousand feet above the green fields of Syria? Like him, she was a free spirit. She allowed herself an unladylike spit over the edge of the cockpit.

She reached Aleppo, staying less than two hours, then flew on, on towards Baghdad, across a desert where columns of dust rose a thousand feet in the air, the sand tearing at her face and lips, the plane tossed around into an upward roll, the next instant spinning towards the earth. Just when she believed she had cleared the sandstorms, another one appeared, so dense that the sun looked like a black sphere. She flew now by her instruments, trying to take a short cut that would enable her to fly around the storm, but the landscape grew darker. Then as suddenly as the storm had hit her, she passed through it, only to discover that it was night again.

Now she was faced with a decision: to fly on towards Baghdad, without knowing if she might encounter more storms, or to land in the desert. The moon was very bright; beneath her she saw a stretch of smooth earth that she would learn later was a camel track. An attempt at a landing seemed her only choice. Turning off the engine, she allowed the plane to glide towards the surface and land. She remained seated for a few minutes, her eyes closed. Her body was bruised, her face cut by the sand, her tongue so dry and parched that it was difficult not to drink all the water in her Thermos in one long gulp.

She walked a little way along the track, trying to determine how much firm ground there was before her. Something soft barred her way. On closer inspection in the moonlight, she saw that it was a dead camel. Something crept away in the darkness, causing her to shiver. By the light of her torch, she saw that it was a land crab of some description. Returning to the plane, she took the cushions out of the cockpit and spread them beside the fuselage. As soon as she lay down she fell into a deep sleep.

When she woke, the sun was blazing fiercely, and eight Arabs were sitting around her in a circle. As she scrambled to her feet, they all rose as one. Were these the Assyrians?

Once, when they were children, Harold had read from one of his encyclopedias what to do if accosted by a sheik. The advice was to shake hands, and say 'Salaam'.

'Salaam,' she said in a shaking voice to one of the Arabs, an olive-skinned man with heavy eyebrows, who appeared older and more richly dressed than the others. He wore a long white flowing robe with a head-dress of striped material kept in place by a twisted cord. He seemed astonished when she grabbed his hand and began to shake it effusively. After a few moments, when nobody seemed to move, she thought of a better, more immediate plan and returned to the plane. From the cockpit, she seized a tin of cigarettes, opened it and, with trembling hands, lit one before passing it to the man she assumed to be the sheik. Smiles of pleasure now covered the faces of the onlookers, and before long they were all seated again, smoking with her.

She was still wearing her heavy flying gear. She had intended to change into tropical kit, but this was impossible in sight of the tribesmen. She decided now that she must get airborne as quickly as possible and began to swing the propeller of the plane. Although the heat was now rising, there had been frost in the night that had settled in the engine. She swung the propeller for nearly half an hour, dashing backwards and forwards to the cockpit to switch the engine on and off, sweat pouring off her.

Suddenly the sheik stood up. She could have sworn she saw a glint of humour in his eyes, as if this was an intriguing diversion, but called on Allah and walked toward the propeller. It was clear that he had decided to help, but she now saw that if the propeller did turn over, the flowing sleeves of his garment would be caught in it. There was nothing to be done, but to roll his sleeves up and tie them around the back of his neck, something he allowed her to do with an air of amusement.

Once again, Jean switched on the contact, and suddenly the engine roared into life. The tribesmen jolted with fear. She saw that they would be injured if they came near the propeller, so she turned the engine off and jumped out, gesticulating violently for them to keep away. They retreated a little way and stood in a group. Leaving the engine running, she walked over to the men, offering a packet of chocolate biscuits by way of thanks, and said goodbye. The sheik pointed along the track where, in the distance, a camel caravan was approaching.

By now it was nine o'clock and the heat was intense. She ran for the plane, jumped in, not waiting to strap herself in, and took off, climbing for a minute or two, then circling back to wave to the tribesmen, who were now almost obscured by dust. They waved wildly in return, and over the sound of the engine she believed she heard an ululating chorus of farewell.

Ahead of her lay Baghdad, in Mesopotamia, recently renamed Iraq, where there had once been the hanging gardens of Babylon. The city lying beneath her shone, the blue and white of the mosques relieved only by the intense green of thousands of date palms clustered along the edge of the Tigris, flowing into the Persian Gulf. Again she was overtaken by poetry, lines Harold had once recited, his lips moving with wonder: *I have set eyes on the wall of lofty Babylon on which is a road for chariots, and the statue of Zeus by the Alpheus, and the hanging gardens, and the Colossus of the Sun.* That was as much as she could remember, an old Greek poem. How much more did Harold have stowed away in his head? What else had settled there before things went so wrong? Before they had all come to the parting of the ways.

Chapter 20

In the distance, on the journey between Baghdad and Basra, Jean saw a mirage. A deep sapphire-coloured lake appeared in the desert, standing out in sharp contrast to the surrounding yellow sand. No such lake was marked on her map, and for a moment she doubted her compass. More than an hour and a half later, the lake disappeared. When she looked back, there was no sign that it had ever been. Like the civilisations that had come and gone in this vast expanse of land, it had simply ceased to exist.

From Basra she flew to Bushehr, where she slept for a few hours in a bare room of a guest house. At midnight she rose again and set out for the town of Jask on the Persian Gulf.

The night was warm and clear, until three in the morning when the moon set, leaving her in complete darkness. As she flew by the light of her torch on the instrument panel, the sense of loneliness she had experienced over Greece settled on her again. Sometimes the coastline she was following took a great curve, so that she would think that she was flying out to sea, and then realise that she was steering towards mountains. These she could just distinguish by their density against the sky, a more intense black than black.

She was saved by the dawn, and in its tender, creeping light her despair melted, and she began to shimmer with excitement. Jean knew she was flying to Australia faster than any person had done before her, and that the record was within her grasp.

At Jask, she slept again for an hour or so, and ate a tin of cherries. She prepared the plane to fly to Kashmir.

But the elements were against her again. Some hundred miles to the south, over Baluchistan, she encountered more sandstorms so violent she was forced close to the ground. The plane jolted this way and that, hurdling sand hillocks and missing bushy coastal trees by inches. Shortly, she came to an area of fields and decided that, at whatever cost, she must land. She eased the plane over an earthen bank and brought it to rest, rejoicing for a moment that the landing appeared successful, until the plane lurched and the wheels began to sink deep into mud, tipping the propeller nose-first into the quagmire. She switched off the engine and leapt in after the plane, standing in the mud and putting her shoulder to the nose. Nearby, some two hundred tribesmen stood looking at her with curiosity. The wheels sank deeper in the mire, until the plane was resting on its fuselage, tail in the air, and she was up to her waist in the mud. Her body could no longer support the weight of the machine. She called upon Allah, as she had learned the day before, shouting loudly.

On hearing this, the tribesmen approached and carried the plane to dry land.

When she inspected the plane, she discovered that one of the propeller blades was fractured. She had no idea how she was going to explain this. She knew she must be only some thirty-five miles from Karachi. If there was some way of communicating with the airport there, it might be possible for them to bring her a propeller. After some thought, she put up a great wail, shouting 'Karachi', all the while pointing at the propeller.

The people shook their heads. Karachi was not possible. Instead, they said 'Bela', and indicated that they would take her there. She knew this to be an ancient town in the hills, a long way to the north-west, in the opposite direction to Karachi. There seemed nothing for it, but to agree to their plan. Between them they picketed the plane to the ground, and two men volunteered to stay with it. She again gathered her belongings, placing them in a bag. Desolation almost overwhelmed her as they turned their backs on the plane. When they reached a village, women of the tribe gave her food, curried prawns, with goats' milk to wash them down.

The tribesmen strapped the air cushions from the plane onto the back of a camel, and helped her to mount, seating her where she could rest her back against the camel's second hump. Her driver climbed in front, and the journey to Bela began. Throughout the long night the driver kept the camel going at a steady pace, shouting loudly when it stumbled.

Early in the morning, they reached the city of Bela, a place that had begun to seem like the mirage she had seen days before, a place that existed only in the imagination. Her driver collected her baggage and motioned her in the direction of a large square white house. He knocked sharply on the door, until a man, heavy with sleep, opened it, demanding to know their business. Some words were exchanged and then he said, in perfect English, 'Come inside, you must be very tired.'

This greeting was so unexpected that Jean thought for a moment she would cry with relief. 'Where am I?' she whispered. 'Who are you?'

'Until recently I was the head man of the Jam Sahib,' he said. 'Come, sit down. I've got English tea, and some rather nice biscuits. When you've had those you can wash and rest until it's time for breakfast.' The room was simple, with whitewashed walls, but furnished with colourful kilims and cushions.

'I need to get to Karachi.' She explained her predicament.

'Well,' he said, 'I will have to give that some thought. It is a shame that Jam Sahib is not here. He was with us until last week.'

'He speaks English?'

'Oh, my dear young lady. Where are you from?'

'New Zealand.'

'New Zealand. And do they not play cricket there?'

'I believe they do.'

'But you are not a follower of the game? Ah well, never mind. Jam Sahib played test cricket for England.

He was described once in a newspaper as the *Midsummer night's dream of cricket*. You may have heard of the name Maharaja K. S. Ranjitsinhji.'

'I'm afraid not.'

The assistant sighed, and stirred another lump of sugar into his own tea. 'He was a prince among men.'

'So where is he now?'

'He is not with us.'

'He has died?'

'Last week.' He bowed his head for a moment.

'I'm so sorry,' Jean said.

'The time for mourning has passed.'

Jean could see no way through this strange conversation. 'So is there no Jam Sahib now?'

'Oh yes, indeed. We have a new Jam Sahib. But he, too, is away, attending to his duties as the new ruling prince of Nawanagar, which is the area where you are now. Hmm.' He scratched his chin, deep in thought. 'The new Jam Sahib has an aged Chevrolet truck which I think he could spare for a few days. He is kind, he would want you to have it. Yes, indeed, that is the answer. And I can signal ahead to your people in Karachi what has happened, and perhaps you can alert them to your needs for this flying machine of yours. Forgive me, your *aeroplane*. The late Jam Sahib liked aeroplanes. He even went for a flight in one once. It took off in a field and brought him back to land in the same place.'

'Cobham's Flying Circus. I asked them for a job but they wouldn't take me because I'm not a man.'

'You can fly a circus plane? You must be a very good flier indeed. But surely Mr Cobham would be right? What does your father think of a young lady like you flying in a circus? No, no, Mr Cobham must surely have been correct.'

The journey that followed had a hallucinatory quality. There was not enough petrol available for the journey to Karachi so, on the way, they took a detour back to the plane, still guarded by Baluchi tribesmen, and drained enough to see them on their way, leaving sufficient fuel for a takeoff. They lurched, then, over dry riverbeds, dashed down banks and across rivers in flow, became stuck in mud, collecting stones, cactus and thorn bushes to place under the lorry wheels. Time, which had seemed so important to Jean, had become meaningless, something not to be measured. She entered Karachi, its streets filled with camel caravans, the animals decorated with red and purple scarves, tinkling with bells. She saw Mohammedan priests dressed in bright orange robes and another man in black wearing what appeared to be the hoof of a cow on his head. This was a priest of the Parsee.

They drove along Drigh Road to the entrance gates of the British RAF compound, where a Commander Watt was in charge of the aerodrome. He invited her into a cool and pleasant room, where she collapsed into an easy chair and sipped cold lemonade. Outside, he said, there was an army of reporters, who had heard that she was missing in the desert. Did she think she could face them?

'I could have a quick word,' she said, 'but I do want

to get away as soon as possible.' Jean had lost some three days, but now that she was back at an airport, all the urgency of her journey returned. She began again to calculate the chances of still breaking Amy Johnson's record. It was not impossible. Now it was 5.30 p.m. She had telegraphed from Bela at four in the morning, asking for a propeller to be waiting for her on her arrival. The propeller wouldn't be available until the following morning. Resigned to spending the night in Karachi, she spoke to the reporters. As well, she sent cables to her mother and to Victor.

Still in her flying suit, she fell onto the bed that was offered to her and slept until the next day. When she woke, the propeller had arrived. The story of the girl aviator who had spent nights in the desert, and was still hell-bent on flying to Australia, was flashing its way around the world. The commander offered her a pilot and a plane to fly her out to the abandoned Moth.

But the machine was not to be found. It was impossible to believe that it had disappeared. After searching the surrounding barren land for more than an hour, they returned to Karachi.

A second search was organised. This time the plane flew all the way to Bela and back. The plane, somebody suggested, must have been dismantled by the tribesmen and taken away. Or, they said, perhaps all the land around there was marshy, and it had simply sunk right into the ground. Jean could not believe either of these propositions. The day had started so well, she had felt so

253

refreshed and light-hearted, and certain that she would be on her way. Convinced that the plane still existed, she saw this as merely another setback to be overcome.

The truck that had brought her from Bela had not yet begun its return journey. She offered the driver money for a journey to the fields. In the evening, they arrived at the village, and again mounted camels. It was impossible to strap the propeller to a camel, so teams of men volunteered to carry it on their shoulders. They set off into the night, six camels, two boys running ahead with flaming brands to light the way, the tribesmen panting with the exertion of carrying the propeller.

Towards midnight, they came to the plane. To Jean's astonishment, a circle of the Baluchi people sat around it. By the light of the moon and the torches, she saw that every part of the plane was covered with camel cloths. A sandstorm had blown up and the local people had covered the machine with cloths to protect it. In the process, they had also provided the perfect camouflage from the air.

To her joy, the engine turned over as soon as she switched it on next morning. Now, at last, she could continue her journey to Australia. She gave money to all who had helped her, and prepared to leave. There was a fair wind blowing, but the space to take off was so short that she vaulted the plane over a bank and into the next field, where there was sufficient runway for the plane to rise. Within half an hour, Karachi lay beneath her.

Suddenly there was a sharp report and her engine failed completely. She was some five hundred feet up, but the airfield was too far away to reach by gliding. Below her lay Drigh Road which ran northwards from Karachi, through a series of sandhills. This seemed the only immediate place that was firm, and where there were no houses. As she glided down in the now totally silent machine, wondering how she could dodge the cars, she saw to her horror that the road was bounded at intervals by a series of white posts that appeared narrower than the thirty-foot span of her wings. Sure enough, as she landed two of these posts caught the plane in an inevitable embrace. The plane turned a complete somersault. Jean clung to the bottom of the cockpit, so that when the aircraft came to rest, she was able to lower herself on her shoulders and crawl out from beneath the wreckage.

A car approached along Drigh Road and the driver stopped. She stood for a moment looking at the remains of her plane, before accepting his offer of a lift. As soon as she could, she resolved, she would attempt another flight to Australia. She learned soon enough that a connecting rod had snapped clean in half and gone right through the engine casing.

Barely a week had passed since Jean had left London. It was still April 1933. As Nellie noted, the bluebells were still in flower beneath the trees at Oakleigh. She had rung the Dorée household several times, but a servant always said that the family was out. Yes, Mr and Mrs Dorée and all the young Mr Dorées as well. She had walked up the familiar driveway and knocked on the door, wearing her best hat. Mrs Dorée came to the door, and, after some hesitation, invited her in. They sat in the reception hall, on hard-backed chairs, beside the curved staircase that led to the upper rooms. Mother to mother, Mrs Dorée said, Victor hadn't really budgeted for this mess. Jean, she intimated, was a resourceful young woman, who would surely find some way to get herself back home. Perhaps, did Nellie think, it might be time to return to New Zealand?

Nellie took her leave, keeping, as she related it to Jean, a civil tongue in her head. 'Embarrassed,' she said. 'That's what she was. They wanted the newspapers in on the act so long as the stories were good. Cheap cosmetics, indeed. They're trade really, not professionals.'

In India, a doctor had ordered Jean to rest in a darkened room for several days, for fear of concussion. After three days, she emerged from her room, set upon finding a way to return to London. A cable arrived from Viscount Wakefield. He had been told of her difficulties and, more than that, he commended her for keeping a steady head in the face of danger. She was to see the Castrol agent in Karachi, Mr Chubb, who would take care of her return journey, the passage of the plane's remains, and anything else she might need.

Four days after the crash, Jean boarded a ship. Late in May, she disembarked in England. That night, she and Nellie sat down to a barren meal of toast, and hot chocolate made with water. Nellie wanted to say a prayer of thanks for Jean's deliverance, but Jean said she was no longer sure about divine intervention, and could they please leave prayer for another day.

'What will you do about Victor?' Nellie asked.

'I should try to see him. Whatever his mother thinks of me, he should have a chance to explain himself in person.'

Before she went to bed she wrote two letters, one to Victor suggesting that they meet, and another to Viscount Wakefield to thank him for his generosity.

A note arrived from Victor. 'I agree that we have some matters to discuss,' he wrote. He didn't propose that Jean visit the house, nor that he would take her to dinner. 'There is that pub in Edgware Road, The White Lion. We could meet at one o'clock on Saturday afternoon if that's convenient for you.' It was the same pub where she and Frank Norton used to meet.

She almost didn't go, but still she supposed there could be some misunderstanding.

Victor had arrived before her and was seated, suave, distant, drumming his fingers on a tabletop, as if impatient. He glanced at his watch when she walked in.

'Victor,' she said. 'What can I say? I'm sorry about the plane.'

'Not half as sorry as my mother.'

'Aren't you pleased to see me?' she said, knowing how pitiful and silly this sounded, yet unable to help herself.

'You know, it was hard out there in the desert.'

'Well, of course I'm glad you're all in one piece. I wouldn't have liked to have that on my conscience.'

She felt herself stiffening. 'I take it that our partnership's finished?'

'Well, it was worth a try. Look, I'm sorry old thing, but you did take some risks.'

'It's my fault then?'

He was silent. His face was as smooth as the satin sleeve of one of his mother's dinner dresses, and, it suddenly occurred to her, almost as pink.

'The connecting rods,' she said.

'Is that an accusation?' he said swiftly, almost before the words were out of her mouth.

'You know I was doubtful about them …'

'You need to keep those thoughts to yourself,' he said. 'De Havilland wouldn't be amused to hear that.'

'It was nothing to do with him. He wasn't working on the plane.'

'I take it you can't pay anything towards the damage?' When she shook her head, he said, 'Well, it's not the end of the world, I suppose. I'm afraid I'm out of it. I've just bought a rather nice Lanchester, it needs a bit of work on it. I've been playing around with that.'

'A car. You've bought a new car?'

'New old. More fun. I might get around to another plane later on.'

He didn't say that he had recently met Mary Swan, whose family owned the Swan kettle factory in Swansea.

Jim Mollison took the opportunity to tell Jean this when she finally showed up at Stag Lane. He gave her a wink, with one of those 'There's something you need to know' expressions. Earlier in the year, Mollison had flown from England to Brazil in three days and thirteen hours, stopping over in Africa. It was a record time, and the first solo flight to Brazil. The word was that he and Amy were planning to attempt a record flight over the Atlantic.

The morning after Victor's engagement was announced in *The Times*, Jean collected up the half-empty bottle of Chanel No. 5, the silk panties and other gifts Victor had given her, and took them in a brown paper bag to the gate of Oakleigh. 'Feel free to check the contents,' she said to the attendant who had once opened the gates for her and Victor as they swept through, seated behind the family chauffeur.

She kept the white flying helmet. Who knew whether it might come in handy again one day?

These were not the only things that happened in 1933. There was hunger, but then, as Nellie remarked, they were not alone in this. The year was memorable for the meals she and Jean didn't eat, rather than the ones they did, for the way they eked their way through the summer, dreading the onset of winter, and the cold. It was a year when Nellie feared for her daughter's life more than she had when she was missing in the desert. The old demons of despair preyed on Jean, so that she would sit for days at a time, barely moving, her dreams again haunted. The resolve to fly again had evaporated. 'I feel nothing,' she said, more than once. She felt quite worthless.

'Is it because of Victor?' Nellie asked gently.

'I thought he loved me.'

'Did you love him?'

'I liked that he seemed to love me,' Jean said. 'I liked the house, and the family, and the idea that he wanted to take care of me. But of course he didn't at all. He should have got in quick with Amy Johnson if he wanted a famous flying wife, shouldn't he?' She gave a sour laugh. 'I hear Amy had a black eye the other day. The joys of being Mrs Mollison.'

This was gossip she'd heard on what would be her last visit to the clubhouse for some time. Her subscription had run out. Besides, in July, Amy and Jim had flown across the Atlantic to the States, but crash-landed at Connecticut after they'd run out of fuel. The charitable view was that the black eye had happened in the crash. And, crash or no crash, the couple had still won themselves a ticker-tape parade in New York.

Over in Australia, Charles Kingsford Smith had established a commercial airline between New South Wales and New Zealand, carrying mail and freight, and a small number of passengers.

In August, John became a father. This, too, Nellie and Jean discovered by reading *The Times*. The newspaper was the one luxury Nellie allowed them. Indeed, she said it was a necessity of life, given what it told one. Madeleine had given birth to a daughter. This followed hard on the heels of her latest book, fittingly entitled *New Soul*. In one of her many interviews, she gushed that while motherhood was both wonderful and inspirational, and she and her husband were thrilled about the baby, domesticity wouldn't stand between her and her vocation as a writer.

'Touching,' Nellie said. 'Such a brave, enlightened little creature.'

Towards the end of the year, a letter came from Frank Norton demanding that Jean repay the money he had lent her for her flying lessons. Five hundred pounds. He wanted it right away. He'd heard she had a rich new boyfriend.

Jean wrinkled her nose with disgust. 'Frank Norton,' she said. 'He can't even keep up with the gossip. Men.' She screwed up the letter and threw it hard at the opposite wall.

The last day of the year was dark and freezing. The weather had driven seagulls up the Thames to London, where they gathered in Kensington Gardens, unable to pierce the ice for fish. Passers-by fed them. Nellie and Jean didn't have bread to spare.

But another letter would arrive before long.

Chapter 21

It was that cold snap that brought Jean out of the depths. All through the autumn the sounds of the Moths overhead had been driving her further into herself. She barely seemed to notice the cold when it arrived. Nellie said that she wasn't going to go to bed freezing.

'Come on,' she said, 'we're going for a walk, get our circulation going. I mean it. Stand up, Jean. Walk with me.'

Jean got to her feet and, with Nellie's help, pulled her coat around her. They walked out into the brisk air, Nellie stamping her feet all the time. A breeze stung their faces. Jean shook her head as if to clear a blockage, and looked at her mother with surprise, as if she hardly knew how they had got there, as if the frost was biting through the blanket of misery with which she had surrounded herself.

Next morning, she got up and began to write letters. She wrote again to Viscount Wakefield, to newspaper reporters on Fleet Street who had singled her out earlier in the year, asking if they could make appeals on her behalf — after all they had had some good stories out of her disasters — and to the aircraft manufacturers. Although all her entreaties appeared to fall on deaf ears, it was as if a spring had been uncoiled.

On a day when snow was still falling, and she and Nellie had shivered through another night without heating, she dressed herself in her fur-lined flying gear, and walked to Stag Lane. She wondered what would have happened if she had walked into the clubhouse. Nobody would have turned her away, she believed, but there would be awkwardness, now that she was no longer a member. In all likelihood, Victor Dorée would be back there. And she preferred not to see Amy and Jim again. Amy would probably have given her a hug, or a warm handshake at least, but Jim had already let her know that she was a failure, without saying it outright. In the air, as well as in love. Instead, she chose to stand on the edge of the flying field, where she watched takeoffs and landings. There had been new intakes of trainee pilots in her absence.

As she was watching a hapless young man swerving all over the field, a voice behind her said, 'We all have to learn, don't we?'

It was Geoffrey de Havilland, his smile as warm as the morning she had left England. He asked how she was, without making reference to the crash.

'I'm well enough, sir. Thank you.' She supposed she must say something about what had happened, but nothing came to mind. 'He just has to learn not to be afraid of the takeoff,' Jean said, indicating the student pilot. 'You can see, he's avoiding the moment.'

'You'd make a good instructor,' de Havilland said.

'Not me, I'm too selfish. To be honest, I'm in it for myself.'

He gave her a long look. 'You've done remarkably well, it seems to me.'

'Me? I've made a pig's ear of everything.'

'You had a faulty connecting rod?'

'It's my own fault. I should have stood my ground. I wasn't happy with them when I left for Australia.'

'I think you did very well to survive. Very resourceful. What are you doing about getting another plane?'

'I've really got nowhere to turn,' she said. 'I've written to Viscount Wakefield, several times in fact, but he doesn't answer my letters.'

'A lot of aspiring pilots write to him.'

'But he was so kind when he got me out of India. I hadn't asked him to help me then.'

'I think you'll find he has a file on you.'

'Really?'

'He keeps an eye on young up-and-coming pilots. He's already talked to me about you. He'd made a note that you'd phoned Wakefield House, and written to him. What were his words? Oh yes. *A young lady of strong determination, as well as charm.* And even though you didn't succeed on your last flight, he reckoned you had it in you to succeed. Gutsy, that's what he called you. And damn pretty to go with it.'

'He didn't really say that?'

'Well, yes he did. Would you like me to write a letter of introduction?'

'Would you?'

De Havilland gave her a grin. 'I reckon he's onto something.'

It didn't happen straightaway. After some weeks had passed, and just at the point when Jean was beginning to think she had imagined the conversation with de Havilland, an envelope whispered through the door by the morning's first delivery. It was a letter from Viscount Wakefield's secretary. Although his employer wasn't prepared to fund her in full, he would advance her four hundred pounds, *which he assumed would be a fraction of what she needed.*

Jean pored over advertisements in aircraft magazines searching for a plane that might come in under this sum. She discovered an early model Gipsy Moth in an aerodrome at Berkshire, advertised for two hundred and forty pounds. When she saw the machine, her heart sank. It was in a semi-derelict state. The wings were propped against a wall, the stripped fuselage of the plane with a four-cylinder engine stored in a wooden crate beside it.

Feeling sick with disappointment, she stood back and surveyed these various remnants. This was hardly a plane that would carry her to the other side of the world. The owner, seeing how dismayed she was, offered to restore it for her, bring it up to the standard required to get a certificate of airworthiness.

'Can you lend me the logbooks?' she said. 'I need to think about this.'

At home, over the following several nights, she discovered the plane had had four owners, and several crashes in the four years since it had been built. One of the owners was a French woman pilot, Madeleine

Charnaux, who had crashed in a desert and survived to tell the story. Charnaux had a reputation as a sculptor, before she turned to aviation, and for a turbulent love life. This seemed to Jean like a portent — an artistic woman who had survived against the odds.

The plane's engine appeared undamaged, but the machine had a top speed of only eighty miles an hour. She did some calculations, and worked out that if she took a shorter route to Australia, she might still beat the women's record. The Moth didn't have the power to break the overall record. None of this was ideal, but she could see no way to acquire another plane at such a price.

She phoned the owner and said that, yes, she would buy it, and would he please paint it silver.

On the morning when the plane was ready to take delivery, she whistled on her way to the bus stop, causing passers-by to turn their heads in her direction. She caught a bus that took her to within two miles of the aerodrome, and walked the rest of the way. After the terrible winter, an early spring illuminated the landscape. As she swung along the country lane, she drew great breaths of fresh crisp air into her lungs, feeling how good it was to be alive. When she arrived at the hangar, she saw that the Moth had been completely recovered with fabric. The silver paint gleamed, the registration numbers picked out in green: G-AARB. Just add an O, she thought, that's me. Garbo. The thought pleased her. The plane was hers, and she thought it beautiful. She paid nineteen shillings and sixpence for a tankful of petrol. Snow was falling lightly when she took to the air, her first flight for several months.

While the restoration was taking place, she had registered at the Brooklands Flying Club. There were triumphs to remember at Stag Lane, and people like Herbert Travers and de Havilland himself whom she would miss, but there had been frustrations and humiliations that were better forgotten. She admired the stylish rectangles of the art deco clubhouse at Brooklands, a long, low slab structure sitting close to the ground, bisected by a tower, the whole building painted bright white, broken only by a scarlet entrance.

It was to this aerodrome that she flew her new plane. That afternoon, she began the process of preparing the machine for its flight to Australia. To her added delight, the plane had been fitted with new connecting rods.

When she arrived home, she sat down and wrote a curt note to Victor. *Do you have any use for the large tanks that were fitted to the Moth I flew to Karachi? If not, I wish to have them. We were, you might recall, in partnership.* She felt hardness in her when she wrote this; it was the very least he owed her. If he parted with them, she would have a large tank with a twenty-seven-gallon capacity to place in the front cockpit, while the fifteen-gallon one would fit in the luggage locker. As with the first plane, this would give her enough for ten hours' flying or a range of eight hundred miles.

After she had posted the letter, she said to Nellie, 'Now read me the registration papers, please. Aloud.'

When Nellie came to the part reading, *Name of owner: Jean Batten*, she felt another surge of delight, and had Nellie read the whole thing over again.

Victor replied: *Do what you like with the tanks. They are of no further use to me.*

Frank wrote to her again, demanding money. *I'll show you up for what you really are, just a little gold digger.*

Within days of her registration at Brooklands, Jean attracted the attention of a divorced stockbroker called Edward Walter. Ted, he liked to be called. One of his forebears had founded *The Times*. He flew a Gipsy Moth the same vintage as hers in the weekends, if the weather was good. He had to admit that he was not a very brave flier. She allowed him to drive her about, and she and Nellie were glad to eat at good restaurants again, although Nellie told Jean he bothered her in a way she couldn't explain. He was said to be the black sheep of his family. There was something desultory about Edward. He was thirty-three, and a stockbroker, he said, because it ran in the family and a man had to do something for a living. He loved aeroplanes. He had parts of them all over his bedroom, he told her proudly. Some day he would put all the bits together.

Nellie decided that she ought to seek John out and meet her granddaughter. When she phoned the Elstree

Film Studios a receptionist told her Mr Batten was not currently working on any films, but she had a phone number for him. Nellie's call was answered by John, only he gave the name of a plastic surgeon in Hampstead, and asked how he could be of assistance.

'John, why are you answering this doctor's phone?' Nellie exclaimed.

'I work here,' he said. 'Is that you, Mother?'

'Of course it's your mother. What work?'

'I'm the receptionist.'

There wasn't much film work on offer right now, John told her, although he hoped to resurrect his career the following year. He didn't think this was the right time to meet Madeleine and the baby.

But a successful meeting was at hand: Jean was about to meet Viscount Wakefield.

She had written to tell him of the purchase of G-AARB, and all the work she had had done on the plane, how she had made his gift stretch to cover almost all her costs, except for the price of the fuel she would use on her journey. By return mail, a note of invitation arrived, requesting that she call on him for afternoon tea the following day.

The office of C. C. Wakefield stood in Cannon Street, dominated by Christopher Wren towers, exuding a sense of weathered elegance. Jean alighted from the train and made her way through the huge glass-domed concourse, and out into the street. She had walked through this thoroughfare before, but today it had special significance. She shivered in her thin winter coat, as she made her way towards the tall Castrol building.

Viscount Wakefield of Hythe was waiting for her, standing facing the window, his hands folded behind his back. Charles Cheers Wakefield, former Lord Mayor of London, and head of Castrol, the biggest oil company in the world. He was seventy-five, with a round face and thin wisps of hair brushed back from his forehead, but his bearing was that of a younger man, and his dress was immaculate. His shirt was high-collared, his tie held with a subtle silver pin. She had heard that his friends called him Cheers. He turned from the window and observed her as she came into the room. After a long, studied look, he beckoned her to the window to stand beside him.

'So, Miss Batten,' he said, 'you are going to fly to Australia?'

'I hope so, sir,' she said. 'I plan to give it my best shot.'

'Why would you want to do something so daring and fraught with danger?'

'Because I believe that the future of transport is in the air, and that its possibilities have barely begun to be explored.'

'I see. I understand you come from New Zealand?'

'Yes, and perhaps that has something to do with my desire to travel further and faster across the world. My family is British, but it's hard to feel as if one is truly so when we're so far away. New Zealand is at the edge of the world. It takes many weeks, and considerable hardship, even now, to travel from one side of the world to another. I want to demonstrate that there are faster routes, better ways to accomplish global travel. I hope to fly from England to New Zealand some day.'

'Really? Not this time round, though?'

'No, sir. The plane I've bought doesn't have the capacity to fly across the Tasman Sea, the last barrier on the journey between here and my country. But if I'm successful with this flight, then I hope to convince the world that I'm worthy of their support in that endeavour.'

Wakefield continued to stand at the window. She wondered if she had said something wrong.

'Look out there,' he said. 'London. It feels as if it belongs to me, which isn't the case I know, for it belongs to millions. But if you've had the good fortune to be Lord Mayor of a city so magnificent, it's difficult not to feel proprietary. I feel as if every brick and stone, every tower and cathedral is in some way a part of me. See down below?' And here he pointed out the window to the street. 'Where this building stands was once the base for the Hanseatic League, one of the most powerful trading organisations in the world. Elizabeth the First threw them out, because she was afraid England would be overrun by the Germans. Well, who knows, she might have had a point. It's a street with a long history. But you know, sometimes I look out here and I think, this is mine,

I own this same piece of land, and the thought makes me humble, that I've had so much of life's riches. Sit down, Miss Batten.'

He insisted on helping her to remove her coat, then pressed a bell on his desk. A woman appeared. 'Please take Miss Batten's coat for her,' he said. 'And bring us a nice hot cup of tea, and some milk and sugar lumps. I think some biscuits would go well, too. You like chocolate biscuits? Of course you do, all young creatures like chocolate biscuits, even when they say they don't.'

He studied her again. She was beginning to feel like one of de Havilland's butterflies pinned to a wall.

'I like your attitude. I will do whatever I can to assist you with this flight, Miss Batten. You're not just the most beautiful aviator who has ever entered my door, but I think you have brains, and courage as well. Don't look so startled. I'm an old man, my compliments are harmless. My wife and I weren't blessed with children, but there are some fearless free spirits about who, from time to time, we like to think of as our offspring. Like good parents, we'll help them as we can. You don't need to worry yourself over the fuel. At each of my depots along your route, there will be Castrol available and, wherever possible, one of my agents to consult if you should run into difficulties.'

He held up his hand to prevent her from speaking. 'Just drink your tea. I could sit here and look at you all afternoon, just for the sheer pleasure of it, but I have another appointment in quarter of an hour.'

As she was leaving, he said, 'Forgive an old man's

impertinent question, but I see you're wearing a ring? You're to be married?'

'I've met someone,' she said, blushing.

'I hope he appreciates you. Is he happy for you to make this flight?'

Jean sighed. 'I don't think he finds my desire to fly across the world my most admirable trait.'

Wakefield laughed out loud. 'Think carefully about this proposal of his. You deserve a man of courage.'

Edward had told her he loved her. He really did. How could he prove it except with the ring he had given her? Afterwards, she wondered why on earth she had accepted it. At least there was an announcement in the paper. She kept reminding herself of the importance of marriage.

When he kissed her, she summoned up what she hoped passed for passion, as if she needed to find the conviction for both of them. She was twenty-four and feared that her lack of feeling was unnatural. Of his first wife, Edward spoke little, other than to say that she was a cold fish. Jean hoped the day wouldn't come when he said the same of her. He placed his hard, long tongue inside her mouth and held her buttocks firmly in both hands as he pulled her towards him. 'We should get married now,' he said.

'We hardly know each other,' she said.

'You'll be ready to settle down when you've got things out of your system,' he said.

By things, she supposed he meant long-distance flying. There was an old familiar chime to this conversation.

Nellie had been asking for advice about how to invest money. She had none, she admitted, but the time might come and she wanted to be prepared.

On 21 April, two newspapers were alerted to the flight Jean was about to make. A small headline in one of them read: *THE TRY AGAIN GIRL.*

Chapter 22

1934. They loaded themselves into Edward's green Armstrong-Siddeley. As he opened the door for Nellie, her hand stealthily stroked the polished surface. She sat up very straight in the front beside Edward, her hat, even at this hour of the morning, tilted rakishly over one eyebrow. As he started the motor, he remarked that Jean's mother seemed content for her daughter to disappear without trace. Jean caught a glimpse of Nellie's face reflected in the side mirror and saw how it crumpled, the glint of unbidden tears. Nothing more was said on the drive to the Lympne airfield. Jean shivered inside her flying suit. It was hard to tell in the dark, but the edges of the road were becoming more difficult to discern, blurring in the headlights. The forecast was for fine weather but she had an uneasy feeling that it was wrong.

When they had parked, Nellie said to Edward, as if out of nowhere, 'That was unnecessary. What you said. Very cruel. My daughter is,' and here she hesitated, 'she's my life. My whole life. Perhaps she'll become yours, too. Or perhaps not.'

Jean had cleared Customs the night before, so that nothing would hinder her departure. She carried with her eight small bags, each containing money in the currency of the countries she expected to land in on her way: guilders and rupees, francs and lira, and others. For months in advance she had compiled lists of the places she would fly over, schedules of petrol and oil depots around the world, tables of times for sunset and sunrise and the Greenwich time wherever she would be, the number of hours of daylight for each day's flight.

There was indeed mist over the field when they arrived, but the ground staff told her it was of no concern, just a light fog that would lift over the English Channel. In France the weather would be fine. The aerodrome officer, a man called Mr Dupe, said that he would leave all the lights on, and instructed her to fly towards the red light on the hangar building. This would give her a point of reference to take off. And to help even further, everyone would leave their car lights on.

Edward saw her looking around her as if searching for someone. A man from Wakefield's Castrol company appeared, and shook her hand, introducing himself.

'You were hoping Wakefield might come,' Edward said, with an edge in his voice. 'Instead he's sent his lackey.'

'Ted,' Jean said in a quiet voice she hoped nobody else could hear, 'you came to say goodbye to me. Don't let's quarrel any more.'

He nodded his head wearily. 'I'm not much good in the mornings, am I? Something I'll have to improve on when we're married. I promise I'll learn to do better.' He kissed her cheek. 'Good luck, old thing.'

It was her mother's turn now to embrace her. 'Darling. Darling. I'll be with you every mile, every moment of the way.'

Mr Dupe, her mother, the man from the Wakefield company and Edward clustered together to form the farewell party, waving through the mist that had become as thick as paste, brushing long, wet tendrils in her face. All she could see was the smudged outline of the hangar. 'Are you sure it's not getting worse?' she called to Mr Dupe.

'Just keep your eye on that red light,' he shouted back, 'and lift her off.' As if to reinforce his point, he called out again that the weather over France was beautiful. '*Le ciel est bleu*,' he added in excruciating French.

Taking off according to his instructions might have been easy, had the plane not being carrying sixty-one gallons of petrol. Fear snaked through her belly as she turned the plane to face the wind. Just before she opened the throttle, she heard Mr Dupe's voice wailing in the distance for her to stop.

The oil company representative came running over. 'The lights seem to have all gone out,' he said. 'I'll ask everyone to put them on again.'

Jean switched the engine off and sat in the plane for several minutes. She was desperate to be on her way. The monsoon rains would soon arrive over Asia and the walls of water that sheeted down for months on end would obliterate her little plane.

In a little while, Mr Dupe came back, shamefaced,

to tell her that all the lights were on, but the fog was now so dense that it was impossible to see them. The oil company man had gone off in a different direction and was lost altogether.

'That fool,' Jean said to Nellie, when they were back in the inn that afternoon. 'I could have killed myself.'

'Duped, indeed,' Nellie said acidly, then laughed. 'Darling girl, I'll have you all to myself again until the weather clears. We'll have a splendid dinner, roast lamb if they have some, as if we were in New Zealand, and lemon meringue pie for dessert.'

Edward had been banished, or rather had banished himself, to the City where he was needed at the stock exchange. He promised to return when conditions improved, however long it took.

'Would you like to be back in New Zealand?' Jean asked. It was a question she had asked her mother many times, but the answer was always the same, that Nellie would rather be with Jean than anyone in the world, and those she had left behind in New Zealand were as nothing to her now.

The delay in Lympne went on for days. She should, perhaps, have stopped then, waited another year, but she had waited long enough. She and Nellie picked bluebells in the damp woods, reminding them that a year had gone by since the first attempt.

When the meteorological office at last issued a fair weather outlook, Jean set off again. The same retinue was there, minus Edward, because there wasn't time for him to make it back to the aerodrome when the all-clear came. They waved until she could no longer see them, her mother's face growing smaller and smaller into a tiny pale dot, not a person any more. She had forgiven Mr Dupe.

And she was alone up there, and soon the English Channel lay beneath her, flecked ghostly white as the light of morning increased, and she felt the familiar exultant surge that always overtook her in the sky.

The weather was clear and still, with a gentle following wind. The conditions were much as they had been on her first journey along this route.

But this time, the weather turned as she neared Marseilles. Visibility worsened, and soon she was flying into thick fog over the south of France. Eight hours had elapsed. There was no question, this time, of flying on to Rome without refuelling.

At the aerodrome, on the edge of Lake Berre, the ground staff told her more bad weather was forecast. The whole southern coast of France now lay shrouded in fog and Corsica was surrounded by an intense depression. When she asked if the weather was likely to improve the next day, the man in the meteorological office shook his head with sorrow. 'It will get worse,' he said.

'Then I should get on my way as quickly as possible,' she said, 'and try to get ahead of it.'

'*Non, non.*' That was not possible, he said, with horror. She would surely die in any attempt at such folly. '*Il fait mauvais temps,*' he said over and over again.

She did some rapid calculations. Since the aerodrome was under water, it would be impossible to take off with a full load of petrol. Instead, she ordered that forty-five gallons be put in the machine, enough for about seven hours' flying, and she should reach her destination in four to five hours.

When she climbed into the cockpit, she shouted 'Contact' to the ground staff, but nobody moved. She looked at the impassive faces of the men on the ground below her. She understood that they were not going to help her. There was nothing for it, but to climb out and swing the propeller herself. At that point the meteorologist reappeared, carrying a piece of paper. It was, he explained, in halting English, a document she must sign to say that she had received the bad weather report and decided to carry on at her risk. He made a throat-cutting gesture and pointed at himself. She took the paper from him and, noting his distress, signed it in her neat round handwriting.

'There,' she said. '*Là.* Don't worry about this. I can turn back to Marseilles if the going gets too bad.'

After an hour, as predicted, the weather did become worse. The fog was now so thick that she could not distinguish the coastline at all. Somewhere beneath her in the swirling mists lay the high mountain peaks of Corsica, but she couldn't see them, didn't know where they were.

She saw herself caught in the trap, neither able to fly back to Marseilles nor in a direct line to Rome. In order to avoid the mountains, she now decided to fly south around the island and over the strait that lay between Corsica and Sardinia.

That took time. When she next glanced at her watch she saw that the plane had made very little headway. The headwinds battered her with relentless force, so that she seemed almost at a standstill.

Hours passed and the coast of Italy seemed further away. Then darkness overtook her. She passed the solitary glow of a lighthouse beam, and thought herself near to Italy, but realised there was still a long crossing over the sea ahead. At least the wind had dropped and the air felt calmer around her.

Within the path of light, she noticed a line of ripples following her on the surface of the water, and understood in a flash that this was the wake of her propellers and that she was just a few feet above the sea. The petrol gauge was reading zero, but still she must climb upwards or drown. For a moment, she longed for Edward's revolver. She found herself praying. God had seemed more absent than usual on this flight. To make sure there was no fuel left in her auxiliary tanks, Jean turned on both petrol tanks, pumping hard, holding the nose of the plane up until it nearly stalled, so that any fuel left would fall back towards the pump. The pump gripped once, twice, and she knew there must be a little petrol left. Enough perhaps, to carry her the last miles to Liguria, the airport in Rome, near the Tiber River. But perhaps not.

She undid the laces of her shoes and the chin strap of her helmet, and loosened the buttons of her flying suit, so that she could slip these clothes off if she had to swim. A great calmness descended on her. Death might come soon, but that seemed insignificant now. Rather, the regret she was experiencing was for her mother, and for those who had trusted her. She deserved a watery death, but her mother did not deserve this, nor Lord Wakefield. She could not think at that moment of anyone else for whom she should feel responsible. Edward didn't enter her mind.

She banked to the right, and for a moment the engine spluttered and cut out, picked up again. Below her, she glimpsed the seaplane station of Ostia, and was tempted to drop her aircraft in the water there. But still the engine purred on and the lights of Rome were visible. If she were to follow the river, she must come to the airport.

And then the engine died, with a cry like a small meowing cat, and the plane began its inevitable glide towards earth. In the dazzling city lights, she searched for a dark space clear of buildings and saw one ahead. She leaned out of the plane, flashing her torch to see the ground. A red light appeared high above her and disappeared. It was on a wireless mast directly ahead; she swerved quickly enough to avoid hitting it, but no sooner had she turned than another one appeared. Turning left, she steered between the two giant towers. She picked out a row of trees ahead, and there was just enough forward speed left to vault them and then this game of weaving and ducking was over and she collided at last with Rome.

She touched her face and felt the sticky rush of blood.

In the afternoon, after consulting with the engineers who would work on her machine, Jean found herself alone in the large hangar where the repairs were taking place. Because it was a Sunday, there was just a skeleton staff on hand. Nobody seemed to mind as she picked her way around piles of machinery parts. The miracle of her landing had been repeated over and again, of how her plane had landed fifteen feet in front of the trees and fifteen feet behind the high embankment of the Tiber. The close proximity of the Church of St Paul had not gone unnoticed. The men who found her had crossed themselves and said that it was certainly St Paul who had protected her and guided her to safety.

She shivered then, and said to Jack Reason, 'But they beheaded St Paul, didn't they?'

When Molly Reason told her, the day following the crash, she had already heard the bad news: there were no spare wings for her Moth anywhere in the country. A propeller and other fittings had been located in Berlin, and two compression legs for the undercarriage in Turin, all of which could be delivered by airmail and train within a day or so, but it would take three weeks to build new wings.

Her journey would be impossible before the monsoon rains set in. And that would be that, 1934 come and gone, another year without an attempt on the record.

Jean leaned against a strut in the hangar. The hours since she had last slept were turning into days. Not wishing anyone to see her giving in to this despair, she straightened up and walked further on into the recesses of the hangar, where cobwebs abounded. She almost fell over as she bumped into an aeroplane, so covered with dust, and strewn with dangling wires, that at first she did not recognise it for what it was. But then her eyes accustomed themselves to the gloom. 'A Gipsy Moth! It's a Moth, don't you see,' she shouted out to the men further down the hangar.

Someone came running. The men clustered around the crumbling machine, minus an engine. 'The wings,' she said. 'I want the wings.'

Jack Reason had followed the men, hearing the excitement.

'Yes, it's a Moth all right,' he said. 'Doesn't that belong to Signor Savelli? He flies on the Berlin-to-Rome service. But look at the terrible state it's in.'

'But it has *wings*,' Jean said. She felt excitement bubbling up inside, like a crescendo.

On closer inspection, the wings could be seen for the sorry objects they were, the fabric covering rotten and broken away, while various ribs were broken.

'They could be reconditioned, couldn't they? That shouldn't take too long.'

'But signorina, they belong to Signor Savelli,' said Signor Chiesi, a Castrol agent who had been detailed to help her.

'Well, find Signor Savelli and tell him I want them.'

Signor Chiesi opened his hands in a wide gesture. 'He should be in on the six o'clock run from Berlin. We can ask him.'

This was how Jack Reason and Jean came to dine that evening with Francesco Savelli. Molly had been invited, but declined at the last minute, citing a headache. Savelli was in his fifties, with a wiry body and direct, clever eyes. His grey hair, cut shorter than the fashion, grew in a peak. At once she was drawn to the Italian; there was something magnetic and charged about him. He held her hand as if it were a porcelain object that might fall and break if he let it go. His touch caused a tremble to run through her fingers.

'So, signorina,' he said when they were seated, 'you are already well known for your skills as pilot.'

'I seem to have left them behind me when I set out for Rome.'

'Ah, that was last night. But correct me if I'm wrong, you have flown the fastest time of any woman from London to Rome?' Again he touched her, this time her cheek, just below her still swollen eye. Although she knew how awful she looked, she felt he was seeing beneath her bruises, to how she might appear on a better day.

'That was a year ago. But it doesn't seem very important, after what happened last night,' she replied,

Jack Reason translating rapidly between them. 'Signor, you know what it is that I'm asking for, don't you? Your wings?'

'Ah yes, my wings, little bird. Let's eat first and then we'll talk.' By then, they were seated in the restaurant. He took her left hand in his again, holding it for some moments before turning it palm down on the table. He fingered the diamond circlet of her engagement ring. 'Some fortunate man must think a great deal of you. You're planning to marry?'

'I'm engaged.'

'But the plan is not yet complete?'

If she had not been so drawn towards Savelli, Jean might have laughed, observing the embarrassment this translation was causing Jack. He looked as if he wished himself anywhere else.

'I don't know,' she said. It was as if she were having the conversation with Wakefield again. What was it that was so obvious when her engagement to Edward was mentioned? But she understood that her head might easily be turned by this stranger, full of assurance and a powerful energy, unlike the men who had courted her in the past. She guessed that he was used to seducing women, but that didn't seem to matter. She had experienced sex, but not desire. This was new and disconcerting.

'Perhaps, it's as well,' Savelli said. 'Flying is men's work.'

'Not at all. I don't know how you can say that, signor. Many women fly aeroplanes. Look at Amy Johnson. And Amelia Earhart. What do you make of them?'

He shook his head, amused. 'They all settle down, sooner or later. I expect they'll make babies and old bones.'

'Surely it's possible to do both?'

Savelli shrugged, his hands flung wide in a gesture suggesting a certain regret. 'No, no, Signorina Batten. That's impossible. Now I'm ordering,' he said, as if to distract her from an uncomfortable topic. 'This dinner is a special occasion to celebrate my meeting with you. We're going to have zucchini flowers. You eat zucchini flowers in your country? No. Tonight you will. She needs an education, don't you think, Signor Reason? Artichokes? Yes, we'll have artichokes. These you will enjoy. They are stripped of their leaves and beaten, dipped in boiling oil. Like the early martyrs.'

'I've already heard a bit about martyrs today. Believe me, signor, I'm not one of them.'

'Perhaps not, but you must learn to eat with style if you're to spend time in Rome.'

'Not for long, I hope.' But as she spoke the food was being delivered, the zucchini flowers first, their trumpets crisp and hot, full of the delicate collapsed flavour of mint and ricotta, then later the artichokes, spread on her plate like the petals of a darkening sunflower. He picked up a morsel on his fork and placed it delicately in her mouth. And she said 'Ah', and 'I can't believe this', and when they had drunk some wine it was hard to remember why she was there, or what it was that she wanted from him. Jack Reason and Savelli talked, the former pausing only now and then to explain their conversation. He asked Savelli how he had found Berlin that day, and what he thought about Hitler's latest plans, and whether Mussolini would go along with them. Savelli brushed the questions off. He did not think Il Duce admired Hitler as much as he appeared to on the surface. Besides, Il Duce was concerned with the Ethiopian question.

'You think he'll strike there?'

'You ask many questions, Mr Reason. How should I know what Il Duce is thinking? He and his Black Shirts are in charge. The Ethiopians are savages, there's no doubt about that. Sooner or later he will want to tame the African continent. And your country, signorina, are there black people there?'

'We have a Maori race. They are brown-skinned. I was born among them.'

'You were? Well, that's interesting. I'm not familiar with the British colonies. The Antipodes.'

His eyes rested intently on her, as if he could see right through her. Surely, she would think later, he could not have known the deep ache of longing that had possessed her, a sensation that was entirely new. She felt as if she might yield, although to what force she was not exactly sure. But it was something unfulfilled, a sense of submission and desire. The evening had become like flying, wild and exhilarating. Somewhere out in the night, a gramophone was playing Ethel Waters singing 'Stormy Weather'. Savelli said, 'Some wild strawberries, perhaps. Picked in the woods this morning. With a small jug of freshly squeezed lemon and a dash of sugar.'

'I love strawberries,' she said dreamily.

'Miss Batten,' said Jack Reason, 'I think you're very tired.'

'The wings,' she said. 'What about the wings, signor?'

He touched her hand again, and when she raised her eyes, she observed the regret in his, as if he had come to a decision and was sorry. For himself? For her? She couldn't tell. Perhaps it was the presence of Jack Reason that restrained him. Or he saw how injured she was, and more than a little strange. 'Oh yes, the wings. Well by all means, you may have them reconditioned.'

'Really, that's wonderful. Thank you.' She knew how girlish and breathless she must sound, even as she sensed a certain withdrawal in his manner, a coolness that had descended.

'They're not a gift, signorina. I expect you to pay two-thirds of the cost of repairing them, and return them to me immediately when you get back to England. Within a month. '

'But I plan to fly to Australia. You know that.'

'And I am offering you the opportunity to take your aeroplane back to London. That is all. It is over to you to decide.'

'Mr Reason?' she said, turning to him for advice.

'I think Signor Savelli has made up his mind. A final offer?'

When Savelli nodded, Jean said, 'Very well, signor. I will return your wings when I get to England next week.'

She tasted sour anger at the back of her throat, the taste of disappointment.

After that evening, Molly was kinder, as if she had accepted the presence of her house guest. Jean guessed that Jack had told her what had happened. Back at the apartment, Jean had gone straight to bed and slept for twelve hours. When she woke up she couldn't remember a single dream. Molly brought the English newspapers for her to read, her manner gentle. 'You'll see these soon enough,' she said, 'you might as well now.' The headlines shouted Jean's disgrace: *BATTEN GIRL DIVE BOMBS ROME, WHY DOES SHE KEEP DOING IT? BATTEN CRASHES AGAIN*. The articles all had a similar tone, implying that she was too inexperienced to attempt the long flight to Australia, and why bother when Amy Johnson had already done it in such style? Although it was not spelled out in so many words, there was another question: Who does she think she is?

There were telegrams, too. One, from Edward, said: *Come home at once. Leave plane behind*. In another, Nellie wrote that there would be another time, and they must think of a new plan. Yet another was from Frank: *See you are in Rome. Must be in the money. Send what you owe, or else*. She felt a shudder of revulsion and tore the cable into little pieces, as if the yellow paper would contaminate her.

Molly looked at her curiously. 'Not bad news, I hope.'

When Jean didn't reply, Molly said, 'Why don't we go and look at some of the sights? There must be places you'd like to see.'

'The place I'd most like to see,' Jean replied, 'is the field where I was forced to land.'

Molly shook her head in disapproval at first, but then she said, 'Well, why not? I expect if it were me I'd want to see what happened, too.'

They set out for the St Paul wireless station, the grassy field surrounded by six masts, each one a hundred and fifty feet tall. There were also numerous high-tension wires overhead that the Moth had glided above, unseen by Jean. She stood and looked at them for a long while, and at the mosquito-ridden marshes through which she had staggered to safety. The area had been drained to make poor farming land, now inhabited by poverty-stricken labourers living in shacks.

'Enough?' Molly asked. 'I think you need to see the rest of Rome.'

She drove them at erratic speeds in her battered Vauxhall. It wasn't so much that it was old, but that 'things kept bumping into it', as Molly put it and they both found themselves laughing. They began to eat at restaurants together. Jean bought bunches of lavender to fill the vases in the apartment, and an air of festivity began to overtake them. Molly, Jean realised, was one of those service wives who went where their husbands were told, with no option but to follow them and make the best of things. The Reasons had two children in English boarding schools. Molly spoke of them with quiet longing.

Often Jean walked alone through Trastevere or to the markets at Campo de' Fiori, inhaling thyme, and rosemary, the bundled masses of sweet basil, or climbed the Spanish Steps, banked with massed azaleas. The mist from a hundred fountains brushed her face, reminding her of the lakes of her childhood, their surfaces ruffled by breezes at evening, or of sunny days swimming with her brothers. With her father, too, supine on a rock, droplets of water still clinging to the hairy pelt of his chest as he dried off in the sun. One evening she came at dusk upon the statue of Marcus Aurelius, the bronze horseman looming against the background of the Palazzo del Senatore, and was moved to sudden tears by its detail, its poised splendour, the way the light played on its surface, the green stipple that spoke of great age.

As she walked, she wondered if she might find Francesco Savelli out strolling, but she didn't see him again, and nor was he at the hangar when she went on her daily excursions to inspect the progress of the repairs to the Moth. All the same, she understood that the Roman education he had begun the night they dined together was unfolding before her day by day, and she believed that if he could see her he would approve. Had she met Savelli, she knew she would have been drawn to him again.

At the same time, she seethed at his dismissal of women aviators, and the hard bargain he had struck, believing that he was ending her ambition to fly across the world. He had succeeded in raising doubts in her own mind about whether she could carry on, and she didn't thank him for that. Or did she? It was possible that, here in Rome, he knew she must face this crisis, the challenge thrown before her.

Most evenings, she returned to the apartment in time to stand at the window, and look across the rooftops as she had on the first night. Each evening, the woman she had seen at the window still sat reading or, once, sewing perhaps, for the movements of her hands were different. She did not raise her head, or acknowledge Jean, but each time her presence reminded Jean afresh of her mother.

Edward had cabled that there were no wings available in England either, as her model of the Gipsy Moth was obsolete. As it was, here in Rome, it would take weeks to build new ones.

One evening, towards the end of the week, the sky had a dark indigo quality, then paler bands of blue, colours such as she had seen in the Mediterranean — a paler scarf of light, like white surf, and beneath, at the edge of the earth's curve, the glow of the setting sun. Against this rose a huge cloud of birds, a murmuration of starlings, thousands, perhaps millions of them, flying in perfect harmony with each other, expanding and contracting into different formations, becoming so dense that they blotted out the last of the dusk light. Jean had heard of these birds, but this was the first time they had performed their aerial display for her. She felt her spirits lift, as if something had been released in her, watching their matchless flight, the birds wheeling through the infinite air. For an instant she saw herself again in the sky.

As she watched, she saw a movement in the far window. The woman had been watching the birds, too. She turned towards Jean, raised her hand in greeting.

The salutation was brief, so that for a moment Jean wondered if she had imagined it. Before she had time to respond, the woman had resumed her position, as if nothing had taken place between them.

On the morning of 6 May, Jean sent a cable to Edward. *Returning today. Must borrow lower wings from your plane.*

Part Two
Flight

1934–1937

Chapter 23

8 May 1934. Tuesday morning. Seven a.m.

Jean flew to Lympne for clearance once again to fly to Australia. At Brooklands she had collected the wings from Edward Walter's Gipsy Moth, and had them attached to her plane. She arranged for the return of those belonging to Francesco Savelli.

Edward had argued with her. 'I beg you,' he said, 'please don't do this crazy thing. Look at you, you've barely recovered from your accident. You've been here less than forty-eight hours. Stay here. Marry me. We can have a happy life together.'

Jean had turned to her mother. 'Do you think Ted's right?'

Nellie had taken a deep breath. 'I think it's for you to decide.'

'Are you sure, Mother? You're the only person in the world who could stop me from going.'

Edward had barely been able to disguise his anger.

'I've told you, you must decide whether you've got the strength for it.'

'That's it then. I'm leaving for Australia.' She had known that if she faltered for another moment, she was lost.

Again she kissed her mother, and climbed into the cockpit. Overnight, Edward's anger had abated. He borrowed a plane from a friend at Brooklands, his own now out of service, with the wings firmly attached to Jean's plane, and flew to Lympne with her. When the Customs formalities were cleared, he took off again, and flew for part of the way across the English Channel with Jean. She knew how much he disliked flying over water, and sent him a blessing of thanks. He signalled farewell, and she was on her own again.

At Rome, the ground staff were astonished to see her back so soon. As she left the city at daybreak the following morning she passed near the St Paul wireless station where she had so nearly lost her life. Already that terrible night seemed like a dream.

So she flew on. From Naples and back to Athens in a gale. From Cyprus to Beirut, and over the Sea of Galilee, in terrible heat and a dust haze. She flew a shorter route this time, going by way of Damascus. She thought again of her brother Harold as she passed over Babylon and felt an ache of sorrow for him.

She landed at the Iraqi town of Fort Rutbah, after following tracks over the desert. On 16 May she flew from Karachi to the Indian city of Bamrauli, landing at Allahabad airport, a day's run of 932 miles. She had now flown further than on any of her previous attempts. Even at 6.45 the following morning the heat was intense as she crossed the Ganges, pumping petrol with sweat pouring from her like water. *Wish I had automatic petrol pump,* she wrote in her logbook. Later that morning, the oil union worked loose and oil sprayed all over the side of the plane, forcing her to land at Calcutta, with only three quarts of oil left.

On 17 May, three air force planes escorted her for twenty minutes, as she rose to an early dawn start. When they left her, the loneliness she had experienced on earlier flights came flooding back. *Lonely now,* she jotted in the log, as if writing it and declaring it to herself would make it go away. Its darkness reminded her of the caves, and the time she had spent with her brother there, the black intensity of the underground space, prickled with the light of the glow worms. She thought then of Kitty, whom she had met on that trip to the north, passing her days alone. Was this what might lie ahead of her, somewhere beyond this empty sky, in this tiny fragile machine?

To distract herself, she ate her lunch, although it was still only breakfast time.

Malaya lay below, rubber plantations and dense green jungle stretching for many miles, before she put down at Singapore. At the Royal Air Force aerodrome, all the station's officers were assembled to meet her, dressed in spotless tropical kit. Her flying suit was stained with oil. 'I'm a sorry sight,' she said, as she climbed down from the cockpit. There were now several adjustments and repairs to be made to the plane. As if in anticipation of these needs, a team of mechanics appeared and the plane was wheeled away.

A group captain and his wife offered her a bed for the

night. Within an hour she appeared in the officers' mess, immaculate in her white silk dress, a glass of champagne in her hand. A maid had whisked her flying suit away to be washed ready for the morning.

When she got up, it was too damp for her to wear. 'How about a pair of my husband's white sports trousers?' the group captain's wife suggested. To this was added a white shirt. Jean wore this outfit on the next leg of her journey, as far as Batavia, the trousers held up with a big safety pin, covered by her raincoat. 'Pretty dashing,' she said, admiring herself in a mirror before setting off.

Flocks of parrots rose from the trees, like large red and green clouds, their plumage flashing in the sun, alligators and crocodiles basking on mudflats. At 8 a.m. on 20 May she crossed the equator. She was back in the Southern Hemisphere. The possibility of success began to seem within her grasp.

From Batavia to Rambang in a storm. From Rambang through hail, then sweltering heat, through a cloud of volcanic ash from the Ender volcano, towering red-hot and dangerous, causing her to veer off-course, until she righted her direction and came to the island of Timor.

She feared she would never see land as she feverishly wrote in her logbook on 23 May:

> *6 a.m. From Kupang on Timor Island on the last hop to Australia*
> *8.30 a.m. Revs 1821, oil 40 lbs, height 600 ft*

9.30 Engine running smoothly — sun shining sea choppy
10.30 Winds seem to have dropped sea calm
11.00 Wish time would pass more quickly
11.10 Hot work pumping petrol by hand —
11.15 Should see land soon now

She trusted her navigation. As a gardener who knew how to prune roses, or a chef who could make a perfect soufflé, she knew how to find her way, whether in sight of land or not. Now was no time to doubt herself. Her fuel was running dangerously low. Even if she were flying in the right direction, would there be enough to get her to her destination? She remembered, with a start, that she hadn't allowed for a deviation error in her compass, caused by the massed metal in her long-range tanks. She compensated by altering the compass seven degrees, even though she was out of sight of land. A rising panic threatened to overwhelm her.

11.30 Headwind must have increased have pumped all petrol through to top tank

She tried to steady her breath. It occurred to her that perhaps she had missed Australia altogether. There was no way back now. Besides, it seemed almost preferable to die than to fail a third time. Her lunch-box had been packed with roast chicken drumsticks and sliced mango.

A Thermos of coffee had grown tepid. She jotted again in the logbook strapped to her knee:

12.00 pm Having lunch must see land soon

The food helped to calm her but now she felt a terrible weariness seeping into her bones.

12.20 No land in sight yet
12.30 Should have seen land by now wonder if petrol will last out

And then, there on the far horizon, she saw a small dark cloud, and the weather was still perfect, so she knew that it must be Australia, and as she flew nearer, the country's red dust and the smoke of fires rose before her.

12.45 HURRAH LAND hurrah must be about 30 miles away
1.15 About 20 miles south of Darwin will have slight following wind up coast
1.30 Landing DARWIN

She remembered later, thinking of the moment as she taxied across the airfield towards a waiting crowd, that despite having flown over some of the most ancient and beautiful cities of the world, none had been as magical as this little township, surrounded by angry bush fires. She had broken the existing solo record for women by four and a half days. Her legs trembled as she climbed out of the cockpit. In the distance she saw reporters running towards her. Hands reached out to grab her, hold onto her, touch the miracle of what she had done. The locals wore pith helmets and threw them in the air. A Fox Movietone camera was trained on her, watching her every move.

An official party now made its way across the runway. The first person to greet her was Captain Bird, the Castrol representative, who had arrived just a few minutes earlier in a plane that was to escort her across the Australian outback to Sydney.

In the morning, she received telegrams. As she opened each one, she understood more clearly what she had achieved. The first one was from Lord Wakefield:

> *Warmest congratulations upon your splendid achievement Stop Your courage and perseverance have won for you a well deserved success. Wakefield of Hythe.*

And then the telegram deliveryman handed her one that made his hands shake.

> *Please convey to Miss Batten the congratulations of the Queen and myself on her wonderful flight. George R. I.*

There were more of the great sheaves of yellow cables with their capital letters — from the Governor-General and the Prime Minister of New Zealand, and the Prime Minister of Australia.

And there was this, from Fernhurst in England:

> *Warmest Congratulations was sure you would do it.*
> *Amy Mollison*

A heart more generous than her own, Jean thought. All she had wanted was to beat Amy's record, and now she felt almost a moment of guilt, her success so overwhelming that she guessed no woman would catch her now. As the newspapers arrived with their enormous headlines proclaiming her success, Jean prepared herself for the reception that awaited her on the other side of the continent.

As she came into Sydney a week later, sixteen planes flew out in formation to meet her. To the right of her Moth, she saw Smithy's *Southern Cross*, filled with waving passengers. The roofs of buildings were crowded, the roads jammed with cars as people tried to reach Mascot aerodrome and join the tumultuous throngs waiting to see her arrive.

She stepped down from the plane, wearing her white helmet and white flying suit, and made her first public speech.

The Wakefield agent discreetly slipped her an envelope. It contained a cheque for one thousand pounds.

In the evening a huge reception had been arranged in the Sydney Town Hall. Jean knew that people liked her in white, the way she dazzled in a crowd. She chose a white lace gown, a short white fur coat and silver shoes, carefully inspecting herself in the mirror of the handsome hotel where she was staying. When she walked through the foyer, she reminded herself of the way Madame Valeska had taught her dancers to carry themselves, with a graceful flick of their hair, chins level, as if they might be going to rise on their toes at any moment, light on their feet. It made heads turn. At the town hall a red carpet had been rolled out for her to walk down, and all along it were women in beautiful dresses, their perfume heavy on the air, and stout men in their straining black evening jackets, like a herd of cattle waiting to charge. Cameras flashed in her face. She kept on walking, smiling, touching a hand reached out to her here and there. It was only a matter of weeks since she had walked the streets of Rome, her face bruised and swollen, seeking parts for her plane, and now here she was, in the hot Sydney night, fêted by the rich and famous, and the Lord Mayor of the city.

Charlie Ulm was there, giving her a hard time for being more famous than him. 'Who am I?' he wailed. 'Just some joker making way for *la belle dame*.'

'Oh go and palely loiter,' she said, laughing at him. 'Do we need Keats tonight?' The banquet laid out for the guests had been cleared away and they were dancing, his hand reassuringly firm and surprisingly cool, resting in the hollow of her back.

'And you want to know something,' he said, 'I just love it that you've made it, kid. I'll never forget the day you turned up demanding to hitch a ride with Smithy.'

Then they were hurried away to do a live broadcast together, to thirty Australian radio stations, plus all the English and New Zealand stations, in what someone said was the largest broadcast ever organised from Sydney. Later there was a shortwave broadcast to the United States.

She told herself, I'm living in a dream. But it's a dream of my own making.

In London, Nellie had gone into hiding from the hordes of reporters pounding at her door. She kept a rolled wad of notes inside her brassiere, waiting for a moment when she could escape and book a passage home.

In New Zealand, Fred Batten was coming to terms with being the father of a star. With some hesitation, he was telling the newspapers how proud he was of his daughter.

Chapter 24

It astonished Jean how easily she could hold people's attention when she spoke. There would be a great murmur of anticipation. Then she would walk onto a stage and the silence was sudden and immense. When she recounted her adventures, the three attempts on the record, the obstacles to overcome, and the loneliness — yes, sometimes she touched on that, too — there was nothing but a rapturous stillness that ended only as she finished speaking, rent by a vast roar of approval.

There were moments when the loneliness came back. It caught her when she least expected it, in beautiful hotels, where a maid had come in and turned back the bed covers and placed a flower or a chocolate on the silk sheet. This was where she would curl up by herself, with nobody to call out to in the night. Or she would walk into a tiled shining bathroom, the brass taps gleaming, and catch sight of herself in the mirror — the flawless make-up, the perfectly arranged hair, the dress that might be a gift from an admirer (some urged her to go into the best shops and 'choose yourself something nice, and the bill will be paid') — and not recognise the person she saw. She would ask herself what she was doing alone with this woman. Who was she? Charlie Ulm's question, though made in jest, had touched a raw nerve. There were days when she was so exhausted that she wondered how she would get up in the mornings.

She felt this loneliness again when the newspapers ran a story about the aircraft wings she had borrowed from her fiancé, Mr Edward Walter. *FLOWN ON THE WINGS OF LOVE*. Edward had sent her a furious telegram demanding why she had spread their private business around. She had thought he would be proud. After all, their engagement had been announced.

Boarding the *Aorangi* and leaving Sydney for Auckland had been a relief. As it turned out, Charlie was travelling to New Zealand on business. He was setting up a commercial postal air service between the two countries, and was going to some meetings.

They had time now to talk about what they did and why. His hero, he said, was the aviator turned writer, Antoine de Saint-Exupéry. It was the French in him, he supposed, but he loved everything he wrote. Jean must read *Night Flight*, a novel about an impossible flight made in Patagonia. The main character, Fabien, flies for the Patagonia Mail Service. His boss wants him to fly in a thunderstorm, then he never comes back, and Fabien's ghost will haunt him forever. But, Charlie pointed out, Fabien has the choice to turn back and he doesn't. The story would break her heart, but it might also explain to her why she found it so hard to resist the temptation of danger, why she'd become a slave to it. ' "Even though human life may be the most precious thing on earth, we always behave as if there were something of higher value than human life",' Charlie quoted. 'That's from the book.'

'Do you believe that?' she asked.

'I suppose I must.'

They were sitting on deck chairs, gulls wheeling past, when he told her this, although it was the end of June and they huddled in their coats to keep out the cold. New Zealand would be upon them the next day. Charlie had come across her in one of the saloons, writing in her journal. This was something she had taken up since her arrival in Australia, in spare moments in hotel rooms — an account of her journeys, the three attempts to reach Australia. Writing it had helped her put together notes for the speeches she had been asked to give. Charlie wanted fresh air, he said, somewhere where they could smoke without old biddies waving their hands in front of their faces and sniffing. They were both smoking Camels.

'I shouldn't,' said Jean. 'You're leading me astray.'

'Tobacco's a dirty weed. I like it. It satisfies no normal need. I like it.'

'You talk rubbish.'

'It's a poem,' he said. 'Honestly. "It makes you thin, it makes you lean, it takes the hair right off your bean." Haven't you heard that one?'

He turned serious again. Although he was full of quips and flirtatious banter, he saw how she was often troubled. He had had these moments, too, he told her, moments when he didn't believe in himself, when he'd been judged.

The Coffee Royal scandal had altered things, changed how he felt when he saw admiring crowds. They could turn on you in the blink of an eye. And, in a way, it had changed his friendship with Smithy. It was hard not to go back to that dreadful year of the inquiry, the things that were said of them.

His first marriage had ended abruptly. He had married at the end of the war, he explained, when he was just twenty-one. The failed marriage had caused his wife more distress than it did him, because he had a life to go on with, the famous aviator with a career, while she was condemned to the status of the divorced woman. So there was that, too. 'I couldn't have stayed alive in that marriage,' he said. 'But I did that to her and it stays with me still.' He had remarried and was happy enough. He and his new wife had custody of his son, his only child, from his first marriage.

'Divorce is hard on women. I do know that,' Jean said.

'I can't dwell on it any longer,' he said. 'It happened and it's past.'

'But you do,' she persisted. 'You've just told me about it. My mother feels like an outcast. Not that my parents are divorced.'

'Do you ever wish they were? Wouldn't you like your mother to get married again?'

Jean looked at him in astonishment. 'My mother remarry? I don't think so.'

'She has you?'

'There's nothing wrong with that, is there?'

He pulled a hungry lungful of smoke and blew it into the sea air. 'What about you? You're getting married?'

'I suppose so.' She sighed.

'Hey, don't pull such a long face.' He reached out his hand and held hers briefly. 'You do know you're gorgeous.'

'You keep telling me that, Charlie. You're the nicest man I know.'

There was something about Charlie that reminded her of Savelli, with his European charm, and his nearness. When she thought about Edward, she felt none of this. Nor had she, really, with Victor, who had become a shadowy figure, someone she could no longer visualise. As for Frank Norton, she tried hard to shut out the memory of what she had done with him. That had nothing to do with how she had felt in Rome, and now, here, on board this ship with Charles Ulm. She felt herself trembling.

'Nice. That's hardly a compliment,' he said. 'I'm a little bit in love with you, you know.'

'Yes,' she said. 'I do. But we like each other too much to spoil things, don't we?'

'That's very grown up of you, Miss Batten. But yes, you're right, of course.'

Their conversation turned back to aviation, to Jean's wish to fly all the way to New Zealand some day, his to open up air routes across the Pacific. In the evening, at the last-night party, they danced close together. Jean put her arms around his neck. He lifted two glasses of champagne from a tray carried by a passing waiter.

'See you in the soup, old thing,' she said, laughing as

they drew apart and toasted each other. 'I need my beauty sleep.'

Jean had been assigned a stateroom cabin. Before she climbed into bed, she took some of the *Aorangi*'s headed notepaper and wrote a letter.

> *Dear Viscount Wakefield*
>
> *In the morning, I will be arriving in my homeland, New Zealand. Now is the moment when I must thank you again for all you have done for me. None of my present success would have been possible were it not for your help. And I was overcome by the generosity of your handsome gift of one thousand pounds upon my arrival in Australia. I will confess to you now that I was hundreds of pounds in debt when I got to Sydney. You will understand how much your generosity really means to me. When I return to London, I hope I may call in and thank you again in person.*

In the night the wind came up and the ship pitched and rolled as it made its way down the coast. When Jean heard knocking she thought at first it was a rope come loose somewhere on the ship, but it was someone tapping on the door. Charlie stood there with a bottle of champagne in his hand.

'I knew you wouldn't be throwing up. The bar's a mess. *Mon Dieu*, some people have no stomach at all. I thought you might like a drop.'

'Charlie, no,' she said.

'You want me to go?'

She shook her head and held out her hand.

Towards dawn she slept for a time, her body languid and at ease with itself. He woke her gently, and pointed out the porthole beside the pillow. The ship was sailing into the harbour, surrounded by boats decked with streamers and bunting. Aeroplanes flew overhead. On the quay crowds of people stood waving and cheering.

'What's it about?'

'I think it's about you, love,' he said. 'You should get dressed and go out onto the deck.'

'Have we missed breakfast?'

'I'll order some for you. You can have it when the ship's berthed; it'll take a while for people to disembark.'

'Will you come back and have some with me?' She grabbed his hand.

'If you like.'

'Order me a big juicy steak.'

'Little savage.'

'Plus two eggs, sunny side up.' That was her brother John's saying, she remembered with a sudden pang, gathered in his Hollywood studio days.

'Let go of me,' Charlie said. 'I need to go to my cabin and change. Make sure Miss Batten keeps her reputation intact.' He slid his hand out of hers and seized both her wrists, holding them briefly behind her. *'Je t'aime*. We can still be friends, *oui?*'

'Friends? Is that all?'

'I have a son, remember? And a wife who deserves better than me.'

'I think she's lucky.'

'Jean, look at me: you'll find somebody soon.'

'A tall, dark stranger?'

'I don't know what he'll look like, but you'll know, and you'll be happy. Now then?'

'Yes,' she said, 'friends. My best friend.'

When she appeared on the deck, a huge cheer went up. She had dressed in a pale blue woollen suit, with a grey mink fur stole around her shoulders, and a cloche hat, so that people could see her face. For a few minutes she stood and waved. It was cold out there, and impossible to distinguish anyone among the crowd. After a time she went back inside.

Her breakfast was waiting. Charlie stood beside the table, tapping his finger and looking anxious.

'Where's yours?' she asked, seeing the place laid for one.

'Your father's looking for you. The captain brought him and your brother aboard. I'm going now. Just eat your breakfast and try not to be afraid. Promise?'

'Promise.'

She watched him disappear, pushing his mop of hair back with one hand, before turning and blowing her a kiss. Then he was gone.

Within a few minutes, Fred and Harold appeared. Her brother had travelled down by train. 'We've been looking all over the place for you,' Fred complained. 'We couldn't find you anywhere.' Neither man had changed much — it was still an effort for Fred to do up his coat buttons — but Harold had had his hair trimmed and slicked back for the occasion, and wore a crumpled white shirt beneath his jacket and an uncharacteristic tie, albeit skewed. He seemed curiously shy to see her.

'How are Alma and the kids?' she asked.

'They're good. Good as gold. The kids did some drawings for you.' He held out an envelope.

'That's lovely, Harold. Tell them thank you.'

'They're waiting for you to come out and wave,' Fred said. 'When you've finished feeding your face.'

'I was hungry. I can get you something to eat if you like.' She knew she looked odd, sitting alone in the stateroom at the long, solitary table, dressed in her suit and furs.

'They've been waiting in the cold for hours,' Fred said. 'There're little children out there. Half of them don't have coats.'

That was the note they started on, bad-tempered from the start, although her father was right. There were throngs of people, women shivering in cardigans, children barefoot, men with cigarettes clamped between their lips. But they wanted to see her. There were banners with her name held aloft, and small bunches of flowers being thrust at her, which she couldn't take because of the huge bouquet that had now been placed in her arms. A brass band was playing, and coming along the street a pipe band was setting up in opposition. 'It's just like when the Duchess of York visited,' someone said. Jean was afraid the woman might drop a curtsey.

'I'll see you later,' she called to Fred and Harold.

A car and chauffeur were waiting to drive her to the Grand Hotel, although the car had to stop often because of the crush of people.

As they drove away, Jean's Gipsy Moth G-AARB was unloaded from the ship, ready to be reassembled. Later that day there would be a civic reception. She had lost sight of her father and brother. By the time she saw Fred again, Harold had left for home.

There would be more receptions. Jean would stay in splendour at Government House in Wellington. The Prime Minister, George Forbes, would address the nation, and announce a gift of five hundred pounds to Miss Batten.

In a few days, Nellie would arrive from England

Chapter 25

Among the hundreds of letters awaiting her at the hotel was an angry one from Edward in the same vein as his telegram:

> *I feel that I am part of a travelling circus. Can you imagine what it's like on the floor of the Stock Exchange with one's colleagues looking sideways at me? Our engagement has been announced, surely that was enough? The wings of love, indeed. Marriage is a private affair. I have no idea what you will say next to the press. If you are going to be one of these famous people, you should think carefully what you say, because others are always involved.*

She didn't understand this reaction, although she had an idea that the wings from Savelli had caused Edward some discomfort. As if he doubted the manner in which she had obtained them, perhaps. Or it might simply have been that, now that her fame had spread, reporters had turned up at his untidy bachelor's flat, looking for clues about their lives. The distance between them seemed immeasurable. She longed to end things with Edward immediately, but Charles Ulm would hardly thank her if she did. It wouldn't do for him to think that one illicit night could claim her heart. She determined to put Charlie from her mind, and settle to being in love with Edward. Besides, the newspapers in Auckland were full of their engagement: *OUR JEAN TO BE MARRIED.* The tone of her reply was conciliatory. *Darling, I will settle down. So much work to be done here, and I must see all the people who are expecting me. I will be paid for my lectures, and that will be useful when we are married. You don't want a little wife who is always asking for pocket money, now do you?*

The rest of her mail was being answered by a secretary, offered her by the government. She sat and dictated letter after letter. Yes to that invitation, and that one and that. In all she would make nearly one hundred and fifty speeches, flying herself from place to place.

One of the fuel tanks was taken out of G-AARB, so that Nellie, arrived from London, could fly with her from time to time, although mostly she found it too cold. In Auckland, she and Fred had resumed talking. 'I suppose he thinks we're rich now,' she commented to Jean, but at least they weren't at war with each other.

An air force Moth was to accompany Jean around the country on a tour that would take six weeks. The first flight would take them to Blenheim, a good aerodrome to start from, with clear signals. And the Marlborough Aero Club's first Moth had been presented to it by Viscount Wakefield. Before she left, she was made a life member of the club.

Sheep roamed free on most of the aerodromes and it was important to phone ahead so that they could be cleared from the landing strip. Bach's 'Sheep May Safely Graze' might well be her theme song, she thought, humming it to herself while she circled various airports as the last stray lamb was shooed away.

In Invercargill, Nellie's birthplace, six planes escorted her in over the town, Jean's silver plane in the centre, red and yellow machines on either side, swooping over the green pasture, spread at the foot of the mountains, as they approached the town. People stood on roofs to get a better view. When the speeches were over, and there were many, she said, 'Please, now show me the Theatre Royal.' She stood in front of the old building and imagined Nellie, as a girl, playing the Fairy Queen. Then she turned and looked at the town, with the ornate water tower looming at its heart, and saw Nellie, in a pair of bloomers, flying along the wide streets on a bicycle. It made her laugh out loud. 'My mother,' she said, 'was a bit of a character when she lived here.' She supposed that a part of her own self, her identity, had begun here, with the wild tomboyish mother who had had dreams of her own and was now living them through her. It didn't bear dwelling on too much.

There were several buildings like the Theatre Royal, with balconies and colonnades and decorated ceilings, scattered through the country, in small towns that were often no more than specks on open plains. When she arrived, they were decorated with flowers and bunting in her honour. People paid one and sixpence a head to hear her speak, and the queues stretched outside the venues, just as they had for Pavlova. Jean gave speeches to aero clubs and women's sports clubs, visited schools and hospitals. Where there were no aerodromes, she landed at the nearest airport and drove herself to and from more distant venues, day and night. When she got back to her hotel room, she spent a few minutes recording her impressions in her journal. She feared if she didn't write everything down she would forget it all: the deserts, the camels, the wild rides over lonely seas, and now the long spines of land that made up her own country. New Zealand was like another universe, and sometimes it frightened her. In Hokitika, a man in the audience yelled, 'What about the workers? None of us got five hundred pounds. Who do you think you *are*?'

'Come and see me and I'll buy you a pint afterwards,' she shot back. She would have, too, but the mayor had a banquet arranged in the hotel.

And at Westport, miners' territory, she saw women wearing dresses made out of flour sacks, and children dressed in sugar bags. She wanted to explain that she had lived on sixpenny steak and onion pies in London, if she was lucky, that she knew what it was like to go to bed with nothing but a cup of tea for dinner, but it seemed like an exercise in futility. She made a donation at the maternity hospital 'For the welfare of the mothers'.

Wanganui, sheep grazing. Hawera, weather report available from the postmaster, prevailing winds westerly, more sheep grazing, a Maori haka of welcome. New Plymouth, gales frequent from the south-east, the prediction true enough as the storm threw the plane up and down in violent gusts of wind.

Late one night, driving by road to Paeroa, she came across a stranded motorist, a middle-aged man hunched over the bonnet of his car, torch in hand.

'You all right, sir?' she called.

'Bloody oath I'm not — it's as cold as a frog's tit out here.'

She got out of her car, walked over and peered into his engine. After tweaking a wire, she told him to turn the motor over. It spluttered uneasily.

'Give me the crank handle.'

'Who the hell are you?'

'Never mind. Just pass it over.'

She cranked a couple of times and the car roared to life. As she got back into her car, the moon came out from behind a cloud. 'You're not …? Strewth, you're *her*,' he said. 'You're Jean Batten, aren't you?'

But she had gone, and the clouds moved back over the moon.

In the morning she was due to go to Rotorua but a surge of tiredness overwhelmed her. Suddenly it was too much, and the idea of speaking and being welcomed again was more than she could bear. She rang Nellie in Auckland.

'I'm going to fly back up and rest. Never mind Rotorua,' she said.

'Darling, you have to go, there's a huge welcome laid on for you there. Guide Bella Papakura is going to meet you and take you onto the marae. It's a huge honour.'

'I thought you didn't go to the meeting houses in Rotorua,' Jean said.

There was a silence down the phone. 'You've done so well, my darling,' Nellie said after a moment. 'I think this is something you should try to do.' Jean noted a dangerous edge to her mother's voice. They were coming close to a quarrel. 'For my sake,' Nellie said, 'I'd like our family to be honoured in that town.'

'All right then,' Jean said. 'All right, Mother.' For an instant she saw a small girl crouched in a hallway, while her parents tore each other apart.

'Jean, don't fly when you're like this,' Nellie said 'You can catch a train down from where you are. I've checked it out.'

Jean booked a first-class carriage, hoping to be alone, but a woman in a brown tweed suit, accompanied by a child, was already ensconced. 'Good morning,' the woman chirped, expectancy gleaming in her eyes.

Jean inclined her head and turned away. Later, as they alighted from the train, the child said, 'Who is that woman?'

'Oh her,' the mother said. 'That's Jean Batten. She flies aeroplanes.' Her face was cold.

Jean wanted to say, I don't have to talk to everyone, I have to stop, I have to leave you all behind sometimes.

But she could see it wouldn't do. The woman wouldn't have understood.

By this time heavy rain was drenching the town. Jean was driven to the elegant new Blue Baths tearooms, faintly Mediterranean, in the Government Gardens. There she ate tiny cakes and cucumber sandwiches and tried to remember her walks through the park. Only the sulphuric smell of the earth's gases was familiar. The rest was a cloud as dark as the sky outside. The house where she had lived with her parents had been demolished.

'I've been looking at all the things I'm expected to remember, but I'm sorry to say that I don't,' she said in response to the civic welcome that awaited her. She felt ungracious and bad-tempered and shook herself, trying to be the Jean Batten the crowd was expecting. The woman in the train had cast a pall over her.

She was greeted by Mita Taupopoki, the most famous chief in the district, held in high regard not just in New Zealand, but overseas as well. She was aware of the honour being accorded her. Taupopoki, wearing a kiwi-feather cloak and a taniko-bordered headband, chose to welcome her in Maori, while Bella Papakura translated. The famous guide was wearing a small hat, not unlike Jean's, with a feather in it; her cloak was finely woven from flax.

'You coming here reminds me of Sir Charles Kingsford Smith,' Guide Bella said. 'He came here and I greeted him. Do you know him?'

'He's my friend,' Jean replied. Some warmth started to

return, as if she had lost blood during the day, and was recovering.

Taupopoki began to speak. 'I knew your father,' he said. 'I never thought that one day I would be welcoming his little daughter to our marae, as the great jewel of the Pacific. You have come here in your flying waka through the skies. Your courage is our treasure, our taonga. In return, we have a gift for you.'

The gift, an ancient greenstone tiki, was placed around her neck. In her reply, she paid tribute to the Polynesian navigators who had guided their waka through the water to New Zealand. The words came easily to her, and she felt a stirring within herself, some chord of belonging. Late at night, when she returned to the Prince's Gate Hotel, a flautist, a pianist and a violinist were playing near the fire in the lounge. She closed her eyes, and saw her father, young, a touch flamboyant, entertaining the guests twenty years earlier.

In the morning, the mayor brought a horse to the door of the hotel, and invited her to mount it and recreate Nellie's journeys through the town. Jean and a group of riders set off towards the lake, just along the road. The rain from the previous day had cleared, and the water lay pale grey and mauve before her. Black swans glided past. She saw it all then. The lake in the summer and the water closing over her head, the sun dazzling her eyes as her father plucked her back, holding her above his head and laughing, the family walks, the nights when they sat in the baths together, all their skins touching. The day when the swans came after her. Harold. John, who was her best friend, and now seemed lost to her. The leaving. Always, the leaving.

She was ready to go, too. The country had begun to fill her with melancholy. Back in Auckland, a visit to Madame Valeska's studio had returned her to a world where she no longer belonged. Valeska told her that Freda Stark was performing in the chorus at His Majesty's Theatre in an opera called *Duchess of Danitz*. 'Her girlfriend's the star — you could get to see her,' Valeska said. 'Thelma Trott, they're a big number.'

'Her girlfriend? Oh, Freda's a good friend to have,' Jean said. 'She was good to me.'

'Not that sort of girlfriend, darling. Freda's in love. And Thelma's husband Eric Mareo is the conductor of the orchestra.'

'I think I'll leave it,' Jean said, nonplussed. 'I'm glad she's all right. If you see her, send love from me.' Afterwards, she wondered if that had been the right thing to say.

An invitation arrived from a Sydney publisher, asking if she would write an account of her three attempts at the record.

'Me, a writer?' she said to Nellie.

'You could do it, darling.'

'Something to do when I'm an old lady, perhaps.'

'You'll have forgotten by then.'

'Well, I've kept all these journals. I suppose I could turn them into something,' Jean said. 'I'd need to get away somewhere quiet.' Her determination to leave the country was growing.

Something else happened a few nights after her return to the Grand Hotel. She had come down to the dining room, and there, beside the gilt-engraved post boxes in the foyer, stood Frank Norton. She recognised his bulky frame bundled up in a navy raincoat at once, even though his back was to her. For a moment, she wondered if she might slide past him without being seen, but he sensed her presence, and turned. His face was blotchy, and puffier than she remembered it. She let him speak first.

'You know why I'm here,' he said.

'I haven't the faintest idea,' she said. 'It's over, Frank. I told you that long ago.'

'I don't *want* you. Why would I? I'm getting married, Jean, that's what. I need the money I lent you, a fresh start.'

'You had plenty of money the last time I saw you.'

'I didn't. I gave it all to you.'

'Keep your voice down,' she said. 'There're reporters everywhere.'

'Oh, that's important to you, isn't it?'

'Well, you just said you gave me the money. Make up your mind. Remember, you offered it to me.'

'You're twisting it, Jean. I lent you money for the flying lessons.'

'You got what you wanted.' She was aware that they were hissing at each other, and drew him away from reception, through the door into the unoccupied dining room. Serried ranks of silver glittered on the tables beneath the chandeliers. She saw Frank's eyes widen as he remembered perhaps his days of officers' messes and better times.

'You're a little tart if you think you've paid your debts.'

'Perhaps I am,' she said. 'A tart without many choices.'

'Five hundred quid,' he said. 'That's what you owe me.'

'Five hundred. You're crazy.'

'That's what I came out of the air force with.'

'Then think about where you chose to spend it, Frank. Five hundred pounds worth of lessons? No. Do the sums and go away. Now, before I call the porter and have you thrown out.'

He turned on his heel without a word. When he had gone, she took the lift to her room.

'What is it?' Nellie asked. 'You look as if you've seen a ghost.'

'It's nothing,' Jean said. 'I really want to go, Mother. I need to leave New Zealand.' But Jean ended up telling her mother about the encounter with Frank, although there were parts she left out. The information was skilfully extracted the following morning, while Nellie was pouring her second cup of tea.

'Back to London?'

'Not London, not yet. I've been thinking about that book. I just need some quiet place where I can think.' Jean put her fingers to her temples, her face pale and strained. 'The publisher wants it soon. We could find a quiet place in Sydney, darling, you and me, and I'll just dash off a chapter a week and drop it into the publisher. It's pretty much all up here.'

'But what about Edward?'

What about Edward? Since she had left England, the thought of returning to him appealed to her less with every passing day. Edward, with the clutter of machinery in his bedroom, his pedantic manners and expectations of her wifely role, seemed appalling from this distance. Perhaps they could reform one another, but she doubted it.

'I'll write to him and explain,' she said. 'I'll tell him that there are still some opportunities for me here, and I need to take them before I settle down. And I'd like to see the end of the air race — he shouldn't begrudge me that.'

The race she referred to had been a buzz in the air all year, a major celebration of Melbourne's centenary celebrations. It was planned to begin on 20 October from Mildenhall aerodrome in Suffolk. Smithy was one of the great names scheduled to start, and Jim and Amy Mollison, too. Charlie Ulm was in the States, and apparently wasn't planning to take part, although she'd heard nothing from Charlie himself. For that she was grateful.

She would have loved to participate in the race, but she knew that her elderly Moth would be no match for the planes that would be competing. As the money from her lectures had begun to accumulate, a new plan was shaping up in her head. A faster, more modern plane of her own was starting to seem like a real possibility.

'The race isn't until October,' Nellie said. 'Do you think that's really fair?'

'I don't care about fair,' Jean said, coming as near as she might to stamping her foot. 'I don't want to go back to London yet, and I don't want to stay here. What's the matter with Sydney? I thought you liked Australia.'

After a moment of startled silence, Nellie said, 'I can see you're tired and upset.'

'Don't you understand that I need to be left alone?'

'Well, I suppose if you can put Edward's mind at rest, there's no reason why we shouldn't go over to Sydney for a bit.'

They took the next ship out of Auckland, the Gipsy Moth folded and stowed away on board. In Sydney, Jean found them a comfortable enough flat for a modest rent near Kings Cross. It wasn't the best of neighbourhoods, someone remarked, another woman flier she had met on her first arrival from London. 'My mother and I can manage,' Jean replied crisply. She saw no need to recite the list of slums they had inhabited, the nights with furniture pushed against doors. That life was over. What was satisfying about where they lived was the privacy it allowed them. People didn't come to the door while she was closeted away writing.

The words came as quickly and easily as she had predicted, her logbooks and journals filling in gaps and reminding her of the exact locations where her adventures had taken place. She was grateful, as she wrote, for the disciplines of Ladies College, the English prizes she had won, and for the history lessons that gave background to the ancient desert sites. In the mornings she wrote at speed, in the afternoons she walked and swam and turned her face towards the warmth of the sun. Nellie, watching her closely, was relieved to see her looking well again.

Solo Flight came out in September. Jean held her advance copy, opened it and inhaled its new paper smell. The dust jacket bore a picture of her wearing her white helmet and the Gipsy Moth against a blue sky. The hard cover beneath was green and strong. The first reviews in Sydney were warm.

An offer, which she supposed must have come on the strength of her written words, arrived shortly afterwards from the Gaumont British Film Company. She was invited to go to Melbourne and broadcast a commentary on the great race, now officially called the MacRobertson Race, after the sponsor, a confectionery manufacturer. The first prize was ten thousand pounds. Jean's contract was for the ten days the race was expected to last.

That was how she found herself in the thick of it, sitting at a microphone, reading cables and telegrams on the progress of the race, and translating them into broadcast material. It was like being in the race itself, not just a spectator from afar, but a link to countries around the world.

Smithy had withdrawn before the start of the race. In America he had bought a Lockheed Altair he'd named the *Lady Southern Cross*, planning to race, but the plane wasn't ready in time. The Mollisons set a record time to India, but had to pull out near Karachi; a British plane crashed in Italy, killing both pilots. Malcolm MacGregor, whose youthful acrobatics had entertained Auckland when Jean was a child, had entered. He was now a squadron leader in the Royal New Zealand Air Force.

Three days into the race, a de Havilland Comet 88, flown by Charles Scott and Tom Campbell Black, flashed past the winning post. It was a perfect, still day; the sun shone on the plane's bright red wings and fuselage as it landed. The winners had made the flight in under three days, the fastest time ever flown. A hundred thousand people had gathered to watch the first arrivals. Jean clung to the microphone as the crowds jostled her, not losing a beat in her commentary. A day later she would scoop all the other journalists when she captured an exclusive interview with the runners-up, two Dutchmen, by the simple expedient of climbing onto a workbench and handing them a microphone through a hangar window. MacGregor arrived in seven days, coming in fifth.

When it was all over, there was a party, of course: champagne that lasted all night, and dancing, and singing, too. She found herself at a piano and vamping out some tunes, the first time she'd played since that evening at Oakleigh, only now her playing was exuberant, a touch crazy. Everyone seemed more than a little mad, laughing and embracing each other, making risqué jokes at each other's expense, spilling drinks as they threw their arms about in expansive gestures. The sponsor of the de

Havilland Comet aviators came over and suggested she might like to buy herself a little memento to remind herself of the wonderful job she had done over the past ten days.

'Thank you,' she murmured. 'I'd love to do that.'

That night, too, she met Beverley Shepherd, a slim, fair-headed young man, two years younger than her. He was training to be a pilot. His eyes were blue and clear, his body supple, and he danced with a dazzling smoothness. The band was playing 'I'm in the Mood for Love', the year's new hit, and he began to croon it in her ear, and she sang right back to him.

'Can I see you home?' he said. Afterwards he would say, 'I didn't think I'd have the nerve. How did I ever say that?'

'Simply because you were near me,' she said, and laughed.

She fell in love with him. Just like that. Love, elusive, sometimes close, always complicated, had suddenly declared itself. Just as Charlie Ulm had predicted, as if he had known that she was ready for this moment.

At yet another dinner, some days afterwards, the sponsor whispered in her ear, 'So what did you get to put on your mantelpiece?'

'I don't think it will fit on the mantelpiece,' she said, and laughed. 'It's a French evening gown by Patou, blue *mousseline de soie.*'

It seemed like the perfect purchase to celebrate falling in love.

Jean wrote again to Edward, delaying her return to London.

In December, Charles Ulm's plane, the *Stella Australis,* disappeared on a flight between Oakland, California, and Honolulu. Theories abounded, but the most common one was that an unexpected tailwind had caused him and his two crew to fly past the Hawaiian islands in the dark.

Jean wept in private. There was nobody, certainly not Beverley, not even Nellie, to whom she could confide her pain. Charlie's last night flight.

Chapter 26

'You need to stop seeing that young man,' Nellie said. 'You're engaged to be married.'

'Be honest, Mother. I never thought you liked Edward all that much,' Jean said.

'Liking him or not isn't the issue, Jean. You've had enough trouble with men already.'

Here in Sydney, a coolness was descending between them. Jean had stopped wearing her engagement ring when she was with Beverley. She slid it off her finger and put it in a pocket, leaving it there until she got home, but sometimes she forgot to put it back on. Nellie always seemed to see through her.

'If you're not careful, you're going to have people talking about you. I don't blame you for Frank, and certainly not for Victor. But I'm your mother. I can see what the newspapers will make of it if they catch you running around with Beverley Shepherd while you're still engaged. All summer, swimming, driving, boating. You think nobody notices where you spend your time?'

'Nobody knows I go to Bev's house,' Jean said, her face flaming. 'Anyway, his family's there. You could try getting to know them, you might like them.'

But Nellie's warning messages were hard to ignore. 'You'll become restless if you don't fulfil your dreams,' she said, in one of their exchanges. 'I wanted to be an actress, and look what happened to me.'

'You were happy enough married to my father. Until you found him out.' Jean felt like a junior at school rebuking a prefect, but Nellie's enthusiasm for a perfect marriage seemed misplaced. 'Well, weren't you?'

Nellie's tone was bitter. 'He thought emancipation was just for men. I didn't *understand* him.'

'That sounds like the Temple of Higher Thought,' Jean said. 'Surely you're not saying it was your fault?'

'You're not listening. If I'd been born in this century I'd have done it differently. I might not have married at all.'

'And then I'd never have been born.'

Nellie blinked and faltered. 'I'm just saying, you and Beverley are both young. Don't throw everything away, not just yet.'

'I don't get it,' Jean said angrily. 'You were happy enough for me to get engaged to the others.'

'I don't think this boy would be happy for you to go flying off around the world.'

'Well Ted's not either, but I stood up to him.'

'After you'd accepted his engagement ring. Did you think you were in love with him, too?'

As if she hadn't heard her mother, Jean said, 'Beverley's different. I can see now what the others wanted: a wife they could boast about when I gave their dinner parties, when I was stout and middle-aged. They could tell about my exploits and make a good story of it.'

Nellie had shrugged, as if Jean was beyond reasoning with, and changed the subject.

People did, of course, know that Jean often visited the Shepherds. The family had many visitors at the Darling Point house, a sandstone mansion with views across the dark blue waters of Sydney Harbour, green bush pressing against its garden walls, the soft susurration of a gum tree on the boundary. The suburb was one of the best addresses in Sydney. Jean, as often as not, could be found slung in a hammock on one of the wide verandahs, sipping lemonade, freshly made by Beverley's mother. He got his looks from her, a lean, tall woman with straight sandy hair, and a wide smile that broke out whenever she looked at Jean.

'I can't believe it,' she said more than once. 'My boy in love with one of the world's most famous women. Are you really in love with him?'

'Oh,' Jean said, laughing, dodging the question. 'I'm not that famous yet.' Her fingers strayed to Beverley's face, tracing its contours. He was seated beneath her on the verandah, leaning back, eyes closed. He seemed oblivious to his own boyish beauty, the perfection of his profile, the morning stubble still soft. Yet. The word hung in the air. Beverley wanted to marry her. 'It's too soon. Yet,' she said to him. In spite of herself, Nellie's words had given her pause.

'Why? Please tell me. Aren't you happy?'

'I've never been happier in my whole life,' she said, and it was true. Some days, since she had met Beverley, flying seemed a chore, something that no longer consumed her the way it had. It was enough just to be with him. 'You're younger than me. I might be a handful.'

'It doesn't matter.'

'It does. You want to be a pilot. You should finish your training. You've got that lovely little plane.' Like Victor's mother, Mrs Shepherd had bought her son a Puss Moth. It was an uncomfortably close parallel. Later, Jean would reflect that this had been a deciding factor. She badly wanted to stay, but Beverley had never had to fight for anything. She didn't want a man like Victor, with ambitions unfulfilled, or worse, lived through her.

The Kingsford Smiths lived around the corner, although there was a question over how long they could afford the address. Beverley and Jean had taken to calling in on Smithy, his second wife, Mary, and their young son at the weekends. Mary was a neat, small-boned woman adoring of her husband. Jean and Smithy spoke only briefly of Charles Ulm, as if saying more would open up a wound too painful to examine. Smithy was sometimes in the doldrums; she assumed he was brooding on Charlie's disappearance. His hair was already thinning, and the lines around his mouth were deepening. Money was on his mind, as well. 'I'm going to have to break another record,' he said morosely, one afternoon.

'Sir Charles,' Beverley said awkwardly, trying to participate in the conversation, 'are you planning to break Scott and Campbell's record?'

'Sir Charles.' Smithy's tone was irritable. 'Jean, tell your boyfriend not to stand on ceremony. You've dropped in for a cuppa, for God's sake. Oh look,' he said, rubbing a hand wearily over his face, 'sorry, I didn't mean to bite. I wish sometimes I'd never had this handle attached to my name. Every man and his dog thinks you're rich. Sir this and Sir that, but when you talk about money it's embarrassing because they think your pockets are full, and you must be greedy to want more. You know what it's like, Jean, trying to raise money, the endless bloody circuit.'

'Yes, I do,' Jean said. 'And sometimes I love it — that's what bothers me. The rush of blood when you look at the crowd, and you can hold them in the palm of your hand, the silence ticking over that only you can break. It's like a spell.'

'And you think, in that instant of silence, that you're God. I've got to get away from it before long or I'll start believing it.' He watched his son, playing on a swing in the back yard. Another Charles. 'Yes, mate,' he said to Beverley, 'I'm going to have a crack at the record by the end of the year. It's there to be taken, although Scott and Campbell were pretty sharp, I'll give them that. If I can crack that one, well, perhaps we can all sit back and relax, eh Mary?' His eyes rested on his wife. 'All I want is to stay at home now.'

'You'll use the *Lady Southern Cross*?' Jean asked.

'I reckon she'll do the job. I can tell you, I was brassed off not making it to the MacRobertson. Ten thousand quid. I could have used that. Bloody hot, isn't it? ' He stood up, shaking himself a little, as if his joints were stiff. 'Couple of beers, whadya reckon?'

This conversation played over in Jean's mind. How long would it last, this life she was leading? She must place her trust in Beverley waiting for her. Jean wrote several drafts of a letter, screwing up balls of paper before she was satisfied.

> *My dear Ted,*
>
> *Thank you so much for caring about me enough to want to marry me. I am grateful for your patience and kindness. I think it only fair to tell you I have decided against marriage and would like to return the ring you gave me when I get back to London. I have still some goals I want to achieve. I cannot commit myself to matrimony while I pursue what, I suppose for want of a better word, you could call my ambition to succeed. I want to be the very best aviator in the world but I'd make a rotten wife. I have made a choice. Count yourself fortunate.*
>
> *Yours, with affection,*
> *Jean*

Then she put the screwed-up pieces of paper in the rubbish bin. As she went out to post her letter on her way to the Shepherds', her mother gave her a knowing look.

'Be careful of what you want. Sometimes you get more than you bargain for.'

Jean left without replying.

'I wrote to Edward this morning. I've broken off my engagement,' she told Beverley.

'About time.'

'But I *am* getting my Moth overhauled. I gave instructions to start work on it yesterday. I'm going to fly it back to England. Bev, don't look like that. When I've flown from England to New Zealand, we'll get married. I promise. Promise. Stop frowning. You'll be a pilot, and I'll be your good little wifey, and we'll have babies.' She laid her cheek against his. 'I know this is best for both of us.' She felt wise and mature. They would grow old and happy together and he would be glad.

As she rode the ferry back across a glittering Sydney Harbour, later that day, she steeled herself to tell Nellie about the broken engagement. Her mother had made baked chicken and jacket potatoes for dinner, an appeasement for their earlier sharp words.

'I've got something to tell you,' Jean began.

Nellie put a finger to her lips. 'You're not pregnant, are you?'

'No, Mother, I am *not*.'

'All's well then. I take it you're not going to marry the stockbroker?'

'No.' She hesitated. 'Are you angry with me?'

Nellie gave a short laugh. 'I wanted you to be sure. As

a matter of fact, I'm glad. A cold fish if ever I saw one. A bit of an odd cod. Are we going back to England, or are you staying here with this new boyfriend of yours?'

'London.'

'We need to book a ship then?'

'You do. I'm flying.'

Nellie shook her head. There had been enough arguments that summer. The following weekend, Nellie paid a call on the Shepherd family. As the ceiling fans turned in Sydney's heat-laden summer air, she looked around the room, taking in the cane and silky oak furniture, the paintings and rugs, then accepted tea and almond cake, served from a Georgian platter that Beverley's mother had inherited from a relative in England.

'He'll do,' she said, when she brushed Jean's hair that evening.

Word got around: Jean was going back to London. As she walked down Circular Quay one morning later in the week, a headline on a billboard caught her eye: *WILL JEAN BATTEN MARRY?*

Somewhere in a newsroom, a reporter had decided that she was returning to England to get married. What was worse, a newspaper in London had already interviewed Edward about why she was going back. He had said, testily, it appeared from the report, that he really didn't know whether the wedding was on or off. Clearly, he had not received her letter.

By then, however, he must have anticipated the news,

and planned his revenge in advance. The day her letter did arrive, he sent a cable — a bill for the wings of the plane.

April 1935. The night before Jean left Sydney, she and Beverley talked all night, holding each other, sometimes weeping. She thought again how young he was and felt him struggling against his tears.

'I couldn't live without you,' he said.

'You would,' she said. 'People go on.'

'How can you be sure of that?'

'I can't, but I have to believe it's true. I'll take care of myself. I'll write to you often, a book just for the two of us, the story of you and me.'

Deep down, she was hoping to break the women's Australia-to-England record. The first section of the flight was across Australia's desert to Darwin. There had been a drought in central Queensland. She flew over lone drovers with great herds of cattle, trekking southwards to greener pasture, and dried-up waterholes, surrounded by hundreds of dead cattle; the stench reached her in the cockpit. From time to time clouds of fine, brick-coloured dust swirled and eddied around her. In an odd sense, she was drawn to the desert, the red heart of the country. A place to burn if you let it catch you. But there was nothing to indicate that all was not well. The journey seemed to be going smoothly.

As she set out across the Timor Sea, the clouds of dust increased, reducing visibility to a minimum. To take advantage of the following wind, she climbed to six thousand feet, and set off for the island of Timor. The carpet of cloud beneath her was still tinged orange by the dust.

Around two hundred and fifty miles from land, the engine coughed. At first she thought she must have imagined it. She listened intently. Then she heard it again. This time the whole plane shook. The engine gave a final splutter and stopped. There was nothing but dead silence. As the plane began a slow glide towards the cloud cover, she was overcome by a dreadful sense of helplessness.

It must be a temporary petrol blockage, she told herself. She gave the engine full throttle, but nothing happened. The only sound was a whirring noise like a sigh, as the plane continued its descent.

It couldn't be possible that disaster had struck so soon. There had to be some way out. The altimeter held her fascinated as it fell to five thousand, four and a half thousand, then four thousand feet. She was among the clouds. At three thousand feet she saw the blue expanse of the sea, stretching limitless before her.

She was possessed by a savage terror. The desire to live had never been so strong. As best she could, she must now prepare to land on the sea. Undoing her shoes and flying suit, she reached for the small hatchet she carried in case of emergency and placed it in the leather pocket at her side. There seemed a last desperate chance that if she were able to land the machine on an even keel, she might be able to cut one wing away and float on it. But who would find her? She carried no radio, no flares. It would be many hours before anyone would think her missing. So much for her promise to Beverley that she would take care of herself. As she neared the water she could see through the waves to the dark eddies and whirls, the vast nothingness beneath. With the propeller still just ticking over, she opened and closed the throttle lever. Still nothing happened.

And then, with a deafening noise, like a great sob, the engine burst into life again. She hardly dared to breathe, as the engine regained its steady note, and she was able to coax the plane back up to three thousand feet. But the next hours, until she reached Kupang on Timor Island, were still filled with fear that the same thing would happen again. The Dutch ground staff listened in horror as she recounted her ordeal. Volcanic dust must have got into the engine, they suggested, causing a temporary blockage in the petrol system.

The filter and the jets were thoroughly cleaned, while she faced the prospect of flying on to England. Her confidence had been shaken in a way she had never experienced before. The following morning, it took all her willpower to get back into the plane and set off for Rambang, on Lombok Island.

It seemed, over the following days, that some demon had entered her plane. From time to time there would be ominous misses in the engine, and then it would revive again, as if she were flying a wind-up toy that might run down at any moment. Sometimes she wondered how much more she could endure. The last engine failure happened in thickening fog as Jean flew up the Rhône Valley towards Dijon. As she approached Chalon-sur-Saône, it cut out again. The Moth was already low, as she searched for a field where she might land, when yet again the engine roared into life. She flew on, hedge hopping to keep the ground in sight, in case she needed to touch down, until more with good luck than skill, she found the aerodrome. There, other planes were fogbound. They all remained in Dijon for another two days until the sky cleared. On the last flight to Croydon, the air was so cold and Jean's spirits so bitterly low, that she landed at Abbeville in order to buy a cup of coffee with her last two francs.

It had taken her nearly eighteen days to reach England, far from a record. For all that, she was the first woman to have flown to Australia and back. It was 29 April 1935.

London was, at that moment, in thrall to the jubilee celebrations for King George V and Queen Mary. As a woman who had flown from one side of the world — or almost — and back, Jean was invited to give an empire broadcast on the BBC the morning after her arrival back in London.

More invitations poured in. Kathleen, the Countess of Drogheda, one of the people from Stag Lane days, sent an urgent invitation for her to watch the jubilee procession from the balcony of her house in the Mall. The chain-smoking countess had remarried since Jean had first glimpsed her in the clubhouse, and taken to motor racing. 'Fancy you remembering me,' Jean said, when she joined the house party.

'Remember you? Darling, I've only just heard of you,' the countess said, half jokingly.

Wakefield took her to dinner at the Savoy. 'Will you have a cocktail?' he asked.

'Champagne, just champagne,' Jean said.

'I tried a very nice champagne cocktail with a dash of gin and some lemon juice, the last time I was here.'

'Just champagne. I like the bubbles.' He stroked the back of her hand. 'I'm so proud of you. You've done wonders for Castrol,' he said. 'But you look exhausted. You need building up. Oysters,' he said, perusing the menu, 'and a nice consommé, followed by filet mignon.'

'Too much food, sir.'

'Miss Batten, what is the trouble?'

She told him then about the Timor Sea, about her terror, the way she had braced her body in anticipation of death. 'I want to live,' she said. 'I have everything to live for.'

He turned her hand over on the crisp white tablecloth.

'It's true, you're not engaged any more?'

'It is, and I'm glad, but I wish it hadn't been in the newspapers.'

'But somewhere there is a lucky man?'

'I'm fortunate,' she said, reddening a little.

'Ah, I see. True love. I like the idea. Let's raise a toast to romance. But I think you need some rest, my dear, if you're to get your spirits back. I've some friends with a house in Scotland. Viscount Elibank, great chap, he's in charge of National Railways. He and his wife would be delighted to entertain you.'

When she agreed that this sounded a charming idea, he looked relieved. 'We can't lose you to flying just yet.'

Back in London, the RAF invited her to give talks to promote a new film. For two weeks she spoke three times a day. The applause was dimmed only by a letter to *The Aeroplane* magazine, wanting to know why on earth a woman should be associated with a film about the Royal Air Force. In a footnote, the editor agreed with the writer of the letter. Jean cut it out and sent it to her mother, accompanied by a big piece of notepaper covered with exclamation marks.

She was famous. Truly famous. Or infamous, if the editor was anything to go by. News came of prizes won: the Britannia Trophy from the Royal Aero Club, the Harmon Trophy for the most outstanding flight by a woman. She shared the latter with the American pilot Amelia Earhart, a woman she longed to meet.

Every day, she wrote to Beverley. *My darling*, she would begin, in letters that poured forth from her over the year or more that followed.

Meanwhile, she had begun the hunt for her new plane.

Chapter 27

She caught her breath when she saw the Gull for the first time, on her birthday in September, its silver surface gleaming under the hangar's powerful electric lights. Like, she wrote in her journal, *some lovely thoroughbred groomed and polished in readiness for a great race, and straining to be away.* When she took to the air, it turned and soared as effortlessly as the seabird for which it was named. It had an automatic petrol pump, and hydraulic brakes, but landing flaps as well and a metal propeller, luxury beyond her dreams.

Years earlier, when Smithy had realised his ambition to fly to Australia in record time, the aeroplane he chose was a Percival Gull 6. What was good enough for Kingsford Smith, Jean had decided, would be good enough for her, although she had purchased a later model, brand-new.

She now wrote to Beverley that, although flying to New Zealand was still in her sights, she wanted to test the Gull on a flight to South America, and that she had already begun her preparations for this attempt. There were, after all, some other records to be broken, and this was not such a long journey. She did not add that it was more dangerous.

It was November when she set off. Nellie, back in London, was there to see her leave. Although she had been so anxious for Jean to follow her ambitions, this new hazardous undertaking had shaken her certainty. 'Make this the last before New Zealand,' she said, the night before Jean was due to leave. 'Please.'

Some disquieting news had been broadcast the day before: Smithy was missing. He had set out in the *Lady Southern Cross* with his co-pilot, Tommy Pethybridge, in the attempt to break Scott and Campbell Black's new record. They had last been seen setting out on an overnight flight from Allahabad in India, to Singapore. There were reports of a typhoon in the area. Smithy had disappeared before, Jean told herself. He would be all right. It was unthinkable that anything could touch him. She vowed to check on the search for him at stops along her route.

She had hardly left Lympne when hail and cloud set in over the Pyrénées. The old loneliness descended, more swiftly than usual. The possibility that Smithy's disappearance was real had been growing by the hour, but she tried pushing the thought to the back of her mind.

In this metal grey space in the sky, with sharp hail like bullets rattling the plane, she was beset with the fear that she might not see Beverley again. She had been side-tracked from her intentions. It was so easy, so beguiling, to be tempted into the drama of risk and glamour. Why had she not said 'Enough', the day they all talked on Smithy's back lawn?

The hail stopped, and there was no sound except for the thrum of the engine. All she had was this solitary confinement in the cockpit of her plane. It was as if she were the only person alive in the world. She shook herself, took a sip of coffee from her Thermos. She thought of Beverley. He'd said he couldn't live without her, and for his sake she must survive. High above the cloud layer, a brilliant blue sky emerged. At fourteen thousand feet, the air outside the plane was icy cold, but her fear, and, with it, the loneliness passed.

She flew over Spain, glimpsing dark green rows of orange groves, castles on mountain tops with roads like cotton threads winding up to them, the shining city of Madrid, on and on, until she landed in Casablanca. Even in the darkness, the city looked porcelain-white. When she landed, there were murmurs of congratulation.

'But I've only just begun my journey,' she exclaimed.

'Mademoiselle,' the French ground staff explained, 'you have flown the fastest time ever from London to Casablanca. It is a record.'

She slept for a few hours in a Moroccan hotel, rose again just after three in the morning, and headed for French West Africa, across the Sahara Desert. Nobody at Villa Cisneros on the Saharan Peninsula knew anything about Smithy; they had not even heard of him. A hundred or so miles north of Thies, in Senegal, a vast flock of flamingos rose up, the blood-red undersides of their cape-like wings creating a ribbon of scarlet tulle across the sky. The airport at Thies was smaller and shorter for take-off than Jean expected. The tanks, filled to capacity, made the plane very heavy. She could not afford to shed a drop of the petrol, but some weight had to be lost. Climbing into the cockpit, she removed a heavy signal pistol, a revolver she had been told was essential in Africa, her tool kit and spare engine parts. Only her logbooks, the emergency rations, Thermos flask and two evening dresses were left on the plane. Now all was in readiness for the crossing to Natal in Brazil. The Atlantic Ocean stretched before her.

The airport commandant said that he had heard some message on the radio about Smithy but the news was garbled. He didn't think the aviator had been found. She slept for a few hours, at the commandant's house. When the alarm clock went off at three, she lay and looked at the flickering shadows cast by a lamp across the ceiling, and found it hard to envisage the next leg of the journey. Light rain was falling and the weather report for the South Atlantic was not promising either. But the commandant's African chef had prepared a packet of sandwiches and cooked a whole chicken for her. At least she wouldn't go hungry, she told herself with grim pleasure.

In the plane Jean adjusted the compass, and set her course straight as an arrow to Brazil. The blackness of the night, and the two-thousand-mile stretch of the Atlantic lay ahead.

Storm following storm battered her, one after another. She flew so low that at times she was only fifty feet above the water, then she lost sight of it altogether. Giving the engine full throttle she pulled the plane up into a climb. The Gull roared up through the dark mass, until at one thousand feet, she put the machine on an even keel. Both her feet were braced against the rudder bar, her hand gripping the joystick fiercely, as she concentrated all her attention on the blind flying instruments and the compass. Heavy rain now thundered against the Gull. Suddenly she saw the compass needle swing slowly around the dial. Imagination, surely.

But the needle continued its horrible, inexorable progress. Beads of sweat gathered on her face. She was lost. If the compass continued this movement she had gone in a full circle. It had now swung a hundred and eighty degrees. I will not give up, I will not, she cried out loud.

Then slowly, as if in some miraculous gesture, the compass needle was swinging back to its former position. Once more there was calm sea beneath. It didn't last long, as dark mushrooms of storm appeared on the horizon again, and she was plunged once more into blind flying through the heaving cloud.

Twelve and a half hours had passed since she left Africa. She was down to her last petrol tank. And then, slowly, a glimmering yellow line appeared on the horizon. The lonely deserted sand dunes on the coast of Brazil, and the undulating ocean waves breaking on the shore. She saw a slight promontory where, if it were Cape San Roque, the north-eastern tip of Brazil as she believed, there should be a lighthouse. In silhouette, against the sandy background, she saw the wire framework of a red painted structure that held a fixed light. She had made landfall within half a mile of her calculations. She crossed a hill, and there was the town of Natal.

An English couple, among the handful of mostly French people who greeted her, invited her to stay the night with them. Together they drove over rough roads into the jungle to a large house, surrounded by a beautiful garden, a riot of wild orchids and begonia, and the heavy, sweet scent of tobacco flowers on the evening air. Jean, at her hosts' invitation, took a long bath, before appearing to join them for dinner in a white silk dress. They looked at her transformation in astonishment.

'If you listen to the radio you might hear the announcement of your flight being broadcast from London,' her host said, drawing a chair close to the radio. 'It's just about time for the news.'

The roar of the engine for so many hours had left Jean temporarily so deaf that she had to strain hard to hear the announcer's voice. And then, there it was: 'Miss Jean Batten completed her flight from England to South America by landing at the aerodrome at Natal, Brazil, this afternoon. Her total time for the flight from England was sixty-one hours, fifteen minutes, and this lowers by almost a whole day the record held by Mr James Mollison.'

She learned, too, that no trace of Charles Kingsford Smith and his co-pilot had been found.

Wherever she went, crowds greeted her. At Rio de Janeiro, she was presented with a brooch made of a large diamond set in platinum. The British ambassador drove her to the house of the President, where she was shown to a large cool room, with a highly polished parquet floor, brocade-covered furniture and walls hung with many mirrors and portraits in oils. An attaché wearing a dazzling white uniform embroidered with gold cord, escorted her into the presence of Getúlio Vargas, a dictator also known as 'the father of the poor', a man said to admire beautiful and glamorous women. He gave her a long look of appreciation. It was the wish of the Brazilian nation, he said, to confer on Miss Jean Batten, the decoration of the Order of the Southern Cross, in recognition of her flight, which had linked England with Brazil in the fastest time in history. Vargas took a green and gold leather case from the desk by his side. Inside it lay a gold cross with a centre medallion of blue enamel, on which were embossed in gold the stars of the Southern Cross. The cross was joined to a pale blue ribbon by a green enamel link representing a laurel wreath. After the insignia was pinned to her dress, she responded in Spanish, and Vargas gave a smile of pleasure, holding her hand much longer than was necessary.

There were more gifts and honours before she left, bouquets by the hundred, receptions by the dozen.

On 6 December, she set sail for London, the Gull perched on the ship's wide deck. The thought of flying back had crossed her mind, but she dismissed it with a speed that surprised even her. She had made a promise to herself, and to Beverley Shepherd, that sooner or later she would return safely to Australia.

And, somewhere, in the warm green Andaman Sea, Smithy, Sir Charles Kingsford Smith, lay lost forever.

Chapter 28

Monsieur Louis Blériot was the most elegant of the gentlemen gathered at the Sorbonne to honour Jean. Blériot himself, the man whose picture Nellie had pinned above Jean's cot. He was still youthful in appearance, with a full head of hair and a spectacular moustache that showed no trace of grey, his eyes bright under heavy lids. His suit fitted him with a particular stylish grace, his tie was striped with golden fabric, his socks silken and fine. Beside him, Jean shimmered in a white evening gown and a white mink stole.

'Mademoiselle, you look like Anna Pavlova,' he murmured.

'Thank you, that's a great compliment. I saw her dance when I was a child in New Zealand. She was exquisite.'

'You have an interest in dance?'

She hesitated. 'I was a dancer,' she said.

'Indeed? That explains many things. Your grace, the way you carry yourself when you walk into a room. You're quite a small lady, if I may say so, but your presence is immediate, powerful. You are the kind of person who inspires others to dream.'

'As you are, monsieur.' She explained then how her

mother had pinned the newspaper clipping above her cot when she was an infant, the way his name and deeds had followed her all her life.

He gave her a long considering look.

'If you are free, I should be honoured if you would dine with me and Madame Blériot at our residence.'

It was February, and the Gull was being overhauled in preparation for Jean's flight to New Zealand. An invitation had arrived inviting her to Paris as a guest of the Aéro Club de France for a month. After many receptions, the prospect of a quiet dinner with her hero was as delightful as it was unexpected.

Blériot took her first to his salon. Straightaway, she noticed a glass case filled with gold, silver and bronze medals from almost every country in the world. His eyes followed hers. 'They are important,' he said, 'but they are not the journey.' Before them, on a table, stood a large glass globe. 'This is where I follow your journeys,' he said.

'You actually follow me?'

'But of course. You can have no greater admirer than me. There are many fine fliers in the world, but I've come to the conclusion that you must be one of the greatest navigators of all time. You appear to have an instinctive sense of direction that is extraordinary. Like an extra sense, a special power. You make me feel humble. Come, I have something else to show you.'

Just off the carpeted hallway, a door opened to reveal a small room, devoid of furniture except for a chair or two. A wooden bench extended its entire length, and on it were various tools, and lengths of spruce. Many blueprints and drawings, and photographs of early planes, covered the walls.

Madame Blériot had followed them into the room. 'Sometimes we have receptions here,' she said, 'and I'll look up and he'll be gone. I make a hasty excuse, say to our guests, forgive me, my husband has had an idea. And of course, he will be here. People of intelligence, the kind of people we invite here, understand ideas.'

She appeared as delighted by Jean's company as her husband. She had made their dinner herself: fish soup — *soupe aux poissons* — followed by roast veal, *fromage*, always *les fromages*, the beautiful cheeses of France that Jean was learning to appreciate, an apple tart, the making of which Madame Blériot described in loving detail. She had made her husband one exactly the same as a treat, the day he flew the English Channel. 'But there, you're not here to talk about the recipes,' she said, ' you're here to talk about aviation. Oh it's a day I'll never forget, my husband flying across that stretch of water. I was on the deck of a battleship that was following him, and then — pouf — he disappeared. For ten minutes nobody knew where he was. I could have cried when he was sighted, safe and sound. And you weren't even born then. How do they bear it, those people who love you, when you vanish across such vast oceans as the Atlantic?'

'I think my mother worries a little.'

'Your mother worries? My dear, you have a talent for understatement. How terrifying for her. Do you have a dear love in your life?'

'Yes, I do,' Jean said. 'But it's a secret. He is a young

man, and learning to be a flier. It's important that he succeeds on his own account, or that's how I feel.'

'That is so wise,' her hostess said. 'But he watches over you, when you set off on your flights?'

'He's in Australia,' Jean told her. 'I'll join him soon.' She did not say that Beverley now had a commercial licence and that she didn't hear from him as often as he heard from her, that a sense of urgency to be on the other side of the world was fast overtaking her. She had so much to relate day by day, while he had a life in Sydney, not as different moment by moment as hers. He had sent her a picture of himself in his Australia Airways uniform, and she could see that he was changing, his profile less boyish. And he was attractive. She knew how girls liked a man in uniform. It made her uneasy, and she disliked herself for feeling this way. There were times when she thought that the flight to South America had been a mistake; it was not what she had promised when she left him in Australia the previous year.

Madame Blériot looked at her husband. 'Shall we show her our secret room?' she said. When he nodded, with a look of merriment, they led her to their bedroom, a room with bare walls and ceiling all painted sky blue. 'You see,' he said, 'even in the midst of winter, even when there is fog outside, I wake up and the first thing I see is clear blue sky. It never leaves me.'

Jean felt that her hosts in France must have been pleased with her. When she was back in London, a letter arrived advising her that the French government wished to bestow on her the French Légion d'Honneur, the first British airwoman to be honoured by France. Before it could be awarded, the permission of the King must first be obtained. While this approval was being sought, Jean and Nellie flew together in the Gull for a holiday in Majorca.

As Jean began the physical preparation she undertook before a major flight, the daily skipping and swimming, they explored the island from end to end, the wild flowers, and the giant olive groves, took a trip into the mountains to the monastery at Valldemossa, where Chopin and George Sand had lived together for a short time. They stood in the room that housed Chopin's piano. 'This is where he composed the "Raindrop Prelude",' Jean said, wishing she could sit where the master had. Her head filled with the swarming opening notes.

It was outside the monastery that they encountered a dog. The large bull mastiff materialised apparently out of nowhere, bounding along at speed, pulling up short of them, teeth bared in a snarl. Jean gave a terrified scream.

'Stand still, Jean,' Nellie said, her voice firm. 'You must not move, do you hear me? Don't look in its eyes.'

The dog had crouched, ready to spring, when a man appeared from behind the monastery wall, shouting commands. The dog sank onto its haunches, saliva dripping from the corners of its mouth. The man led the dog away, muttering apologies in Spanish.

Later, that evening, as they sat on the balcony of their

hotel, Jean said, 'You were so brave, Mother. How did you know what to do?'

'There were dogs running loose in Rotorua. Don't you remember? Oh, perhaps not, you'd have been too little.'

'I remember the swans.'

'Well you chased them away.'

'Dogs are different.'

'True, these ones are. I've read about the dogs on this island, Ca de Bestiar is the breed — they've been here for hundreds of years. They used them for hunting, and bull fights. The dog held the bull until the matadors could finish it off.'

'That's horrible,' Jean said. 'I've had a few frights in my life, but nothing like that. I don't know what I'd have done if you hadn't been there.'

'Just remember not to challenge a dog. If you look it in the eye it'll think you want a fight. Look away.'

Jean shivered. 'I'll try to remember that advice.'

Nellie seemed unruffled, the incident of little consequence. 'I should so love to live here,' she said, over breakfast on the sun-drenched terrace, a day or so later.

Jean looked doubtful. 'Well, perhaps you could,' Jean said, as the coffee was poured. This was not the first time the subject of where Nellie would settle once Jean and Beverley were married had arisen. 'We could visit you.'

'You don't sound keen.'

'Yes, I do like the island. Truly, Mother, we could help you find a place here later on.'

'You don't want me to live in Sydney then?'

'Mother, you know I always want to be near you. You just said you liked it here. But you know there's talk of a war in Spain.'

'Pray God, it won't happen,' Nellie said.

They left it at that. The holiday was almost over. This, Jean thought, would be a time she and her mother would remember as their own. They would meet for lunch in Sydney, perhaps, in years to come, and Jean would have her children with her. 'Remember that time in Majorca?' they would say and it would come back to them, the scent of orange blossom rising up to meet them in the mountains from the valley floors, the rustle of leaves in the olive groves, the dark layers of blue in the ocean beyond the white beaches, the music of Chopin. Her mother was right, the dog was not important.

That night there was a blood-red moon, casting a mysterious light over the sea.

The flight to New Zealand was delayed again. Jean had been made a Commander of the British Empire, and the King now required her presence. In the interval, in order to maintain her fitness for the journey, Jean organised a rigorous eighty-mile walking tour for herself and Nellie, through the South Downs. Her mother's eyes had widened at the proposal. 'If you think you're old, that's what you'll be, I suppose. I'm not ready for that yet,' she said, as they set off. She was sixty-two.

While they were away, they heard that New Zealand runner Jack Lovelock had won the mile race at the Berlin Olympics. He was already famous, and now he and Jean vied for being the best-known New Zealanders in the world, if the newspapers were to be believed.

'I'm glad to leave the limelight to him,' Jean said.

'Something's bothering you, Jean. What is it? Are you worried about the flight?' They were walking from Eastbourne, but had stopped for a light lunch in a pub.

Jean fiddled with the handle of her teacup. 'I just want it over with now,' she said.

'Are you worried about Beverley?'

'I told him I'd get back there safely. But then there's the Tasman to cross. It's a flight all in itself.'

'Don't do it if you're that concerned.'

'Don't do it? What do you mean? Mother, of course I'm going to do it. That's what I said I was going to do.'

'Then I don't know why we're having this conversation,' Nellie said.

'I'm sorry, Mother,' Jean said, as they gathered up their packs to start walking again. 'Sometimes it all seems to have got too big.'

Some people, it seemed, were destined not to grow old. Back in London, news arrived that Louis Blériot had died of a heart attack in Paris. He was sixty-four.

'Everyone I touch,' Jean cried, in disbelief and pain. 'Why him?'

But she still had the King to meet and, although her pleasure was dimmed, her spirits rose at the prospect. And with this behind her, there lay the flight ahead.

The new decoration glowed back at her, sitting in a box alongside her Brazilian and French orders. She remembered what Blériot had said. 'They are important, but they are not the journey.'

It was 5 October 1936 when she at last left on the first leg of her journey south.

At Lympne, in the early hours of the morning, reporters and a camera crew flocked around her. She was in no mood for making speeches, but agreed to make a short one before the filming of the takeoff.

As she climbed into the cockpit, a desperate-looking young man waved to her in a frantic manner. Thinking there was some emergency, or a problem with the engine, Jean got out of the plane. The cameraman had forgotten to turn on the sound. 'Please Miss Batten, would you repeat your speech for us.'

She heard herself, imperious and suddenly angry. 'There's no time. I have a schedule,' she said, turning away.

'Please,' he said. 'Please. I'll lose my job if I don't capture your words.'

Jean looked at his dazed and pleading face. This might be the only job he had ever had.

Leaning into the cockpit, she turned off the engine. 'All right then. Make sure this time, please. I want to leave England today.'

As she spoke, she tried to modulate her voice, to keep it slow and calm, aware of the rising panic inside.

Chapter 29

Jean landed at Darwin in the early hours of the morning on 11 October, five days and twenty-one hours after leaving England. She had lowered the solo record for both men and women by a day.

The continent of Australia now lay between her and the hosts of people who awaited her in Sydney. Again, the rooftops were crowded with onlookers, as she circled the city, the harbour bridge.

'The flight isn't finished yet,' she told the crowd at Mascot, over the massed swelling roar of their voices. 'I have yet to fly to New Zealand.'

As they had arranged, Beverley was waiting for Jean at the Hotel Australia, in a suite of rooms booked for her. It was better, they agreed, that their reunion was out of the public eye. It would be brief. If the predicted weather conditions were accurate, she would be on her way again in two days.

Beverley seemed taller in his uniform. His fine, fair hair

was brushed straight back from his forehead, making him appear older than when she had left him. He put his arms around her and held her within their circle.

'I thought you'd never come back. I was so afraid for you.'

'I promised you,' she said.

'And now you're here, I'm not going to let you go any further.'

She took a step backwards from him. 'What do you mean, Bev?'

'Look,' he said, 'I don't want you to go on. Why not rest on your laurels and just stay here?'

'You can't be serious.' She felt her voice rising.

'There's already talk in the newspapers. There was a headline this morning, suggesting that it was madness to carry on over the Tasman. You know it's one of the most dangerous seas in the world.'

'That's part of the challenge. I've crossed that water often by ship. I know what the storms are like out there. I've studied the charts. What do you think I've been doing all these years?'

'You have been known to crash.'

'I don't believe I'm hearing this,' she said, still trying to keep her voice down. She knew people would be within earshot.

'Jean, you're not to go. I'm telling you.'

'Nobody tells me what I'm allowed to do.' He looked as if he were about to walk out of the room. She could hardly believe that this was how her sprint across the world was ending. 'Beverley,' she said, her voice breaking, 'this was always the plan.'

'What's the reward of trying to link England and New Zealand if you end up losing your life? What will you gain?'

'I'm very tired,' she said. 'I think we need to talk about this tomorrow.'

They ate together that evening. He gave her news of his family, talked about the passenger route he was flying on from Sydney to Brisbane. It was a peaceful sort of route, he said, over the mountains, the gum trees a sea of moving colour. He loved it — all the adventure he needed.

'It was rough over there today,' she said. 'I had trouble keeping the Gull level as I came into Sydney.'

'That doesn't happen often.'

He left her then. She needed to sleep, he could see — or this is what he told her. Nothing had been resolved. It felt as if they had quarrelled, even though the subject of the Tasman crossing had been dropped.

But, in the morning, nearly two thousand telegrams awaited her, hundreds of them from people begging her not to make the flight. This seemed incomprehensible. The Tasman had now been flown seventeen times. But not yet by a woman, or, as some of her opponents pointed out, by a plane that had just flown across the world. Some said she must surely be tired. This was true, but she was not going to admit it to anyone. At a newspaper interview, a reporter asked, 'Miss Batten, if you fail at this attempt, surely it will be a terrible setback to aviation in both Australia and New Zealand?'

'In that case, if I succeed, the reverse must be true,' she snapped. 'I'd say it will give a tremendous impetus to aviation.'

A headline the next morning, contained an appeal from the Governor-General's wife: *WOMAN TO WOMAN, I URGE YOU NOT TO GO ON.* In New Zealand, Fred Batten had announced his opposition to her flight. His daughter had been 'a sweet little girl' he told the reporters, but she always had a mind of her own. This was a step too far in his opinion.

The Civil Aviation authorities stepped in, and announced that they would not permit a takeoff with an overload of one thousand pounds, unless she could produce a certificate of airworthiness with an endorsement authorising her to do so. She produced the special permit she had obtained from the Air Ministry before leaving England, and the tone of the argument changed.

The RAAF stepped in and offered her the use of their runway at Richmond, so that she could take off on a hard surface, rather than grass. They would also light a flare path to guide her on the early morning departure. This seemed a good omen. It was at Richmond that she had had the first flight of her life with Smithy and Charlie Ulm.

The newspapers had not finished with her yet: *Miss Batten seems oblivious to the vast amount of money and resources,*

and the risk to the lives of others that would be involved in a search
for the Gull if it goes down in the sea.

In the afternoon of that last day in Sydney, Fred Batten rang his daughter from his dental practice in Auckland, with reporters listening in.

'Do you promise not to take off unless the weather's perfect?' he asked.

'Yes, Dad, I promise.'

'Are you feeling up to it?'

'Dad, I'm in the pink,' she said. 'I'll see you in Auckland about four tomorrow afternoon. No, Dad, no. I won't come if the weather is bad.'

She had a late lunch with Beverley in the seclusion of her rooms. He had wanted to take her to Darling Point to see his mother, but she reminded him she had to get to Richmond, where she had been offered a bed in the officers' mess, and some sleep. 'I'm still waiting,' he said, as he kissed her. It was a peace offering of sorts.

'I love you,' she said. But already he had gone.

At Richmond more telegrams were waiting. All these wished her good luck, and Jean wondered if the secretary who had been assigned to her had sifted out all the negative messages. One from Nellie: *My prayers go with you and I am confident you will succeed.* Telegrams from Lord Londonderry, and Viscount Wakefield, from the French Air Minister, and a group of ex-servicemen. *Good on you, Jean,* they said. *Don't be put off by all the Jeremiahs. You will make it all right.* She laughed out loud.

At half past two she rose and spent a long time looking at the weather chart. An intense depression was moving over her route. The decision had to be made quickly: wait for the weather to pass, or alter her course and land at New Plymouth. In the back of her head, a small voice was asking why Smithy had not listened to the weather report that he must have surely received that morning in Allahabad.

'I'm going,' she said.

The Gull was wheeled out. She did the last check of her maps and charts.

A long line of flares burned brightly along the runway, lighting a path in the darkness. A small crowd had assembled. As she turned the Gull into the wind, pausing to make a final check, a man ran forward with a microphone. 'Say a few words, Jean,' he shouted.

'Very well,' she shouted above the roar of the engine, 'but I want the group captain to hear what I have to say.' She cut the motor and spoke to tense white faces looking up at her. 'Listen, if I go down in the sea no one must fly out to look for me. I've chosen to make this flight, and I'm confident I can make it, but I have no wish to imperil the lives of others or cause trouble or expense to my country. Goodbye for now. I'll be back.'

She released the brakes, gave the engine full throttle. The bright line of flares flashed past. Nearing the last one, she eased the plane off the ground. The Gull climbed swiftly through the darkness.

Chapter 30

In London, Nellie Batten leaned close to the radio to hear the broadcast from New Zealand. The announcer was honking with excitement.

'Jean Batten is arriving. They can just see her way down on the horizon, right away, miles away, but she is coming along very fast and bearing straight down on the clubhouse, coming straight through. Here comes Jean Batten right now ... her silver plane is shining away there and round she comes. She's taking a circle round the aerodrome and losing height and round she comes.

' ... the first message we got was that she was sighted from New Plymouth flying north at 4.04. She did not land at New Plymouth. The next message we got was that she was ... Mokau 4.15, then ... three miles south of Kawhia at 4.35 and well out to sea.

'Here she is, coming just past the tent now on the right-hand side. She is coming over the crowds and is losing height all the time. Everybody is tensed up and they are all ready to cheer her. It won't be long before you won't be able to hear me for the cheer they give Miss Jean Batten, the New Zealand aviator ... The crowd surges forward, a large crowd of police, mounted police, foot police and traffic inspectors and they are having a great job to keep the crowd back. Here's Mr Batten very anxious to get down and meet her.

'Here she is coming down, she is down about twenty feet now, about ten feet, she is nearly on the ground, just very near the tops of those motor cars and nearly touches them. A beautiful three-point landing she is going to make … Here she comes … I don't know whether you can hear me or not … We can see a white … a white helmet …'

In Auckland, the speeches had begun. First the mayor spoke. 'Words fail me to express adequately to you the feelings of all the persons here today. But Jean, you are a very naughty girl, and really I think you want a good spanking for giving us such a terribly anxious time here. We knew you could do it, but we did not want you to run the risk.'

Jean decided to let this go. What was the point of a quarrel when she had barely landed? In Australia, she had been reminded forcibly that, here in the Antipodes, she was in a man's world.

This had been one of the loneliest flights of her life. The storm had broken soon after she left Richmond. The rain was intense, just like the tropics, only very cold. The cabin began to leak, and the water soaked her shoulders. She was flying blind in low cloud. An albatross provided some company for a few moments. Soon after, emerging from the cloud, she had looked down at what appeared like a wreath in the water, and saw that it was a whale swimming just beneath the surface, so that its back looked green. She thought of the spirit of Moby Dick, and wished intensely that she could see land. At this time of year, whales swam through Cook Strait, and she had a sudden fear that she was passing through the strait and out beyond towards the Pacific Ocean. In a few minutes, in teeming rain, she had seen that her course was true, as she flew over New Plymouth.

She was tired and cold, and there were still speeches from dignitaries of every kind, the government, and women's organisations, and the air force. There were cheers for her father, whom it seemed must now be counted as one of her very best friends in the world.

Finally, her teeth chattering with cold, she was able to speak. 'Ever since I had my very first flight,' Jean said to the huge gathering, 'I had in mind the linking of Great Britain and New Zealand by air. I left England on October fifth, and although I wasn't trying to break the solo record to Australia, I was able to break the men's record and arrive in Australia just a little over five days after leaving London'.

The crowd screamed with delight, an animal herd braying.

'By continuing my flight from Darwin the following day I was able to fly on to Sydney and arrive there from London in the fastest time ever — one week. Before I left

England I didn't think of the Tasman as a separate flight but just as one hop of the complete flight, and I had in my mind the thoughts that, as you all know, New Zealand is the only dominion of Great Britain that has not yet been linked, that had not yet been linked to Great Britain by air in direct flight.

'I'm very happy to arrive in New Zealand today, and incidentally, nine and a half hours after leaving Australia, thereby creating another record, and actually today I am just ten days, twenty-one hours out from England, so in this flight, I was able to fly through from England to New Zealand in the fastest time in the history of the world.'

The mob had become hysterical. Ambulances were moving in to pick up people who were being trampled.

'I don't need to add how pleased I am to see you all here to greet me, and I think I can say without doubt this is the very greatest moment of my life.'

The crowd now began to sing 'For She's a Jolly Good Fellow'. The mounted police carved a path through the crowd as she was driven in a motorcade to her hotel. If it were peace she was seeking, it wasn't there. Already, the first of thousands of telegrams and letters had begun to arrive. The reception area was heaped high with flowers. Within a day or so, four secretaries would be employed by the government to help her deal with the correspondence.

The London newspapers had new classical names for her. *The Times* dubbed her the *New Diana*, while the *Morning Post* referred to her as the *Atalanta of the Air*. She wasn't sure that either of these descriptions applied to her, but the image of herself as Atalanta, the virgin huntress, unwilling to marry, was particularly unsettling.

There was a cable of congratulation from Beverley, followed by his silence.

News of friends and family began to surface. Harold had gone bankrupt and shifted further north. John and Madeleine were living in Tahiti, where Madeleine could write in peace and the living was cheap. Fred was cagey about this. He said something to the effect that Madeleine was planning to spend some time on her own. Freda Stark was working as a clerk somewhere. There had been a scandal when Thelma Trott, Freda's lover, was murdered by her husband Eric Mareo. Freda had been a star witness for the prosecution. Valeska said Freda was thinking about dancing again, and how nice it would be if they got together. Jean agreed, but there were days when she was overcome with a great lethargy, and when she thought about the drama of Freda's life, and that of her own, she found it hard to muster the energy to pursue this meeting. Malcolm MacGregor, whom she had got to know in the days following the Melbourne Air Race, had died in an air crash in Wellington. She had heard this, of course. He was part of the roll call.

Fred Batten, now a doting father, appeared at her door late one afternoon. He had special access to his daughter, and nobody questioned his right to knock whenever he came up the stairs by the side entrance.

'A quiet word if I may,' he said to Jean. 'Something private.' He looked around with a meaningful glance at the secretaries, and a photographer who had just finished a sitting with Jean.

'I wish you'd called up, Dad,' Jean said when the room was cleared. 'You can see what a lot I've got to deal with. Is this about the family?'

'It might be if something isn't done.' He held his hat by its rim and turned it around carefully with the tips of his fingers. 'I had Frank Norton to see me this morning.'

'Frank *Norton*? That man …'

'I seem to remember you liked him well enough once.'

'I can't bear to even think about him. What does he want?'

'He tells me you owe him a lot of money. Five hundred pounds.'

'That's not true.'

'He says he paid for your commercial flying lessons.' There was a silence. 'Well, Jean?'

'It's not quite like that, Dad.'

'I have to know.'

'Why? Why do you have to know?'

'Because he's downstairs now, and he says he's going to the press if you don't pay up. He says he met some woman he wants to marry and that it's impossible because all his pension is gone, and he can't support a wife.'

Jean jumped up from her chair, shaking, her fists

clenched, the muscles in her neck taut with fury. 'The pig. The rotten blackmailing pig. And don't you look at me like that. I'm not your sweet little girl any more.' She collapsed onto a sofa, and put her face in her hands. 'He did help me with some money. It wasn't five hundred pounds, nothing like it. He had five hundred when he came out of the RAF. God knows what he did with it. Drank it, probably.'

'Why didn't you pay him?'

'He had his money's worth.'

'Jean. What are you saying?'

'Oh, never mind. You say he's downstairs?'

When her father nodded, she said at last, 'Tell him I'll bring him down a cheque in a few minutes. Please, stay with him. Don't let him near me. Do you promise?'

After her father left the room, she gathered herself together as best she could. Her hands were still shaking as she wrote a cheque for two hundred and fifty pounds. As she emerged from the lift, she saw the two men talking, and wondered what Frank had told her father. He looked at her, his face bloated and red.

'Hello, Jean,' he said, his voice too hearty.

Jean held out the cheque without saying a word, turning away without waiting to see what he made of it and retreating up the stairs. As she left, she heard him say, 'Well, I know when I'm beaten. She always was a tough bitch. A man-eating bitch, if you'll forgive me, Mr Batten.'

Her father returned to her room.

'What are you doing here?' she said.

'I came to see if you were all right. I'm worried about you, my little Mit. Look at you, you look as if you've seen a ghost.'

'Your little Mit, no, I told you those days are over. You shouldn't have interfered.'

'I didn't ask to be in the middle of all this,' he said, his tone sharp. 'I'd been quite content with my life until you brought all this on me.'

'You should go now.'

They stood gazing at one another, her expression steely, until he made a futile gesture and left.

The tour of the country she had promised to make now began, but the crowds turning up to hear her were not as great as in the past. There was a certain dull resentment in the eyes of some in her audiences. She was rich and they were on the bones of their backsides. The prospect of flying around the country was daunting. She couldn't understand why she felt so tired. Instead, she asked that she go by train or by car from one destination to another. She made it to Hamilton on the train; from there she was driven by a chauffeur to Wellington. In the middle of the Desert Road, with the mountains high and white in the distance, and the purple heather dark with spring growth at the edge of the red clay banks lining the road, a car came towards them. The chauffeur called out to say that he knew who it was.

'Does it matter?' she said, as he pulled over to the side of the road, hooting the horn.

'Yes, yes,' the man said, jumping out to open the door for her. The other car pulled to a halt and the two chauffeurs greeted each other. The passenger, a slim man with a shock of fair curls got out, and walked towards them. Jean saw no option but to get out, too.

The passenger held out his hand. 'Hello there, good to meet you, Miss Batten. I'm Jack Lovelock.'

'Well, what about that,' Jean said. 'Goodness, what would the cartoonists make of us now? You should be running and I should be flying.'

He grinned. There seemed nothing more to say. They climbed back into their respective cars, and drove off in opposite directions from each other.

Jean made it to Wellington, but the ominous stretching of her nerves had reached breaking point. Something inside her snapped. It was time to stop. The Prime Minister, Michael Savage, on learning of her state, offered her a holiday at the expense of the government, and suggested that a hotel on the West Coast of the South Island might be an ideal retreat. He had not been told the exact nature of her illness (it was first reported as pneumonia), but he seemed to sense her need to be relieved of the public's attention. A bachelor who lived a secluded private life, he, too, was mobbed wherever he went. At the Franz Josef and Fox glaciers, she might have privacy and complete rest. In the meantime, he intended to take up a public collection on her account.

Fred sent a telegram care of Thomas Cook in London, praying it would find its way to Nellie. *I am worried about our daughter. Please telephone me. Here is my number.* The phone woke him in the early hours of the following day, Nellie's voice crackling over a distance that seemed as long as the time since they had last spoken.

They spoke at length. Jean could not manage alone, he said, and what he had to offer seemed inadequate. He thought she was half crazy, or worse, and now it had come to this, that the Prime Minister had got involved. Savage was probably a madman himself, who knew, but he was kind. Could they not, he suggested, put their differences aside, and try to help Jean? If they could spend Christmas together as a family, it might heal some of the wounds of the past. There was a very long silence at the other end, punctuated by Fred saying, 'Are you there? Are you there, Nellie? Nellie, it's a bad line, can you hear me?'

'I can hear you, Fred,' Nellie said. 'I understand what you're saying.'

She was standing in a little booth in the post office at Hatfield. She put the phone down, and paid the postmistress the enormous bill for the call.

When she got back to her flat, Nellie picked up her suitcase, which she kept packed for emergencies, walked out the door and pushed the key through the letterbox, waiting only an instant to hear it land on the floor. She walked to the Tube and caught a train to Kings Cross, where she made a booking. In the morning she boarded a ship bound for New Zealand.

At Franz Josef, the hotel where Jean was now in hiding was almost deserted, the winter season over. She walked by the lakes, or watched the great river of ice, framed with dark green bush and ferns, with a fixed fascination. The glacier, pale green, thrust like a gigantic tongue out of the mountains. It was known to advance and retreat, sometimes quickly, other times inching backwards and forwards. When the days were clear in the mountains, the snow-covered peaks of Mounts Cook and Tasman could be seen; as the sun set they glowed with dazzling orangeade reflections, while down below, at the level of the glacier, the evening turned dark purple. On other days, the rain fell in steady insistent downpours and the fog lingered on the valley floors.

The quietness began to fill the empty spaces in Jean's head. A pure and absolute silence descended on her — a white silence was the way she saw it. She sat for long periods of time, absorbing the stillness. This was how it must be, she thought, time to rest from fame and move to the next chapter of her life.

When she had been there for ten days or more, she wrote a letter:

> *My darling Bev,*
> *I long to hear from you. Our meeting in Australia*

was not as either one of us expected. What did I expect? I don't know, really. I suppose that I wanted everything to carry on just where we left off. But how could it, with me dashing off to New Zealand? I know that I flew here against your better judgement, and, if we are to be together, I need to pay more attention to what you think about things.

I have done the things I wanted to do. The only thing I want now is that you should hold me and tell me that you love me, and that all the dreams we had may still happen. I am looking at this glacier, this huge stream of ice from the mountains, and I feel that for many months now, I have been like ice, not myself at all. It's as if I've taken stage fright from my own life. I want to start it over again.

My parents have made friends with each other for the moment. It is all about me, I suppose. They are worried. My mother is on her way to New Zealand. I'm going over to meet her when her ship arrives in Sydney on 12th December. I thought I would come a few days early. We'll stay until we can get the ship back to New Zealand. I have promised to go with the parents to Rotorua, the place where I was born, after Christmas, when I have recovered. I feel I must. Perhaps it is as near to being a family again as we might ever be, even if it is a pretend family. So when I'm in Sydney we can have a whole week together, just you and me, and all that means to us both. Oh how I've missed you, my love. Time flees, we mustn't waste any more of it. Dearest, you have never left my heart. Say that it will be all right. Please.

Jean

A few days after this letter had been posted, the Castrol agent in Wellington, a man called Bob Smillie, persuaded his wife Doris to travel to Franz Josef to keep an eye on Jean. He didn't want to have to account to Lord Wakefield if anything happened to her, and what on earth Savage had thought he was doing, posting the poor girl off to the mountains by herself, he had no idea.

The appearance of Doris put an end to the respite at Franz Josef. She was kind, to extremes, Jean thought. She felt herself becoming hostile the moment the older woman arrived. 'You will have to excuse me,' Jean said after an awkward dinner, on their first night in the yawning cavern of the dining room, 'but I think I need to lie down.' She had fallen in love with the darkened corners of the room, lit only by the flickering light of a huge fire on a stone hearth. She wanted them all to herself.

In her room, she paced up and down. She knew that Doris's arrival marked the end of her stay, but, at the same time, she knew that if she were rude this would be interpreted as a further sign of madness. The best thing, she decided, would be to go along with her presence for two or three days, and fill the time with activities that would distract them both, to prove that she was capable of looking after herself. If she weren't careful, she would find Doris on board the ship she was planning to take to Sydney.

This ploy worked well. One day they hired horses to ride along guided trails, and another day was spent on a fishing expedition. Jean caught a large trout that the chef cooked for them that night. She declared herself as never better, fit and well, and Doris had to agree that she looked in good health, and it was amazing what a bit of mountain air could do for one.

A letter from Beverley was waiting for her back in Auckland. He was longing to see her too. What was she getting herself all worked up about? He had already booked their favourite restaurant table for the night of her arrival in Sydney: *The one near Circular Quay, where we went on the first night back in Sydney, after the race. Two years ago now, time we got together again.*

So in time to come, that was the week she would remember as the best. The summer beaches and drives in the country, and nights when she seemed lost in who she was, abandoned in him. She didn't know any longer where she left off and he began. I love you and I love you and I love you, she said to him over and again.

Nellie was happy to rest at her hotel after the voyage, or to spend time at the Shepherds' house, being entertained by Beverley's mother. Jean didn't ask them what they talked about. Nellie never did tell her that they had started gleeful plans for a wedding that seemed sure to happen.

There were moments when things were not all that they might have been. Like the evening when they entered a restaurant, and the diners got up and applauded Jean.

Beverley looked irritated. 'So I'm destined to be regarded as Mr Jean Batten, am I?' he muttered.

'They will forget who I am in no time,' Jean said, placating him. 'Just ignore them.'

But he had insisted on a table where he could sit with his back to the room.

On another afternoon, Jean had agreed to speak to some school children. It was a day when Beverley had taken leave from work. 'It will only take an hour,' Jean insisted. 'I shouldn't disappoint them.' Beverley bore it, but only just.

When they parted, he kissed the top of her head and told her not to worry about things too much, everything would be all right in the long run. Just hurry back, he told her.

Soon after Jean and Nellie arrived back in New Zealand, Nellie and Fred met at Smith and Caughey's. Over lunch, Fred said, 'Ellen, that girl is sick. There's something wrong with her.'

'She gets a bit down to it at times,' Nellie said. 'But she's perfectly fine now. You should have seen her in Sydney, on top of the world.'

'Things have gone wrong in our children's lives,' Fred said. 'You can't deny that. There's Harold.'

She put her cup down. 'Jean is not like Harold.'

'Perhaps not. But she's different, all our children are different.'

'Well of course, if you're talking about John, that's another matter.'

'John is who he is, Nell, you have to accept that. I didn't always but I do now. It's not been easy for him, you know.' His voice was gently persuasive.

'I don't care who John is. He can't say I haven't tried. Anyway, he's got that woman he's married to.'

'Yes, but for how long? There might come a time when John's on his own again.'

'I thought we'd come here to talk about Jean.'

'All right,' her husband said. They stared at each other across the table, until Fred's eyes fell. 'I know it was my fault,' he said. 'The family falling apart.'

Nellie sat back in her chair as if some small victory had been achieved. 'Jean will be fine when she's married,' she said. 'Her hormones are all over the place, you know how it is.' As if to concede a little ground of her own, she added, 'I suppose mine were, too, when I was young. I did go off the handle a bit.'

'A bit.' He chuckled, remembering. 'You will keep an eye on her, won't you?'

After Nellie had agreed that she would indeed be around for as long as possible to watch out for Jean's welfare, they set to planning the family holiday they hoped would right some of the wrongs of the past. 'Separate rooms, mind you, Fred.'

He looked at her in astonishment, and laughed. 'Oh, I think so, Nell.'

In Rotorua, Nellie and Fred were charming and funny and kind to one another, making jokes when they all met for breakfast at the Prince's Gate Hotel. Jean and Fred played a duo on the hotel piano one evening to great applause, and then Nellie and Jean offered to do high kicks together, something Jean had taught her mother in her dancing days, which caused a riotous party to erupt in the lounge. The manager came in and said that, really, he knew there were famous people present, but some guests had come for peace and quiet as well.

The lake lay cool and blue in the mornings. They walked in the gardens and swam and fished. Jean said that if she ate another trout she would start to look like one. If Fred had had a past in the town, it was not in evidence, except for the occasional person who stopped him on the street to thank him for the best dentures they had ever had. Te Arawa held another welcome for Jean, this time at Ohinemutu, not far from where the Battens had lived, the village where the children had been forbidden to roam. Nellie's chin trembled a little when the moment came to press noses in greeting with the chief. Jean was presented with a feather cloak of her own, and bestowed with the name Hine-o-te-Rangi, Daughter of the Skies.

Beverley, impatient with this extended family reunion,

wrote to her regularly, asking how soon she would be back. Now that they had had their time together before Christmas, he knew how much he needed her with him. If she didn't come soon, he would come and collect her himself. She told him that she planned to be back in Sydney in mid-February: *Can we meet straightaway? I will be all yours. Let's meet at our special restaurant again.*

Within a matter of days, the Gull was lifted onto the deck of the ship that would take her and Nellie to Sydney. A huge crowd gathered to say farewell. If it were possible for Jean's fame to increase, it had in the past week. She had received news that the Royal Aero Club had awarded her the Britannia Trophy for the greatest flight of the year by a British subject, for the second year in a row. And there had been two more trophies.

When their ship berthed in Sydney on 19 February 1937 Jean and her mother made their way to the hotel, where Jean planned to change and go to meet Beverley. But before she could leave for the restaurant, the doorman asked her casually if she had heard the news. He thought she might be interested, given that it was about a plane.

'Yes?' she said, impatient to be away.

A Stinson airliner bound for Sydney from Brisbane was missing, with seven passengers and two pilots aboard.

'Did you say a Stinson?'

When the doorman agreed that, yes, that was what he had heard, she turned deathly pale. 'Excuse me,' she said, 'I have to make a phone call.'

One of the pilots was Beverley Shepherd.

Chapter 31

That night, the night Beverley Shepherd disappeared, Jean Batten ordered that her Percival Gull be unloaded off the ship from which she had so recently disembarked, and taken to Mascot aerodrome. Mechanics, she insisted, were to work all night to put it together, ready for her to join the search for the missing Stinson in the morning.

The distance between Brisbane and Sydney is just five hundred miles. Somewhere, in a clearing, the Stinson would be found. It wouldn't be too hard. She would go to it like a homing pigeon, the first to see it. She would find him. He would stand up, his fair hair shining in the sun, and put his arms out to greet her. 'I knew you'd come,' he would say. Everyone aboard the plane would be safe, and she would be glad for them all. But most of all, she would be glad for him. How careless of you to miss our dinner date, she would say, and he would laugh and say that she had kept him waiting long enough. What was another day or so?

These were the things she told herself as day after day she rose around 5 a.m., before taking off to search over the mountains and rainforests. By now there were dozens of planes in the sky, whirling around in the heat of the summer. They had to watch out for one another.

Every day she circled the mountainous country, searching ravines and areas dense with ancient beech trees, pigeonberry ash and rosewood. Beneath them grew peach myrtle and everlasting daisies. She remembered the daisies because these cool glades, buried away from the sun's harsh light, were the only place in the world where these relics of the last Ice Age had survived. This should have told her what was quickly becoming apparent to the searchers — the trees were so dense that the plane might never be found. The trees hid their secrets well. They didn't admit the sunlight, or the gaze of strangers.

When Jean had flown for some thirty-eight hours, over five thousand miles of terrain, she stopped to rest, because she could go on no longer.

In the morning, after her return to Sydney, the Stinson was discovered by a man called O'Reilly, who lived in the mountains. On a hunch, he had gone out on foot to search. The headlines shouted the news. Two survivors.

Neither of them was Beverley.

One of the survivors told of how the two pilots had laughed and chatted as they crossed the mountains. They had flown lower and lower. The passenger had grown anxious. He had looked at the face of the co-pilot, a fair young man, and seen that he was worried, too. In fact, he had said, as they boarded, he wasn't flying on his normal run. He had to get back to Sydney to meet his girlfriend. She'd chew his ear if he didn't turn up. Fine young fellow. Last thing he remembered before the crash, this young chap had an awful look on his face as he leaned forward to adjust something on the control panel. But it was too late.

'I'm cold,' Jean said to her mother, again and again. 'I'm so cold.'

Outside the temperature was close to a hundred in the shade. Nellie fanned herself, desperate for air, as Jean closed all the windows to stop the draughts.

'You need to get dressed for the service,' she said.

'Service. What service?'

'You know, dear. You know whose it is.'

'Are you mad? Why would I go to that? It isn't a funeral, there isn't even a body. How can you have a funeral when the person is lost in the mountains?'

The decision had been made to leave the four men who had died at the crash site, buried alongside the plane that had taken their lives. The terrain was too difficult, the forest too dense, and the cliffs and ravines so perilously steep that the call had been made not to bring them out. Some of the families were holding a small service to commemorate their lives.

Jean wrapped her arms around her knees and rocked backwards and forwards. 'I wanted to hold him again. I wanted to touch him.'

'His mother,' Nellie said, helplessly. 'We should go for his parents' sake.'

'What am I supposed to do at their damn service?' Jean

shouted. 'Press their hands and say, "Oh, I'm so sorry." And they'll look at me, sorry for themselves, and sorry for me. Well, I won't have it, I don't want their pity.'

'Jean,' Nellie tried again, 'it's not their fault.'

'I don't care about his parents. I don't care, do you understand? Get me a blanket if you want to do something useful. You hear me? Get me a bloody blanket.'

Cold. Everlasting. The everlasting bloody daisies.

She huddled under the blanket and whimpered. 'You don't understand,' she said in a voice that Nellie could hardly hear.

'What is it, dear? What did you say?'

'My heart. My heart is frozen, don't you see?'

'It'll pass,' Nellie said, trying to hold her.

'I'll always be on my own now. I didn't want to be alone.'

'You won't be,' Nellie said. 'So long as I live, you'll never be alone.'

Her mother brought her hot chicken soup. She rang Fred in New Zealand. 'No, don't come,' she said. 'I'll get her back to New Zealand if I can. Treatment? We'll have to wait and see.'

In the end, Jean said she just wanted to stay there for a bit, get some sun, swim, try to get warm. The months passed. Some days she drove alone to look at the sea. John and Madeleine were passing through Sydney, on their way from Tahiti to New Zealand. Nellie met them, but Jean said that she would rather go for a drive that day. Nellie could tell her all about them. Nellie reported that John looked very tired. The little girl was a dear wee thing, and seemed very bright. Madeleine hadn't had much to say for herself. Apart from that there seemed little more to tell.

Amelia Earhart, the American pilot with whom Jean had shared a trophy, but never met, disappeared in July while on a round the world flight. She and a companion, Fred Noonan, had been flying a Lockheed Electra. They had last been heard of on their radio above the Pacific. 'It's what happens to us,' Jean said, resignation in her voice.

But Jean didn't mention the cold again, and Nellie decided that some kind of thaw was setting in. An Australian pilot called Jim Broadbent now announced he was planning to break Jean's record England–Australia time. He had already set a number of records of his own. This appeared to galvanise Jean into action. She drove to Mascot and ordered the Gull wheeled out. She hadn't flown it since Beverley's death. That day, she took to the skies again, flying over the city and above the Blue Mountains. It was a salute and a farewell.

'I've decided to fly the Gull back to London,' she told Nellie. 'Then I'll be the first person to hold both England-to-Australia and Australia-to-England records at the same time. Just see if I'm not.'

Nellie shook her head. 'There have been too many accidents. I couldn't bear anything to happen to you.'

'I don't especially care,' Jean said. 'It's the way to go if one must.'

Lord Wakefield had continued to write to her from London. He didn't mention the loss of Beverley, although

Jean imagined word might have got back to him. He sent her a diamond brooch. She turned it over in her hands, delighting in the sparkle of the exquisite stones, but wondering if he had forgotten an earlier gift of a brooch. When she wrote to thank him, she told him that he hoped he wouldn't mind, but she had decided to exchange it for diamond ear clips.

She showed them off to Nellie. 'People will be missing us back in London,' she said. 'We need to get back, Mother, have a good time, paint the town red.'

Her mother suggested again that they return to New Zealand. 'Your father would like to see you.'

Jean gave her a blank stare. 'I don't want to see him. After what he did.'

Nellie looked puzzled. 'I don't understand.'

'You must. He betrayed me to Frank Norton.'

'But you and he were happy when we went on holiday.'

'Holiday. What holiday?'

'Jean. Listen to me. Your father didn't betray you. He saved you from embarrassment. We all went away together. You do remember that, don't you?'

Jean had a bewildered look in her eyes, and shook her head, as if to clear it. 'You go back to New Zealand if you want to.'

'Jean, listen to me, my darling, I've told you, I won't ever leave you.'

'I know,' Jean said, and put her arms around her mother. They clung to each other. 'Best get a ticket for London.'

'Two tickets?'

'Just one. I've told you I'm flying. And it would be so wonderful if you were there waiting for me.' Jean had recovered herself, as if nothing odd had happened. 'You've never seen me land at the end of one of my big flights. I have to get the Gull ready. That'll take a few weeks. So if you were to leave now, you'd be there for me.'

'If you're sure.' Nellie was still doubtful.

'I'll be all right. I promise.'

Jean set out for Darwin on 15 October, battling through red dust storms, flying low over kangaroos that hopped out of her path, following cattle tracks and causing stampedes amongst herds on the ground. After four days in Darwin, she took to the air again. News had come through that Jim Broadbent had set out upon his journey from England.

Before her lay one of the most difficult flights she had ever embarked upon, storm after storm battering the plane. She flew on, through monsoon rains, through the nights ahead, over the lonely Burmese coast where Smithy had disappeared. As she neared the edge of Pakistan's Sind Desert, she was so tired she leaned her head against the side of the cockpit and propped one eye open at a time to stay awake. Death or a record, it didn't really seem to matter. She took out a bottle of eau de Cologne and dabbed some on her burning face with a handkerchief, ate an orange, and drank some black coffee. Near Karachi, the heat was so intense that the crêpe soles of her shoes melted and stuck to the rudder bars.

She slept at Damascus for four hours. When she left, more storms hit, and she decided to turn back. Later she would think that, after all, some instinct for self-preservation still lurked within. Besides, her time was now so far in advance of the record that she could afford to take this break.

Storms confronted her again, but this time she determined that she would ride them out. Lightning flashed, the strange phenomenon of St Elmo's fire creating thin blue circles of light around the propeller. Somewhere near Greece, she and Jim Broadbent passed in the air without seeing each other. Not that he would make it much further: his plane ran out of fuel, stranding him in the Iraqi desert.

At Naples, Jean was lifted from the plane, gaunt with exhaustion. A doctor called to the airport advised her not to continue for the sake of her health and there were grim warnings from the meteorological office of more bad weather ahead.

She flew on.

On 24 October, she arrived at Lympne, unable to walk. She recovered sufficiently to fly on, after twenty minutes, to Croydon, where vast crowds awaited her. She had flown from Australia in five days, eighteen hours and fifteen minutes, breaking the record by fourteen hours.

She was the first person to hold both outward and inward records at the same time. Two policemen carried her from the plane head-high so that people could see her.

And there was Nellie, waiting, as she had promised.

Part Three
Following the Sun

1938–1970

Chapter 32

'So there Mother was,' Jean said, to the audience of New Zealanders and other dignitaries who had gathered to honour her at a special luncheon. 'She has been and always will be my inspiration, and I think I owe all my success to her.'

As three cheers for Mrs Ellen Batten rang out, Jean continued her speech. 'You know there was a time when I was refused a job in Sir Alan Cobham's Flying Circus. In fact, it seemed that the pilots thought I ought to go away and get married. One of the pilots gave me that impression so much that I asked him, "Is this a proposal?" He didn't say any more about it.'

A man jumped to his feet. 'Miss Batten, I'm Sir Alan Cobham.'

'Oh my goodness, so you are. Now how did I miss you?' Jean said, laughing and shaking her head. Nellie, seated beside her, sighed with relief. Jean was giving and taking quips, as she had in the past. She was dressed in an elegant white suit, with a matching hat that had a tilted brim.

Cobham said, 'When my pilots demanded to know if I was going to let a woman in on the show, I thought there would be a riot. No, no, we couldn't have had that, and what would have happened if we'd damaged the most famous woman in the world? We wouldn't be here today. I think you should be thanking me, Miss Batten.'

They bowed to each other as the laughter and clapping continued.

At another function she was presented with a bouquet of crimson carnations and, just as she was burying her face in their scent, a note was put into her hand. King George and Queen Elizabeth would be honoured if she paid a visit that evening and joined them for supper. If she were driving herself, she just needed to present this note at the gates, as she was expected. This seemed a charming way of delivering a royal command.

It emerged, on her arrival, that she was first to meet with another king. A butler bowed and said, 'King Leopold would be delighted if you could spare him a few moments. He's staying here at the moment.'

Jean was puzzled. 'Won't he be joining us for supper?'

'My instruction was to show you to his rooms, Miss Batten.'

She expected servants in attendance, but when she entered she found King Leopold III of Belgium alone, sitting on one of a pair of matching Regency chairs.

He was a tall man with a long face, pushing unruly hair back from his forehead. 'Please sit down,' he said, indicating the chair opposite. 'I'm very interested in aviation. Belgium's colonies are so far-spread, I've had to travel great distances myself, someone else at the controls, though I often wished it was me who was flying the plane. I've followed you on all your routes.'

'Really?'

'Indeed, I sit by the wireless whenever you are in the air, listening for reports of how you are faring.'

'I'm honoured, Your Majesty,' Jean said, bowing her head.

They talked then about their journeys, and advances in the aviation industry. After a time, he gave her a long, intent stare, and cleared his throat, as if he were nervous. 'Miss Batten, I hope you don't mind me saying this, but you're even more beautiful than I expected. Your photographs don't do you justice.'

'Thank you, sir.'

'I'd like to think we could be friends. I'm a widower by the way, did you know?'

'I'd heard that you lost your wife. I'm so terribly sorry.'

'It's a while ago,' he said, tucking his chin into his hand. 'I was driving in Switzerland. Queen Astrid was by my side. She was due to have a baby. I lost control of the car, it plunged into the lake. I lived, but she did not. Nor our child. It should have been me.'

Jean felt hard knots of tears pressing behind her eyelids but she looked at him, stony-faced.

'You'll think me impertinent. It's not for a king to pour out his sorrows. Sometimes — it seems there is nobody. I can't think why I've told you. Miss Batten, I'm so sorry. When I saw you, I thought you might understand.'

'We all have our sorrows,' she said. 'When you're an aviator you become accustomed to the loss of your friends.'

'I heard something …' His voice trailed away.

Jean was wordless. She had not spoken Beverley's name since his death. She hoped that the King did not intend to speak of the matter now.

'Perhaps you'll come to Brussels some time?' he said at last. 'I should so like to see you again.'

'Thank you, that is a very kind invitation.'

He sighed heavily. 'So long as Germany doesn't bring war upon us all.'

There was a discreet knock at the door and a messenger entered. 'Queen Elizabeth will receive you in her private apartment, Miss Batten.'

The Queen, seated on a blue brocade sofa, rose and greeted Jean as if she were an old friend. Her eleven-year-old daughter, also Elizabeth, was there, too, rosy-complexioned, wearing a dark pink crushed-velvet dress.

Jean curtseyed, first to the Queen and then to the Princess.

The formalities over, Jean turned to the child. 'The children in New Zealand and Australia love you, ma'am,' she said. 'They'll be so envious to know that I've met you.'

Elizabeth blushed. 'I've got a new puppy,' she said. 'Would you like to see it?'

'Oh, how lovely,' Jean said, trying to sound enthusiastic and hoping her reply hid her nervousness of dogs.

As the child disappeared to fetch the dog, the King entered the room.

'I'm so pleased to see you, Miss …' and here he stopped.

'Batten,' said his wife swiftly. 'It's Miss Batten, Bertie.'

Jean had heard of the King's stammer. 'I'd so like you to call me Jean,' she said quickly.

The King looked relieved, as if this were one less thing to worry about in his new and unexpected role as a monarch. It was barely a year since his brother had abdicated to marry the divorcée Wallis Simpson, and already he looked exhausted. Jean smiled inwardly, remembering Edward being rolled in and out of a laundry van. She couldn't imagine this man ever being in such a predicament.

Toasted crumpets were being served with tea. The Princess dashed about with her corgi, demonstrating its tricks to Jean, until her mother remonstrated, and the conversation turned, as it had with Leopold, to talk of aviation.

So 1937 slid into 1938 while Jean gave speeches, met more royalty, received prizes, had her likeness created at Madame Tussaud's — and partied, her clothes always remarked upon. When the parties were over she would disappear into the night, a taxi waiting to bear her off to her lodgings with Nellie. In the early afternoons, she sat down and wrote. She called her new book *My Life*, though there was only so much of her life she would reveal. She and Nellie took a cruise in the Caribbean, and when they stopped off at Jamaica declared themselves in love with the island. Now here might be a place to live some day. The Spanish Civil War had put paid to thoughts of going to Majorca.

There was talk of a wider war on the continent. Week by week, unease was spreading throughout England, as Hitler's menacing behaviour pushed the stakes higher. It was not as if Jean hadn't noticed, but the talk had gone on for so long that somehow it had stopped being real. Or perhaps it never was for her. If you went to a party and danced until you dropped it was easier to sleep. 'I want to just keep following the sun,' she said to Nellie. 'I want to feel warmth on my face every day.'

Late in August 1939, when the Swedish countryside was simmering with gentle heat, she visited Axel Wenner-Gren and his wife. When she had first met them they said they would be enchanted if she could find time to visit them in their country residence. Wenner-Gren, who looked like a king, immaculate and suave, with fine Nordic features, was reputed to be one of the wealthiest men in the world, having made his money in international electronics, developing Electroluxes and refrigerators. The last guest of the Wenner-Grens had been the reclusive Greta Garbo. Jean hoped she might return while she was still there. Her own 'Garbo of the Skies' tag had lingered, long after the years of Gipsy G-AARB, and she was keen to meet her namesake. There were picnics and car trips, and in the evenings Jean played Chopin on her hosts' grand piano. The war wasn't mentioned in her presence, so that the sense of living in a golden bubble where no harm could come to them all, persisted through the summer. Then, just as Jean was preparing to fly the Gull home, she received a telegram from the Foreign Office in London, warning her that she was not, on any account, to fly back over Germany. At once, she went to her hosts and asked them what on earth she should do. To her surprise, Wenner-Gren picked up the phone, and asked for a number in Berlin. It was done in a trice, her clearance to use German airspace obtained. 'I spoke to my friend Göring,' he said. 'There's nothing to worry about.'

On 27 August 1939, Jean flew over Germany, its skies curiously empty of air traffic. She passed above the rivers that streaked the countryside, the fields golden where the grain harvests had been cut, the dense forests and mediaeval castles. It was to the south that she saw a sight that made her catch her breath. Lined up on an airstrip alongside a huge factory, stood a hundred, perhaps even two hundred Messerschmitt Bf 109s, fighter planes, stretching almost as far as the eye could see. She was tempted to circle back and fly over them, but thought better of it.

When she landed in Lympne, a man was waiting for her at the airport. The man wore a striped suit and a Homburg, and carried a rolled umbrella. He had a polite warning for her, which he delivered in a quiet voice. It might be better, he said, if she were not to discuss her flight. Best for all concerned. He was interested in anything she might have seen.

The following week, Chamberlain's fateful announcement was made from 10 Downing Street. Nellie and Jean sat by the radio, their faces pale, as they heard that England was at war with Germany.

'I must do something,' Jean cried.

'What will you do?' Nellie asked, not understanding.

'It's my duty to offer to help the war effort. I'll write a letter straightaway.'

The response was swift.

> *Dear Miss Batten,*
>
> *Many thanks for your letter of the 4th September offering your services and your Percival Gull G-ADPR for dispatch or communication work. I am at once communicating with Sir Francis Shelmerdine with a view to your name being included in a pool of civilian pilots for employment on Royal Air Force organization and delivery work or general communication flying, and I am asking him to communicate with you directly in the matter.*

The letter was signed by a secretary in the War Office.

The correspondence continued for a while, then tailed away. The enthusiasm for Jean's services appeared to dwindle. The Gull had been put in storage since the outbreak of the war.

In June the following year, the Air Registration Board wrote to her wanting to inspect the Gull and 'assess its suitability for impressment'.

'Impressment,' Nellie said. 'What does that mean?'

'It means,' Jean said bitterly, 'that they're seizing my plane. The one I paid for myself.'

'And they won't pay you for it?'

'Oh, I think so. But that's hardly the point, is it? Mother, don't look at me like that. I'm not sick, you don't need to go phoning my father. I'm angry, that's all.'

The Air Transport Auxiliary did not, after all, require Miss Batten's services.

They did require Amy Johnson's.

Victor Dorée, she learned, had become an RAF flying instructor.

In New Zealand, the Royal Navy accepted John Batten, now divorced from Madeleine, as a dental mechanic. He would serve on the *Achilles* and the *Gambia*, seeing action on both.

Jean's eyesight was a problem, she was told. But then so was that of several women who took to the air wearing spectacles.

The requisitioning of the Gull felt like the ultimate loss. She couldn't put it alongside the loss of love, but in her bewilderment she felt lost to herself. She no longer recognised the person she had believed she was. It was less than three years since she was being described as the most famous woman in the world. It had been said as a joke, and the joke had turned out to be on her.

Her flight across Germany proved to be her last.

Chapter 33

Nellie and Jean, mother and daughter, chose the place to build their house in Jamaica together, although not without some hesitations and misgivings about its location. The land they bought, in 1948, was beside the sea at Tower Isle, on a stretch of coast east of the town of Ocho Rios. It was a rough, winding ride to the sea, through countryside dotted with wooden shanties occupied by West Indian locals, and by places they called the balm yards, thatched covered huts clustered together, a bright red flag flying overhead, where revival meetings were held every night. Black cattle strayed among sparse coconut palms that barely moved in the almost non-existent breeze. Cane fields stretched into the distance, tended by West Indian labourers clad in white robes and white turbans. Towards the sea lay mangrove swamps that reminded Jean and Nellie of Auckland. And then they came upon the sea, so clear that they could see the grains of sand, the life of fish, when they stood above it. The beaches were the colour of pale champagne.

This is where it will be, they said, in almost one voice. It was not the first time they had lived on this part of the island. When they arrived, two years earlier, they had rented a house in the area, one with a long view of the Caribbean, surrounded by an exotic garden, darting with humming birds. Jean was enchanted. This was perfect, it gave her heart ease, she said. But Nellie hadn't been so sure. There was something wrong with the house, she said, something evil was going to befall it.

'Mother, don't be so silly,' Jean said. 'You're going back to that weird old church of yours. Just because you've come to a place where everyone believes in jumbies and ghosts, doesn't mean you have to go spiritual on me again.'

'I don't believe in jumbies,' Nellie said in a sharp voice, although she shivered. Jumbies, the islanders held, were the souls of live people who lived in the bodies of the dead. 'Listen to the music, and all that chanting. It's been building up louder and louder the last few nights. There's something sinister going on. I don't understand what it is, but we need to get away from here.'

She had been so insistent that Jean had agreed to them packing up their possessions and leaving the next day. Nellie was right, though. The day after they left, the young gardener, high on ganja, had run amok with an axe, breaking every stick of furniture in the house.

'Perhaps he was unhappy because we left,' Jean said, but Nellie would have none of that. They landed up in a cottage in a British army camp, high in the Jamaican Blue Mountains, for the next year or so. The trees, native cedar and teak, were high and thick; the mountains took their name not from the colour of the trees, as in Australia, but from the blue mists that shrouded the forest for much of the year. The rainfall was high, and there were more days spent inside than out. Besides, the proximity of the camp meant that well-meaning residents sent constant invitations to dinner. Jean wanted none of that. Nor, she told her mother, could she bear the constant memory of the Blue Mountains in that other country 'where things had happened'. It was she who planned their escape route, consulted a builder and chose the piece of land at Ocho Rios, and, in the end, Nellie had to agree that it seemed the perfect spot.

The house was not all Jean had dreamed of: the one she had planned in her imagination cost more than they could afford. Nellie kept a careful eye on the stocks and shares she had managed with such skill and thrift over the years. 'Totally impractical,' she said, when she saw the plans, and what the house would cost.

They settled for something more simple and conventional, not unlike an Auckland villa, with three bedrooms, a good-sized kitchen and a verandah looking out to sea. As if to stamp some sign of wealth on it, Jean had a swimming pool built that stood between the house and the sea. She chose the name Blue Horizon for the property. It was her decision, too, to have a high fence built around the house, with a gate that locked. Inside its walls, Jean planted a garden full of brilliant colour. After lunch, they sat in low-slung deck chairs, under large sun umbrellas, and read.

A man stepped through the gate one afternoon in January, when the gate had been left ajar for the delivery of groceries. He was tall, hollow-cheeked, with a crooked nose, as if it had been broken and badly set, like a scar on his otherwise perfect features. His eyes were heavy-lidded. 'I was just passing,' he said, holding out his hand. As soon as he spoke, Jean noticed that his teeth were rather long, so that, after all, the symmetry of his face was flawed. She still noticed teeth, remembering the way her father used to give an involuntary glance at people's mouths before he looked at their eyes. 'Excuse me if I've interrupted anything.'

Jean was slow to take his hand. The man could have been fifty, it was hard to tell his age, but he smelled of cigarettes and gin. 'We were having a rest, Mr—?'

'Fleming, Ian Fleming. And you're Miss Batten?'

Jean nodded. 'We enjoy our own company here,' she said crisply. She was dressed in a floral patterned halter-neck top and wide-legged shorts, not what she would have chosen to wear to receive guests. Her feet were bare.

'I've heard of you, Commander Fleming,' Nellie said, getting to her feet. 'Royal Navy? You're one of our neighbours, aren't you?' She was in her seventies now, but she was still strong and supple in her movements. Her hair formed a silver cloud around her shoulders when she released it from the pins that held it in place in public.

'Not all the time. I come here when it's winter in London.'

'Ah yes, you're in newspapers now, aren't you? You own that house, Goldeneye, on the cliff at Oracabessa?' Nellie said.

'Very well observed.'

'It's a little hard not to know who's who in this place,' Jean said. 'Which is why our gate is generally closed.'

'A pity,' said Fleming, with a casual shrug of his shoulders. 'I'll remember it the next time I'm in this neck of the woods. I'd been going to suggest dinner at my place.'

Nellie said, 'Commander Fleming, dinner at your place would be delightful. Did you have a date in mind?'

He suggested the following Sunday — drinks around six and they could watch the sun going down, then Violet, his cook, would prepare them some fish. He hoped they were partial to the local fish.

Jean had moved away from her mother, her back rigid, as this conversation took place. Fleming came and stood beside her for a moment, before he left. He looked down at her, sideways, his hooded eyes resting on her. 'I like solitude, too, as a rule. But now and then I like a change. We could get on well, you and I.'

'I doubt it. I don't care much for men.'

'Really? Well, I wouldn't have picked that.'

Jean shut and locked the gate firmly behind him. 'Why did you do that, Mother?'

'You don't want people to think us odd, do you?'

'They do already. What does it matter?'

'Well, just say I'm curious. I understand he's the foreign manager of the Kemsley group — the *Sunday Times* and all that. Quite an important position.' Nellie, who had grasped the patois of their servants more easily than Jean, often had conversations with them, and had become well informed on local matters.

'You know I don't want newspapers anywhere near me,' Jean said.

'Well, of course not. But Mr Fleming comes here for a rest. All I'm saying is, he could be interesting. Now come on, dear, you should have a swim, and I'll brush your hair out for you afterwards. You'd like that, wouldn't you?'

Fleming's house had a rough, do-it-yourself quality and was Spartan in its furnishing. The canvas chairs, once blue, had faded to grey, and the concrete living room floor, originally intended to be navy blue, had turned out with an odd but not unattractive marbled effect.

The Battens were not his only guests. A man, wearing a patterned satin tunic over white linen slacks, held out his hand before Fleming greeted them. His face was long, saturnine and smooth-skinned, his smile white. 'My dears,' he said, 'welcome to Golden Eye, Nose and Throat.'

Fleming now appeared from behind a wreath of smoke. 'Take no notice of my dear friend Coward. He can't resist a dig at my lodgings, although he makes himself perfectly at home when it suits him.'

'I stayed here once,' Noël Coward said. 'It was perfectly ghastly, no hot water, iron bedsteads. *And* he charged me fifty pounds a week for the privilege. And he's still got this awful stool thing to sit on at the dining room table.'

'There's hot water now,' Fleming said, sounding grumpy.

'I have my own house along the road these days,' Coward said. 'You'll have to come and visit me next. Miss Batten, I expected you to be wearing wings of diamond. I'm a great admirer of yours.'

'Well, nobody could admire *you* more than my mother,' Jean said, laughing in spite of herself. She wore a sleeveless white silk dress, like many she had worn in the past, only shorter, the hem swirling around her knees, and silver sandals. The only diamonds she wore were her small ear studs, which she touched a trifle self-consciously.

'I'll never forget *Blithe Spirit* in the West End — 1941,' Nellie said. 'The war, and all of us so down-hearted, and then that wonderful play.'

'You enjoy the theatre, Mrs Batten?'

'My mother is a thwarted actress. Worse, she's a thwarted spiritual medium,' Jean said, mocking Nellie. 'Of course she loved *Blithe Spirit*. She could see herself in it.'

'Now then,' Fleming said, fitting another cigarette in his holder, 'what's it to be? A vodka martini? Whisky soda?' An ample West Indian woman had appeared from the kitchen.

'Have you got champagne?' asked Jean.

Fleming looked put out. 'Champagne, oh well yes, if you insist.' There was nothing welcoming about him at all. Jean wondered why he had bothered to invite them. Nellie agreed to a whisky soda, as if to humour him.

'Violet, Miss Batten wants champagne, if you please,' he said.

Violet put her hands on her hips. 'Oh Lordy, Lordy,' she muttered, as if there had been an invasion of locusts. 'Champagne.' But she was soon back with a bottle of Dom Pérignon.

While the drinks were poured, Coward asked, in a desultory way, whereabouts exactly they had come from in New Zealand. When Jean said she was born in Rotorua, he clapped his hands.

'I've been there,' he said. 'You can pop an egg in the ground and boil it.'

'You could,' Nellie said, 'although we never tried it.'

'Oh. But such a bonus, hot water everywhere. Although I've heard you boil up some poor devils out for a walk as well.'

'We did have to keep an eye on Jean. She was a very adventurous little girl.'

'I can imagine. I have to say, in spite of all the domestic possibilities, I wouldn't find it compensation for having to live immediately on top of the hidden fires of the earth.'

Dinner was now served, conch gumbo and fried octopus tentacles with tartare sauce. 'Violet's food is perfectly vile, too,' Coward said. 'Fleming, pour Miss Batten some more champagne.' They were all perched on the narrow banquette seating that ran along either side of the table.

'So what did you do in the war, Miss Batten?' Fleming said.

'I worked in munitions until I was released to give talks for the war effort. I raised a considerable amount of money.' Fleming appeared to be listening intently, but he made no comment. 'I spoke at factories and dockyards, textile mills, town halls. I went to coal mines, and another time I spoke to thousands of dock workers at the Chatham Naval Base.'

'But you didn't fly?'

'My plane was requisitioned at the outset of the war.' Jean's eyes filled, and she raised her napkin to catch the unbidden tears. 'I wanted to fly for the Air Transport Auxiliary. I was disappointed, to say the least, when they turned me down.'

'Now, why I wonder was that?'

'There was something wrong with my eyesight, or so they said. So, as I couldn't fly for the Auxiliary, they took my plane. I suppose I got lucky. Look at Amy Johnson, the war had hardly begun and she was killed. I was surprised at that, but then her health wasn't good and she was a wreck after her divorce. All those things going wrong for her and they took her on. I don't think *she* was fit to fly.'

'Tell me then, when was your last flight?'

'I flew back from Sweden, right at the outbreak of the war.'

'Hmm, I see. That was over Germany. You must have been the last British plane to fly over Germany?'

'Possibly.'

'How on earth did you get permission?'

'I had friends.' She fell silent again, sensing that Fleming knew more about her than she did about him.

'Oh, now who might that have been?'

'Really, Fleming, my dear chap. Surely Miss Batten doesn't have to be interrogated at the *dinner* table,' Coward said.

'Axel Wenner-Gren,' Jean said carefully. 'He was suspected of being a spy for the Germans. I didn't know that at the time.'

'Ah, Göring's mate,' Fleming said. 'You know he lives in the Bahamas now?'

'I haven't followed his movements. They don't interest me.' Jean returned to her meal.

The conversation continued, while Jean picked around the tentacles of the octopus. If Fleming noticed his guest's lack of composure, he made nothing of it.

Suddenly she asked, 'Mr Fleming, who did you spy for?'

He looked at her and snorted what might have passed for a laugh, although there was a touch of contempt in it, too. 'I've had Violet mix a special cocktail,' he said. 'We call it Poor Man's Thing. Orange and lemon skins. A bottle of Three Daggers rum. In a minute she's going to bring it through and set it alight. I'm sure you'll like it, Miss Batten. Jean, you said I might call you Jean?'

Coward was apologetic about his friend Fleming. He had finished showing them around his own house, and they were settled in deep comfortable chairs. The fourth chair was occupied by a young man called Graham Payn. 'What could I call this place, except Blue Harbour? Look at it, isn't it magnificent? Well, blue horizon, blue harbour, we're not meant to be original here. Mind you, Graham's here to work, aren't you? Graham's got two new films coming up. He has to rehearse his lines. Don't you, Graham?'

'I am, I am, I've been at them all day.'

'You have to practise. You can't carry the script around when the action starts. I've written this screenplay with Graham especially in mind.'

'How immensely fortunate to have a film written for you,' Nellie said. 'What's it called?'

'*The Astonished Heart*,' Coward said. 'I'm going to be in it myself.'

'It's quite gloomy,' Graham said, frowning a little. 'I'm not sure it's quite me.'

Coward looked at his watch, and then at the door. 'Graham, be a dear and fetch us some water please.'

Graham stood up in one quick, graceful movement. He wore a deep purple shirt and a gold bracelet. Jean noticed that Coward was wearing a similar bracelet.

Nellie raised her eyebrows slightly. Coward inclined his head towards her, as if to say that it was all right, it wasn't catching. Or that's what Jean thought.

'Fleming will be joining us soon. He's a good chap, really,' he said, during Graham's absence from the room. 'He's had a spot of bother. His little girl died shortly after birth.'

'That's dreadful,' Nellie said. 'I'm so sorry. I didn't know Mr Fleming was married.'

'He's not. This happened some little while ago, you understand, but the trouble still raises its head.'

'So — where is the mother of the little girl now? Is she all right?' Nellie asked.

'She hasn't been well, but I hear things are improving. She's at home in London with her husband. This is between us, you understand. But you might find the situation here a little unorthodox. You're bound to come across Ann, that's the lady's name, if we're all going to visit one another. Something I should like, by the way.'

'Ann? It's an ordinary enough name. Would we know her?' Nellie asked.

'She's the Viscountess Rothermere. Before that she was Lady O'Neill. Her first husband was killed in action. Goodness knows who she'll end up as, but I do think she's rather set on Fleming.' He put his fingers to his lips, motioning them to silence.

Fleming had appeared at the door, dressed as he was each time they had met him, in baggy pants and a loose blue short-sleeved shirt.

Graham returned, bearing a tall jug of iced water, floating with slivers of lemon.

'Well, here we are all together,' Coward said. 'Sit down, Ian. We're not having one of our edgy days, are we?'

'I was reading a good book,' Fleming said. 'I almost couldn't put it down.' He sighed, and cast his eyes around the room. 'Your collection of colonials is assembled.'

'Now, now, that's enough. I want you to be civil to my guests. Better than that, I want you to be nice. Graham is from South Africa, you understand,' their host said, by way of explanation to Nellie and Jean. 'Which reminds me, what's happened to that brother of yours, Miss Batten?'

There was a silence that neither Jean nor Nellie was willing to fill. 'Do you mean my brother John?' Jean asked, finally.

'Yes, of course. He did that rather good war movie, *For Those in Peril*. I hadn't seen him acting in anything for years.'

'We don't hear much from him,' Nellie said. 'He joined the navy as a dental mechanic. We heard he served on the *Achilles*.'

'With distinction, I gathered. And then they released him to do the movie.'

'He seems to live his own life,' Nellie said.

Coward gave her a curious look. 'Well, I suppose his divorce was inevitable. I mean to say …'.

'Madeleine was a flighty girl,' Nellie said stiffly.

'We used to bump into him from time to time, didn't we, Graham? I gather he's gone back to New Zealand.' Coward looked at the two discomforted Batten women, with a faintly apologetic, or was it amused, expression, and changed the subject. Had Fleming been writing any articles today, he wondered aloud.

Ian Fleming looked weary, his gaze not leaving Jean's face, his expression impenetrable. He shook his head.

After dinner, Coward asked Jean to play his piano, and accompany Graham while he sang. They produced sheet music, mostly of Coward's own songs, and finished the evening all singing 'London Pride' together, even Fleming.

'I sometimes wish we could go back,' Nellie said. 'We had such a nice time in London, didn't we, Jean? Before the war.'

The fragrance of frangipani was heavy on the air as they took their leave, the petals glimmering in light falling from the doorway as Coward and Payn bade them all goodnight.

In the morning, Jean drove to Goldeneye, parked behind the house and walked around to the front verandah. It was past eight. Fleming was sitting with a mug of shaving water beside him, lathering his face. His expression darkened when he saw Jean.

'What are you doing here?'

'I wanted to see you.'

'I don't have sex before breakfast.'

'That's not what I came for.'

He completed the lathering, took up a razor and began shaving. 'You see,' he said, stopping between strokes, 'I have my rituals in the morning. I go for a swim out to the reef at seven. I come back and I shave. Then I have my breakfast in the garden. In a minute, Violet will bring me some paw paw and scrambled eggs, and coffee. I like to do this in isolation, except for the company of the birds. You see the humming birds out there? I like to watch them. I feed the kling klang. If I wanted company I would find it for myself. What do you know about the kling klang?'

'The black birds that come to the garden? I don't like the sound they make, it's very shrill.'

'Not if you feed them nicely. I like the blackness of the kling klang. I like birds.'

'So do I. They tell you when land is close when you're far out at sea and believe yourself lost. I've studied birds, too, Mr Fleming, more than you might believe.'

'Oh yes, the aviator, I almost forgot. Birds of the air. You haven't always been rich and idle, Miss Batten.'

'Rich? You call me rich. You have no idea.'

'Of what? You weren't born with a silver spoon in your mouth?'

'If you call living on three pounds a week in London, year after year, rich, well that's over to you. To tell you the truth, people around here make me sick. If it's silver spoons in the mouth, you were all born with them welded into your fillings.'

Suddenly he laughed. 'Oh that's quite a nice line. Do you want to have breakfast with me?'

When they had finished eating and Violet had cleared up, with a flounce and raised eyebrows at the sight of Jean, he took out a cigarette. 'Why don't you like men?'

'Because they die. Every man I've ever got close to has died.'

'So that's why you won't go to bed with me? You're afraid you might kill me off.'

'You have no idea what it's like.'

He leaned forward. 'I know about death, in the same way you know about birds. More than you think. I'm willing to take a chance.'

'No,' she said, 'no.'

'I'd like to sleep with you. You're a bit past your prime but I think you could still make it a pleasant enough pastime for both of us. I could whip you if it would make you feel better about all those dead blokes. I like whipping women.'

She stood up. 'You're disgusting. I have to go.'

'You still haven't told me why you came.'

She took a deep breath. 'The Swede. Axel Wenner-Gren. I knew nothing about his connections with Germany. I swear that.'

He tapped another cigarette on the table, his fourth since her arrival. 'We decided he probably wasn't a Nazi agent anyway. What does it matter now?'

'What does it matter? I lost everything, every last thing that I valued. There was nothing more to hold onto.'

'You got paid for your plane.'

'It didn't bring it back.'

'Buy another one.'

She clenched her fists. 'Stop it. Just stop.'

As she got into her car, he called out to her. 'Let me know if you change your mind about anything.' She saw his face behind the flame of his cigarette lighter.

The war. It was still there, behind her eyes some mornings when she woke. The war where she never truly belonged. She believed herself patriotic. When she made her speeches she had spoken about the ties of empire, which she had helped to foster. The King and Queen had received her as if she were a friend. It was no time to abandon her country, but her country seemed to have abandoned her. She turned to the French, whom she was sure would find a role for her. The Anglo-French Ambulance Corps ran a mobile hospital in France, staffed by some British doctors and nurses. The French did indeed welcome her, and she was soon wearing their uniform, driving ambulances in Britain, in preparation for being mobilised to France. Before that could happen the German army had over-run France and that door was closed behind her. She found herself working in a munitions factory in Poole in Dorset, inspecting the guns that were used on Spitfires. Her twelve-hour days on the assembly line began at 7.30, six mornings a week. At nights, pieces of plaster from her bedroom walls fell around her ears during the German bombing that Poole suffered night after night. When she had leave, she retreated to the Hertfordshire countryside, where Nellie was now living. She would be waiting with whatever nourishing hot soups her ration cards could run to, pressing her daughter to go to bed and sleep. While Jean slept, she sat beside her bed and watched.

'I'm not going to be invalided out, Mother,' Jean said once, opening her eyes unexpectedly. 'I told you, I'm not sick.'

Perhaps she was not. Perhaps it simply happened that way, but Jean would wonder if her mother had a hand in what happened next. An organisation called the National Savings Committee was raising money for the war effort. They saw, in Jean, an ideal person to promote their message. The Air Inspection Directorate, to whom she was responsible, opposed her discharge from the factory, but in the end the committee won the day. And so, as she told Fleming, and repeated the next time she confronted him, she had travelled the length and breadth of the country.

He had narrowed his eyes through cigarette smoke. 'But I knew all that,' he said. 'Why do you think I sought you out? You were bloody brave. Now tell me something I don't know.'

He didn't like to be bored. 'Tell me a story', he would say on the days when Jean came and sat on the edge of his verandah. So she would tell him. About how she came from a little country far away on the edge of the world. About caves and glow worms. About wanting to fly, and running off to Australia to meet up with Smithy, and ride in his plane. About Stag Lane, and rolling the Prince of Wales into the back of a laundry van, and the day she saw the R101 on her first solo flight. Of the nights stranded in the desert, alone with the Baluchi men in their robes. Most of all, she recounted the way she was supported by a frail wooden craft in the limitless dark nights, the immensity of the sky by day.

'You knew Kingsford Smith?' Fleming said, awe in his voice.

'But of course I did.' She told him then about the ups and downs of her hero's life, and the Coffee Royal scandal, and how it altered the course of her own life — things she hadn't written in either of her two books.

Fleming had laughed when she told him that she had written her autobiography when she was twenty-nine. 'How could you have thought that your life was over then?' he had asked her.

'It was,' she said, putting her head in her arms. 'Believe me, it was.'

'But that was before you lost your plane.'

'That was the last straw,' she said. She didn't tell him about Beverley.

There were some things she couldn't say to Fleming, whatever the things were that she could do with him.

'We don't really wish to receive Mr Fleming and his wife,' Lady Mitchell said. 'Mrs Fleming, of course, knows everyone in society, but I think she's beyond the pale now.'

Sir Harold Mitchell and his wife, Mary, owned Prospect Plantation near Ocho Rios, a thousand acres planted in pimentos, allspice and lemons. Their house was a vast eighteenth-century mansion set among gardens tended by dozens of West Indians.

Mary Mitchell was as close to a friend as Jean had had, apart from her mother, since her years in Auckland. Mary's husband had made his fortune from coal and oil, coffee and farming, in widespread interests across the world. He had withdrawn his money from Great Britain when a rail company he owned was privatised after the war. The couple had a daughter, a little girl called Mary-Jean.

The child had taken an instant liking to Jean, following her about and asking questions.

'I think she sees you as her aunt,' Mary said.

'She's a beautiful little girl,' Jean said. Mary-Jean made her think of her brother's children, and the summer she had spent with them. 'Do you think she'd like to learn dancing? I could teach her, if you like.'

This was an arrangement that suited everyone. Jean called more and more often at Prospect, and Mary-Jean's dancing improved with every visit.

'I hope you don't mind that I see Mary-Jean so much,' Jean said, on one of these occasions.

'Mind? Of course I don't mind. Why should I? She adores you.'

'I have to remind myself sometimes that she's your little girl.'

'You'd have liked one of your own?' Mary said.

'I would have liked children,' Jean said, her voice suddenly wistful.

Important guests arrived in a steady flow at Prospect. Mary faithfully invited the Battens to dine on each of these occasions. Often, they declined, and Mary never seemed ruffled. The invitations still came. Nellie's eyes sparkled when Charlie Chaplin was about to be entertained, but when it came to the point she begged off. She was coming down with a cold, she decided.

Winston Churchill was a different matter. There was no question but that they would attend. Already Nellie had bought herself a new, fitting black velvet dress, with full silk net sleeves. It was this occasion that had Mary worrying about the Flemings.

'What else could Rothermere do but divorce her, when she got pregnant again?' Mary pondered. 'All so quick, so public. And now here she is, six months gone, and the pair of them holed up there at Goldeneye, as large as life. Or in her case, rather larger. Have you met her?'

'Yes. She looks remarkably like the Duchess of Windsor,' Jean said, without elaborating further. She had, indeed, met the sharp-tongued woman with shrewd green eyes and a bright red mouth. Noël Coward had insisted that they pay a visit. Coward had been shaken by his part in the drama. Ann, it seemed, had been saying for years that she was visiting him in Jamaica when really she was with Fleming. It had been an embarrassment. Fleming was disturbed by the prospect of marriage. He was forty-four and he'd managed to evade it up until now. Yet Coward had been a witness at the wedding, one of the two people present.

Now his friend was writing a book to help him get over the loss of his bachelordom.

'I think we should put him off the whole idea, don't you?' Coward said to Jean.

When they arrived at Goldeneye, Ann Fleming was sitting in front of an easel dabbing away with a paintbrush, a palette perched in her hand. On the verandah, Fleming sat with his cigarette holder clenched between his teeth, typing at furious speed on a gold-plated typewriter.

'I'm writing a novel,' he said to Jean, without really pausing. 'It's a spy story called *Casino Royale*. Sound familiar? Royale-des-Eaux, it's the name of a town in France. I've just made it up.'

'And the hero is called Ian Fleming, I suppose?'

He stopped typing and grinned. 'I reckon James Bond sounds good. I've pinched it from some ornithologist fellow. You know I like birds.'

'Won't he mind?'

'Oh, who cares? I don't expect he'll ever read it. Anyway, my chap's got a code name. It's 007.'

Ann turned her head in Jean's direction.

'Get rid of her,' she said.

Nellie struck up an instant rapport with Winston Churchill. She told him her age, something she called her 'state secret'. Churchill was seventy-eight. During a conversation with his host, he turned in Nellie's direction and remarked: 'I am the oldest person here. By two years.' He raised his glass to Nellie. 'To the most beautiful woman in the room,' he said.

Nellie raised her glass back to him, with the air of a girl.

Noël Coward rushed over and kissed her while she pretended to faint with delight.

'It doesn't come much better than that,' Nellie said, as they drove home later that night. 'Did you enjoy the evening, Jean?'

'Oh, it was pleasant enough,' Jean said, keeping her eye on the winding road unfurling beneath them.

'Not a sign of the Flemings,' Nellie said.

'I'd say she was a little overripe for dancing right now, wouldn't you?'

'From what I've heard,' Nellie said.

'You know, I think I've seen enough of the people here,' Jean said. 'The same people, every time. Don't you ever get sick of them?'

'Just like that? We had such fun tonight.'

'Perhaps that's as good as it gets.'

'What would you like to do instead?' Although her

voice was cautious, Nellie's interest had quickened.

'Europe should have calmed down by now. We could have a look around.'

'I would like to go back, yes. There are a lot of places we haven't seen.'

'Just you and me, darling, just you and me.'

'I can't think of anything I'd rather do,' Nellie said.

'I'll miss Mary-Jean,' Jean said softly. 'I'm sure we'll keep in touch.'

The gate was unlocked, just like the first time Fleming had let himself in. Nellie and Jean were surrounded by boxes and packing cases.

'You didn't have to go,' he said to Jean.

'I do,' she said. 'You knew I would.'

'The publishers like my book.'

'Well, congratulations. You must send me a copy. Send it care of Thomas Cook.'

'I'm writing another one.'

'You must have found your vocation at last.'

He came up and stood close to her. 'There's a beautiful woman in it, with dark hair. She wears white silk dresses, and she doesn't like men. Or so she says.'

'How fascinating.' Jean didn't look at him.

'Her name is Solitaire. A game for one player.'

'Goodbye then, Mr Fleming,' she said. 'Or should that be 007?'

He narrowed his eyes against a coil of smoke. 'Jean, I could never figure out,' he said, 'why you put a swimming pool between your house and such a beautiful stretch of the sea. Was it something you were afraid of?'

Chapter 34

Nellie had taken good care of their money in Jamaica. They declared it 'their' money because, although Jean had earned it, it was Nellie who had invested and made it grow. 'Thanks to good old Edward Walter's tips,' she would say. 'Ted did have his uses.' She once said to Noël Coward, at dinner, 'I started out with horses and did very well. Now it's the stock market, and it's as big a flutter as the gallops. Amazing how it works out.'

On the island, Nellie and Jean had bought land here and there. When it came time to divest themselves of the various properties, the money mounted higher. They were ready to spend some of it. It was enough to keep them drifting through Europe for the next seven years.

After they left, Jean wrote often to Mary, always giving their address as Barclay's Bank. *We're in Monte Carlo, and guess how much Mother won? No, she wouldn't tell me, the wicked old thing.* The climate suited them better than that of Jamaica, the air was drier. Provence was all that they dreamed of. They would spend days walking in the mountain villages. At the village of Èze, near Nice, Jean had discovered an artists' colony and taken painting lessons. She thought her watercolours weren't too bad, and they would return so she could learn more later on.

Spain delighted them. Jean had long spoken fluent Spanish and found it easy to blend in with the locals. Granada especially appealed to them. They stayed in an old monastery within the palace gardens. *We could have stayed there forever. It's hard to describe the Moorish palace. The gardens were exquisite. Almond trees were in bloom, with the snow-covered Sierra Nevadas in the background. Everywhere we went the Spanish people were so kind to us, hospitable and untouched in their manner by tourists.*

Every letter was finished with an enquiry about the progress of Mary-Jean. Mary would reply with the details of local fêtes, and how her poppies had won first prize at the garden show. Of the locals, she wrote little, and nothing at all about Ian Fleming. Sometimes she enclosed a photograph of her daughter. They made plans to meet in Paris in the spring of 1954, though somehow they missed each other.

Nellie now fulfilled some ambitions of her own. She had always wanted to go to Italy. 'Everyone should see Venice once before they die,' she proclaimed, once she had been there, but really the whole country stole her heart. From Venice, she and Jean drove to Verona, because Nellie wanted to see the presumed home of Juliet Capulet, with its courtyard and stone balcony. And then nothing would do but that she saw Leonardo's fresco of the Last Supper, so they drove to Milan. They spent some weeks in Florence, where Nellie succeeded in climbing all the stairs to the top of the Duomo. But her ashen face at the end of the ascent frightened Jean.

'I think we should stay put for a while, Mother,' she said.

'Well, as long as it's warm,' Nellie replied, 'I'm sure I can cope. Don't write me off just yet.' She had caught her breath, and put her shoulders back after the descent.

For a long time they were torn between Provence, Italy and Spain. In the spring they found themselves often at Cap d'Ail. They would be in London and the sky might be grey one morning when they woke. Let's go to the Riviera, one of them would say, and they would be packed by lunchtime, ready to take the night train to Dover, followed by the morning train to the south.

Churchill took his holidays at Cap d'Ail. One day in 1955 a letter came from his private secretary, inviting Nellie and Jean to cocktails, and from then on they were often the Churchills' guests. Sometimes they went together, other times Jean was alone, driving the Austin she kept in France over the winding road to the Churchill villa. When they had eaten, everyone would stand and look along the sea coast, while they marvelled at the lights, the dazzling colour that swept around the bays, then up to the mountains, towards Italy. One evening in late spring they ate a simple entrée of rock melon and ham — *le jambon*, Clementine Churchill murmured, testing her French — a chicken dish to follow, some caramel custard to finish. Jean was sipping a glass of champagne.

'Now don't you go drinking too much of that stuff,' Churchill said, 'not when you're going driving around those corners. You know the bloody French, you have to watch them.' He'd drunk four whiskies before dinner, a bottle of champagne with the meal, and had just begun his second Cointreau. 'I'm laying off on the drink,' he said. 'Doctor's advice. I've given up the brandy.'

'Very wise, I'm sure, Mr Churchill,' Jean said.

'You're quiet tonight, Jean. In fact, if I may say so, you're getting like that Greta Garbo. She's got a place around here. You bump into her at all?'

'No, I've always hoped we might meet, but we never have.'

'Yes, I can understand that, what is it they call you, the Garbo of the skies? Now she's what you'd call a recluse, keeps herself to herself.'

'So they say.'

'You don't want to turn into one of those. You need to get out and about. How old are you? Forties, eh? Same age as my daughter, Diana. She's a bit melancholy in her ways. Are you melancholic, Jean?'

'I'm not sure what you mean.' She had met Diana Churchill once, and found her an agreeable companion at dinner, although she sensed a despair never far from the surface. She didn't want to compare her own state to that of the other woman.

'Down in the dumps? You get that way sometimes?'

'I think everyone gets sad when they remember the past.'

'Anything in particular?' he persisted. 'Oh, excuse an old man's impudence, but I like you, damn it.'

'Flying was my life, and now it's gone. That's all, everything has gone. I tried to get over it in Jamaica. Well, it didn't seem to work really.'

'You shouldn't have stopped flying.'

'Your government decreed it,' Jean said.

He paused, his stomach rumbling, while he cleared his brain. 'Oh yes, that Nazi fellow, of course.'

'Only he wasn't, as it turned out.' She turned the stem of her glass around in her fingers, before placing it on a side table. 'That's life, I suppose, always half-full.' Churchill blew a long stream of cigar smoke towards the window. 'We couldn't be too careful in those days.'

'I think I should be going now, Prime Minister. If you'll excuse me.'

'Well, we can talk about it another day,' he said.

His wife had remained seated at the table while this exchange took place.

She looked anxious. 'Winston, that's enough. Jean, you'll come back and see us again, won't you?'

'Oh yes, I expect so, some day,' Jean said, her voice deliberately vague.

Jean *had* seen Garbo at Cap d'Ail. She had glimpsed, one day, a woman sitting alone at a table in an outdoor cafe, smoking a cigarette, a glass of rosé in her hand, seemingly unguarded. A large hat shaded her face, and she wore dark glasses. But Jean knew. She had studied the angle of the woman's head, a certain way of turning it, for so many years, that she knew she wasn't mistaken. Garbo had not worked throughout the war and there had been rumours about where her sympathies lay — unfounded, as it had turned out, just as they had been about Jean. She hadn't worked since then, and in this, too, Jean saw herself as a kindred spirit. Garbo knew the work that had gone before was its own statement.

Jean hovered, wondering if she might approach the star. Garbo moved uneasily, as if she felt eyes on her, the aura of self-containment about to be undone. Jean understood then, that what she had seen was enough. They were connected, even if the actress did not know it, never would.

Sooner or later she knew that she and Nellie would have to stop moving and find a home. Jean wanted a place that was quiet, somewhere where she didn't have to make an effort any more.

Nellie was now in her eighties and a decision about a home couldn't be delayed much longer. It came about quite suddenly. They were in a small fishing village called Los Boliches in the south of Spain. The houses were white on the hillsides and the twin bays as blue as any they had ever seen, even in the Caribbean. Nellie caught a chill, despite the warmth of the sun. A doctor was called, who suggested bed rest for a week or two. She recovered quickly, but their weeks in the village stretched into months, and before they knew it, they had found the perfect villa on a hillside and bought it.

They called it La Paloma. The name was suitably Spanish and, Nellie claimed, it was the song Fred was playing in the room next door while she gave birth to Jean. She spoke of Fred more often, of late, and with a fondness that appeared to overlook their parting. Jean didn't always respond warmly when Nellie's memory stretched back into the past.

'Remember how happy we were in Rotorua? I can still see you climbing that gate and setting off down the street. You were a determined little creature even then. And Fred coming home and lighting his pipe while I prepared the dinner, and all five of us sitting round the table.'

'I'm happy now,' Jean said.

'I know, I know, dear. I was just saying.'

'How happy we were in Rotorua. Well, perhaps, but I was too young to remember much. Thank goodness we're in a place where nobody knows us now. That makes me happy. No one can find us.'

They may have believed they were the only people to have discovered the village, but soon others came. Tourists filled the streets and the villas on the hillsides began to fall into British hands. Jean found herself glancing behind her, as if someone might tap her on the shoulder, say her name. It was time to go again. They sold La Paloma, and all their possessions except for their clothes, and some battered suitcases containing documents and old newspaper clippings, then set forth for a holiday in Morocco.

From there the car was shipped to the Canary Islands. They decided that this was where they might stay, on Tenerife, a place that seemed remote and too difficult of access to attract any but the most dedicated traveller. They liked the wild and varied nature of the landscape, the mountains and the ravines below, and the steady climate. The Island of Eternal Spring — warmth all year round, without excessive heat. The population had dwindled during the Spanish Civil War, as thousands of its inhabitants had fled, and parts of the island seemed virtually uninhabited.

In the village of San Marcos, Jean found rooms for them to stay in while they searched for another perfect home. There was a tiny kitchen, and a toilet outside. The main room was airy and white-walled, furnished with two beds that served as couches during the day, a gate-legged table and two upright chairs standing near the window. Behind the house stood a volcanic mountain, and before them lay the sea, lapping against a shell-shaped beach of black sand.

Nellie would turn ninety in three months' time. Her movements had become slower. When Jean suggested a walk Nellie would agree, on condition that it be short. If they were to do more travelling, they must keep fit, Jean would remind her mother.

Nellie said to her one day, 'Darling, I think I'm going downhill a bit.'

'Of course you're not,' Jean cried. 'You're just not eating enough.'

Nellie folded her hands in her lap, and didn't reply.

Jean looked at her mother, her thin frame supporting shoulders that had become slight. She took up her basket and set off for the markets, choosing freshly caught parrot fish, oranges and green beans. When she returned to the room, where Nellie still sat in the same position, Jean steamed the delicate seafood and the beans, and sliced an orange.

'Come on,' she coaxed, 'eat up, darling.'

To please her, Nellie sat at the table Jean had laid and decorated with a small vase of white daisies. She picked at the food, and murmured, 'Delicious.' After a few mouthfuls, she put her fork down. 'I'm sorry, darling. That's all I can eat for now.'

She didn't eat the next day, or the day after. 'I'm going for the doctor,' Jean said.

'I don't want you to leave me,' Nellie whispered, 'not just now.' She had dressed that morning, with Jean's help, putting on a grey silk dress and a cardigan, even though it was midsummer.

'I'll ask the landlady to call him,' Jean said firmly.

She left the room for a few minutes and returned to find Nellie standing at the window, her face towards the sea. She turned to Jean, her eyes glazing, as she began to fall. Jean rushed forward to catch her, holding her tightly as she guided her towards a couch, where Nellie collapsed. 'Mother, don't leave me, darling,' Jean implored.

Nellie murmured, 'Now none of that or you'll make me feel unhappy.'

And then she was gone.

The Spanish doctor, who had been called, pushed open the door, walked over, closed Nellie's eyes and crossed himself.

'She's not dead,' Jean cried frantically.

'Her spirit is moving away from us. Talk to her for a little while, perhaps she's still listening to you,' the doctor said. 'Let her hear that you are releasing her in a joyful way.'

Jean had now to find a place to bury Nellie. She turned to the vice-consul in Puerto de la Cruz, some distance away. 'It must be Protestant,' she said.

He suggested the Anglican cemetery there — very old, very respectable, he said. Jean prepared her mother for burial. She ordered a mahogany coffin, lined with glass and padded with mauve satin and, when the time came, lifted her mother's seemingly weightless body, and placed her in it. How, she wondered, had she not noticed how tiny Nellie had become?

As she asked, a white hearse took Nellie to the All Saints Church, a simple stone building. Jean stood alone at the front. The vice-consul and the vicar's wife arrived for the service, but when they saw Jean, her manner warned them that she didn't want company. They stood at the back. An organist played 'The King of Love My Shepherd Is', and the vicar, as Jean had discussed with him, delivered a eulogy. The casket was placed in a niche in a wall, so that, if she wished, Jean could take it with her if she left Tenerife.

When the service was over, the vicar suggested she might like to return to the vicarage where his wife would make some tea. Jean gave him a withering look and turned on her heel.

Later, she returned to see the vicar and apologised. 'Mother's service was beautiful,' she said, 'just what I wanted. But I had to be on my own, you understand?'

When he said, gently, that he did, she explained that she planned never to leave Tenerife without Nellie.

Soon she would buy a tiny apartment in Puerto de la Cruz, a small desperate act of self-preservation, before grief overtook her, like an illness.

Melancholy was how Churchill might have described it. She had heard how Diana Churchill had committed suicide, some years before. Now she, herself, was fighting to stay alive, but she didn't have a name for this continuous sadness. She slept black, dreamless sleeps, eating when she remembered, walked endlessly when she finally dragged herself from bed, and visited the wall where Nellie's coffin had been placed each day. 'I love you, darling,' she would whisper.

After a time she did begin to dream again. Slowly, at first. There was a morning she woke up and thought she smelled sulphur, heard mud bubbling in the ground. Another night, towards morning, she was woken by a dream she had to fight to remember. She saw vaguely the depth of caves, a woman in black. The next night, it was the scent of wild strawberries. She put the light on to see if her hands were stained with juice. This seemed better. She rose early and went to the markets, a basket over her arm to collect fruit.

Sometimes people tried to speak to her, but she would turn away.

She began to dream more often of Kitty, the woman in the house near the caves, and wished she had returned to see her again. She was, surely, long dead. Jean would have liked to talk to her about solitude. She imagined the morning light, by which the old woman could decide how to spend her day, whether to lie in bed a little longer, or go to the verandah and listen to the cicadas in the grass, the sound of the birds or, in the winter, to listen to the sweet singing rain on the tin roof of the old house, creaking near the sea. Then she remembered Kitty's deafness. But I still know it's there, she had said of the sighing macrocarpa.

As she knew Nellie's bones were close, she wanted to stay near them. If she stayed there long enough she believed, sooner or later, her mother's face would come back to her, too. For now, it escaped her.

Tenerife would be her home for the next sixteen years broken, in time, by forays back into the world. But these were still a long way off.

Chapter 35

Fred wrote to Jean and asked her to come home. It was his last letter before his death, a year after Nellie's. John wrote and offered her a home with him. He had stayed in New Zealand until Fred died, but now he was going back to England. Jean didn't reply.

This was the pattern of her days. She would eat breakfast, put on a large hat and leave the apartment to walk the town, or into the hills, have an early meal at a café where she usually read a newspaper, and then retire home to bed. Apart from regular haircuts, and laundry that kept her clothes spotless, her appearance didn't concern her much. Sometimes she read books, but the words soon blurred and lost their meaning.

Jean wondered if she were dying, too. It was the dreams that persuaded her that she wasn't. There was light in them now, even though her days appeared dark. Three years had passed: it was 1969. On an impulse, she booked herself a flight to London, and made an appointment with a Harley Street specialist. After a thorough check, he told her she was in perfect health, her body more like that of a woman half her age. He listened with patience when she described the shadowy life she was living in

Tenerife, the way her hands sat in her lap some days and she didn't know what they were doing there and who they belonged to, the way she woke each day with a sense of hope behind her eyelids, and how it disappeared the moment she opened them.

'That is grief,' he said. 'One day, you'll wake up and your mother's death will seem a little further removed. There will come a morning when it's not the first thing you think about.'

'How can you be sure of that?'

'It's true that some people die of grief, usually because they take their own lives, or neglect themselves so badly that they perish.' His voice was measured and kind. 'But, Miss Batten, you've come to see me, which suggests that deep down you want to survive. You've had a great deal of practice at surviving the odds, wouldn't you agree?'

He talked to her at length, prescribed some medication and made another appointment for her to visit him. He was sure, he said, that she would come back to London.

On her return to Tenerife, almost on cue, an invitation arrived for Jean. British Petroleum and the Royal Aero Club were planning to commemorate the anniversary of Ross and Keith Smith's first England-to-Australia flight, fifty years earlier. Would she like to start the race at Gatwick, with yachtsman Sir Francis Chichester?

Requests had arrived from time to time through the circuitous Barclay's Bank address that she now used. She had sent routine brief notes of thanks and a refusal. But that morning, as she ate breakfast on her balcony, something stirred inside her. In her bedroom, she looked at her reflection in the mirror. It was a long time since she had studied herself. The woman who looked back at her now was sixty years old, and small lines had developed around her eyes. The dark hair was streaked with grey. This was the face of a woman who had been noted for her beauty, and now she would be lost in a crowd. That was what she had wanted, of course, but suddenly she wasn't sure. The invitation was tempting. And the moment she recognised this temptation for what it was, she understood that she might recover from the grip of her despair, that the thaw had truly set in.

Her reply to the invitation was swift. *Thank you, I will be there*, she cabled.

But before the race, there were things to be done. She flew to London where she attended a round of beauty clinics, make-up lessons, hair-colouring sessions, and shopped for clothes. The way women looked astounded her, their tiny skirts just covering their bottoms, their long boots, their eye-liner a work of art. Carnaby Street was the place to go, a girl on a bus told her, when she asked where she bought her clothes: Mary Quant. The Beatles in Abbey Road. This was all news to Jean. Her spirits soared.

Her re-emergence startled people. Some had to be reminded who she was. But there were scores of photographers and reporters at the beginning of the air race, and the newspapers and radio stations soon picked up a story at their elbow. Her face was in the limelight again. A reporter was foolish enough to express the belief held in many quarters that she had died. She demonstrated how alive she was with a number of high kicks.

The race organisers had booked her into the Waldorf Hotel, where she held court for the media, while the race was in progress. None of the competitors managed to break her own solo record, which had now stood for thirty-three years, and this was cause for still more excitement.

She was asked frequently to comment on women's liberation. This puzzled her. In spite of the new styles, she couldn't see that anything else had changed. 'When I was flying, I was usually the only girl,' she told one reporter. 'But I was accepted as just another pilot. There wasn't any antagonism, oh no. But then nobody took me seriously until I started breaking men's records.'

When it was all over, she found herself standing in the street by herself. The thought of going straight back to Tenerife didn't appeal. In another impulsive moment, she walked into a travel agent's office and bought herself a ticket to New Zealand.

Part Four
Home

1980

Chapter 36

The queue waiting to have their books autographed snaked along Queen Street in Auckland. The author, Jean Batten, looked up and flashed her famous smile as she handed back each copy. It wasn't the first time it had been in print, but now the story of her life had a new title, *Alone in the Sky*, and a shiny fresh cover with the Percival Gull pictured against clouds. On the back cover, she was pictured in a flying helmet, with goggles on top of her head. The inside of the dust jacket dated the picture: Jean Batten at Stag Lane aerodrome, on gaining her pilot's licence in 1930.

Over forty years had passed since then. If you didn't know, it would be hard to tell how old the writer was, nor would there have been many clues in the book, for the text was almost exactly the same. Her new publishers had tried to persuade her to update the story, but she had been adamant that there was nothing more to tell. Let the records tell the story, she said.

Her hair was blonde at this appearance, although in recent times it had been black, and again flame-red. Over the past ten years, since she turned sixty, she had become a public figure again. The 'come back kid' she sometimes called herself.

Her looks had changed from the cool glamour of the 1930s. At first, she wore incongruous mini-skirts and high white boots and floppy leather caps, as if she were much younger. 'I suppose I'm young at heart,' she said, 'because I've never really grown up. That's what my mother used to say, anyway.' She referred to her mother often. Sometimes her eyes would fill with tears when she alluded to her. 'She didn't need glasses until she was eighty-nine,' she would marvel. 'She was tall and elegant, with a beautiful head of hair until she died. In my arms,' she added once, before hastily turning away. When asked, she would describe her life in Tenerife. 'I swim there every day, and paint, and cook very nice meals. After I've had my daily swim I always have a small bottle of champagne,' she told one interviewer.

For there were still interviews to do when she came to New Zealand, and talks to be given to schools. One school had been named in her honour. Her dress style had toned down since her new beginning. More often she wore a white kid coat with a mink collar, and stylish, form-fitting dresses.

She saw family, too, when she came to New Zealand. In the north, she had a niece and nephews, her brother Harold's children, and they had children, too. 'Fancy,' she said. 'Grown up, all grown up.' She had hired a white chauffeur-driven limousine to drive her to their farms on her first visit back. Strange, she hadn't meant to lose touch with them all, but that was the way it had happened. She was sorry she hadn't seen Fred one last time, but she couldn't bring herself to leave the place where Nellie was buried in Tenerife. She just couldn't.

The niece and nephews took her to see their father. Alma had died, but then so had the marriage, long before. Jean didn't recognise Harold, shrunken and wizened, ranting at the people who took care of him in a hospital. But then he didn't know her either, his eyes dulled with medication.

'Our mother died, Harold. Did you know that? I put a blue scarf over her hair when she was in the coffin — you know how nice she always liked to look. I put some perfume in a little sachet in her pocket. And I got a great big spray of red roses. Ninety red roses, can you imagine that?'

When he didn't answer her, she put her hand briefly on his restless head. 'I'm still here,' she said. Something in him stilled for an instant, and then he moved away from her touch. Now Harold had died, too.

And then there was John to think about, who had come back to New Zealand, then left again. For a long time, he had been a radio announcer in Auckland. People who had heard him on the radio said his voice was beautiful. So that was another lapse of time to contemplate, one she found difficult to dwell on. But yes, it was fifty years since they had seen one another. Why had they quarrelled? She didn't really recall. She had thought they were at one with each other when they were children, but they turned out to be different. That was all she could really put her finger on. Perhaps she could have tried to understand more, at least when she grew older. But where would one begin after so long?

That afternoon, as she sat signing books, a woman came up and presented her purchase.

'Are you going to catch up with Freda?' she asked.

'Freda?'

'You know, Freda Stark,' the woman said with a touch of impatience. Her severely styled hair and black-rimmed spectacles suggested an academic. Jean glanced at the woman's shoes and, sure enough, they were brogues. 'You and she were friends, weren't you? That's what she told me.'

'Oh yes, Freda. I do remember. She had some trouble, didn't she?'

'That was a long time ago.' The woman's voice sounded sharp. 'You'll know about her dancing of course? She was simply amazing.'

'I thought she gave it up.'

'But surely you know what she did in the war?'

Jean shook her head. 'I've been away a long time.'

'Goodness, she was sensational. She entertained the troops at the Wintergarden cabaret every night. Our boys and the Americans. They called her the Fever of the Fleet. She used to be covered from head to foot in gold paint, just a G-string and a feather head-dress. You don't know about that? Well, she was a breath of fresh air, absolutely famous in her own right.' Again, there was a hint of rebuke as if to remind Jean that she was not the only person who had made a name for herself. 'Freda shook New Zealanders up, they needed it.'

'I had no idea. Where is she now?'

'Oh, she works at the university. I'll tell her I saw you.'

Out of the corner of her eye, Jean saw an elderly man standing at the door, looking in.

'Well, it was nice to meet you,' Jean said, signalling that the encounter was over. The woman collected her book, raising her eyebrows as if in some disbelief at Jean's ignorance.

The man still stood at the door, frail-looking, nearly bald, just threads of hair springing from the back of his head. He wore a shirt and tie knotted under a pullover, and a heavy woollen zipped jacket. But she knew those eyes, the high cheekbones.

The next woman in the queue noticed her distraction. 'I'm sorry, Miss Batten,' she said, 'but I've got to pick up the kiddies after school, and the book's for my dad's birthday.'

Jean picked up the pen, and wrote her name quickly, still in the round hand of her girlhood, with a slight flourish, an ornate round capital 'J', the top stroke missed off the first 't' in 'Batten', a firm line beneath her surname.

'Thank you,' she said. 'Thank you for coming today.'

He would wait for her, surely he must.

'Excuse me,' she said to the next person in the line, 'I'm sorry, but there's someone I have to catch.'

She ran to the door of the big shop. 'John,' she called wildly down the street. But he had gone.

One of the booksellers had been guarding the door, directing customers to the queue. 'There was a man here,' she said.

'Yes, Miss Batten. He said he knew you from a long time ago.'

'Did he tell you who he was?'

'He said his name was John.'

'Batten? Did he say his name was John Batten?'

Recognition dawned on the bookseller's face. 'Of course, I thought I knew that voice. I'm sorry, I did suggest he wait a minute or two. But he said he was on a cruise ship and it was just in port for a few hours. He said it was a bit of a shock to see you, because he thought you were in Tenerife.'

In the afternoon, when the shop had cleared, she walked along Queen Street to the port, the old ferry building, the wharves that she remembered, only everything was built up now, familiar but changed. A big liner was pulling away to sea. She stood and waved until it was out of sight.

For a moment, she thought that she was back up there in the sky, and that while she was up there, the whole world had simply disappeared.

Postscript

Jean Gardner Batten died in Palma, Majorca, in 1982. She had shifted from Tenerife, to a modest serviced apartment in Palma not long before. Some time earlier, she had told a couple in England who had befriended her that she was 'going to ground for a while'.

There is no account of why Jean moved from Tenerife to Majorca, nor any real information about what she did there. Perhaps she returned to the ancient monastery at Valdemossa where Chopin had composed his music on a stormy night, and listened in her head to the scattering raindrops of his prelude, her fingers flexing over an imaginary keyboard. Or she may have sat under a large umbrella in the town of Palma, and watched the sun dropping and a dark red moon rise over the sea. Somewhere, on one of her walks, she may have caught sight of a shadow among the trees, and called out her mother's name, listening for a voice to come back to her.

But nobody knows any of these things.

What we do know is that Jean had been ill in the days before her death. She had gone for a walk and been bitten by a dog. The wound had become infected. She declined medical assistance until the hour of her death when, it appeared from later reports, she became aware of the seriousness of her condition. The maid, who had gone for help, returned to the room and found Jean Batten lying dead, fully dressed, on her bed.

The authorities, not knowing who she was, buried her under the name Gardner, in a paupers' common grave.

Because it had been her habit to disappear for long periods of time, five years would pass before anyone became seriously concerned about where she was. Nobody sought her until 1987. Two television documentary-makers, researching a film about her life, discovered her whereabouts that year.

By then, it was impractical to disinter her remains from the common grave where many lay buried.

Her body had disappeared, in a sense, as did those of so many of her fellow fliers: into infinity.

Acknowledgements

I wish to acknowledge that some phrases used to describe Jean Batten's flights come from her own early writing as do her logbook entries. The final words attributed to Ellen (Nellie) Batten were quoted in *Jean Batten: The Garbo of the Skies* by Ian Mackersey (Macdonald, 1990). Copyright for letters written by Jean Batten is unclear. The letters on pages 312 and 435 are written in the spirit of her writing only. All the other letters are fiction.

The poem 'Tobacco is a Dirty Weed' quoted on page 309 was written in 1915 by Graham Lee Hemminger.

The names of some characters on the fringes of Jean Batten's life, and their circumstances, have been changed.

I thank many people who have given generous advice and information to assist me with writing *The Infinite Air*. In particular, I thank my research assistants Alice Janssens (London) and Oliver Peryman (Wellington), as well as the following: Dominic Alessio, Jean Anderson, Philip Andrews, Jim Batten, Jennifer Beck, Bev Brett, Anne Collett, David Colquhoun, the late Cherie Devliotis, Peter Downes, Anne Else, Billie Farnell, Lesley Gunson, Michael Harlow, Anna Hoffman, Simon Johnson, Ian Kidman, Joanna Kidman, Marie-Claude Lambotte, Des McLean, Lachie (Lachlan) McLean, James McNeish, Alison Morgan, Jill Nicholas, Vincent O'Malley, Vincent O'Sullivan, Noel T. Robinson, Jennifer Shennan, Allan Shields, Judy Siers, Peter Wells and Redmer Yska.

I acknowledge a number of institutions that have made their material available to me, and whose staff have helped me. These include: Wellington Public Library; Rotorua Public Library; Dunedin Public Library; Invercargill Public Library (with special thanks to Linda Teau); National Archives of New Zealand; the Alexander Turnbull Library; Wellington College Archives; MOTAT (Museum of Transport and Technology, Auckland); Rotorua Museum (with thanks to Ann Somerville and Manaaki

Pene); Croydon Aircraft Company at Old Mandeville Airfield (Gore); Department of Research & Information Services, Royal Air Force Museum (London).

I am grateful for permission to reproduce the radio commentary in chapter 30: a transcription from archival recordings held by Sound Archives Nga Taonga Korero ID 31502, Jean Batten's record-breaking flight, 16 October 1936.

The letter from the War Office (1939) on page 408 is reproduced with the kind permission of the RAF Museum, London.

My editors Harriet Allan and Anna Rogers continue to give me support beyond the call of duty, and I can never thank them enough.

Many thanks are due, too, to Kimberley Davis and Sarah Thornton.

During my research the following books and texts were invaluable:

Batten, Jean, *Solo Flight*, Jackson & O'Sullivan, 1934

Batten, Jean, *My Life*, George G. Harrap, 1938

Batten, Jean, *Alone in the Sky*, The Airlife Publishing Company, 1979

Bell, Elizabeth S., *Sisters of the Wind: Voices of Early Women Aviators*, Trilogy Books, 1994

Churchill, Sarah, *Keep on Dancing*, Coward, McCann & Geoghegan, 1981

Civil Aviation Handbook, Air Department New Zealand, *The Air Pilot*, 1939 edition

Collacott, Bertram A., 'Memories of Stag Lane', unpublished manuscript, RAF Museum, London

Collett, Anne, *Jean Batten and the 'Accident of Sex'* (with Clive Gilson), Faculty of Arts — Papers (Archive), University of Wollongong, 2009

Coward, Noël, *Future Indefinite*, Heinemann, 1954

Devliotis, Cherie, *Dancing with Delight, Footprints of the Past, Dance and Dancers in Early 20th Century Auckland*, Polygraphia, 2005

Everett, Susanne, *London: the glamour years 1919–39,* Bison Books, 1985

Haworth, Dianne and Diane Miller, *Freda Stark, Her Extraordinary Life*, HarperCollins, 2000

Horrocks, John, *Something in the Waters*, Steele Roberts, 2010

Howgego, James, *London in the Twenties and Thirties*, B. T. Batsford London, 1978

Hughes, Robert, *Rome*, Weidenfeld & Nicolson, 2011

Jillett, Leslie, *Wings Across the Tasman*, A. H. & A. W. Reed, 1953

Lenart, Judith (selected and compiled), *Yours Ever, Ian Fleming: Letters to and From Antony Terry*, privately published, 1994

Mackersey, Ian, *Jean Batten: The Garbo of the Skies*, Macdonald, 1990

McNally, Ward, *Smithy, The Kingsford Smith Story*, Robert Hale, 1966

McNeish, James, *Lovelock*, Hodder & Stoughton, 1986

Mulgan, David, *The Kiwi's First Wings: The Story of the Walsh Brothers and the New Zealand Flying School, 1910–1924*, Wingfield Press, 1960

O'Malley, Vincent and David Armstrong, *The Beating Heart: A Political and Socio-Economic History of Te Arawa*, Huia, 2008

O'Reilly, Bernard, *Green Mountains*, B. O'Reilly, 1940

Pearson, John, *Ian Fleming, Creator of James Bond*, Jonathan Cape, 2007

Simpson, Tony, *The Sugar Bag Years: A People's History of the 1930s Depression in New Zealand*, Alister Taylor Publishing, 1974

Verran, David, *The North Shore: An Illustrated History*, Random House, 2010